To Lauren,

You are a great daughter,

Out For Blood

Private Diary of a Gossip Vampire

By
Mike Walker

First published by The Writer's Coffee Shop, 2013

Copyright © Mike Walker, 2013

The Writer's Coffee Shop
(Australia)   PO Box 447 Cherrybrook NSW 2126
(USA)   PO Box 2116 Waxahachie TX 75168

Paperback ISBN- 978-1-61213-157-3
E-book ISBN- 978-1-61213-158-0

A CIP catalogue record for this book is available from the US Congress Library.

Cover image by: © Depositphotos.com / Andrejs Pidjass, © Depositphotos.com / aarrttuur, © Depositphotos.com / Francesco Cura, © Depositphotos.com / Andrey Bayda

Cover design by: L.J. Anderson

www.thewriterscoffeeshop.com/mwalker

Foreword

Mike Walker has made a breakthrough in writing style not seen since Thomas Wolfe caused editorial desks to tremble 50 years ago. Strange indeed that a man who has plundered journalism now for four decades should write in a way completely different to that which made him famous. He spews words and he doesn't care if they splatter here or there. Mike Walker is having *fun*, jumping up and down in his sandbox with wild abandon.

Out for Blood is more than a good story, cultivated in the rich fields of Hollywood gossip; more than a revealing look at celebrity culture and its impact on the world; more than red-hot sex in a blood sucking world of vampires that is Hollywood at its worst and best. It tells a story in a way that is as original today as was The Electric Kool-Aid Acid Test half a century ago. With this work, the circle around the campfire just got a little tighter. *Out for Blood* not only glows in the dark, it turns its own pages.

Colin Dangaard
Journalist
Syndicated Columnist
Author, *Talking with Horses*
President, Australian Stock Saddle Co.

To Crystal Ball, my vampire muse.

"Quiet on the set, please . . . and . . . *action!*"

Prologue

"Is Tom Cruise gay?

"That *is* today's question, friends, and you're listening to *The John Phillips Show* here on KABC Radio, broadcasting live from the heart of Hollywood! We're back from our break, and hoping to get an answer to that *query*—no pun intended! And, we'll also dig into today's most shocking news story: Major Hollywood celebrities getting *kinky* in so-called 'vampire sex' sessions! Bite on that, people!

"My in-studio guest this hour, the man *Newsweek* calls 'the world's most powerful gossip columnist!'—Clark Kelly of the *National Revealer*. His column hooks millions with sizzling scoops about the hottest boldface names in Hollywood . . . and today, Clark, you've got a shocking new exclusive that's breaking worldwide headlines, like this one from London's *Daily Mail*: 'Major Hollywood Celebs Hook Up For Secret Vampire Sex Games?' Wow! Welcome again to the show, Clark!"

"Great to be here, John."

"Okay . . . now, before the break, I got you to reveal the *most-asked question* when gossip fans recognize you in public, but for listeners just tuning in, tell us again. What's the most-asked question for Clark Kelly, aka 'the man who knows everything'?"

"Well, John, gossip fans hit me with all kinds of . . . uh, queries, as you put it. But over the years, *the* most-asked question, hands down, has always been, 'Is Tom Cruise gay?' "

"Clark, I'm dying to ask how you answer *that* burning question! But first, *everyone's* talking about your latest shocking scoop, which is making headlines from BevHills to Beijing to Bucharest: Roma Kane, world-famous Hollywood celebrity and billion-heiress to the Kane Industries fortune, allegedly went . . . 'full vampire' in an in-character, full-costume sex session with Damon Strutt, that handsome young British actor who stars as Kragen the Vampire on TV's top-rated *Bold Blood* series!

"And here's Clark Kelly's kicker, he reports that sexy, bad-girl movie star

Taylor 'TayLo' Logan secretly *pimped* this sexual encounter between her two mutual friends as a so-called, 'surprise early birthday present' for BFF Roma. It's a shocker, Clark! The usual tabloid trashers are blowing your story off as unbelievable, but no one's denied it, right? So, for the record, Clark Kelly, are stars really playing *vampire sex games*?"

"John, I print stories I believe to be true. Period!"

"Okay, but as I said, many tabloid-phobes are saying—"

"What they're *actually* saying, John, is that this story sounds too good to be true. And that's my definition of the perfect story. Because here's the lesson I've learned, over and over, as a journalist—truth is often stranger than fiction. And nobody's ever caught me printing fiction as fact, pal!"

"True enough, Clark. You've got an amazing track record. You break so-called unbelievable stories that are later confirmed, independently, to be absolutely accurate. Do you get *upset* when people question your accuracy?"

"No, John. Because that means my story is *so* sensational that they're actually dying to believe it—they're secretly *praying* it's true. And that's when you know you've got people hooked! So when—and please note that I'm not saying *if*—I'm proven right, *The Revealer* will sell even *more* copies and I can keep affording Louis XIII cognac at $130 a shot. Look, John, if I'd published, let's say, that Damon Strutt took Roma Kane out to dinner at Spago, would people be so quick to question that?"

"Probably not, no."

"Exactly! But *why*? Because what makes a story irresistible is the 'you'll *never* guess what happened next' factor. Whenever I lecture at journalism schools like Berkeley and Columbia, I teach students my 'Sweet, Sweet Sundae' analogy. Like, if I said to you 'Hey, John, want a scoop of vanilla ice cream?' You might resist the temptation because . . . oh, maybe you're on a diet. But, if I *upped* the ante by offering a scoop each of vanilla, strawberry and chocolate, *and* promised to drizzle it all with hot chocolate fudge, *then* threw in whipped cream, a sprinkle of chopped nuts *and* . . . hey, John, let me top it *all* off with a bright red cherry! Aren't you now totally tempted? Sure you are. And *why*? Because every new tidbit makes it tougher to resist, right?"

"Curse you, Clark Kelly. Now I'll have to order hot fudge sundaes for the entire show staff. Look behind the control room glass wall—our producer and technical director are both giving me a thumbs-up. By the way, Clark, will you have a sundae with us?"

"Not for me, thanks, John."

"*No*? How about if I throw in one of those steaming hot cappuccinos you're so addicted to, Clark?"

"I see you've learned my lesson, John. Which is, of course, that when you have a story with two boldface names . . . top it with a *third* boldface name . . . and top that all off with—"

"Wait, wait, *don't tell me*! Today's cherry on top is *vampire sex*?"

"Right! Pick up your degree, John, you've just graduated from Clark Kelly's Gossip U!"

"Wow, thanks! Now before we get back to the 'Is Tom Cruise gay?' question, let's talk about the vampire craze that's still gripping Hollywood and, if you'll pardon the expression, shows *no* sign of dying, right, Clark?"

"Vampires won't be going back underground anytime soon, John, if *you'll* pardon the expression. Vampires have been scaring us on Hollywood screens for decades, but the genre suddenly exploded—especially on TV—when vampires started emphasizing sex instead of scariness. Ladies *love* offbeat bad boys, and that's what vampires represent—exotic sex with dangerous, otherworldly men. Just look at the last *Twilight* movie! It did north of $500 million, and why? Because of the sex! It's a craze so universal that even teenage girls understand the erotically charged term you used earlier in the show, John, going '*full vampire.*'"

"Right, Clark, because 'full vampire' doesn't just mean killer sex. It means sex that can literally *kill* you! It didn't kill Roma Kane, of course. But that's because Damon Strutt—dressed up, according to your scoop, in full 'Kragen the Vampire' costume during the deed—isn't a *real* vampire. Okay, we'll bite deeper into vampire sex later this hour. But first, Clark, what about persistent rumors that real vampires exist in Hollywood? Can you confirm *that*?"

"Yes, I can, John. One runs a major studio, and uh . . . there's Harvey Weinstein, of course. Plus most Hollywood agents: you listening, Ari Emanuel? . . . Oh, I'm just kidding! John, when vampire rumors become truth, you can bet I'll print them."

"I know you will, Clark, but hey, that brings us back to a star who *played* a bloodsucker onscreen, Tom Cruise. So answer this . . . is *he* a vampire?"

"No, Tom Cruise is *not* a vampire. Nor is his *Interview with the Vampire* costar, Brad Pitt. Though, I'm not too sure about Brad's hot lady, Angelina Jolie. And that's the dull truth, John."

"Okay, Clark Kelly, we always believe you, but now, let's get down and dirty. Is Tom Cruise GAY? That's the question we'll demand you answer when we come back after a quick break. This is *The John Phillips Show* on KABC Radio. Stick with us as we dish even *more* dirt with world-famous gossip columnist Clark Kelly . . ."

. . . who, believe it or not, John, is a real, live Hollywood vampire himself, I was dying to add.

I didn't, of course.

And for the moment, dear reader, let's keep our little secret hush-hush . . . and very confidential!

Chapter One

Even for vampires, there are funny moments. On that Saturday night when it all began, a pinch-faced Hollywood publicity chick, too young and too boozed to know better, abruptly got in my face at the Roosevelt Hotel bar, spitting mad about an item in my *National Revealer* gossip column. My scoop had exposed, so to speak, her supposedly "macho" movie star client's penchant for sniffing coke off the manhood of a hunky young stud he secretly kept on retainer to bang his sexually frustrated wife—*and* him, of course. Worse, as the item in my column teased, "cell phone pics got clicked and *might* break online!"

Like most primitive life forms, public-relations types are ill equipped to express subtle, nuanced emotion, but this PR princess was more than easy to read. She was *pissed!* Red faced and hyperventilating, her silicone fun bags heaved spasmodically as she sputtered and raged.

Then the bitch bared her teeth at me and hissed: "Bloodsucker!"

I fought to suppress a grin. Oblivious to the irony of her insult, this fried flack had unwittingly thrown one of the funniest zingers I'd heard in centuries, and I'm really a sucker (pun intended) for a funny line.

I mention this to apprise you of a trait that, hopefully, will amuse and not annoy—my sense of humor is highly attuned, even over the top, some might say. It's a quality quite unique among my kind. Vampires truly are, as human lore depicts us, a damn somber bunch. "Funny vampire" ain't no proud sobriquet among *my* undead homies.

Quickly eyeballing the crowd to make sure no one was observing, I stared down at the fuming flack and—drawing my lips back in a wicked smile— unsheathed my long, shiny-wet fangs. Instantly, her legs went rubbery and she collapsed like the blood had been sucked from her body. It hadn't been, of course. I'm fast, but not *that* fast.

Poor thing, I thought as she hit the floor. Probably reads vampire novels. And what woman doesn't, these days?

I flicked a quick glance at the milling crowd. No one had seen her hit the floor. Good.

I smiled, imagining the hilarious scene that would ensue Monday morning when this terror-stricken twinkie would babble to her bemused bosses.

"You've got to believe me! The *National Revealer*'s gossip columnist is actually . . . a vampire!"

But, not gonna happen, gossip fans. She'll keep her mouth shut. Because even if she didn't get fired for incipient lunacy, she'd be forever fearful of waking some dark and stormy night to find me perched on her windowsill. Like a giant bat.

"Omigod!"

A woman pushing through the crowd suddenly spotted the carcass at my feet. She and her date looked at me questioningly. I shrugged.

"Don't know her. We'd started chatting, but she seemed . . . high. Excited . . . trippy. You know . . . then she just . . ."

Oh, yes, she'd been excited all right. Because even in today's wild-on Gollywood, when headlines blaze with the sudden revelation that your A-list movie star client—a tough-guy action hero and supposed *hetero*—gets his kicks snorting snow off a dude's dingus, it's *bad* no matter how you cut it (the news, not the coke).

It's a titanic fucking *disaster*, however, if your faux macho man gets caught doing it, as I'd reported, behind a hedge at Will Rogers Park in Beverly Hills—the playground for kids that's barely a coke spoon's-throw from the public toilet where cops once arrested Brit singer George "I Want Your Sex" Michael for boy-*oh*-boy skanky-panky.

Funny old George. He'd uttered one of my fave celeb quotes ever when he'd said, "Vaginas bother me the way spiders bother some people!" (Oh, wait . . . that was *Boy George*!)

Anyway, despite the flack attack, it had been a good day. I'd served up steamy gourmet gossip that had Hollywood and the blogosphere giggling, Googling, tweeting, texting and sexting! My iPhone jammed with e-mails and voice mails. My Twitter tweeted nonstop. Even the archbishop's office had called. Not His Grace himself, but a handsome, young gay priest/gossip fan who uses a code name whenever he phones (which is often), begging me to "confess" secret celebrity sins deemed too hot for even my column.

Imagine, a gossip junkie priest!

Why do I humor him? Because he hears the confessions of Hollywood's rich and powerful. And while what's whispered in the confessional is supposedly sacred, I'd be willing to swear on a stack of Bibles that someday, Father Flamer will tip me to a sensational sin 'fessed up by one of his boldface-name parishioners. From lips queer to God's ear, so to speak—with a quick whisper to Kelly in between, eh?

How do I know that will happen?

Fact: Even notoriously close-mouthed folks experience a sudden urge to regurgitate dirt whenever they encounter me in the clubs or on the street. They know I'm a pro so they're dying to impress by proving that they, too, are privy to Hollywood hush-hush. It is absolutely overwhelming, this deep-seated human need to confess. And . . . *hallelujah!* Where would the Church, or I, be without the urge to purge? After all, if everyone kept their secrets *secret,* there'd be no gossip, *n'est-ce pas?*

But gossip, thank heaven, spreads eternal, due to one immutable rule: Everyone tells one person!

Even those who swear they'll *never* pass a secret on, and genuinely mean it when they say it, are nonetheless driven to tell the one person they absolutely trust—after abjuring them to keep their mouth shut, of course. So, precisely because we *all* have that one person we absolutely trust—best friend, lover, spouse, mom, etc.—once we stumble on something hot, we cannot wait to whisper it in their ear. And it doesn't end there, of course. Because *that* person—after solemnly vowing their silence—will invariably whisper the "inviolate" new gossip secret to that one special person *they* most trust.

And on, and on, and on . . .

Think about it. Gossip serves a serious function in human society. It's much more than a prurient, pounding jungle telegraph for transmitting naughty tales. It's the conduit by which we learn about human nature, and intuit just how much aberrant behavior the tribe will condone before it condemns. Hot gossip will *not* be contained! The second you hear it, you're desperate to share it. Especially with someone like . . . *me*, an aficionado who'll truly savor your tantalizing morsel!

But more about my beloved profession later.

Suddenly, hotel staff were milling around our fallen Flackette, attempting to revive her. She moaned, her head twisting sharply, then barfed on a security guard's highly polished shoes. Turning away, I pushed through the crowd and grabbed a just-vacated stool at the bar. I ordered a sidecar and toyed with a sudden idea for a new gag: "Why do vampires love/hate drinking Bloody Marys?" Then I found myself chuckling again at PR Patty's "bloodsucker" line. Now *that* was funny! Even the most humorless vampire would crack up at that one.

Trust me on this because—pardon me for endlessly belaboring the point —I am a *real* vampire.

Really.

And let me be absolutely clear that I do *not* mean, as Flackette did with her hilarious "bloodsucker" crack, that as a tabloid gossip columnist I'm a metaphorical sucker of celeb blood. I am that also, of course, but I am literally *nosferatu* . . . vampire! A centuries-old member of the undead. Transylvania branch, y'all, and dang proud of it! (See, there I go again.)

And, *no*, I am *not* one of those sunken-eyed Alice Cooper-esque Goth freaks who prowl Hollywood Boulevard in black mascara and eyeliner, getting chicks hot by pretending to be a supernatural creature. I am the real deal—an undead being who emerges from the grave at intervals to live among you "live ones" and feed on your hot, succulent blood—just like in the movies.

Which reminds me, let me note right here that in my opinion Hollywood has done a damn fine job of portraying my kind accurately, give or take a few details I'll fill you in on later. And if I seem overly quick to praise moviemakers, let the truth be told: I am a total sucker (having *pun* yet?) when it comes to glittery, glam-tastic TinselTown.

Burt Lancaster, playing evil gossip columnist J.J. Hunsecker in the iconic fifties flick, *Sweet Smell of Success*, said it first:

"I *love* this dirty town!"

And I second that home-erotic emotion. Which is why, after three centuries of wandering the earth, I have happily settled here in the city of my vampire dreams, Hollywood.

I *love* this silly, scary, sexy town.

And now, in the immortal words of Mick Jagger, please allow me to introduce myself.

Chapter Two

Page from history: I was born of good family and christened Dragomir Craiovescu.

A moldering gravestone bearing that name lies forgotten somewhere in eastern Romania. It marks my unexpected death in 1733, the memorable year of my first youthful passion with an older woman, a devastatingly beautiful friend of my dear mother. It was she, the intoxicating and dangerous Countess Drina Pavlenko, undead and living undetected among mortals, who finally gave in to my endless pleadings one moonlit night and bit deeply into my neck, slaking her savage thirst and beginning the conversion that finally made me one of her kind.

In that one blinding moment, as I drank Drina's succulent essence from a vein just a handsbreadth from her vulva, her fangs sank into my neck and I spasmed in terminal ecstasy, slipping the surly bonds of life, but not of Earth.

Call me crazy, gossip fans, but I think of that day as my *true* birthday; the first day of the rest of my undead life.

After surfacing at Hollywood and Vine in the late thirties, I danced my carefree way through the forties with Fred Astaire and Ginger Rogers. No, really . . . I actually socialized with Fred and "hubba-hubba" Ginger. The lady even had quite the crush on me. I kept her at arm's length, though. Ginger had no idea what I really was, of course. She knew me only as the "sexy, but scary" *Los Angeles Times* showbiz writer with the unpronounceable name, who absolutely idolized her.

But ladies do get jealous. So I made damn sure Ginger never knew about my affair with Rita Hayworth. Or Lucille Ball. Yeah, Lucy, that funny, sexy lady. A chorus girl who was just breaking into movies when I first enjoyed her favors, Lucy was a lithe, long-legged, milky-skinned redhead. Ah, did the carpet match the drapes, you ask? That naughty question invariably cracked Lucy up.

"People *always* ask me that," she'd giggle.

The answer? Sorry, but I *loved* Lucy, and I *never* gossip about lovers. Even gossip columnists have principles. Well, the good ones, anyway, who are artfully filthy and funny, but always fair—cutting, but never cruel. That's why all but a handful crash and burn.

Through Fred and Ginger, I got to hang with all the greats—Gable, Grant, Hepburn, Tracy, Cooper, Bogart. And later, the younger crowd—Garland, Rooney, Taylor, Brando, and Monroe. Fun times! In 1951, I met my fave tough-guy screen idol, the lantern-jawed Lee Marvin, at a snack shack on Sunset Boulevard. I'd ridden into the parking lot on my brand-new Harley Davidson, and there was Lee, perched on his Triumph Tiger, looking so raffish, so cool and genuinely scary that I suspected for a moment he might actually be one of *our* kind.

Especially when he effortlessly pronounced my Romanian name correctly.

"Dragomir *Craiovescu?*"

Cocking his massive-aggressive chin at my bike, Lee leered and rasped, "Hey, Drag. Wanna drag? For beers?"

Lee Marvin; Marine Corps. Caught a Jap sniper's bullet at Saipan; got the Purple Heart. "Shot in the ass," he'd say, and it was true. Buried with the bravest at Arlington National Cemetery, after finally winning his well-deserved Oscar, thank God, for *Cat Ballou* with then-red-hot costar Jane Fonda. But it wasn't Jane who Lee thanked as he clutched his golden prize at the Oscars. Famously and hilariously, he gave full credit to "a horse somewhere out in the Valley" that he'd ridden in the film. Loved that guy.

It was Lee who finally introduced me to the electric young star who became my best pal ever: James Dean. Jimmy and I forged an instant friendship based on fabulous motorcycle rides that always began on the Sunset Strip, and ended God knows where. Malibu, Big Sur, Frisco, Laguna Beach, San Diego (Jimmy called it "'Dago"), Baja, or Tijuana. Jimmy and I were tight, inseparable. He schooled me on being cool, and loved the name "Clark Kelly" when I decided to get hip and dump "Dragomir." But fate ended the fun in 1956 when Jimmy crashed and died in his Porsche.

Suddenly desolate and hopeless as never before, I chose to enter the earth for a long, deep sleep. I mourned my pal deeply. So right after the funeral, I burrowed deep beneath Jimmy's grave in his hometown of Fairmount, Indiana, never emerging from the seductive weight of earth until about seven years ago. Then, refreshed and suddenly raring to go, I could hardly wait to experience this new, young, hyper-digitalized Hollywood!

Just one point I'd like to make about burying myself beneath Jimmy for nearly fifty years: I'm not gay. Hollywood gets very hung up on which way guys swing—ergo, straight studs Brad Pitt and George Clooney trigger giggles by lounging in each other's laps. So let me be clear that I've sucked male blood, but nothing else! Pursuant to that, let me tell you about my instantly visceral reaction that Saturday night at The Roosevelt when I suddenly spotted that truly sultry, female vision across the crowded lounge —my Hollywood dream girl, Miss Scarlett Johansson.

Wow! *Total* gonad jolt! (Oh, yes, we *do* have gonads.)

Angel Eyes was seated in semidarkness at a banquette toward the back of the Roosevelt lounge, but was clearly visible to me. My kind, as you may know from vampire lore, are often equated with bats, which is strange, really, considering the time-honored cliché, "blind as a bat." We're actually blessed with the night vision of hunting owls.

From across the darkened lounge, an ethereal glow emanated from Miss Scarlett's pale, porcelain skin. This halo'd angel, this living representation of a portrait by Vermeer, has no equal among the countless women I've laid eyes on over several centuries. Even among The Clans, as we call ourselves, I'm notorious for being what my kind term "a thirsty bastard" when it comes to pale young virgins. Not that Miss Scarlett, who's dallied at marriage and diddled the dashing Sean Penn, is an actual virgin. But to steal a phrase from Mr. Penn's kinky ex, Madonna, shining ScarJo will forever be "like a virgin" in my mind.

And before you ask, no, that pale white neck has not felt the sharp prick, so to speak, of my affections. I would never dream of invading Miss Scarlett's sleeping chamber uninvited; although once, in the dark of night, I winged to her mansion and hovered outside a second-story window as she prepared for bed. The dazzling images I spied that moonlit eve will illuminate my dreams in every tomb I inhabit from now 'til Doomsday.

But wait, you may ask, will I ever surrender to my barely suppressed lust for Scarlett Lady? Will I not slake the unquenchable thirst that grips me whenever I see her? Sadly, no. *Never.* I am not some sleazy celebrity stalker. When I dine gourmet, I prefer to be an invited guest. Color me old-fashioned, folks.

So tonight I will do what I always do when overwhelmed by ScarJo's incandescent presence. I will depart this place before I'm seized by what you human beings would quaintly refer to as "blood lust." A condition that, were it to overtake me, would leave the joint looking like a bloody abattoir. That phrase is not necessarily oxymoronic, by the way. An abattoir is "bloody" by definition, of course, but what if nothing's been slaughtered there for . . . weeks, *eh*? Ah, word games! Love 'em. But I digress, as—you've surely noticed—I often do!

Oops, sorry. Again, how typical. In blathering on about *what* I am, and what I'm *not*, I haven't formally introduced myself, although you did hear my 'now' name during that radio broadcast on KABC; the boldface byline over my column in the *National Revealer*, America's most-read tabloid:

Clark Kelly.

Sirs and Madames, pleased to meet you.

Now, Clark Kelly's not my birth name, as you already know. I'd assumed it, after three centuries of wandering the earth, when I finally settled here in the city of my dreams. And let me be clear, when I say "dreams," I do not mean the kind of pale, shadow-box images that flitter through the shallow, nocturnal slumbers of human beings. My kind measure sleep cycles in years, even decades. Our dreams, experienced during catatonic suspensions of a depth incomprehensible to mortals, feel more vivid, more real, if you will, than reality itself. Don't even *try* to imagine it, human pals! So, awake or asleep, above ground or below, my dream is my life, and life is my dream of Hollywood.

I *love* this silly, scary, sexy town.

TinselTown.

Early in the fabled fifties, I'd assumed the *nom de plume* by which you, not to mention millions who read my tabloid gossip column in *The Revealer*, might know me by today. It's admittedly a "square" name, picked simply because it felt just right for those innocent, pre-Elvis times: Clark Kelly.

My name was inspired, as you might guess, by silver screen legends Clark Gable and Gene Kelly. My admiration for the great Gable needs no explanation. "Kelly" was a tip of the hat to my abiding passion for dance, tango and tap especially. Macho hoofer Gene Kelly was actually my second favorite among the male dancing legends, but Clark Astaire sounded incredibly stupid. Ergo, I became—and remain today—Clark Kelly. Like any fresh-faced hick from Hicksville seeking Hollywood fame and fortune, I exchanged the exotic kitsch of *Dragomir Craiovescu* for an all-American generic designed to play well in the Corn Belt.

Clark Kelly. My first-ever pseudonym. In previous stints above the firmament, I'd never felt the need to adopt a "stage name." When I'd surfaced for the first time here in my adopted city during the late thirties, my given moniker, however baroque and exotic it might sound today, fit the tenor of those melodramatic times perfectly. It was The Golden Age of Hollywood. Marquees were lit with names like Bela Lugosi, Theda Bara, Eva Gabor, Greta Garbo, etc. So Dragomir Craiovescu sounded quite natural in those times.

Today, I'm just plain Clark Kelly, Vampire Gossip Columnist.

Chapter Three

I tossed a fifty-dollar bill on the bar and winked as the barman gushed, "Thank you, Mr. Kelly."

I knocked back my sidecar, moved to exit the Roosevelt bar, and passed Miss Scarlett's table. Unwisely, I let my mind reach out to touch her psyche —just lightly, mind you—and was immediately trapped in the powerful pull of what felt like an industrial-strength electromagnetic tractor beam. Our eyes met directly, for the very first time; I'd never before dared to stare full-on into those huge, limpid orbs. She eyed me impassively, and, to use tabloid terminology reserved for throbbing first encounters: *Sparks flew!*

Focusing my energy, I disengaged myself from ScarJo's powerful force field with some effort, sensing the seductive, intoxicating heat of blood pulsing through the delicate tracery of veins beneath that translucent skin.

Ah, blood. It's food, it's sex, it's . . . everything.

I willed myself to march toward the main entrance, but suddenly became aware of a hostile male presence blocking my way. Almost grateful for the diversion, I refocused the energy roiling within me and approached the impudent human obstacle.

Smiling broadly, I brayed, "Well, well, well . . . if it isn't Danny Payne!"

My florid, cheery tone made him grimace. This creepy, so-called "street magician"—who'd achieved fame hanging off buildings while holding his breath, or whatever—was one of the nastiest narcissists you'll ever meet, even in Hollywood. Payne's face twisted into his trademark sneer as he responded, mimicking my inflection and doing it quite well, I must admit.

"Why . . . if it isn't Clark Kelly."

Okay. I had *no* time for this asshole. It was just after one in the morning, practically midday for me, and there was vampire work yet to be done. Magic Prick needed to be dealt with swiftly.

Loudly, sarcastically, Payne bellowed. "Look, everyone, it's Clark Kelly, the *famous* gossip columnist."

Hambone was playing to the crowd, which now sensed something was up. What, they knew not, of course. But I did. Not because of vampire prescience, but because we have something of a history, Payne and I. He'd once implied, during an appearance on the Howard Stern Show when I was also a guest, that my gossip column was a pack of lies. I'd skinned him alive, flaying him with vicious insults honed over centuries as Howard, along with his Wack Pack, cracked up.

Laughing, Stern had told his listeners, "Good thing Clark's broadcasting from the West Coast, or these guys would be killing each other!"

Right on, Howard.

But now, here we were, Payne and I at last, and I knew exactly what was coming next from this arrogant bullyboy. He'd conjure up some kind of bullshit "street" magic, magically calculated to make *me* look like a fool.

"Hey, Kelly," Payne barked. "Wanna see a magic trick?"

Lee Marvin had said it best in *The Killers* while terrorizing a sightless receptionist at a school for the blind, who'd delayed him momentarily in his quest to ice a teacher, who'd double-crossed a mob boss: "Lady, I got *no* time for this shit!"

Loudly, jovially, I said instead, "Hey . . . sounds like *fun*, Payne."

And I smiled.

"I love magic," I told him, waving a hand at the buzzing crowd. "So . . . *dazzle us!*"

In that split second, as my broad gesture directed the crowd's attention to him, I focused the terrible inner power my kind can command and fired it through my narrowed vampire eyes. Instantly, violently, Payne was blown off his feet and shot backward at warp speed. He slammed into the wall with an awful thud and slid slowly to the floor. Pointing at the dazed chump, I started applauding, yelling in feigned amazement to the stunned crowd.

"*Wow!* How the hell did he DO that? Great trick, Payne. Give the guy a big hand, people!"

Sure enough, the crowd applauded like trained seals; proving once again that people are innately programmed to do what they're told. Such an endearing human trait.

Still applauding, I strolled past Payne, who was being lifted back to his feet by his stunned posse—including longtime groupie Leonardo DiCaprio, I noted—as I waved buh-bye and exited. Hmmm? Leo sporting a mustache? For a new role, perhaps? Have to check that out for the column. I memoed myself as I exited the Roosevelt, and hit Hollywood Boulevard.

As if on cue, the always-present pack of paparazzi camped on the sidewalk surged forward, then suddenly retreated, snarling and growling as one of their number noted my barely bared fangs and barked, "It's Kelly!"

Not that I needed to flash my equipment. These slavering beasts knew they were in the presence of a superior creature. Because *they* are creatures, too. Especially the ugly lycanthrope who'd shouted my name.

Fact: Wherever vampires appear, werewolves are never far behind.

And here's Hollywood's dirty little secret: quite a number of modern-day camera-flashers—the so-called *paparazzi*—are actually werewolves. It had happened gradually over the years. All those polite, professional, white-guy photographers (like Peter Borsari and Roger Karnbad, who'd once clicked celeb pics outside Wolfgang's, The Ivy, Nicky Blair's and the Polo Lounge) retired or died off, only to be replaced by today's gibbering, bestial paparazzi pack that celebrities love to hate. And when did that begin to happen? Just as I came back into my current wakeful state in the mid-2000s. Coincidence? No. Vampires and werewolves are like hot dogs and buns, beer and pretzels, Frank and Dean, Brad and Angie; find one, you'd best start peeling an eye for the other.

That's right, Hollywood stars. Your worst fears realized.

Paparazzi *werewolves*!

To be clear, vampires do not fear werewolves. All things being equal, they are the lesser species. Still we are wary of the treacherous beasts. They are a menace because they are primitive and single-minded, lurking endlessly once they mark you as prey. Drop your guard and the next sound you hear could be your skull popping in the grip of those fearsome teeth.

The Roosevelt Hotel valet came running up. "I'll get your car right away, Mr. Kelly!"

"No, Billy," I said. "I'm going to take a walk. Should be back in an hour, but if not, just keep it in the lot and I'll drop by tomorrow, okay?"

"Yes sir," he said, palming the twenty I slipped him.

I walked briskly down one long block, faded into a dark alley . . .

. . . and rocketed straight up, up, up into the night sky, finally reaching my fave cruising altitude—about six hundred feet. It was high enough for panoramic viewing, but low enough to avoid the ubiquitous Trauma Hawk helicopters whirring to and from Cedars-Sinai Hospital, or the hard-charging LAPD choppers with blazing spotlights perennially scanning the streets for perps.

Below me, the ribbon of neon that was Hollywood Boulevard flickered and faded.

I banked south, then west, soaring through the cool night air over Beverly Hills, then Sunset Boulevard, and the UCLA campus. I veered north at the beach, peering down at one of my favorite after-dark views, the Santa Monica Pier, with its gaily lit Ferris wheel, jutting into the Pacific Ocean swells. Ah, dead or alive, we're all kids at heart, aren't we? Below me, the Pacific Coast Highway snaked north along the shoreline.

Kicking it hard, I blasted up the coast. Destination? Malibu.

Chapter Four

As I ruminated on the pressing gossip business I'd transact this night in that fabled celebrity paradise surfers and punks call The 'Bu, I took in the twinkling lights of ships and oil rigs dotting the black Pacific void below. Man, what a beautiful night. I felt, you'll pardon the expression, truly alive. Flying like a bird, free and at will, the powerful winds lifting me to the skies, the joy irresistible.

Running late, dammit. But it was okay. Malibu's just twenty miles away, as the vampire flies.

Okay, *that* was a truly corny line. Comedically obnoxious, and a perfect example of how I'm "always on," as one of my human stand-up comedian pals puts it. Worse, it ruptured the mood of the tale I'm spinning here. By twisting the cliché "as the crow flies" into a corny crack, I dissipated the dramatic tension of my rocketing leap into the moonlight. *Now* can you imagine how annoying my own kind find me?

Unlike human beings, vampires have almost no sense of humor. You guys, at least, can find grins even in how totally *lame* some of my jokes are. (*Some*, okay?) But not my undead homies! NO grins there, bro'! That's why I don't hang with vamps much, because when it comes to cracking gags, I can't help myself. I love going for the belly laugh. I've even thought of trying stand-up comedy myself.

Can you imagine? A vampire *comedian*?

"Good evening, folks. Great to be appearing here tonight at The Improv! As a vampire, I'm excited to see so many 'live ones' here tonight! Hey, what a great-looking audience! Or, as I like to call you, *energy drinks*! . . . (*Rim shot!*) . . . Folks, if you think vampire comedy's easy, you're making a *grave* mistake! . . . (*Cymbal crash!*)"

Ah, 'twas a grand night to be flying. I felt fired up, like I always feel when I'm tracking a hot news story—not to mention a hot girl. I looked down and smiled, experiencing a sudden surge of love for Mother Earth.

And I was seized with euphoric gratitude that my kind had been granted the precious gift of flight. It's no secret that we often yearn to be reborn and feel warm blood coursing through our veins again. I've been gripped by this longing sporadically over the centuries. But each time I arise from the earth and shake off the grave's chill embrace, a smile touches my lips as I anticipate the thrill of soaring above the world like a great predator bird, or a great predator vampire, if you will. And, although I prefer night flight for obvious reasons, sunrise and sunset are breathtaking when viewed from aloft.

But wait, you ask, don't vampires die if exposed to sunlight? Strictly speaking, we do, yes, but only if the exposure is prolonged and incessant. Contrary to Hollywood myth, brief sojourns in daylight are not instantly destructive, although the risk does increase with exponential swiftness. The symptoms, while quite bearable initially, grow progressively worse—like a severe allergy attack—bearable until they suddenly blow your body wide open.

Vampire moviemakers exploit this dramatic device endlessly, showing us exploding like fireballs and dissolving into powdery ash whenever we're exposed to even a stray ray of sunlight. And who can blame them? It's an irresistible bit of lurid dramatic license, a guaranteed crowd-pleaser. But pure bullshit. Exposure to daylight does *not* trigger instant vaporization, although you do start feeling like crap if you push it much past an hour or two. After excessive direct exposure to That Lucky Old Sun, you feel the urge to seek a dark, quiet grave and pull it in over your head.

Sorry. Didn't mean to go all "Vampire 101" on your ass. Time to cut to the chase. What you really want to know right now, of course, is why the hell is the world's only vampire gossip columnist swooping through the night skies toward Malibu like a bat out of hell?

Wait, there it is! Just coming into view below. Malibu Beach. *The 'Bu!* That laid-back-but-exciting playground to the stars. And, as a point of interest for all Olde Hollywood fans, I'm looping down, down, down, toward a wooded estate once owned by that fiery forties movie bombshell, dazzling Dolores Del Rio. Today it's a modern landmark, one of TinselTown's rapidly proliferating celebrity rehab centers. Malibu Colony's infested with luxury detox joints catering to troubled, substance-abusing stars. They keep popping up *everywhere*. Detoxing the rich and famous has burgeoned into a big-bucks industry.

So many fucked-up stars, so few places to put them!

You've heard of the famed rehab hideaway Promises that's often in the news, right? Well, the even newer one I'm headed for tonight is called Miracles! Is that just too totally *precious*, or what? Truth be told, the only fucking "miracle" is how they keep these joints perennially packed with rich dope fiends, who casually hemorrhage five thousand dollars a day *minimum* for treatment.

Rehab! Hollywood's hot new growth industry.

No surprise, you say? You're assuming that A-listers crowd these places so they can heal their substance-abusing asses in a drug-free atmosphere, right? *Wrong!* As readers of my gossip column know, Miracles and other rehab centers like it often double as luxury spas for filthy-rich celeb head cases who want to score the finest addictive substances money can buy and then cook, snort and savor it at their leisure in a secure, swanky facility, safe from the prying eyes of paparazzi. Then, through the lying mouths of their PR peeps, they can piously announce to the world that they're "in recovery."

Hear what I'm saying, gossip fans? Behind those high rehab walls, celebs can safely sniff, scarf or inject drugs, guzzle booze and even enjoy discreet sex with other celebs or with super-cute nurses and interns these places tend to hire. Best of all, Beverly Hills is just a limo ride away. So when the dreaded drug munchies make you suddenly ravenous, no problemo! Fave celeb snackeries like Wolfgang Puck, Mr. Chow's and The Ivy are ready to roll gourmet takeout up the Pacific Coast Highway by limo. Shocking? Sure. But it all makes perfect sense when you think about it.

Ask any real Hollywood insider where's the best place to score drugs without fear of getting busted, and they'll tell you, *"Rehab!"*

Ask big-time dealers offloading primo shit from the same Golden Triangle warlord who supplies world-class connoisseurs like Keith Richards. They'll tell you there's one place where you can *always* find rich-and-eager junkies: *"Rehab!"*

And please, don't go all dumbass and ask how drugs can filter into a locked-down facility. Just remember, people *love* to make celebrities happy. And many of those people work in *"Rehab!"*

Breaking the "strict" rules and smuggling contraband goodies, like pills to pop and sniffy to sniff, to these larger-than-life folks is virtual child's play. Very *lucrative* child's play.

Aah! There's Miracles below, just coming into sight and affording me the perfect moment to demonstrate my theory! Casting my night-vision vampire orbs down at the front entrance of this celeb rehab Mecca, I suddenly spot an obsequious valet ushering a world-famous face out the front entrance to her equally famous car—a much-photographed Bentley convertible sporting a custom pink candy-flake paint job.

It's the only car in the world like it, and it belongs to the flaky, young, rich-bitch mega-celebrity and heiress, Roma Kane.

"Well, well, well," I yell exultingly into the night air. "Visiting a friend in rehab when you could be out partying, Roma? Why, I wonder?"

My rhetorical question floats in the air as she hops into her ostentatious, hot-pink ride—The Pepto-mobile, as I'd sneeringly dubbed it in my column —and races out of the Miracles driveway, heading south on the Pacific Coast Highway toward LA.

So "Roma Does Miracles!" How very, very interesting. It played into the nagging gossip hunch I'd been nursing lately, and one I'd be investigating tonight.

Descending through the darkness, I slowed and hovered about thirty feet above the roof of Miracles, carefully reaching out for a mind I knew quite intimately, but in a far different way than when I'd reached out to Miss Scarlett earlier. That had been a relatively difficult exercise. This would be child's play.

To explain; movies, television, Anne Rice and various so-called vamp "experts" posit that infiltrating the wary, sentient mind of a stranger requires enormous expertise and power. This is true. We call it "mind-rolling," by the way. It's how I'd seized Payne's mind and triggered his muscles to collide with that wall. But reconnecting with the mellow psyche of a *previously satisfied* blood donor? An absolute cinch, folks. Happily, the focus of this evening's exercise happened to be a young woman of somewhat intimate acquaintance, as shall be explained in due course.

Her name? Taylor Logan.

Yes, *that* Taylor Logan.

Or, as she's known in even the most obscure corners of the planet, *TayLo*!

Once again, I was about to encounter that sex-sational, brilliant young actress who, although barely twenty-three, had suddenly taken Hollywood by storm then, just as suddenly, burned her ass halfway down the road to Hell, indulging a mind-blowing appetite for booze, drugs, fast cars, and marathon sex. Who was it who said, "Taylor Logan knows all, ingests all, and *balls* all—male and female alike"?

Why, that was . . . Clark Kelly, I believe. In that wonderful gossip column he writes.

Ah, sweet, doomed, talented TayLo! She'd become my gushing new font of gossip news, truly a dream source for a scandal-starved columnist, and a gift that will never stop giving. *If* I played my cards right and to be honest, you would not be incorrect if you sensed a certain yearning beyond a lust for news in the phrase "a gift that will never stop giving." Just saying.

Oh, yes, friends. Gossip business of a high order *would* be transacted here tonight.

Chapter Five

I felt her mind stirring, sensing my probing intrusion. She twisted in her bed, fighting the impulse to wake, which was a good thing. I probed deeper, detecting what might be the tiniest trace of drug residue in her system; also a good thing for my purposes. Ah, she's pulled back from the abyss of Morpheus, and . . . good, she was wide awake now, her mind calling out to me, so desperately, plaintively . . . sweetly.

"Master, come to me. I need you . . . please come!"

Wow! She actually called me "Master". Where the hell did she get *that*? Old vampire flicks, probably. *I* certainly never told her to call me Master, but coming from her, the term could grow on me.

Anyway, as I was saying, you can see that unzipping Taylor Logan's mind was no big deal for me. Why? Because unlike Scarlett Johansson, Miss Taylor Logan is, as I have mentioned, an intimate acquaintance.

I will reveal how that came about forthwith, but for the moment, let it suffice to say that on a night not long ago, under a full moon, this incredibly sexy young star lay thrashing and gasping as my fangs grazed her neck, screaming out her sexual ecstasy as I punctured two holes in her fair skin and hungrily sucked her rich, steaming life force.

This occurred just once. But once, as we V-Men like to say, is enough. Tonight, blood was calling out to blood. My voice reverberated in her aroused brain.

"Get out of bed, precious . . . walk to the window. Open it wide for me."

As she obeyed, I sailed down onto the roof of Miracles—a four-story edifice poised dramatically over a cliff. Landed on the building's top ledge, I slithered face-first down the front wall, keeping an eye cocked for wandering security personnel. Descending to the second story, I glided in through the window she'd opened.

Instantly she flew into my arms, a pretty picture in a diaphanous nightdress, one breast carelessly exposed as a strap slipped off her shoulder.

I was overpowered momentarily as she embraced me. I felt blood heating her skin. I pushed her back, gently at first. She resisted. My mind slammed her backward. She fell onto the bed, whispering hoarsely.

"Please . . . please . . . you know what I want. Please do it to me again, like before . . . I need you so badly . . . I need . . . goddam you, you know fucking well what I want. *Give it to me!*"

I looked directly into her eyes, holding a finger to my lips. She opened her mouth to speak, then recoiled from the punishing touch of my power, feeling it coil inside her.

"You're hurting me, you bastard," she cried, then subsided quickly at the warning in my eye.

Feisty little devil, this Taylor Logan! Irish blood, of course. Invigorating, mercurial, and riding a dope-driven roller coaster of emotions.

"Hello, TayLo," I said.

She rolled her eyes, giggling just a little. "Ever since you called me that in your column, *everyone* does. *'TayLo!'* Fuck, I hate that nickname. It reminds me of that old fat-ass, J.Lo."

I smiled. "Don't worry, babe. No one will ever make *that* association."

Looking down, I marveled as she squirmed seductively on the bed. What a beauty. Full lips, red-blond hair, magnificent legs, and a bosom worthy of mounting on the prow of a Viking ship.

I gestured at the slipped strap. "Nip needs a tuck, sweetie."

She didn't move.

Looking up at me, she faked a pout and asked, "This time, will you *fuck* me, too?"

I laughed. Was this a fun girl, or what?

"When's the last time you actually *did* get fucked, may I ask?"

She shrugged and covered her tit before she rose and walked to the minibar. Pulling a Gatorade from the fridge, she popped the top, and smiled sweetly.

"Sorry, I'm all out of *blood*. Can I get you something else?"

I shook my head, still waiting for her answer.

She guzzled the Gatorade, thinking it over, then said, "Let's see, I got fucked . . . yeah, it was the day before yesterday. A young intern, really cute guy. Did me doggie-style at the desk over there."

I glanced at the desk and nodded. "Pretty picture. Thanks for putting it in my head, bitch. I am *so* jealous, okay? Now, let me ask an important question, and *no* bullshit! When's the last time you did drugs?"

She guzzled again, raising her eyebrows quizzically.

"Drugs? Dude, get real, this is *rehab*—or didn't you notice?"

I smiled sardonically; the way a vampire is supposed to smile, the classic one-raised-eyebrow-lips-compressed-in-a-sneer, Frank Langella-like evil smirk. I used to practice it in front of my mother's bedroom looking glass when I was a Transylvanian teenager.

"Very amusing, TayLo, but rather puzzling, considering that I sensed a trace presence of drugs when I meshed with your mind. Seems you've miraculously found a way to score sniffy stuff here at Miracles."

The minx flashed a coquettish smile. Had to admire the cool little cucumber. Tell most girls you'd just popped into their mind for a look-see, they'd be terrified—wondering if you'd detected any lingering fantasies about booty sex or replayed their latest super-session with the Pink Pearl Bunny.

Instead, our heroine said, "Hmm, you checked the tank by looking inside? Doesn't sound very accurate. Why not *siphon out* a few drops and do a real test, big boy?"

I suppressed the urge to bust out laughing. I had to maintain dignity and control, but goddam . . . the *balls* on this girl! She had true bravery; a unique fierceness of spirit. She wasn't nuts, and had the healthy sense of fear necessary for self-preservation, but her feistiness was genuine, not false bravado. I've been scaring girls for centuries, so take it from a guy who knows. But her raging courage had a downside. It fueled her appetite for danger-tinged pursuits like sex, drugs, crashing cars, and flirting with vampires.

A light film of sweat on her half-exposed breasts glistened in the moonlight. I looked deep in her eyes, remembering her as she was on another moonlit night I am now driven to tell you about; the magical night I first met TayLo, as she's known to the untold millions of males who want to fuck her . . . and the females who want to *be* her.

Okay, roll film for a fascinating flashback, vamp fans. It gets a tad twisty, so *stay alert.*

Chapter Six

Fury! A klieg-lights-and-limousines, red-carpet gala ballyhooed the grand opening of Fury, a venue destined to morph instantly into Hollywood's most happening club, five blocks south of Santa Monica Boulevard on La Cienega.

On that moonlit night, Taylor Logan, the screen's hottest young female star, rolled up to the club in her black stretch limo. Hustled past the surging crowd of rope-a-doped wannabes by three rhino-sized bodyguards, TayLo barely cracked a smile. Her surprise arrival had been madly texted by reporters from *Star*, *TMZ*, *The National Enquirer* . . . pretty much everyone. The club's management was ecstatic. Only an hour before, they'd been alerted that TayLo had graciously agreed—at the very last possible minute —to accept their $1 million cashier's check and grace them with a twenty-minute visit that would put Fury on the worldwide gossip map.

TayLo's handlers had demanded super-heavy security—and here it came, a flying wedge of fifteen brutes who literally exploded through the crowd massed at the entrance. People went down hard, screaming in pain. Stray flecks of blood spotted the sidewalk.

"*Mon dieu!* Zey are such fucking bastards," said my favorite Hollywood restaurateur, Jean-Claude Chatenet.

By sheer coincidence, I'd decided to dine *alfresco* that very evening on the patio at Jean-Claude's petite French bistro, directly across the street from Fury. I'd seen TayLo arrive and watched the paparazzi erupt in a feeding frenzy as her limo rolled up. Firing their cameras like weapons, desperate for the money shot, they'd surged and shoved like the tough little bastards they are—until the club's bigger, tougher bastards slammed them back into the gutter.

"Just a normal night in Hollywood," I told Jean-Claude as I paid my bill.

I strolled across the street, skirted the crowd outside Fury's front entrance, walked to an alley just a few doors down, and then doubled back to the unmarked, locked back entrance. I banged on the door in a code the owner and I had prearranged twenty minutes earlier when I'd texted him from the restaurant.

The door swung wide.

"Clark, my dear friend. Come in, and welcome to my latest fantasy."

Sami Kardanian, a super-rich Shah of Sunset, embraced me. Then we exchanged fist bumps—keeping it Old World and real at the same time.

"It is so wonderfully convenient, Sammy, that you now own more than half of the hot clubs in this town. Instead of dealing with thirty people, you've become one-stop shopping for me. And I see that your fabled Persian charm has enticed the lovely TayLo to grace the place."

Sami smiled and said drily, "That, and a few of my fabled Persian dollars."

Taking me companionably by the arm, he escorted me from the quiet of the back room and out into the thumping roar and flashing lights of the jam-packed club. He led me to a private booth. We sat. Two bouncers posted themselves on either side of the table.

"Some Dom, Clark? The '91, isn't it?"

I paused, but shook my head. Sami snapped his fingers. A waiter nearly dove across the table.

"If I know Mr. Kelly, we can tempt him with a slightly warmed snifter of Remy XO. In fact, bring two. I'll join you," he said.

I smiled. Class act, this guy. We sat, sipped and watched the scene. Familiar faces drifted by . . . Justin Bieber, Selena Gomez, Miley Cyrus, Lindsay Lohan, Channing Tatum, Emma Stone, and Paris Hilton with her pathetic, smelly boy/BFF—the fabled sweaty asshole known as Grease Man—in tow. Then P. Diddy plus posse, Avril Lavigne, one Jonas Brother, both Olson twins, a Kardashian sis whose first name began with a K, of *kourse* . . . and on and on and on.

The only major movie star in the joint was old-timer George Clooney, sporting a gorgeous European-looking brunette. Female, let me add quickly. Kinda ancient for this crowd, but whatever. George dropped by the table to greet Sami, gave me a decidedly curt nod, then headed over to the table where TayLo was holding court and fending off—but totally enjoying the attentions of—a pack of panting, young and not-so-young studs.

She rose to give Clooney a hug, then bounced out on the dance floor to shake off a little sexual energy. She shimmied and shook, her body tight and toned. God, she looked sensational, despite the booze and drugs she consumed so ferociously.

Sami looked over and rolled his eyes. "She's a great beauty and a great talent, but I fear for her. I would marry her if I thought it would save her, but I don't think it would. Not with me, at least. What mere man could control her? Can she survive, Clark?"

I shrugged. "God, I hope so. Look, Sami, you can sum it up in two back-to-back clichés. TayLo still has youth on her side—but she's burning the candle at both ends. Drugs, booze, two car crashes in the past year. She parties 'til dawn, sleeps until midafternoon, causes production delays on every movie she gets. Her agents have warned her that insurance underwriters are starting to balk about covering her projects. My column that hits the streets tomorrow says the studio grapevine's buzzing that she'll be unemployable very soon—if she doesn't OD on drugs first.

"But here's the *really* sad part, pal—studio execs and producers actually like her, because even though she can be a diva, she's not a nasty bitch. She remembers the names of girlfriends, wives, kids and dogs. Even remembers to send birthday and Christmas gifts."

Sami smiled. "And it doesn't hurt that she's a world-class piece of ass."

We sat there, enjoying our cognac and the ass-and-tits parade, idly exchanging nasty gossip about the star faces floating by. Just two tough bastards who still cared whether a young girl killed herself or not.

Suddenly, there was a commotion near the DJ booth. Piercing shrieks of cat-fighting girls rose above the din. Sami jerked his chin. A bouncer guarding our table barreled through the crowd. He was back in thirty seconds, reporting to his boss.

"Paris Hilton's screaming shit at TayLo. Grease Man's egging her on, as usual. Stupid fucking no-tits bitch just can't get used to the fact that TayLo's a star, but she's *so* not. What should I do, boss?"

Sami sighed. "Throw her out, and that fucking Grease Man with her."

Before the bouncer could move, the club's head of security, Eddie Scanlon, rolled up.

"TayLo's pitching a fit about that cunt Paris. She wants to leave immediately. But, boss, she'll be mobbed by those paparazzi waiting for her, and then she'll be pissed at us for not controlling them."

Sami thought it over and smiled. "Actually, throwing Paris out will create the perfect diversion. Let the paparazzi chew on her and Grease Man when the guys escort them out to her car. Make a big production out of protecting them, but let the paparazzi mess with them a little bit. Meanwhile, Eddie, you—and I mean *you* personally—slip TayLo out the back door."

Eddie nodded and took off, the other bouncer in tow. I threw back a last sip of Remy, and then said, "Thanks, Sami. Love the new club, and you'll love the write-up in my column."

Sami nodded. "I trust your discretion, Clark."

I slipped out of the booth, moved quickly through the crowd and caught up with Eddie. He was an ex-LAPD cop, a hard-as-nails guy I'd known for years. He was at TayLo's table, whispering urgently in her ear. She nodded. He muttered a command to his bouncer. The guy high-signed the chief headbanger of the club's gorilla pack. Seconds later, a new commotion erupted behind me. Paris and Grease Man, screaming protests, were being hustled, gently but firmly, out the front door.

As all eyes turned to the new action, Eddie discreetly took TayLo by the arm and guided her toward the back office area. I fell in behind, staying far enough back that they didn't notice me.

When they reached the locked back door, Eddie opened it cautiously, and peered into the alley. I heard him tell TayLo, "Stay tucked close behind me. This alley spills into the next street. A car's going to meet us there. We couldn't tip off your limo driver because those friggin' pappa-*rats* will be watching him. But my driver will get you home, don't worry. Okay? So here we go . . . *let's roll*!"

Pulling her close, Eddie hustled out the door. I waited until it swung shut, then moved to follow them. Hearing a faint scream, I shoved the door wide open and blinked at the blinding flash of a camera strobe.

Eddie yelled. "Back *off*, goddammit!"

The camera flashed again.

"Okay, you fuck . . . I WARNED you!"

Chapter Seven

Eddie charged the lone paparazzo, a guy who hadn't been fooled by the Paris/Grease Man diversion. Slamming into the creep, he knocked him flat. But the guy bounced up fast, face contorted in outrage. Now we had trouble. In the light of the moon, which was waxing gibbous and nearly full, I recognized this foe-tog, a burly bruiser with reddish hair and thick eyebrows that grew together over the bridge of his thick nose. I'd seen him more than once in daylight, and noted that his middle and index fingers were exactly the same length.

The signs were classic. Werewolf! No doubt about it.

Before I could move, the monster paparazzo lashed out with inhuman speed, knocked Eddie unconscious, stepped over his body and charged TayLo, firing his flash as she screamed in terror. Instinctively, knowing the moon's phase was working in my favor, I pulled an old Transylvanian trick. I suddenly howled. Like a wolf . . . or a werewolf.

Done correctly, this triggers the lupine instinct and this time it worked perfectly. The transformation was instantaneous, frightening. The paparazzo's shoulders, chest, and arms suddenly doubled in size, bursting through his clothing. His nose thickened into a snout. Hair sprouted on his face. Hands became nailed claws.

Now he was . . . The Beast.

Jaw thrust forward and opened wide, the monster displayed huge, wolfen fangs as he howled in ancient obedience to the call of the pack and the irresistible command of the lunar cycle. But then, disoriented by his sudden and involuntary transformation, he got tangled in his own feet. He fell to the pavement. His camera shattered. Struggling to rise, confused but enraged, he saw me behind TayLo and roared his challenge.

"Nosferatu . . . Drakul!"

TayLo suddenly turned and caught sight of me crouching behind her. She shrieked in sheer hysteria as I opened my jaws wide, unsheathed my fangs and hissed another ancient word.

"*Bikli* . . . Werewolf!"

Baring his teeth, the man-beast bunched his muscles and sprang. But a werewolf is no match for a vampire. In the blink of an eye, I vanished, instantly materializing behind the hairy bastard. He whirled, sensing my trick, but . . .

"Too late, Wolf Dude!"

Reveling in the dreadful power my kind can summon when our blood is surging, I cupped his hairy head between my hands and twisted sharply. There was a sharp crack of bone as I ripped the creature's bestial skull right off his neck. I held up my bloody trophy, gloating as his acephalous carcass spasmed wildly and slammed to the asphalt.

Then, like a showboating sports jock trying to impress the pretty cheerleader—which I was, I guess—I set my feet, neatly one-handed the hairy lump at a trashcan fifteen feet away and . . . *ka-ching!* . . . made the shot.

Yeah!

No time to pump a victory fist. I heard approaching shouts and howls, feet pounding up the alley. The maddened paparazzi pack, a good fifth of whom were werewolves themselves, had sensed, as their kind always do, that a pack member was down. And while it's true that no werewolf is a match for a vampire one-on-one, I had little stomach for facing a snarling, snapping pack of these ugly bastards with a girl to protect.

TayLo, frozen in the grip of horror so dreadful it choked off her screams, cringed when I put finger to lips and told her, "Don't be afraid. You know who I am?"

She nodded, then gasped. "You're the gossip guy from the *National Revealer*. But you're . . . a . . . a . . . fucking *vampire*?"

I'd retracted my fangs, so I smiled. Reassuringly, I hoped.

"Let's just get you out of here, okay? And trust me, I'll explain it all later."

She nodded, eyes wide. Reaching back over my shoulder to the neck of my suit jacket, I fumbled under the collar and extracted the magnificent swath of exquisite black silk I kept secreted in the lining. As I shook it out behind me, TayLo—fear momentarily submerged by that primal female fascination for fashion—gasped in admiration.

"You . . . you've even got a fucking *cape*?"

I nodded. "Yes. Hopeless traditionalist, I'm afraid."

In an eyeblink, I gathered her up in my arms, feeling her tremble as I unleashed the power and rocketed up, up, up into the moonlit sky.

Looking down, I saw Sami's security guards pouring out the back door of Fury. They lifted Eddie Scanlon and rushed him back inside, just as the ravening paparazzi pack reached the scene of carnage. Frustrated and furious, the fucking beasts were clustered around their fallen pack member, agitated, hopping up and down.

And then it happened . . .

In the sudden excitement of battle, the scent of fresh, hot blood and the power of the waxing moon caused three more paparazzi to transmogrify into werewolves. Evil snouts sniffed the air. Then, as one of them lifted the freshly severed head from the trash can, they clustered around their decapitated bro' and looked skyward, catching sight of my silhouette rising high against the silvery lunar globe. Gnashing their wolfen fangs, the deceased's brother beasts howled, *"Drakul! . . . DRAKUUUUL!"*

My laughter drifted down on the wind. And feisty TayLo—suddenly in the moment, bless her salty little soul—screamed down at the snarling beasts,

"Fuck you! . . . *Fuuuck youuuuu!"*

Understand; this was hardly the first time I'd swooped up a terrified maiden for impromptu flight through night skies. But in my experience, without exception, ladies instantly shrieked, struggled, cried for Mommy, or begged to be taken back to Earth. And who can blame them?

But not our TayLo. The girl didn't stay scared for long. Oh, she was still wide-eyed and keyed up, but this chick was far, far from terrified.

Sniffing the blood roaring under her skin, I sensed only the faintest residue of drugs. She wasn't high. Yet, she'd quickly accepted her somewhat startling situation with the weary sophistication of a jaded chanteuse warming up to warble that exquisite Cole Porter lyric: *"Flying too high with some guy in the sky . . . is my idea . . . of nothing to do . . ."*

She threw back her head, her long hair whipping in the wind as she stared up and embraced the night sky, drinking it in like she'd never seen moon and stars before. Then she shifted her pert little ass, getting downright comfy in my arms.

Her gaze shifted. She stared back over my shoulder, looking utterly fascinated.

I raised an eyebrow. "What?"

She yelled in my ear. "Your cape looks *so* fucking cool, man! Fluttering in the wind, moonlight on silk, it's like . . . black waves."

Girls. Born for fashion.

Then Ice Cool Cutie popped her next surprise. Lips to my ear, she purred, "Your place or mine?"

I almost dropped the bitch!

Chapter Eight

"OMIGOD, what a night that was," she giggled, sucking on her Gatorade as she lounged back on her bed at Miracles. "The look on your face!"

I shook my head, rolled my eyes a bit. She was right. I pride myself, like most vampires—and most men, I suppose—on being a pretty cool tool. But a human girl like this was a first for me. We'd had all kinds of scary vampire/werewolf shit going down that night, but this little pistol had acted like it was just another party night in Hollywood; score some sponsor goodie bags, get high, get laid, crash at sunrise, sleep 'til twilight.

Now *this* was a girl a vampire guy could take home to mother.

If we *had* mothers.

I still remember mine. Still miss her.

She swung her legs over the side of the bed and sat there, remembering that apocalyptic night we'd first laid eyes on each other.

She glugged some more Gatorade, wiped her lips and asked, "Do you remember the very first thing you asked me that night, Mr. One Track Mind?"

I grinned. I'd said to her, "Lady, you fucking high?"

Her coquettish answer had been, "Not yet!"

I don't know why I'd even asked the question. I'd smelled her blood earlier that night at Fury, and blood doesn't lie. No dope to speak of in her system. No STDs either. Hey, even a vampire can't be too careful these days. We're just about totally immune to human disease, but fucking dandruff can be a bitch. Hooray for Head & Shoulders.

TayLo put down her Gatorade deliberately, got up from the bed and walked over to me, ending up thisclose.

"Well," she purred, "how about it?"

"Why, Ms. TayLo," I said in a seductive Gable-as-Rhett-Butler drawl, "you hardly know me."

She rolled her eyes. "Oh, I *know* you, Clark Kelly. Everyone in

Hollywood *knows* you. I'd just never *met* you properly—outside of car crashes and parties—before that crazy night. But I'd read your snarky, sex-obsessed column just like everyone else in this lousy town, and, honestly, I'd always fucking loved it! Even though you always printed the worst shit about me! But you were always *funny*!"

"No, you're always funny," I said, with a playful fingertap to that irresistibly turned-up, freckled nose. "Remember the first time you really cracked me up that night?"

"When I said that I lived at the Château Marmont, so we'd have to make it your place and not mine. The staff was used to seeing me drag in all sorts of strange creatures, but I thought a gossip columnist might be way too weird. Even if they *didn't* know you're a vampire."

"Yeah," I said, "that's when you asked me if I lived in . . . fucking *Forest Lawn?*"

She'd giggled hysterically. So had I. A dead-funny line.

She smiled almost giddily, recalling our first night together. "Then I got in close and told you that I was trying to get you in a good mood so you'd drink my *blood*! And you totally lost it when I asked if you were ready to make me your . . . Bride of Dracula!"

Oh, did I ever remember *that*! I'd started laughing so goddam hard my focus wavered and I lost a hundred feet of altitude before I got it back under control.

That had scared her.

Finally.

Now get a tight grip on your psyche, vampire fans, we undead are far more adept than you live ones at darting back and forth in time, but once again, try to keep up, okay?

Chapter Nine

"Omigod, don't drop me. I'm really scared . . . please, let's stop flying!" She was babbling hysterically and her fingers were digging into my shoulders. Damn! If I were human, I'd scar.

"Calm down, lady. Never lost a passenger yet," I said. "Hey, speaking of stuff to drink . . . how does a chilled bottle of Cristal sound?"

I smiled my most charming, non-sardonic, cute-vampire-boy-next-door smile.

She perked up instantly, forgetting I'd nearly dropped her. "Cristal champagne? Fuck, yeah!"

"We'll be serving it when we land at our destination."

"Which is?"

"Just below us now. Look!" I hovered at three hundred feet, letting her eyeball the neighborhood.

She gasped.

"Omigod, isn't that . . ."

"Yes! That is the legendary Beverly Hills Four Seasons Hotel."

"You live *there*?"

"Sort of."

"What do you mean, 'sort of'?"

"Attention, all passengers," I intoned like a cool pilot guy. "Fasten seatbelts for landing. Local time is three thirty-six. Thank you for flying Transylvanian Airlines."

I descended slowly, keeping a sharp eye out for the security personnel who sporadically roam the Four Seasons rooftop. It's really easy to be spotted at night in the glow of the massive aircraft navigation beacons atop the hotel. But the coast was clear. I swooped down onto a canopied balcony dotted with fragrant blooming flowers and decorative trees, set TayLo down carefully, then stepped back and bowed.

"We are proud to welcome you, Taylor Logan, legendary star, to this legendary Hollywood landmark hotel. If you'd care to enjoy the magnificent view for a moment, I'll just step through those French doors over there and return momentarily with a flute of bubbly from Madame's already-chilled bottle of Cristal."

As I turned away, she gasped. "Omigod, this is a fucking penthouse suite. Britney Spears used to live one floor below, until they told her to leave because she made too much fucking noise."

I grinned at her excitement. Walking inside, I headed to the wet bar and popped the cork of a nicely chilled 1982 Cristal. A moment later I rejoined my guest on the patio, handed her a crystal flute, then raised mine in a toast.

"To new friends," I said.

Her compelling green eyes locked on mine as she sipped her champagne. She said, "You saved me from a fucking werewolf—that's what it was, right? *Wow!* I owe you big time."

I shook my head. "You owe me nothing."

She smiled a very seductive smile. "I *want* to owe you."

I chuckled. "Be careful what you ask for."

She laughed, knocked back the rest of her Cristal and held out the empty flute.

"But I don't *like* being careful," she said when I took the flute from her. "Didn't you say that about me in your gossip column? More than once, if I remember correctly."

She followed as I turned and walked back into the suite. I set our empty flutes on the bar, refilled them with bubbling Cristal, and served up one of my vintage lines.

"Wine," I said portentously, "is sunlight held together by water."

She was *so* not impressed.

"I've heard that line a million times since that fucking wine movie."

"Right. *Bottle Shock.* What a great film."

"It was *Sideways*, schmuck!"

"Whatever."

She paused, sipped her Cristal, and said, "I . . . look, I've got a lot of questions—like, how did that paparazzi guy back there suddenly turn into a . . . " She stopped, shaking her head. "Never mind, I don't want to talk or even think about it now, or I won't be able to stop, so . . . um, thanks again."

Pause. Sip.

I said, "Let me ask *you* some questions. You mentioned that you aren't high . . . yet. Does that mean you intended to get high tonight?"

"*Der!* That's why I was at Fury! One of my girlfriends said she'd meet me there. Said she was holding. Bitch never showed up." She shot me a naughty-little-girl smile. "Got any blow?"

Omigod, or as we like to say in Hollywood: *OMFG!*

Chapter Ten

"Drugs have no effect on the undead," I said taking a pull of Cristal. "Our physiology is, well, complicated. Fortunately, we can taste food, fine wines and liquors. But let me ask you . . . why isn't the buzz of champagne enough for you? And more than that, why overindulge in chemical substances that literally paralyze the body and the brain?

"You've had two DUIs, one of which almost killed you. You've been in rehab twice, and you've only just turned twenty-three. You've fucked over two major studios by delaying production because you were too high to work. Yet you don't strike me as suicidal, or stupid, so why are you screwing up what started out as an incredible career? You're not just some hot little bimbo like Paris, Britney, or Lindsay. You're incredibly sexy and sensual, to be sure, but you're also a sensitive actress with incredible talent."

She rolled her eyes and shrugged. "Omigod, listen to him. I'm getting lectures from a vampire. Like, why do you drink blood, asshole? I mean, what is this shit? You sound like . . ."

She paused. It was cruel, but I said it anyway. "I sound like . . . your *dad*? Surely, you weren't going to say 'like my mom'—or were you?"

TayLo's mother, Alina Logan, was a typical lunatic stage-mom from hell. She'd pushed her child into showbiz before she could walk, pimping her out as a baby model.

And Dad! A failed movie studio exec and aggressive drunk, he was reduced to "managing" low-rent club acts and strippers.

Parents from hell as far as I was concerned.

She scowled fiercely. Goddam. Even scowling she looked cute.

"Why don't you just shut the fuck up, anyway?" she raged, with a flip of her red-blond locks. "Do you always give little lectures when girls ask you to jump their bones? What are you, fucking *gay*? Jesus!"

"Let me answer those in order," I said. "Okay . . . no . . . and *no!*"

She laughed. "So, you gonna show me the place?"

I shrugged. "There's not much to see beyond the balcony and the rather magnificent dining-living area." I waved a hand at a corridor to the right of the suite's double-door entrance. "Nothing back there but bedrooms—three of them, actually."

She sipped her champagne and did a little dance step.

"Well, actually, I *love* bedrooms. You've mentioned that fact in your column many times, too," she said archly. "But, hey, I'll take a rain check if you'll put some music on."

I walked to the stereo, punched in a number. "Just got this. Lady Gaga. Her new one."

The beat kicked in. She discarded her champagne before her head snapped back and her limbs jerked spasmodically as the dance gods yanked her to life. She bopped, twisting and shaking that magnificent body. No question about it, of all the hot young stars in Hollywood, Taylor Logan was totally the hottest. Which made her unholy dedication to booze, sex, drugs, and debauchery a tragedy waiting to happen. Because even a healthy young body will finally, inevitably, break down under constant assault.

Reminds me of an old joke that'd work well for my "vampire comedy" act: "If I'd known I was going to last *this* long, I'd have taken better care of myself!" *(Cymbal crash!)*

Vampires, of course, never have to worry about getting old. You stay at the age you were converted at—so I'm glad I "died" young-ish. I still looked like a late-twentyish Central European; pale white skin, black hair with two premature white streaks, aquiline face, high cheekbones, and a lean but muscular body that topped out at just over six feet. Yes, I'm attractive to the undead and the living. And to both sexes; but no, I am not *gay*!

TayLo boogied close, her jiggling breasts brushing my chest.

"Come on, Dracula, shake your ass . . . let's do 'The Vampire'!"

Setting my flute to one side, I shuffled my feet a bit, following her lead. Despite my passion for Terpsichore, and a couple of quick lessons from Astaire himself, I'd never been any great shakes as a dancer, dead *or* alive.

She cocked her head and said, "You know, I come by the Four Seasons a lot, and I've never heard that you live here. I mean, you're pretty famous, and I run with the town's hottest in-crowd. So how come nobody's ever told me to watch my ass at the Four Seasons because Clark Kelly, the *gossip columnist*, lives here?"

I shrugged. "Nobody knows I live here."

"What? But . . . the hotel staff knows, right?"

I shook my head.

"*What*? That's fucking impossible!"

"Not really. First of all, I rarely spend more than two or three evenings a week here. This is my getaway, my retreat, my private place to unwind. You've seen the view from the balcony. It's spectacular. Beverly Hills,

Hollywood Hills, Century City. I fly in, I fly out. Nighttime only, so *nobody* sees me, just like tonight.

"If I order room service, they just leave it on the dining room table and get out while I'm in the bedroom. The suite is cleaned twice a week at prearranged times. My bill is paid automatically from a bank account. There is a permanent "Do Not Disturb" notice on the door, and no one on the staff has ever seen me. Nor do they know my name. If the hotel should have an emergency inquiry, they contact a lawyer who handles my affairs. So here's a lesson for celebs like you who want to duck guys like me. Remember, whatever hotel staff know, *I'll* know in five minutes. So tell no one where you are—and no one can tag you."

She'd stopped dancing. "That's so fucking weird. But it's so cool too. Wish I could sneak in and out of my hotel. The worst part when you're famous is that everyone wants to see who you bring home for sex. So where do you really live? Marilyn Monroe's crypt?"

I shook my head. "Too crowded. But I did live right under Jimmy Dean's grave."

She laughed, unsure whether I was kidding. I walked back to the bar, snagged the ice bucket and two new flutes. "Let's go back out to the balcony, and I'll show you my abode."

As we moved toward the French doors, the stereo suddenly switched from boogie to classical. She looked at me suspiciously.

"Did you change that with your mind?"

I shrugged. "You've been seeing too many vampire flicks, girl. I didn't touch it. Damn thing has a mind of its own."

But any mind, even an electronic one, is quite easily controlled, I chuckled to myself. Yeah, that's the kind of B-movie dialogue me and my ego conduct in my mind. Hey, I'm *alone* a lot. Make allowances, okay?

I took her arm, and guided her to the east side of the terrace. We looked out over Beverly Hills.

"My apartment is over there, about four blocks away," I said, pointing in the direction of trendy Robertson Boulevard.

She smiled. "You live right in the middle of the greatest girlie-shopping area in LA? And near my favorite restaurant, The Ivy. That is so hot!"

I lifted the bottle from the ice bucket and filled a flute for her. She took a deep quaff of Cristal, and was quiet for a few moments, looking out over the city. Then she asked:

"What it's like . . . you know, being a vampire?"

"The answer lies in the inevitable question," I said. "If you were dead, yet still possessed the consciousness to *know* that you were, what would be your first thought?"

"I don't want to die."

"Exactly. And if you roamed the earth undead for, say, three hundred years, what thought would overpower all others?"

"Uh . . . will I ever be alive again?"

"*Good* answer."

She looked at me steadily. "Is that what *you're* thinking?"

"Every minute."

"Wow."

She held out her glass for more Cristal. As I poured, she asked, "Do you think I'm hot, dude? No, wait, I mean, are you attracted to me?"

I smiled. "Oh, yes! And you? Do I turn you on, dude?"

"Totally. I am, like, so . . . hot. And *hellloooo*, I'm not even high. Maybe it's because you're a vampire."

"Bad boys are often irresistible to ladies, *hellloooo*."

She giggled. "Yeah, that's part of it. And I've always liked older men."

"Even *centuries* older?"

She stepped in close, sipping her champagne, looking up into my eyes deliberately, willing me to feel her desire.

"Show me the master bedroom now. Please."

I smiled, sipped.

She pouted.

Chapter Eleven

It was *too* amusing. What a bizarre time to be a vampire in Hollywood. America's great entertainment machine was literally spewing out movies, television series and books about our kind, making millions of people our adoring fans. But where we'd once struck fear in the hearts of whimpering young maidens, we now ignited erotic heat in their tummies.

The Irish novelist Bram Stoker never knew what a craze he'd create when he wrote *Dracula*, novelizing age-old Middle European folklore about gargoyles, werewolves, vampires and the like. A hundred years later, a marvelously creative writer named Anne Rice published *Interview with the Vampire*, jump-starting Bram's *Dracula* craze all over again. Incredibly, in this digital age, vampires are newly hot and sexy (and so is the deliciously kinky *Sleeping Beauty* Anne published under her pseudonym A.N. Roquelaure). And Hollywood's turned bloodsuckers into stars.

If I suddenly revealed my true nature, I'd nail an eight-figure series commitment and/or a three-picture movie deal overnight. But only a handful of mortals know I'm vampire. And without exception, every female among them has ended up begging me for vampire sex after learning my secret. Not that I'm complaining, mind you!

TayLo's eyes held mine for a long moment, unblinking. I smiled. Human beings blink constantly, hardly noticing these involuntary tics during normal conversation. But skilled screen actors like this cutie are adept at freezing their blinks during dramatic scenes, and for good reason. When an actor's eyes are boring into your soul from a sixty-by-twenty foot movie screen, the sudden twitch of eyelids and lashes—even though it takes just two hundred and seventy-five milliseconds—can be a jarring mood-breaker.

I knew TayLo was about to say something . . . dramatic.

"So, really, what's it *really* like being a vampire?"

Sweet Jesus. Again?

I shrugged. "You've heard the expression, 'Life sucks, then you die.' It's like that, kind of, except . . . you never die."

She blinked. Then her eyes flashed.

"Don't patronize me, you prick. Just because I've got big tits and the tabloids call me a boozy cokehead who fucks way too many boys *and* girls, I assure you I'm *not* a moron. Are we having a goddam conversation here? Or don't vampires indulge in the dying art of stimulating intellectual exchange?"

Whoa! It bites. And not at all like a bimbo. I smiled my most maddening smile. "Of course we do. Didn't you see *Interview with the Vampire*? Or read the book?"

She laughed. "Okay, you condescending son of a bitch. If we're going to play 'professor and student,' at least let me sit in your lap. I want a good grade."

"Not necessary. Just keep wearing those miniskirts to class, babe."

"Okay. Like, I know I sounded a bit *recherché* with my dramatic, thematic, portentous opening gambit, like, 'What is the meaning of life?' or *whatever*. But I do have intellectual curiosity, *excuse* me, and I just couldn't help wondering what . . ."

As she nattered on, I sat down my flute on the portable bar I keep out on the balcony, extracted two crystal cognac snifters and a bottle of the grape's greatest gift to mankind. I poured and lifted my snifter in salute.

"It was an excellent question, my dear. And my rejoinder reveals a great flaw in my personality that even death could not erase. You see, I love to annoy pretty girls. I just can't help it. Especially, pretty girls who are able wrap their lips so erotically around a word like *recherché*."

I poured her one. She smiled. Dazzling.

She raised her snifter, slowly opened her lips and drank.

"Mmm, yummy. Hennessy?"

"Bitch, *please*. It's Louis XIII."

"Black Pearl?"

Now *I* was surprised. "You know Black Pearl?"

"I know that less than eight hundred bottles were sold at auction a few years ago for about ten grand each. Snapped up mostly by rich Japanese. I checked it out when I let a cute, young Nipper movie star get in my pants after about four pops of the stuff. It's crazy fucking delish!"

Ah! The yearning. It hit me hard. It was the mention of things Japanese.

She looked at me and said, "What was that?"

"What?"

"I . . . don't know. I felt you, like, react, or something."

"No. Just an involuntary twitch."

Yeah. A twitch. Triggered by my sudden appetite for that special blood warmed by the Rising Sun. It was nearing time to feed again on that unique essence, because its properties allowed me to savor my beloved spirits to the fullest. Be cool, I told myself.

"So—or perhaps I should say, '*Ah, so!*'—you've visited Japan?"

"Yeah. Promoting my first big movie hit."

"*Girlie Girl.*"

"Yeah. You see it?"

"Did. Fell in love."

"Uh-huh."

"No. I mean it. You were a fucking revelation. I'd gone to the Laemmle Sunset to see a Polish art flick. It was sold out, but your mean-schoolgirls movie was about to start, so I went in."

"Dirty old man."

I chuckled. "Babe, think about it, I'd be a dirty old man if I dated your great-*grandmother*. I'm a vampire, remember? Anyway, the next day I told everyone I talked to that you were totally on fire, the next hot young star."

She did the unblinking thing. Drama time again.

"Like, how old *are* you?"

"Damn, you're relentless. Okay, let's see, in vampire years, I'm, uh . . ."

She giggled. "Oh, is that like dog years?"

"Exactly. You can't really count our age like people."

"Okay, okay, you look like you're maybe thirty-two passing for twenty-seven, so . . ."

"Let's leave it at that. Age is such a relative thing, after all."

"That's what all my two-hundred-year-old friends say."

"Good one, girlfriend!" I didn't bother telling her she was off about a century.

We leaned forward, laughing, and high-fived. I poured more Black Pearl. We clinked snifters.

She stretched like a kitty, moved to the balcony rail.

"God, what a gorgeous night. And what a gorgeous place to view it from. I love this place."

She smiled back at me, throwing a cue. I joined her. We leaned on the rail quietly for a while, staring out over the carpet of lights sprinkling across BevHills to Century City.

"So," she said softly, "let's try again. What's it like . . . being a vampire? And why won't you fuck me?"

I chuckled. "I don't think you know what that might entail."

She started to smile, her eyes widening in mock fright.

"Oooh, are you talking about drinking my blood? And turning me into a vampire? Or are you warning me about the well-known fact that full-on sex with a vampire can actually break a girl's bones?"

Here we go again, I thought.

"Look, forget what you think you know about my kind. You're young, but you're certainly intelligent enough to know that your so-called knowledge, based on what you've seen in movies or read in books, can't be accurate because fictional facts about us vary so widely as to be ludicrous. Anne Rice and Bram Stoker are the most accurate, by far. But even though they agree on many aspects in imagining who and what we are, they still differ on many basic facts. They can't even agree on how vampires pee, for Chrissake."

She laughed. "So how do you . . ."

I held up a hand sharply.

"Please, I am not going to answer the endless questions I know you're dying—you'll pardon the expression—to pose. I am not in the mood for Vampire 101 tonight. So far, you've observed that I possess supernatural strength, and I can fly through the air with the greatest of ease. So if you have any imagination at all, and I think you do, I'm sure it has occurred to you that I might also possess the vaunted vampiric ability to cloud the human mind through hypnosis. In other words, you're aware that your eyes could suddenly close this very moment, and you'd find yourself waking up in your cozy Château Marmont bed—with absolutely no memory of our evening together."

She leaned forward urgently, eyes wide and agitated. This time, the fright was not mock. "Omigod! *Please* don't. Please. I want to remember tonight more than any night of my life."

I laughed, and knocked back the last of the Black Pearl in my snifter. Phenomenal. I could still really taste it. Thank God for Japanese blood that's deficient in a certain enzyme that processes alcohol efficiently, thereby heightening the pungency of liquor, which is why I adore it and . . . oh, I'll explain it all later.

"Look, I'm not inclined to do any such thing, actually," I told her. "You are totally hot, intriguing and intelligent. You're also the best young actress on the Hollywood scene today. I enjoy your company, as I think you enjoy mine. But make no mistake about it. On the rare occasions I reveal my identity to a living creature, I need to judge whether that person might decide to suddenly reveal who I really am, because I so do *not* goddam need hysterical Beverly Hills villagers gathering in the streets with torches, screaming for my fucking head on a pitchfork. So . . . *can* I trust you?"

She smiled her dazzling smile, leaned back, raised her glass and purred, "I know you've already made your decision. If you thought I was stupid enough to blow the chance to hang with an honest-to-god fucking vampire, I'd already be in a fucking trance. Or dead, right?"

I nodded. We smiled and sipped a tacit toast. "Besides," she said, "I want you to fuck me. And you will . . . eventually."

She giggled again, then stopped as I went silent, reaching for her mind and stoking the fire inside. Her hand moved and she found me. Her eyes widened. I felt her sudden fright; her realization that she was not dealing with the usual actor, model, or rock star boy.

I answered her question as it formed in her mind.

"No . . . one does *not* become a vampire simply by having sex with one."

Chapter Twelve

She opened her mouth, but again, I had the answer to the question forming in her brain.

"No. A vampire is not necessarily driven to drink a partner's blood during sex. It's a fun diversion, of course, but it's . . . well, 'vampire's choice,' I guess you'd say."

I saw relief flood her eyes. Her hand moved again, more urgently. Her breasts pressed into me and I felt her hot breath as she turned her mouth up, offering her lips.

"I want you, I want you now. In the bedroom, or . . . right here . . . please . . . now . . . .I want you!"

"No," I told her. "No."

God, I was aroused. And an aroused vampire is no . . . uh, *small* thing!

"But . . ."

I pressed my hand gently over her lips. "I cannot easily explain the complexities of this situation, but please accept what I say. I can't have sex with you tonight. And, as you've discovered, it's not because I am indifferent to your charms. I find you intoxicating; you've had ample proof of that. But I am far too aroused. And that means I wouldn't be able to control the power surging in me. I'd hurt you badly, at best, and . . . well, not to frighten you, but . . . you might not even survive the experience."

She threw herself into me, lifting her arms up to encircle my neck, thrusting her hips up toward mine. In an instant, I'd grabbed her by the neck, lifted her off her feet. She gasped for breath, twisting helplessly as I roared.

"Stop!"

Her eyes rolled back in her head. She went limp. Swiftly, I scooped her up in my arms and took her back into the suite, rushing down the corridor to the master bedroom. I laid her on the bed, patting her cheeks. Her eyes fluttered open.

I leaned over, kissed her gently on the lips.

"You *must* have patience," I whispered.

She smiled up at me. A sweet, brave, winsome smile.

"Fuck patience," she said. "Just fuck me to death! I'm ready, believe me!"

I laughed. "You mentioned getting high. I'm going to make your soul sing tonight, my sweet. If you'll trust me, that is."

I kissed her again, stood up.

She held out a hand to restrain me. "Where are you going?"

I walked over to the door, turned back to her and said, "It's such a beautiful night. Who needs electric lights?"

I flicked the wall switch. The suite went black, took on the pale glow of moonlight pouring in through the French doors.

"Perfect, now I'll join you," I said. "But first, lie back and close your eyes. I am going to transport you to a level of ecstasy that a six-part *Cosmo* series on self-pleasuring couldn't begin to describe. And you must not be afraid, you exquisite, exciting creature. This experience, I promise, will not harm you in any way. This is a drug that will *not* make you crash and burn. Now, do you trust me?"

She nodded.

"And . . . are you ready to *r-r-rrrumble?*"

She giggled softly as I leaned over her. I whispered, "Now . . . slowly open your eyes again."

Her eyelids fluttered, opened, and she gasped.

I was hovering two feet above her, looking straight down into her eyes.

"You are so beautiful," I said.

My silk cloak brushed her skin. Feeling its touch, she looked down at herself and cried out in sudden surprise.

"My clothes . . . omigod, what happened to my clothes?"

I flicked my cape, covering her heaving breasts, and winked.

"Why, you're *naked*! Gremlins, perhaps, my sweet?"

She breathed in sharply as I floated down and my body melded with hers. My fangs, not to be restrained any longer, were now unsheathed and delicately raking her tempting, vulnerable neck.

"Yes, yes . . . oh yes," she cried softly, sweetly tilting it toward the pain.

"Now," I told her, "now, at last, you will experience the seduction of eternity."

Okay, it was a corny line, right out of a Hammer Films flick, but it just felt . . . right.

And she purred, loving it.

"Surrender yourself," I commanded gently.

"Yes. Oh . . . yes. Please . . ."

Her body twitched, just once, as my fangs raked lightly and broke through her skin, already hot from the roiling life force coursing through her veins. And then I tasted it at last—her blood, rich and earthy, like a fine wine hitting all the notes she had created. I sucked it in, reveling in its sweetness, careful to keep myself in check. It had been a while since I'd drunk of sexual elixir, but this had to be a gently sipped nightcap, not an orgy of unslaked thirst. My head spun with her deliciousness. Soon her body began to shake, and finally, she exploded, crying out again and again. My fangs retracted. I was sated . . .

. . . for now, anyway.

Moments went by as I lay beside her in the moonlight. She said, "It was like sex, but not like sex. It was better."

"Better than drugs?"

"God, yes!"

"You will sleep as you have never slept before. You will wake up refreshed."

She sighed. "But will I be able to have this . . . always?"

"No, not always. From time to time, perhaps, but *only* if you stay off drugs. Got that?"

She laughed softly. "I'll quit. I'll do anything you want if we can do that again."

I didn't react. But inside I marveled at how the little minx was trying to control me. I was amused. And aroused.

"And," she whispered seductively, "I'll give you great scoops for your column."

There she goes again, but on that score I believed her; indeed why was I here in the first place? As for that crap about quitting drugs? First rule of gossip: *Never* believe a junkie.

I said, "Can you feel the need for sleep overtaking you? Just let it happen. When you awake, you'll be safe."

She stirred, as if to answer, then her limbs relaxed completely. I wrapped her in my cape and lay there, savoring the moment. Then I called up the power. We lifted off the bed, floated through the suite out to the balcony—where I snatched up her purse—and rocketed into the night sky, en route to Sunset Boulevard and the fabled Château Marmont hotel.

Two minutes later, give or take, we were overhead. For those who like to do the math, my kind fly at about the speed of a military attack helicopter. Swooping down, I jacked an unlatched window, entered the suite that matched the number on the key I'd found in her purse, then tucked her into bed and flew back out into the night. I headed straight for the Griffith Park Observatory, where Jimmy had filmed *Rebel without a Cause*, and burrowed into my hidey-hole beneath the monument dedicated to him, a stone column topped by his bust.

Something had changed.

I needed to think about it in deep sleep.

Emerging three days later, I showed up at *The Revealer* and heard the news that TayLo had overdosed at a Las Vegas club, and been rushed back to rehab. Stay out of it, I'd told myself. But on that fateful Saturday night at the Roosevelt, after knocking out raging PR Pattie, knocking back a drink —and knocking off Danny Payne—I surrendered to this new force that was driving me.

Just as I'd known I would.

So, unlimbering the trusty old cape, I'd flown back to The 'Bu and found her in Miracles; unrepentant, unafraid and unabashedly itching for more hot fangs-tasy. Man, did George Hamilton get it right when he titled his vampire comedy flick (one of my all-time favorites), *Love Bites!*

Chapter Thirteen

I shook my head and sighed.

"So *why* are you back here in fucking rehab again?"

She flashed a maddening smile.

"That's a rhetorical question, right? I mean, we know why *you're* here, Clark. You're the predatory vampire who's come to ravish the young maiden . . . I *wish*. And you *know* why I'm here. Just had a teeny-weeny blackout after a hard night at the Hard Rock, that's all. Figured if I partied hard enough, you might hear about it—and remember that I actually exist. Hey, the story was in *your* tabloid, right? So I'm guessing your *real* question is: Why do I keep fucking up?"

I nodded, not smiling. "At our last meeting, you said, 'I'll quit . . . I'll do anything you want if we can do *that* again.' Remember that?"

Her eyes narrowed to mean-girl slits. "Yeah, well, how would you even *know* what I've been doing? I didn't hear from you. Why are *you* here at all?"

Touche, bitch.

"Actually, I'm hot on the trail of a great gossip story." I cleared my throat. "Not involving you, of course," I lied. "Just happened to be in the neighborhood, thought I'd drop in. By the way, wasn't that Roma Kane's car I just saw headed back to LA?"

"So?"

"So she visited you."

She shrugged.

Then screamed.

I had suddenly . . . vanished. *Poof!*

One minute standing in front of her; the next gone. In an eyeblink.

She recoiled, screamed again as my hand snaked over her shoulder from behind, clamping her mouth, muzzling the shriek. My fangs grazed her neck delicately, barely piercing the skin.

My breath soothed hotly in her ear as I whispered, "Just a tiny sting, baby . . . *easy now*! Okay, all *done* . . . just relax."

Her eyes popped in a terrified stare. Suddenly, I was standing face-to-face with her again. She shuddered, swayed. I steadied her.

"Easy, girlfriend!"

"*Jesus!* How did you . . ."

Her eyes focused, watching my tongue flick hypnotically back and forth across my teeth as I tested her blood. I sighed.

No question: Positive.

She flinched as I touched the tiny pinpricks I'd left on her neck, then showed her the crimson droplets on my fingertips. "Blood never lies, my sweet. You have tooted primo sniffy in the past hour. Not a lot, to be sure, but it's a fresh trace. *La Coca*."

"Look, you can't—"

I shook my head. "Ask yourself a simple question: Why is your dear friend Roma feeding you drugs in fucking rehab? *Why*, goddammit?"

Her eyes flashed and her chin went up. "Because I fucking *begged* her to, that's why. It was just a taste, that's all. *Fuck you!* I do what I want. She . . . she's my friend. She was just helping me out. Jesus! You're worse than my dad!"

Worse than her *what*?

It happened then. Like she'd pulled a trigger. Memory slammed me back three centuries in a heartbeat. Not that I *have* a heartbeat, of course.

Swiftly, violently, the efflorescence of Romania, circa 1730, zoomed up in my mind's eye, hitting me by surprise—as it usually does for the undead. Sudden memories, as experienced by human beings, are reveries drifted into gradually, but for us, memories even from decades or centuries past can slam up instantly, literally hurling us back into the past.

So . . . BANG! . . . and suddenly I was walking swiftly, eagerly, through a verdant meadow on her father's farm.

Romania. Springtime, and . . .

Ludmilla!

My first true love. She was running toward me with laughing eyes. Beautiful, blond Ludmilla. Skirts flying, breasts bouncing, out of breath, wildly excited. She reached out, grasped my hand, pulled me along. Then disengaging, giggling, she ran on ahead. I continued walking at a measured pace, smiling.

She shouted back at me, "Come on, silly fellow, you've got to catch me! Don't you know *anything*?"

Then we were trembling in a haystack, dizzied by love, sexual yearning, and the heady redolence of fresh-mown grass.

For the undead, most memories of human life are attenuated to a mere murmur in the subconscious, but some still burn bright. For me, it's the image of that golden-hued day when I first kissed Ludmilla. Whenever my dreams of being reborn to mortal life recur, as they do eternally, the emotion I most yearn to experience once again is that head-spinning, heart-thumping thrill of first love.

That emotion was, and is, my heart's true desire.

I'd known Ludmilla, the busty but virginal, blond daughter of a prosperous farmer, Nicolai Niculescu, for years during adolescence. Though she was hardly the first girl I'd tried to tumble in the hay. In those halcyon days, the Romanian countryside teemed with lusty peasant girls only too willing to make the acquaintance of a young man born into a family of minor nobility, who galloped around the countryside on a spirited black stallion. Well, to be honest, my beloved Valentino was actually a gelding, but he raged across field and forest as if still possessing a potent third gonad, a phantom nut that the farrier's blade had somehow missed. Strictly speaking, that animal was my *actual* first love. As the Bedouin say, "The wind of heaven is that which passes between a horse's ears."

After tasting Ludmilla's achingly sweet lips for the first time, I swore off other girls, even skirt-raising peasants. I courted her earnestly for many months, and finally confessed I was in love with her. Then, in that haystack, driven by urgent youthful passion kept too long in check, I pressed my precious angel to surrender her virginity and consummate our love, sensing that her burgeoning passion had brought her, at last, to the moment of sexual submission.

But amid a sudden explosion of bitter tears she tried desperately to suppress, Ludmilla finally confessed a terrible thing: Her father had molested her.

Worse, the foul fiend had taken her virginity.

The unthinkable attack had occurred only recently, Ludmilla sobbed, and she astounded me by admitting that her first thought after the brutal rape ended had been of . . . me.

Her heart had broken then, she said, as she was struck by the realization that her father's vicious assault had changed her forever; she felt she would never be able to experience connubial pleasure with me, or any man, ever.

Ludmilla's chilling revelation changed my life—my afterlife, especially —forever.

In the days that followed, I found myself driven by two overwhelming passions: an unrelenting sexual desire that made me ashamed because I didn't understand it—and a hot, murderous bloodlust for revenge. I ached to kill her father.

Sensing my churning thoughts, as women are so naturally skilled at doing, my dear mother—who knew of my sudden obsession for Ludmilla, and whose distant ties to royal blood made her unsympathetic to the idea of her only son becoming romantically entangled with a simple country girl— subtly nudged me in the direction of a beautiful and thrilling older woman, her best friend, the Countess Drina.

In due course, my mother summoned the countess, who lived in our capital city. She arrived at our estate for a visit with her entourage of servants and a mountain of luggage filled with magnificent *haute couture* gowns, hats and shoes from Paris and London.

On her second night with us, perhaps an hour after my mother and father had retired to their wing, Drina entered my bedchamber and launched an hours-long seduction. It was an indoctrination into exotic sexual practices that most men, I knew instinctively even then, would never be fortunate enough to experience.

I was wild for Drina, of course. And she was very clever in not revealing to me—not immediately, at least—what even my clever mother did not know about her friend of many years. Drina was a *vampire*, an undead creature enjoying an undercover life among the living.

I learned of her dark secret just days after our first encounter when, in the dead of night, she crept into my chambers again, aroused and mounted my manhood, then unsheathed her fangs and sank them into my neck, sucking great draughts of my blood. Within weeks, smitten by her psyche, my youthful spirit was as malleable in her hands as her taut breasts were in mine, I began begging this irresistible succubus to convert me—to transform me into one of her kind, a vampire.

And so, one night, on the stroke of midnight, Drina opened an intimate vein and let me drink my fill of her hot, delicious essence.

I swooned.

I died.

And my eyes were opened.

Chapter Fourteen

All through those dizzying days it appeared, judging by knowing looks directed at Drina, that Mother knew full well I was enjoying her friend's favors. Hell, they might have openly discussed it, for all I knew. Whatever the case, Mother obviously approved. But she knew nothing about the Dracula stuff, Drina had assured me, so I can't really blame her for my conversion. Although, one might question why a loving mother would consign her first-born son to the erotic ministrations of a sophisticated, older woman.

On the other hand, one might also advise me to stop looking a gift whore in the mouth.

For my own part, despite the fact that Drina made me wildly, ecstatically happy, I was not as faithless, stupid and callow a youth as you might think. Although my sexual desires had been slaked, the powerful throes of first love had not been eradicated, even after my conversion. Far from it! An unquenchable yearning for Ludmilla pulsed through my vampire heart more strongly than ever—as did a sudden and consuming bloodlust, a mounting desire to commit murder.

I'd had one of my servants spying on Ludmilla's father for a considerable time. One day my man came to me and said: "Young Master, Ludmilla will be alone except for her mother and womenfolk for nearly a week while her father travels to the capital on business."

Excellent!

The time for killing was at hand.

I knew what I had to do, and—instinctively—exactly how to do it. Becoming a vampire had crystallized and focused my thoughts as never before. I now arrived at decisions quickly and without equivocation. I had always been counted a clever young man, but during my life as a human being I had never experienced such confident clarity of thought. One cannot explain the inexplicable, but there's no question that when the mind evolves from human to vampiric, there's no dithering or quibbling about which path one should take.

I knew what to do. And I would do it, swiftly and ruthlessly.

Days later, I intercepted Ludmilla's father and the five sturdy yeomen protecting him, miles before they'd reached his farm, in the deepest reaches of a wilderness known as Dark Forest. The journey would have taken me two days on horseback, but I traversed the route handily in less than an hour via God's blue skies after discovering that, true to the ancient lore whispered by superstitious humans, *vampires can fly*.

What a joy! If asked to name the one thing that makes the afterlife truly worth it, I'd answer unhesitatingly: the gift of flight.

I intercepted my prey and dropped in on them, literally, as they entered a good-sized clearing in the woods. The yeomen instantly gripped their weapons. Ludmilla's father held up a hand and said, "Why, it's young Dragomir! What tree did you drop from, pray tell?"

I smiled, baring my fangs. The yeomen stepped back, drew their swords.

I said, "I bring you greetings from Hell, where you shall soon find yourself."

Please, dear reader, allow me to pause in the narrative, briefly, for yet another of my annoying tutorials. It's important to note that in my new vampiric persona, I was still operating purely by instinct, being what you might call a "baby vampire." Barely a week before, I'd been a human being. Suddenly, I was one of the undead, a creature extraordinary. Imagine what it felt like to suddenly discover I could do the oddest things—leap into the air and fly, for example—purely by instinct. Vampires, like most humans, are not given much to deep, introspective thoughts like, "Wow, I'm a vampire now. What, I wonder, does that mean? What new skills do I have? And what's my purpose in life . . . or rather, death?"

I quickly discovered that, to put it simply, you mostly just think up stuff . . . and it sort of . . . happens. Magically. (Eat your heart out, Danny Payne!)

So here I was, about to launch into my first foray as a "scary vampire." And at first, I was still trying—as a human being would—to ruminate seriously on what moves I should make next. But I quickly discovered that all I had to do was decide to be scary, and the mayhem would take care of itself. Literally.

So . . . the instant my melodramatic words consigning Ludmilla's father to Hell passed my lips, his sword-bearing yeomen charged. The first to reach me, a tall fellow with long, well-muscled limbs, swung a vicious cut aimed at separating head from body. With no conscious thought, I caught his arm on the downswing, yanking sharply. Instantly, his limb was ripped from his shoulder. Great gouts of blood spurted as his separated arm, still gripping the sword, hit the ground and bounced crazily into the underbrush.

My next assailant, a brutish, bandy-legged fellow, ran straight at me, aimed a thrust at my heart. He was mightily confused when I vanished. A crushing blow on the back of his head was the last pain he ever felt on this earth. Whirling to face Ludmilla's father and his remaining three warriors, I roared.

"STOP!"

They froze in their tracks.

I told the yeomen, "I have no quarrel with you three. Take your weapons and run, NOW . . . 'ere I scatter your bloody heads and limbs as feasts for the wolves. Leave your master to me. He is a man without hope. No power on earth can protect him."

Eyes wide with terror, they turned and scattered into the forest. As the crashing sounds of retreat subsided, Ludmilla's father regarded me in horror, jaw agape.

"How young Dragomir has changed," I could almost hear the old fool thinking.

"It is time you knew your fate, and why it is about to befall you," I told him. "First, look at me carefully. What do you see?"

Riveting him with my eyes, I bared my fangs, shot fire from my eyes and watched as realization slowly dawned. His mouth moved erratically, working to form the dreaded word. He finally spat it out:

"DRACUL!"

I roared: "Well observed, swine! Prepare to die in unimaginable agony. I shall drink your blood, strip your head and limbs from your body, then scatter them here for others to find and be warned. But first, shall I tell you *why* you're about to die?"

Staring out at me from his fright-filled brain, he rasped, "What does it matter? To die is to die. I need no lessons from you in how I should have lived."

I must admit to a certain grudging respect for the man. He showed fear, but refused to display craven cowardice in the face of death. But before I could explain why he was about to die, he cut me off.

"I beg you, Dark Lord, if your kind is capable of mercy, to grant just one boon—not for me, but for my young daughter. Let me show you where I have buried my gold, which is, I am sure, of no importance to you. Please let my daughter know where my treasure lies, so that she can retrieve it and support herself and her mother, my good wife. Please, sir, grant me this death favor, I beg you."

Astounding. I marveled that the man's final plea in the face of death was for the welfare of his daughter—even though I had not yet divulged that it was his unspeakable molestation of her that had doomed him this day. Were I still a human being, I might actually feel a pang of sympathy. But a vampire is not so easily swayed.

In one swift swoop, I lifted us both straight up to the sky.

"Look below and point the way to your gold," I told him. "Be quick about it, for I have little patience. And if you think to trick me, be warned that I will take great pains to make your death slow and painful."

Soon enough we were hovering over a wooded copse on the edge of his vast farm. He pointed down at a good-sized rock positioned between two exceptionally large oak trees.

"Standing at the edge of that rock and facing toward the rising sun, one should take ten steps out and dig there," he said. "You will find my gold. It's at the depth of a grave."

I snapped his neck, killing him instantly.

His final gesture of respect for his daughter deserved that slight concession to a merciful death. Still carrying his body, I flew back over the Dark Forest, dropping him from a great height into the clearing where I'd found him, then hastened back to my darling Ludmilla.

I had much to tell her.

Chapter Fifteen

". . . and he *molested* me, the filthy bastard. *My own father!*"

What?

Who spoke?

"You heard me! *Now* do you know why I hate him? Does that answer your fucking question? Well, DOES IT?"

It was TayLo. I was . . . suddenly . . . back with her again.

In The 'Bu. At Miracles.

Momentarily disoriented, I shook my head.

She burst into tears. "Why doesn't anyone understand? You ask me why I do these things—the drugs and the booze and the car crashes and the fistfights? It's because I was programmed to be this way, and no one can help me . . . *no one!*"

Now she was sobbing, shaking. Then it all welled up and burst from her like vomit.

"When my mother told me my daddy had molested me, it was like my life was ending. She said I didn't remember it because . . . because I was just a little girl when it happened. And I kept screaming, 'Why are you even *telling* me? If I couldn't remember it, how could it hurt me like I'm hurting now, you *fucking bitch!*' It was like, in one horrible minute I'd lost both my father *and* my mother, goddam her! I hate them *both!*"

I blinked, still disoriented, my mind spinning. Abruptly dragged back from the 1700s into the present, I was facing yet another beautiful young woman weeping about an unspeakably villainous father. It was a coincidence beyond weird.

Ah, girls and their daddies, I thought, watching TayLo sob uncontrollably, pacing the room like a caged wild thing.

"He fucked *at least* two of my so-called girlfriends after we came out to Hollywood, but then *she*—my mother—actually fucked my boyfriend from high school one summer when I was away at camp. My own *mother!*"

Suddenly, she stopped, stared at me with crazy eyes and snarled, "Why am I telling you this? Why? *You don't care!*"

I started to speak. "Sorry, I wasn't quite keeping up with what you've been saying because I . . . I wasn't . . ."

How to explain to her that while we'd been speaking, Elvis had temporarily left the building, so to speak, for an unscheduled trip down Romanian memory lane? That was why her abrupt, shocking revelation of patriarchal abuse—coming so soon after my vivid flashback to Ludmilla's identical rapine—had thrown me into total confusion.

Before I could say another word, TayLo made a desperate move; did it so swiftly my superior reflexes were caught flat-footed. In three quick bounds, she ran straight out through the open French doors leading to the tiny balcony, vaulted its rail—and vanished down into the inky blackness.

Even factoring in my aforementioned superhero-like reflexes, my work was cut out for me. The drop into the rock-littered canyon beneath her window was just three hundred feet—about four seconds to splatter-ville, I estimated, launching through the doors after her and accelerating instantly to Mach 3.

Much as I'd like to milk this dramatic moment—telling you how I plummeted down, down, down, finally catching her a mere instant before her beautiful body splattered on the rocks—the truth is, I was hovering nonchalantly below her well before she'd fallen halfway down, and caught her neatly in my arms. Hate to brag, people, but I am greased fucking *lightning.*

Hugging her as she trembled and wept in my arms, I wafted slowly back up to the balcony, glided into the room and set her gently on the sofa. She sobbed helplessly, body trembling and heaving in spasms. My poor girl had literally tried to kill herself. Or had she known, instinctively, that I'd never let that happen? I hugged her close, wondering why vampires can't cry. I felt her press into me, holding desperately. After a while I got up and snagged a Sprite from the tiny fridge, poured it for her, and said briskly: "Get yourself together, girl. And go slap on an even prettier new face. I'm taking you to a party."

I had her instant attention. "Taking you to a party" is one of those surefire buzz phrases—like "designer dress" or "really hot shoes"—that snap females to attention.

"*What* party?"

See! Still sniffling, but all ears!

I smiled my warmest smile. "It's a secret deal with a really tight guest list. I'd rather surprise you, so trust me, okay? Point is, you need a little fun in your life right now, my love. So go fix your face. This party's strictly casual, by the way, so don't overdo it. And switch your bra and panties for a bikini. You'll need it."

"Why? Where are we going? And don't say 'panties.' I hate that word. Will there be industry people there?"

Ten minutes and fifty questions later, we were face into the wind, headed north. She squealed in delight.

"Omigod, you're wearing the cape! I *love* your fucking cape. And I love, love, *love* FLYING."

Leaning back, she flung an arm back theatrically, belting out my favorite old Cole Porter standby . . .

"Flying too high with some guy in the sky
Is my idea of nothing to do . . .
But I get a kick out of you . . ."

She broke into a big laugh when I belted right back,

"Some get their kicks from cocaine . . ."

Below us, moonlight bathed the Pacific shoreline, transforming the surf into molten silver as it lapped up onto the sand. In moments, we were well north of Malibu, hovering over our destination.

"Zuma Beach," she squealed. "I haven't been here in ages."

I swooped down, landed on a deserted stretch of beach just north of Zuma, took her hand and started walking briskly. Looking around, she wailed, "Why are we walking on the beach? I thought were going to a party? There are no houses here. Where are you taking me?"

"Over there."

I pointed to a small fire burning in a pit just ahead. We were there in a moment and I sank to the sand in front of it, pulling her down with me. She started to protest, but I held up a hand and told her, "Whatever you do, *don't* look into the fire. It will ruin your eyes for the moonlight—and the unique spectacle you're about to see. This will be a very special night for you."

She glared at me imperiously, drilling me with the look that had intimidated Hollywood types from studio heads to headwaiters—even paparazzi, werewolves excepted. I stared back at her mildly, and she suddenly laughed.

"Please allow me to play the silly, dumbass girl and ask scary Mr. Vampire again—where's the fucking party? And don't say, 'In my pants!' Unless you *mean* it, of course."

I pointed out at the crashing surf and massive, moonlit waves rolling in ominously from the dark horizon.

"What do you see?"

"Omigod," she said snarkily. "What *is* this, *Hidden Planet*? Have you brought me out here to see adorable fucking whales break the surface? Like, okay, dude, the waves are big, it's all very beautiful. But I'll want a cocktail if things don't get exciting pretty quick. Hey, wait, my new bikini might turn this into a party. Wanna check it out? I took a peek in the mirror when I changed. As Miley Cyrus would say, it's *prrretty* hot!"

I said nothing, waiting. Then she heard it. Faint yells out on the water. She leaned forward, suddenly excited. She peered hard at where I was pointing. Now she got excited.

"Oh, wow! There's someone way out there . . . *surfing*? In the middle of the fucking *night*? Who the hell would do that? It must be sooo scary, out there alone with all those sharks."

I shook my head. "Alone? I think you'll find our moonlight surfer's not alone. Look . . . just behind him there. Now listen."

She jumped up suddenly, jazzed like a kid at Disneyland, pointing out at the breaking seas as she picked up distant cries.

"Omigod, it's fucking unbelievable. There's a whole gang of them, riding in on that huge wave. I've hung lots with surfers—but I've never heard of surfing in the middle of the goddam *night.* Jesus! WOW! Look at those guys—they're almost naked in those tiny Speedos. I've never seen surfer guys wearing anything but board shorts. They are so incredibly hot-looking and . . . *oh*! Look at that wave break! It must be twenty feet high, but they're all hanging in. No one's gone down yet."

She was jumping up and down now, wildly excited, yelling.

"These guys are GOOD! *Rad, dudes! Hang ten!* COSMIC! . . . *YEAH!*"

I stood, walked up behind her.

"Yeah," I said. "Not bad for a bunch of vampires."

She whirled, gasping as she looked up at me.

"Vampire surfers?"

I smiled. "Yeah—oh, except for that blond girl, maybe. I don't know her."

"Blonde?"

Chapter Sixteen

Her head whipped back to face the ocean and she leaned forward, squinting; a female checking for female competition.

Now the surfers were close enough to view in all their glory. There were a dozen vampire dudes, and one blond, bare-breasted female, expertly riding their boards down a towering wave. Awash in moonlight, they shouted and waved as they skittered crazily to elude the crashing, foaming crest that chased and snapped like a ravening sea beast.

Throwing her fists in the air and pumping wildly, TayLo shrieked into the wind, totally thrilled by the spectacle. Suddenly, she began yanking off clothing. Stripped to her bikini, she grabbed my hand and pulled me to the surf, wading in knee-deep and shouting encouragement at the wave riders as a massive, silver-tipped black swell propelled them shoreward.

And finally, as the curl collapsed in on itself and the wave began to level off, the exultant riders straightened and stood tall on their boards, executing crazy little war dances as the shadowy high-breaker they'd ridden so perfectly smashed the shoreline and whipped them into the shallows.

Surfers in moonlight. How unreal they look, I thought.

TayLo, suddenly uneasy as the vampire gang hit the beach running, clung to me. I felt her tremble as they bounded off their boards, yelling as they splashed toward us.

"Look, beasts, it's dear *Dragomir*!"

"Hey, Drag, you made it!"

"Long time no see, *Dracul* . . . who's the hot babe?"

TayLo's fingers dug into my arm. Her eyes were riveted on the alabaster-skinned, topless female, who hopped gracefully off her board, bent to pick it up, then padded past us with a casual wave of the hand.

"Hello, Dragomir," she said, smiling sweetly. "How nice to see you're not lonely."

My turn to tremble. Senses spinning. First stupid thought: *Can't be!* How could it be?

But it was . . .

Ludmilla.

A *vampire*? But, how . . .?

I unleashed a mental wave, felt her repel it. The message was clear. No mind-rolling tonight. And as she passed me by, I felt the grip of a strong, yet undefined suspicion.

Trailed by the males, Ludmilla walked over to the fire pit, sat, and began finger-combing her long blond tresses.

TayLo looked at me, bug-eyed.

"*Dragomir?* Is that your real name?"

"Yes, and I congratulate you on pronouncing it perfectly. You have a quick ear for accents."

"So you and these guys . . . you're, like . . . foreign vampires?"

"Yes. Despite my impeccable accent and American attitudes—and trust me, I'm a patriot who loves my adopted land—I am not a born-and-bred homeboy."

"So where—"

"Was I born? Transylvania, my dear."

"Get out! Like in the vampire movies?"

I bowed. "Clark Kelly, formerly Dragomir Craiovescu, at your service, *mademoiselle*. Having fun yet?"

Music wafted across the beach. Someone in the crowd by the fire had broken out a boom box. A voice yelled out, "Come on over here, Dragomir. We've got some fine champagne in the cooler for you and your lovely friend."

I waved back. "Sounds good. Hey, I'd like to borrow somebody's board first. Okay?"

"Whichever one you'd like," came the answer.

TayLo, sensing what was about to happen, looked at me in sudden fear.

"Oh, no, I don't want to—"

Before she could react, I threw her over my shoulder, snatched up an abandoned surfboard and shot up into the night sky. Leveling off at about a hundred feet, I headed straight out half a mile, dropped the board into the massive swells undulating toward shore, and glided down to land on the roiling, foam-flecked surface.

"Easy, cowboy," I murmured, trying to catch my balance.

TayLo hadn't stopped screaming since we'd left dry land.

I slid her off my shoulder, cradled her in my arms and soothed her like a baby, cooing, "Easy, girl, just *chill* . . . it's okay. I've got you. Calm down. Let's have some fun."

Awestruck and terrified as she looked around us, she finally went silent. But there was no silence in this surging, scary water world. In darkness, sound is greatly amplified. Even in relatively calm seas, the ears pick up the noise of every slosh, splash and ripple. At this moment, we were positioned in a deep trough between two wave crests. I could sense, rather than see, another starting to build below and just behind us. Despite the moonlight, eyesight—even a vampire's—is not the best sense to rely on in a dark ocean. Better to close one's eyes, feel the roiling ocean and predict its moves via the gyroscope of one's inner ear. When treading water, trust balance, not sight.

"I am *so* goddamed scared."

"Hey, I'm terrified, too. And I'm a *vampire!*"

She actually laughed. "Very funny, you prick. God, it is so scary and dark out here. *Please* take me back to shore. By air, if you please."

"Stop being such a girl."

"I *am* a girl."

"Okay, so just hang on tight to the big, strong vampire and get into the fun of it all. Here, let me situate you so you can *really* eyeball the action."

I hiked her up onto my shoulders. She squealed, and her thighs squeezed my neck so tight I could barely wheeze.

"Strangle me and you're dead, bitch! Literally. Because to surf you back to shore properly, one *must* concentrate."

Then there was no time for chitchat. I'd spotted swirling boils bubbling up from holes on the reef beneath. That meant the impact point was immediately below us. I felt the dark swell building behind us pick up speed. A monster, no question about it. Before this thing crested, it would tower nearly twenty feet. Fantastic.

Here we go, I thought. TayLo felt it, too. She howled in my ear, "RIDE this sucker! Ride its *ass*, Dragomir. Don't wipe out! I wanna fuck you on the beach, right in front of your hot blond girlfriend! Vampire surfing! . . . *WoooHOOOO!*"

Tension triggered peals of wild laughter. And suddenly it all exploded into one wild and crazy ride. As I zigzagged up and down the huge wave, picking up speed and accelerating away from the curling break, TayLo dipped and glided in perfect balance atop my shoulders, never throwing me off the rhythm. We howled and yelled . . . but even I shut up as things got hairy right at the end as the wave's curling lash nearly swallowed us whole.

Then it was over.

We whipped into the shallows and I hopped off the board in knee-deep water, taking a deep bow—awkwardly, as one does with the weight of a girl on one's shoulders—and the vampire crew ran to greet us, cheering and applauding.

Chapter Seventeen

TayLo hopped off me and was immediately squired to the fire pit by two of my Speedo-clad, studly homies. The rest stuck with me as we strolled up the beach, making chitchat—mostly Hollywood gossip, believe it or not. Vampires, like most humans, can't get enough of the celebrity life; the pulsing, twisting tango of who's fucking whom. And some wouldn't know a "Bieber" if it jumped up and bit 'em on the ass.

In due course, we reached the fire pit, where the Euro-vamps had broken out a cooler packed with champagne, cognac and fifty-year-old Scotch.

"Glad you could make it, Drag," said Dmitri, an undead from Minsk now living in Paris—the city where so many of our kind settle.

"And why not? If you're fucking gonna be dead, you might as well do it in Paris," Dmitri had told me about a hundred years ago.

Now he added, "Thanks for bringing a hot movie star. You obviously have TayLo under . . . control."

It was more a question than a statement.

I said, "Not to worry, Dmitri. It's always a decision fraught with angst when we allow a live one to share our precious secret. But TayLo's cool. I trust her."

Then Milos, an exceptionally handsome homeboy who'd crossed into eternity two hundred years after me, and not fifty miles from where I'd lived, walked up and said, "Drag, I'm sure TayLo's totally devoted to you, but could you extract her from her two admirers over there and let us *all* enjoy her charms . . . so to speak, of course."

I winked. "Took the thought right out of my mind, Milos."

Strolling over to TayLo, preening under the flirtatious attentions of two vampires I knew only slightly, I mock-pouted when I said, "I think you need to share the wealth a bit, my dear. Everyone's just dying—you'll pardon the expression—to meet you."

One vamp grinned. The other glared. I uttered a low warning growl, disguising it just enough so it would sound to TayLo like I'd simply cleared my throat.

"See you later, boys," she chirped, putting her arm in mine.

I hesitated a beat, my eyes meeting the glaring one's gaze.

"Another time," he grunted, and walked away.

TayLo, getting it now, flashed a knowing female smile.

"Dead or alive, boys will be boys," she purred.

I walked her back to the fire pit. Within moments, she was in her element, knocking back champagne, surrounded by admiring males. Someone turned up the boom box, her hips cranked and she undulated seductively, nodding and smiling as the vampire boys howled and dirty-danced around her.

I walked to the cooler, poured two flutes of champagne, and headed over to a large piece of driftwood where Ludmilla—no longer bare-breasted, and rocking some kind of slinky sari thing—sat brushing her hair with an actual brush.

The phrase "giddy as a schoolboy" described me perfectly as I handed her the chilled bubbly.

"Ludmilla, I can't . . . I mean, I don't . . ."

"Don't know where to begin?"

She laughed like the Ludmilla of old and took a deep draught of the wine.

"Well, you might start by telling me how lovely I look after all these centuries. But the bigger question in your mind, Dragomir, is . . . why am I not dead, and how did I become a vampire? Correct?"

"Well, yes . . . but I just want to say . . ."

"Stop!"

She held up her hand commandingly, motioning me to sit down beside her. Laughing in that charming, girlish way that still made my knees go weak, she said, "Let me just say it all at once so that you know everything. And then, perhaps, we can talk like the two old friends we are. Agreed?"

I nodded, and sat.

"I remember that day you came to me after I'd told you of the awful thing my father had done," she began. "You shocked me when you revealed that you had become a vampire, having been converted by the Countess Drina. And you begged to convert me to the 'vampire life'—you actually used that silly phrase—and I told you I would not, because I now looked forward to dying naturally and finding release from my pain, and perhaps even joy, in heaven.

"Wasn't I a silly little thing? But after you disappeared and I discovered that you had killed my father—I knew it was you, of course, even though the note you had delivered to me with the map showing where to unearth my father's fortune was not signed—I realized that my soul was dying even as my body stayed stubbornly alive. I knew there would never be joy for me on this earth, because I could never surrender to natural love with you, or with any man.

"That's when I began praying that you would return again, Dragomir, so that I could ask you to convert me. I realized how stupid I had been to reject you because of what my father had done. I knew that I should have at least tried to relate to you as a man. It might've been impossible, but perhaps not. And who better to help me find myself again than you, my first true love. But you never came back, and one day—thinking to at least reconnect with your memory—I journeyed to your family estate, even knowing, as I always had, that your mother disapproved of me as a lowly farm girl, despite my father's wealth.

"And it so happened that on that day, your father and mother had taken their coach to town. But Countess Drina, who was visiting, as she often did, was at the estate alone. A miraculous happenstance, as it turned out."

I stood transfixed as Ludmilla recounted astounding events—beginning with her sexual seduction by Drina, which hardly surprised me. That sensuous Circe had enjoyed inciting me with lurid tales of her sexual adventures with beautiful women of the Romanian court, admitting she was especially excited by comely girls in the first blush of youth. So Drina worked her wiles and Ludmilla, grateful at being able to enjoy sexual intimacy with another human being, was truly happy for a time.

"It was not the way that it would have been with you, Dragomir, but it was far better than anything I had believed possible in my ruined life. The next decision that I made, as you might guess, was based on the romantic, girlish impulse that I still might find you and resurrect our love, even if there might be no sexual communion. But you never returned."

In due course, Ludmilla swallowed the blood of Countess Drina and crossed over, joining the legion of the undead. For a long while, the lovers stayed together, but eventually drifted apart. Sex alone could not bond them permanently.

"I loved her, Dragomir, but I was not *in* love with her."

Not disposed to travel too far from the land she knew, Ludmilla eventually slipped beneath the earth for a time and finally found peace. After she emerged, she stayed close to home until times changed so drastically she realized there was nothing left to hold her in Romania.

"That's when I faked my death. I left my shoes and dress at the deep cliff near our farm knowing people would think I'd been despondent and leaped."

That's why, when I went back years later to find her, I was told that she had died. Stupidly, I never investigated further. I assumed her body had never been found. But it had been. Her cold, wet "corpse" was finally found downriver by searchers dispatched by Countess Drina—who lamented loud and long with her kin and the villagers, then "buried" Ludmilla near me in that long-forgotten cemetery. Had I visited her vacated grave, I would have sensed the deception and known she was not dead.

Suddenly, she'd mind-rolled me.

"Yes, damn you, you would have sensed that we were now two of a kind —but you never came back, Dragomir. And when I finally knew that you would never, ever come looking for me . . . I went looking for you, my love."

And that's when realization slammed me. Ludmilla suddenly appearing on the heels of my budding romance with TayLo was no fucking coincidence, goddammit!

The bitch had been stalking me for . . . centuries?

But that was putting it a bit harshly, really. As Ludmilla and I caught up that night after our centuries of separation, I came to realize that she didn't want me as a lover, she simply wanted to see me again. And even though each time she found me, she couldn't bring herself to face me, she still cared for me, as a friend. The very best kind of friend, as she put it.

"Not only an old friend, Dragomir, but a childhood friend. So over the years, I'd observe you. And I suspected, perhaps stupidly, that you still cared deeply for me because, for all the women you seduced—and there were so many, weren't there?—you never truly fell in love with any of them. So why didn't I just approach as an old friend? The timing was never quite right—until our surfers invited me on their California holiday." She laughed. "See what a silly old girl I've become? But I can't help myself when it comes to you, you monster."

Chapter Eighteen

After faking her death, Ludmilla had left Romania to travel in Europe, occasionally connecting with Drina, who'd introduced her to the delights of Paris, Rome, London and other capitals. She finally settled in Paris. I had never met her there, or been aware of her residence, but I guess she'd known that on my last trip to that city. I'd met up with the good old gang now assembled here on Zuma Beach, and invited them to join me for this exotic night of moonlight surfing—and a few days of tasting Hollywood's delights.

"So," I said to Ludmilla. "Here we are again . . . and . . . well . . . I suppose . . ." Suddenly despite all our "I don't love you anymore" business, her face in the moonlight mesmerized me.

She began to laugh, and for a long moment could not bring herself to stop. Finally under control, she looked at me and shook her head.

"Oh, Dragomir, the look on your face is priceless! Don't worry, my dear —as I told you, I love you, but I'm no longer in love with you. I'm not maneuvering to go walking in the moonlight with you to pursue my girlish dreams of romance. I know you have feelings for me still, and perhaps we can be great friends again. But after all, I am now 'Ludmilla, Lesbian Vampire.' Quite different from that simple farm girl you knew."

She laughed, not cruelly, and told me, "Go now, join everyone again and dance at the fire with that lovely film star creature of yours. I'll be along shortly. Go on. We'll talk later, especially about her. I totally approve, by the way."

I bowed, turned and walked away. Vampires never fall victim to fainting spells, but I suddenly got a sense of what sudden involuntary loss of motor control might feel like.

And just what is your problem, wimp-ass? I asked myself. *Okay, you were just reunited with the first love of your youth, and she's not that fresh-faced, country girl who smelled of clover and honey—she's a vampire. But aren't you always bleating about rediscovering the ineffable flush of first love? So now you can enjoy an encore, right? The problems of old have been resolved—because now she's a vampire, just like you. So what's the problem? That she's a lesbian vampire? Oh, come on, a mere speed bump. So she likes girls—so what? Think creatively. (Whoa, did somebody just say . . . threesome? Like, Ludmilla, me and . . . TayLo? Now, that's the kind of creative thinking that had made me Hollywood's greatest gossip columnist!)*

I shook my head sharply. Why can't I just think normal, scary vampire thoughts?

Heading back to the fire pit, I detoured at the cooler, extracted a bottle of Louis XIII cognac, poured myself a snifter and joined the others, happy to be diverted by lively conversation. I smiled at TayLo, who was still dancing and flirting audaciously. *Always in my thoughts, my dear.*

But when I looked again a few minutes later, she'd disappeared. Instinct turned me toward that driftwood log up the beach. And there she was, sitting next to Ludmilla, chatting animatedly. She caught my eye, smiled and turned back to her newfound friend.

Well, I thought, *what are those two gossiping about?*

Me, maybe?

Sorry. It's no surprise that my favorite T-shirt—white letters on black—reads: "It's all about ME!"

I kicked back more cognac, tried to get back into the flow of what was supposed to be a fun night. And after a while, I felt better. Lord knows I enjoy the company of human beings, but there's nothing quite so satisfying as chillin' with your homies. The guys all wanted to hear stories about my adventures in Hollywood, so I related a few tales—and they really went nuts when I told them how I'd ripped the head off that paparazzi werewolf and slam-dunked it into a garbage can. There's nothing vampire guys like better than stories about werewolves being ripped limb from limb, so everyone launched into tales of their own monster fights and physical prowess.

Hey, we may be vampires, but we're still guys!

I took the opportunity to slip back to the liquor locker for a refill, then glanced over at the driftwood.

TayLo and Ludmilla were nowhere in sight. Probably taking a walk, or . . . *something?*

About an hour later, the ladies materialized out of the darkness and joined us. TayLo immediately cranked up the boom box, and she and Ludmilla—now clad in a micro-bikini that showed off her bitchin' bod—began to bop and boogie, looking way hot.

What was the bitch going to do? Seduce TayLo away from me? Despite all her talk about being friends, that would be revenge, vampire-style.

In a moment, all of us were up and dancing with them like it was a goddam hoedown—yelling, stomping, clapping hands. The moon kept working its magic, as did the primo booze, and we shook and shimmied like wild things with no sense of time passing until—as vampires always do —we sensed the dawn well before the first fingers of light pierced the night sky.

We said our good-byes. Ludmilla kissed TayLo and hugged her. Then she shook my hand, smiling primly.

Dmitri said, "Dragomir, we're going to be in town for a few more days. How about guiding us on a Hollywood pub crawl before we leave? Take us where we can see a few stars, that kind of thing. Or maybe we could shoot over to Vegas?"

I handed him my card. "Call me. I'll set something up."

The vampire gang cheered, then swarmed TayLo, gushing about how they loved her work and were so thrilled to meet her. Just before I gathered our star up in my arms, Ludmilla came close and whispered softly in my ear.

"I'll give you a call, too, if that's all right. We should catch up."

"Oh, I thought we had," I said, rather archly.

"Dragomir, make no mistake—I am not the simple little country girl you once knew. Do not dare to condescend."

"I'll say you're not—you're quite a scary lady. But please call, by all means."

TayLo, suddenly beside us, said, "You two sound like a bad movie I saw once—or maybe I was in it? Please don't stop. The dialogue's fucking hilarious!"

I slapped her tight little ass. She yelped. The vampire gang cheered as I snatched her up and rocketed into the night sky.

Chapter Nineteen

I flew at top speed, pushing into the wind so hard she couldn't open her mouth to speak. Minutes later, we landed on her balcony at Miracles. Just as I was about to put her down on her bed, she kissed me full on the lips. It was exquisite, but now was not the time. I pulled away and said, "You'd better get some sleep."

She pouted. "No, I don't want to sleep! I've just had the most exciting night of my life, and I don't want it to stop. It's been like a revelation. I know what to do now. And I finally know what I want. I love vampires. Vampires are fun. I want to *be* one. I love how you guys can drink all you want and not get fucked up."

"Right," I said. "Unless you consider being *dead* fucked up."

She smiled lazily. "I also want to *be* a vampire . . . so I can deal with my new love rival."

"Love rival?"

Suddenly looking serious, she asked, "I've read tons about you guys and seen all the movies and TV shows, but in real life . . . do vampires ever fuck each other, or live people only?"

"In real . . . life?"

She started laughing hysterically. I shook my head.

"Oh, we do each other, yes, but live girls are far more fun. You blood-filled babes represent the unattainable for us, arousing our lust for life itself. You saw how my homies were flirting with *you* more than Ludmilla. They all wanted you."

She threw her arms around me again. "But I want *you*. Please stay here with me tonight, Dragomir. Or better yet, take me back to your wonderful vampire lair at the Four Seasons. Omigod, I want you so much . . . *please!*"

I raised a hand and cut her off. "Enough! And call me Clark, please. Not another word, because this is not the time. You are in rehab and need rest. Just look directly into my eyes and you will sleep . . . *now!*"

Mike Walker

Instantly, she swayed. I caught her dead weight in my arms, carried her to the bed, pulled off her shorts and top, but left the bikini in place. Then, reconsidering, I unhooked her top and tossed it. Those straps had seemed to cut so cruelly into her tender, Irish-pale skin. I tucked her into the blankets, regarded her finally peaceful face for a long moment, then surprised myself by kissing her, rather tenderly, on her forehead.

A second later, I was in the wind. Hollywood-bound.

Seconds after that, I was deep inside TayLo's mind; talking to her, desperate to know *what* had transpired between her and Ludmilla when they'd disappeared into the dark at Zuma.

"Where did you go, after you and Ludmilla left that driftwood perch?" I whispered. "Tell me everything."

Back in the quiet closeness of her room at Miracles, TayLo stirred. Her lips moved, forming silent words as she murmured into her dream . . .

". . . Ludmilla was so beautiful, and I wanted to hate her because I sensed you and she had meant something to each other, and maybe still did. But she was so nice. At first, I figured she was just kissing up to me, pretending to be friends like girls do to get at you later. But after a while I thought, this is a really upfront chick. So I finally asked her, straight up with no bullshit, if she was still hot for you. She started laughing so hard she couldn't stop. And then she started crying. Oh, Clark, it was so sad. She told me everything, about how you two had been in love, but it ended when she decided to tell you the truth about what her father had done to her. That bastard! Do you know how betrayal by a father ruins a girl? It's ten times worse than being fucked over by your mother—and trust me, I know all about that.

"Then she told me the saddest thing of all: that her reaction had been to turn to another woman for love and sexual comfort. It's such a goddam tragedy. What a screenplay it would make, especially the horrible irony of not letting you convert her into a vampire—then falling in love with Countess What's-her-name, and getting converted anyway. It was so sad when she talked about losing you and your love.

"The two of us were bawling our eyes out. I hugged her . . . and the next thing you know, we were kissing like crazy. She suddenly snatched me up, just the way you always do, and we went shooting into the sky. I don't think it was thirty seconds later that she dropped us down onto the patio of a swanky gated mansion up the beach, then was all over me on the sofa inside this adorable little pool house. I was scared shitless, thinking someone might come out of the main house, but she told me she'd cased the place earlier that day and no one was at home. She made me laugh when she said, 'You can have some great, cheap house-sitting vacations when you're a vampire.' Then she was all over me again. It's no secret I've done a little girlie-banging, but I just wasn't into it. You're asking me why? I don't know. Somehow it felt like it might be a . . . betrayal. Of you, I mean. Does that even make sense?

"Then Ludmilla said that she approved of me—for you, that is. I was upfront. I told her there was nothing going on between us, but admitted it wasn't because I haven't tried. I told her I'd fuck you in a minute. It was the wrong thing to say. She started crying again . . . but finally she said, 'I would have fucked him in a minute, too—but he waited a minute too long, I guess.'

"Then we both started crying and laughing like crazy.

"My God, Dragomir . . . Clark . . . please, please, let's write this as a screenplay. Starring me as Ludmilla, and Johnny Depp . . . no, Javier Bardem, can play you. It would be the most sensational comeback of all time, don't you think? Oh, goddammit, Clark . . . Dragomir . . . Master, come to me, make me your slave . . . please . . . I want you to possess me . . . forever . . . Master . . . oh, Master . . ."

And all I could think was, what the fuck's *wrong* with me? I've got *that* lying back there begging for it, and I'm on the return flight to Beverly Hills?

Before you ask again . . . yes, there *are* gay vampires.

NO, I'm not one of them.

Jesus.

Mike Walker

Chapter Twenty

My cell phone started vibrating. I was six hundred feet over Moon Shadows, the surfside Malibu watering hole on the Pacific Coast Highway where Mel Gibson made those career-killing headlines with his infamous anti-Semitic rant. I answered, not bothering to look at caller ID. I knew it'd be Wally Tate, my ace reporter, a driven newshound whose secret ambition, no shit, is to convert. Seriously. Wants to be a vampire. Hell, he might as well be, with the ungodly hours he keeps.

"Hey, Wally, I'm in the wind, literally. Can it keep, or . . ."

I heard his dry chuckle and sighed. Wally never puts off until tomorrow what he can annoy/tantalize me with immediately.

"Master, I am here only to serve you. Your wish is my command."

"Really, Renfield? Then go home. Get drunk. Get laid. Any or all of the above would please me greatly."

"Of course, Master, but . . ."

Knowing from long experience this was going to take *way* more than a fucking minute, I swooped down, landing on a massive rock jutting from a cliff face high above the PCH, peered down at the neon sign spelling out "Moon Shadows." This had been Mel's favorite hangout until the night he'd got busted with a load on and sprayed spittle in a Jewish deputy sheriff's face.

Okay, time to deal with Wally, or, as I call him, "Relentless Renfield." Guy's a dog on a bone when it comes to news or gossip, and he's unswervingly, even fanatically, devoted to me. Which is why I'd jokingly dubbed him Renfield, the name of that creepy, bizarre-but-brilliant character who famously declared to Bram Stoker's Dracula, "I will *never* betray you, master, I am your *slave.*"

Early on in the years we'd known each other, Renfield had ferreted out my secret in a rather clever way, a story I'd like to tell you sometime. Then, talk about a hardcore news guy, he'd begged me to convert him—because possessing the superpowers of the undead would make him an even more formidable reporter.

"Convert you? I've never even *fed* on you, Renfield," I told him.

His instant response?

"My neck is yours to command, Master. Feeling peckish *now*, by any chance?"

That's our Wally. Subservient, but with a wicked sense of humor. And my calling Wally Renfield is an open joke in *The Revealer* newsroom—where no one knows, or even suspects, my true nature. Everyone figures we're just making a jape about our master-slave relationship. And that's amusing to my colleagues, who love to perpetuate the, uh . . . myth that I'm an arrogant know-it-all, and a slave driver who never sleeps. Ah, if they only knew.

"Wally, I'm perched on a rock high above the PCH like a giant condor about to pounce out of the windy darkness. I've had a night of extreme sensory overload, so be brief."

Again, the dry chuckle.

"An exquisite gem of a gossip item just materialized a couple of hours ago, and would have been written and on your desk in the morning, Master —but things took a funny turn when I learned something that you might want to hear before you get to your destination. It's connected, I think, to that which you've been involved with of late—the Roma-TayLo connection. You know that hot little mess who stars on the new high school-oriented sitcom, *Making the Grade*—Jenny Bliss, the baby-doll blonde? Well, last night, sweet Jenny attended a super-exclusive party thrown at the estate of Glenn Burnham, our favorite movie mogul, and got herself really burned on booze, plus lotsa hot smoky-smoky.

"She got dizzy and disoriented, wandered outside—and suddenly needed to pee. So she faced herself away from the lighted part of the house, where the party was happening, squatted and spread—not realizing that the darkened wing she was facing is where Glenn has his huge screening room. The lights were dimmed because he had a crowd in there watching scenes from his studio's latest flick.

"Anyway, someone glanced out a window and yelled, 'Oh my God— LOOK!' And there was sweet little Jenny, thong panties down around her Christian Louboutins, legs splayed to the max—pissing like a wild pony. Our little actress never knew she was performing for the best audience she's ever had. People were *screaming*! And—as happens in today's digital age— at least a dozen cell phones instantly started clicking pics of her pussy. Can you believe it, boss?"

I choked back a laugh. "Wally, cut to the chase! Do *we* have a picture?"

Even as I spoke, my cell phone vibrated. A text! Wally had fired the photo to my phone, and . . . oh, *wow*! There crouched poor Jenny Bliss, blissfully unaware that scores of eyes were riveted on her neatly shaven cooch. Bad enough being exposed to the world, but she'd die when she saw the dopey, shit-faced expression on her kisser.

"Cute, Wally. But I'm waiting for other shoe to drop. You said there was something I needed to know tonight, so . . ."

I heard him start breathing faster. Whenever he's got a hot story in his sights, Wally hyperventilates—pants, almost—just like the "real" Renfield.

"Master, I think you're going to like this. It just so happens that one of my long-time sources, a chick who used to be in PR but now works at Paramount, was at the party last night and managed to call me about the pee-pee scandal. Unfortunately, she didn't have her cell phone with her, so she didn't snap a picture. But when I started asking her who was at the party, she happened to mention Derek Brewster, that very-much-married cop show star—who just found out that *we* know he's banging his costar, a fact he's hoping desperately we won't print, *or* mention to *Mrs.* Brewster."

I chuckled. "So, you got Brewster on the phone, and told him he had a get-out-of-jail-free card from us *if* he texted you the pic. Good work."

"Boss, you're way ahead of me. Actually, we met after he left the party because he was paranoid about texting a picture like that. So we hooked up, and I downloaded it to my iPhone. But here's the interesting part—we sat and chitchatted a bit, and he mentioned a *very* interesting conversation his wife had overheard between Roma Kane and Cara Prescott in a ladies' room, and—"

"Wait, they were at the same party with Derek?"

"No, sorry, they were all at *another* party, last night in Beverly Hills. Mrs. B. was in a stall and overheard them whispering about drugs. No big deal, girls often talk drugs in ladies' rooms. But she cocked an ear when she heard Cara and Roma mention TayLo. She couldn't hear everything, but it was a lot of 'mean girls' shit, stuff about them making TayLo feel bad. Brewster's wife says Roma Kane kept repeating the phrase, 'keep her off balance.' And, get this, she told Cara she was going to, 'keep feeding her that really heavy shit the old man had sent up from Brazil.' Then Roma got a really nasty tone in her voice and said to Cara, 'You'd better keep making that old man real happy, bitch, if you want to be a star.'

"It didn't make a lot of sense to Brewster's wife, but she remembered it because it just sounded like pure evil. Also, Brewster's wife hates rich-bitch Roma—as do ninety percent of the people in this town."

I sighed. "How reliable is Brewster's wife?"

"Before she married him, she was one of the best script supervisors in this town. You know that job—you need total memory recall. I think she's solid."

Renfield paused, then . . .

"So, what do you think, boss? I know it's weird, because Roma always comes on like she's TayLo's best friend, right? Yet here she is talking about fucking her over. And why's Roma suddenly hanging out with Cara Prescott? They hate each other, last I heard. But you know how girls are. They'll team up with their worst enemy to fuck over another chick they hate. Main thing is, there's no doubt Roma and Cara were at the party together. I checked that out myself."

An image whipped through my mind like a speeding bullet: Roma's distinctive pink Pepto-Mobile pulling out of the driveway at Miracles.

"Son of a bitch!"

"Yes, Master?"

"Not you, you sonuvabitch. Listen, where are you? We've got to talk."

"I'm already in Venice, boss, about three blocks from home. And until you grant my fondest wish, to be a 'being' just like you, I can't work much more than twenty hours a day—which is where I'm at right now. Look, it's nearly four, so let me go down until about eight. Breakfast at nine, okay? I'm beat."

God, I loved this guy.

"Be careful what you wish for, Renfield. If you keep lying down on me like this, I just might make your dream come true. Okay, Dupar's at The Grove? Nine sharp."

"You got it, Master. Have a safe flight home. Oh, almost forgot. Ready for your joke of the day?"

I sighed. It was a long-standing ritual between us. "We both know that's a rhetorical question, Renfield. Get on with it!"

"So a dyslexic guy walks into a bra . . ."

He had me for about three seconds; two expended as I stupidly waited for him to complete the sentence, and one to finally get the dyslexic twist on the ancient "guy walks into a bar" riff. Hey, even vampires get punchy after a long night. We need our deep sleep.

I sighed. "Pray for forgiveness, Renfield. Sleep well."

"Thanks, boss."

Chapter Twenty-One

I lifted off the rock above Moon Shadows, got in the wind and rocketed down to LA, hugging the coastline. I wanted to relax, watch the sunrise from where rays can't shine, mull the sudden infusion of new info about Roma Kane—and analyze why the *hell* I was suddenly so obsessed with this Taylor Logan story. I had my suspicions on that score . . . and so, I'm sure, do you.

Twenty minutes later I sat lounging beneath an awning on my terrace at the Four Seasons. Sipping a cup of Earl Grey, I watched the blood-red fingers of dawn claw up from night's dark horizon. And what a night it had been. The shock of Ludmilla's resurrection had me in turmoil. It didn't take a mind matured over three centuries to deduce that I was reacting to the shock of unexpected reunion with my first love, and a feeling that I'd lost her all over again.

Boo HOO! Poor vampire!

Yet, considering my penchant for mawkish sentimentality, I should be feeling totally devastated, I thought, but I wasn't! Why? All together now, people . . .

TayLo!

It struck me then that whenever her name popped up in my mind, I didn't simply say it—I fucking *sang* it!

TayLo! . . . TayLo!

I wrenched my mind back to my developing story—developing even faster based on Wally's hot intel. The good news: It had all the overtones of a classic gossip tale; sex, drugs, big buck$$, famous Hollywood players acting out everyman's fantasies in trendy eateries and nightclubs, plus a disturbing undertone—illicit, dangerous drugs that can literally kill you smuggled in from foreign locales—which boded well for it to burgeon into a front-page blockbuster. And that's my mission: serving up the stories the world can't stop talking about.

So thanks to a snatch of ladies' room chitchat incorporating these classic gossip elements—*and* an eye-popping pic of a star peeing!—I now had the ingredients of a spicy stew ready to serve up after a bit of vigorous pot-stirring (okay, shit-stirring) by experienced hands.

Ah, but who cares, you ask?

Answer: untold millions, worldwide. And to those who dismiss gossip as a trivial pursuit, I retort, "Gossip is human history in the making."

Astute aficionados of gossip are avid historians, experts in the psychology that triggers human nature. They are guided by the one precept you should never forget—so write it down or stitch it on a sampler: GOSSIP IS JUST ANOTHER WORD FOR NEWS!

Gossip is also a metaphor for passion. Just as the vampire is a metaphor for sex, right, ladies? Trivial? Hey, it's only rock 'n roll, but I like it.

I closed my eyes and dozed. The first image swirling up from the mist was Ludmilla . . . gradually replaced by TayLo . . . then Ludmilla again . . . and TayLo!

Two hours later, after a shower and a cup of my hand-brewed Cuban *cafecito*, I phoned my office at *The Revealer*. Elspeth picked up instantly.

"Gossip Desk."

"And why is an important personage like Clark Kelly's deputy editor answering the phone? Where's our Lorna? Day off *again*?"

"Good morning," chirped my unflappable Girl Friday, without whom I'd be just another disorganized vampire gossip columnist. "You're surfacing very early. No, Lorna's here. She's in the ladies' room."

"Ah, she's on the job, then. Ladies' rooms are ground zero for good gossip. Which brings me to why I called . . ."

I filled Elspeth in on everything she needed to know. She ran my Gossip Desk, coordinating the labyrinthine activities of five full-time reporters, eleven contract freelancers, an army of contributing freelancers, plus our most trusted sources and the office support staff that included her assistant, Lorna—not to mention little old me. Elspeth needs to know everything I know, but just to be crystal clear, I did *not* make mention of flying high with a girl in the sky or our rollicking vampire surf party. No, Elspeth does *not* know my secret. Although she often says—even in my presence—that "Clark has strange ways! That's why he's . . . Clark."

And while I aver that she doesn't know my secret, I wouldn't put money on it. Elspeth plays it so close to the vest that even if she did suspect something, she wouldn't press for an answer. She'd wait for me to volunteer it. I trust her completely, as do all my staff and our carefully shielded behind-the-scenes sources, and that's no small thing in our twisty, spy-counterspy world of closely held, scandalous secrets.

"So that's it, Elspeth. I'm off to meet Wally at Dupar's. But I need to speak urgently to Vanillo when she surfaces. I know it's far too early for her now."

How's that for a Hollywood hottie name, eh? *Vanillo!* And it's her real moniker! Vanillo is *The Revealer*'s "club girl." Which sounds like a dream job, but it's actually a nightmare assignment no experienced journalist would dream of taking on.

Every evening, Vanillo Pezzullo (swear to God!)—who looks like Marisa Tomei's smokin' hot baby sis—slaps on her war paint, slips into barely there designer frocks, then click-clacks off on fuck-me heels to make the rounds of every in-spot club from Hollywood Boulevard to the Sunset Strip. Vanillo's paid handsomely to dig up on-the-spot dirt from eyewitnesses who've observed partying celebs do what they do, night after night, i.e., getting drunk, fucking in the john, spitting at paparazzi, throwing dough at the homeless as they exit the clubs, or just vomiting in the street.

Vanillo's got one great advantage: She knows *everyone* on the nightclub scene. But she's got one great *dis*advantage: Everyone on the club scene knows *her*! Celebs freeze at the sight of Vanillo. Club staffers are afraid to act too friendly with her, fearing backlash from celebs. In fact, hers would be an impossible assignment if it weren't for an intriguing fact that *everyone* on the Hollywood night scene knows: Vanillo packs a purse bulging with *Revealer* dough that she loves to spread around. And her personal expense account? It's legendary among workaday journalists.

But it's a grueling gig! Vanillo's got to keep bouncing in and out of clubs, hour after hour, night after night; drinking companionably, but never getting drunk, shaking her booty on the dance floor, but always staying fresh enough to work the insiders who have pipelines to celebrity naughtiness. The girl rarely rolls in before five ayem.

"I just spoke to Vanillo, actually," said Elspeth. "She got some great stuff last night, and she's writing it up now so we won't bother her later. Today is deadline day, as you may recall."

"Really?"

Ignoring my sarcasm, Elspeth said, "So shall I connect you to Princess Pretty Butt?"

"Please."

Chapter Twenty-Two

"Vanillo?"

"Good morning, incredibly handsome boss. I'll be going to sleep soon, so I'll dream of you."

"Vanillo, I've told you before—flirt with anyone you want, *except* me. I *am* your boss. So you must be, accordingly, discreet."

Emitting a throaty chuckle, the minx purred, "You are *so* funny, Clark. Or should I call you '*Mr.* Clark'? Hey, the minute we're off the phone, I'll send an e-mail for your files confirming that I sexually harass *you*! Then I'll think of you as I pleasure myself to sleep."

I adore my little killer, but her chain often needs a yank.

"Vanillo!"

"Okay, *work time*! Hey, boss, did Elspeth tell you I got you great stuff last night? Like, Keanu Reeves disappearing into the john at Fury with a leggy blonde nearly as tall as he is. And boy, *is* he tall! I ended up standing right in front of him when Christina Aguilera jumped onstage to jam with the band. I kinda hoped he might dry-hump me discreetly—even if it would have been between my shoulder blades; I'm so tiny and he's *so* giant. So I finally kinda leaned back into him, and his little big man stood up to say hello. I walked away then, hoping he might catch me later. He smiled, but ended up with some blond slut after *I* got his motor running. *Bitch!* But, hey, I got two great items you're gonna love! One is that Kim Kardashian went—"

"Later, mighty reporter girl. What I need from you right now is deep background on Roma Kane and her posse for an angle I'm working."

"Okay. Like what?"

"Tell me about Roma and drugs—as in, when and how heavy."

"Well . . . she's not heavy at all when she's out on the scene. She's usually straight when she arrives anywhere. When it's a late-nighter, she'll sneak a snort in the ladies' room. But she's always under control. I've seen her turn down prime blow from pals over and over. No, Roma's m.o. is to suddenly drag her posse to her house above Sunset Strip where they all get down with stuff. Roma never goes falling flat on her face when she's out partying, like Lindsay or Britney. You remember that pretty-boy actor she was banging that I got really . . . umm, close to . . . until they had that huge slapping match and she dumped him? He told me some *great* shit, remember? How she'd have 'nude nights' once a month and how she loved getting banged underwater with just her head sticking up above the surface so everyone could see her orgasm face, but not the action down below. Roma's kinky. But as for the drugs, no. She's not what I'd call a heavy user, ever."

A memory kicked in. "Didn't you once tell me she supplies *everyone* when they come to her house for those all-night parties?"

"Oh, yeah. That's why the Hollywood scene kisses up to Roma. Her parties are the best. She stocks killer booze—especially primo French champagne—and she's got the best drugs. Also, she doesn't get uptight if you slip off into one of her spare bedrooms for hokey-pokey."

"Who—besides you—are regulars?"

Vanillo giggled. "I *wish*! But first and foremost, it's whomever she's currently fucking. Roma's funny. She always has so-called steady boyfriends, but they rarely last more than a month or so. Then she's on to the next steady *du jour*. Her in-crowd keeps changing. That disgusting guy Scummy Bear's always around, of course. Her tight girlfriend circle is TayLo, Cara Prescott, plus Britney when she's sober, Lindsay (who never is), and her own two sisters, Hilary and Camille. And sometimes Kim . . . but Big K's got her own posse. I'm always angling like crazy for an invite into that, and I think I'm making progress. A friend of Scott Disick's is totally hot for my bod. And the only way *he* gets in, is if *I* get in . . . *capisce*?"

I grinned. Adopting a stern tone, I said, "Vanillo, it is *never* a condition of your employment that you should sacrifice that which is most precious, even in pursuit of a hot story, and—"

"Oh, shut the fuck up, boss. I do who I want to do, and if getting hot helps a story, so be it! I just want to be clear that—"

She burst out laughing as she heard me humming my don't-wanna-hear-it "Happy Birthday" song under her rant.

"You are *so* funny. Any other questions, Clarksie?"

"Yes. Is Cara Prescott *really* part of Roma's inner circle? I keep hearing they hate each other."

Vanillo sighed. "Men never understand it, but girls are kinda like the Mafia—they love keeping their friends close, and their enemies closer. Even girls who hate each other can have great conversations, help each other with suggestions on fashion, boy problems, taking revenge on common enemies—all kinds of shit. They *use* each other. That's what females do. They're quite comfortable in bitch mode. And keeping someone you hate around means you always have someone to sharpen your claws on. So Roma sorta, quote-unquote, 'hates' Cara, but she's also helped her by getting her introductions to movers and shakers—like that agent of hers . . . uh, what's-his-name?"

"Mark Olson."

"Yeah."

A bell went off. TayLo had dumped Mark Olson, one of the meanest young agent sharks in town, because he openly despised mom Alina. He once had the lunch crowd at the Château Marmont garden gasping as he loudly ripped into her for being an "amateur meddler" in her daughter's career. A real momma's girl, our TayLo. But she'd made up with Olson later, and was lucky he'd taken her back. She'd gotten so toxic with her car crashes, booze and drug binges, showing up late for shoots, etc., that she couldn't find another agent of his caliber to handle her. Then I recalled that during the period TayLo and Olson were on the outs, Roma sent Cara to him—the very agent her good pal TayLo hated. Why would she do that, I asked Vanillo?

"That's not so weird, really, boss. First of all, Cara's no major talent prize, not like TayLo. She just needed an agent, so Roma made the call to help her out. But, so what? I mean, what are you looking for?"

"Tell you when I find it. But, uh . . . are there any old men Roma sucks up to? I mean, like, really old."

"*Old men?* What would she be doing with old men?"

"If you find out, let me know. Back to drugs . . . you think she's a dealer?"

"Like a *dealer* dealer? Hell, no. Roma's always got plenty of rooty-tooty for her friends, like a lot of rich bitches. But she's no dealer."

I sighed. "How about her relationship with TayLo? Are they *really* friends?"

"Hell, yeah. I mean, they bitch at each other, like all best girlfriends. But, omigod, have you forgotten my killer story about TayLo's special gift for horny Roma—the night she helped her get off with Kragen, the TV vampire? You gave me a bonus for that one, remember?"

I laughed, recalling it; the kind of gossip gem that comes along rarely. Vanillo had picked up on it one night at Beacher's Madhouse on Hollywood Boulevard when TayLo, totally smashed, came wandering into the club with a couple of girlfriends. Spotting Britney, Lindsay, Nicole and a few of their other pals, she noted how they suddenly started giggling and shrieking as TayLo—looking around to make sure she wasn't being overheard—started whispering some super-hot secret.

Their table was right next to the hallway leading back to the johns, so Vanillo walked their way as if headed for a pee. But she quickly doubled back and stood right around the corner where they couldn't see her. As she eavesdropped, and heard TayLo telling the girls how she'd done Roma the favor of a lifetime, Vanillo clicked on the tiny, super-expensive digital recorder we'd equipped her with and caught the whole sizzling story in TayLo's very own words:

"Okay, ladies . . . so, we all know Roma's got the hots for Damon Strutt, who plays the vampire Kragen on the *Bold Blood* series, right? I mean, the girl's always had fantasies about vampire sex—like, who *hasn't*?—so I actually fixed her up with Damon, who I know real well 'cause we bonded during that stage play we did together, remember? And, NO, I'm so not doing him! Anyway, I told Roma that Damon was paranoid about the tabloids finding out he'd dated her. He wants to keep the image of being a single guy for his female fans—the usual star shit, right? So he told Roma he'd drop by her house late, and she had to be home alone. He parked his car a block away that night, then walked around to the back of her place—just in case the paparazzi were out front—and knocked on the kitchen door. When Roma opened up, she almost fainted. Damon was in full Kragen drag—fangs and all!"

Recalling the day I'd listened to Vanillo's amazing tape, I'll never forget how the girls had screamed at that point—then shut up fast as TayLo dished more dirty details:

"Okay, so . . . Damon grabbed her all hard like, started chewing on her cheeks and her tits, then growled at her, 'Your bedroom—NOW!' So he chases her upstairs and throws her on the bed real rough, acting like a crazed, horny vampire. But then, Roma told me he stopped joking around and really started kissing her and . . . well, he got kind of into it, acting all tender and shit, so Roma suddenly sat up and begged him, 'Stay in character, okay? Please?' Can you fucking *believe* that bitch?! So she made him go all 'full vampire' on her—and he did, too. Roma says she couldn't walk right the next day, and he even broke some furniture! But she fucking LOVED it!"

Vanillo's tape was fabulous! Even today, my reporters request replays. It's a rare treat, hearing a gossip blockbuster straight from a star's mouth. TayLo had those girls in hysterics. Vanillo reminded me what had happened next.

"But just then, OMIGOD, boss . . . who walks into the club and spots them? Remember? Yup, Roma! TayLo and the girls tried to get it under control, but were so drunk they finally copped—right to Roma's face—that her vampire sex secret was out! They promised not to tell a soul, of course. Then they started cracking up again, and Roma turned all red. But she was so damn thrilled by her own sexy story that she finally 'fessed it was true, and started cracking up herself!"

Vanillo had nailed it. When I'd broken the item in the column, every two-bit gossip site on the Internet ran with it hard! The story made headlines in rags and on websites worldwide.

Vanillo was giggling. "See what I mean, Clark? Fix a girl up with a hot vampire, she's your best friend forever, right?"

"Uh, I guess. Again, great job, kiddo. Now, one last thing. Where's that slob Scummy Bear fit in?"

"Total asshole, as you know, and he's sorta Roma's male slave. She's known him since they were kids. He comes from minor money. His Persian grandfather made out okay importing rugs and shit from the Middle East. He's not in Roma's class money-wise, but he gets a pretty fair allowance from his mother. He doesn't do shit except run errands for Roma, and gets fatter eating those disgusting gummy bears that inspired her to give him his 'Scummy Bear' nickname. Actually, I'm working on something about him, but it's way early in the game. One thing I'm sure of, though . . . I'm hearing some weird stuff about how he lets Roma's miniature dogs get killed by coyotes."

"*What?* What do you mean—he accidentally leaves them outside at night, or what?"

"More like he leaves them outside on purpose, or something. I don't know the details, Clark. Just heard about it. Still trying to check it out."

Goddam.

"Vanillo, how many times have I told you—if you get onto something that sounds like front-page potential, call it in immediately and we'll put reporters on it. I know you're trying to be a hero and get it yourself, but you can lose a story that way. What if *The National Enquirer* hears the tip, puts on a full-court press and nails the story first? Be a pro, dammit! Ask for help and nail the story. You'll still get credit for it, trust me."

"Sorry, boss."

"Don't worry about it. Now keep checking out the dog thing, but quietly. Animal cruelty's always a seller. Meanwhile, we're on it. So, got anything else for me on Scummy Bear?"

"Well, just that he's a creepy sadist. I know some girls he's knocked around, and I know he really fucked up a guy Roma didn't like. A source of mine told me he passed the guy some of that scary drug from Brazil called Oxi. The guy overdosed, and had to be pumped out at a hospital. He's such an evil prick."

Brazil? That rang a bell, in a ladies' room, specifically.

"Yeah, I just heard from a story Wally's chasing that this Oxi stuff is heavy. If it's so dangerous, why's it on the street? Brazilian crackheads are one thing, but who'd use it here?"

I heard the catch in her voice as she said, "Clark, you . . . you remember my old boyfriend? He was such a heavy user, I had to dump him. He was always looking for something with a more powerful kick. Guys who use like that can shoot or snort shit that would literally kill you and me, or even light users like Roma and her posse. I know Scummy never touches that Oxi stuff, so I think he keeps it around to fuck up people he doesn't like. That's just a guess. Look, I'll get into that and whatever's going on with Roma's dogs. I'll let you know when I have something."

I sighed. I knew her boyfriend had finally OD'd and died.

"Okay, but be careful, Vanillo. You're a club reporter, not part of our heavy mob. Not yet, anyway. Get some sleep, girl."

I clicked off, got Elspeth back on and said, "I'll be at Dupar's."

"Okay," she said. "Have the Belgian waffles. Blueberry sauce. Seriously."

Chapter Twenty-Three

Dupar's. The gustatory legend at LA's fabled Farmers Market and my favorite breakfast place. Chomping on the waffles, I enthused, "Man, these are really great."

Wally Tate raised an eyebrow. "You're a maple syrup guy, boss. *Blueberry* sauce?"

"Yeah. Who knew?"

"Elspeth, right?"

I wiped my mouth with a napkin, grimacing at the blue stain. "You're a great reporter, Renfield, but how'd you know that? She tell you, too?"

"Nope. Deduction. Elspeth's your mother hen, always trying to make sure you eat right."

He shot me one of his lopsided grins. "If she only knew what gourmet delight you *really* crave . . ."

I shot him a look. Instantly, off went the smile, out came his reporter's notebook.

"Ready for duty, Master."

Chewing the last chunk of fruity waffle, I took a long pull of coffee and told him, "Finish your French toast. You'll need all the strength you can get, the way I'm going to work your ass. And stop taking notes for a minute. I've already filled you in on the background stuff re Roma via Vanillo."

Wally opened his mouth, but I beat him to the cheesy quip he was contemplating.

"No, there is *no* major thoroughfare in Rome called *Via Vanillo*. Very funny. Applause, applause. But seriously, folks! . . . Jesus, Renfield, why do both of us have this maddening affinity for lame jokes? It's sick!"

Wally nodded seriously, then said, "A guy walks into a doctor's office . . ."

"Okay, down to business, dammit. In the context of everything Vanillo just told me, that ladies' room conversation your source's wife overheard between Cara and Roma really starts to make sense now. But we've got a lot of work to do. So, to begin . . . what do you make of this thing about Scummy Bear, and Roma's dogs turning up dead?"

Wally shrugged. "Everything that we know about the gruesome Scummy indicates that he's a classic sociopath/psychotic. Stage one, torturing and killing small animals. Stage two, killing human beings. So let's hope tomorrow never comes."

I nodded. "Unless it's already come and gone. Wally, I want you to assign somebody very fucking experienced, maybe one of our contract private dicks, to hide up in the brush on the hill that slopes down to Roma's backyard. Not every night, but on the weekends when she has her posse over to party. If coyotes are killing her dogs, I doubt that a whiff of human scent will make them turn their backs on Chihuahua snacks. Those coyotes who hunt in the hills above Sunset Boulevard are used to human scents. Now . . . what about a tail for Scummy Bear?"

Wally shook his head. "Don't think we need one. He's easy to find, always in the open. And a tail can't follow him inside Roma's house."

"Yeah, right. And what would we tell the tail to look for? If Scummy's passing killer Oxi to anyone who pisses him off, he sure won't do it in the open. It's just not . . . oh, *fuck*!"

I put my coffee cup down, leaned back in the booth and cursed myself. "What am I, the world's first *senile* gossip columnist?"

"Master?"

"A highly inappropriate salutation. Unless you mean Master *Asshole*."

"What—"

"I can't believe I'm just *now* remembering this. Okay. Remember my longtime source, Darren Fernald?"

"Yeah. That young guy who was a Mondrian Hotel front desk clerk until you helped him land a job at Horizon Public Relations."

"That's him. A few months ago, Darren came to me with a weird story. A former girlfriend of his, a struggling actress named Janet Carter, had gotten heavy into drugs because she was depressed about her career going nowhere. She finally turned to Darren, who's a real straight arrow, told him she was sick to death of Hollywood and disgusted with herself because she'd started selling her body to raise drug money—but not on the streets. She'd made a connection with a very old, very rich guy who paid her handsomely to play weird sex games. But she'd had enough, she told Darren, and she was going back home to Idaho. 'But you don't have to leave town,' Darren told her. 'Just stop prostituting yourself.'

"She said she'd stopped, but was now out of money. She just wanted to go back home to her parents, get help, do rehab. But she needed a loan for the plane ticket. Darren asked if anyone else knew what she'd been doing. She floored him then—told him that the only person who knew was Roma Kane, because Roma *set the whole deal up*!"

Wally blinked. "Say what?"

"That's exactly what Darren told her," I said. "He was stunned. Didn't believe her at first. Doesn't make sense, he told her. Why does Roma Kane need to pimp young girls? She's an heiress to one of the greatest fortunes in the world. Why would she get involved in something like that? It's crazy. Then Janet told Darren she'd said too much already. She begged him not to tell anyone. Then she left. Said she'd call him later.

"That's when Darren came to me. I didn't really see a news angle. Young actresses sell their bodies all the time in this town. But Roma Kane allegedly involved? I had to check it out. So Darren arranged for me to talk to Janet Carter. But the girl gave me nothing I could print. Then, two weeks later, she dies in her apartment of a supposed drug overdose. Cops rule *no* foul play. End of story."

Pausing for a sip of coffee, I ran it down in my head. A story always begins as a mosaic of splintered, jagged pieces. Fitting them into a coherent picture takes patience, skill, intuition . . . and luck.

"What the hell have we got going on here, Wally? Based on what you heard last night, do you have any ideas about the identity of the 'rich old man' the young deceased was selling her body to? Because Roma Kane's involved, my mind immediately jumped to her grandfather, Montague Kane, but that doesn't really compute."

He shrugged. "I thought the same as you, boss. But Cara Prescott's fast becoming a person of interest, wouldn't you say? And what does 'keeping that old man happy' mean—as if I couldn't guess. But how's all this tie into TayLo?"

My turn to shrug.

"Well, Roma has a track record of eventually turning on every female friend she's ever had, sometimes for very little apparent reason except that she's a 'me-first' bitch—but my guess is she's trying to push Cara's career, make her a star. And that could impact TayLo, of course, because Cara and TayLo are the same type, and they're often up for the same roles. So, to push Cara's career, you sabotage TayLo. Ergo, Roma feeds her pal fucked-up drugs—not to kill her, necessarily, but to keep her fucked up."

Wally shook his head. "Master, you're always at least two steps ahead of me. I am not worthy, but what's Roma's motive for whoring her girlfriend out to her grandfather? I mean, what rich old guy can't find his own young pussy in *this* town?"

That made me smile. "Very good point, Wally. And I doubt Roma would pimp girlfriends *just* to keep old Grandpappy happy. But keep an open mind, young reporter. Do you have any idea how much Montague Kane is worth? He owns a major hotel chain, a major airline, a major banking empire and one of the world's top ten shipping companies. Kane controls more money than most small countries."

Wally sighed. "But, boss, Roma's got a huge trust fund. It kicks in when she's thirty years old. Right now, Daddy and Mommy give her quite a hefty little allowance—and I'm sure her doting granddaddy kicks in, too. So why does she need nickel-and-dime pimp fees? It just doesn't add up, unless . . ."

"Unless . . ." I said, thinking about it, "Roma *don't want no steen-king trust fund, amigo.* Because maybe . . . just maybe, Roma doesn't want Mommy and Daddy getting to control Grandpa's fortune. Maybe Baby wants the whole fucking *enchilada, comprendo?*"

Wally shook his head. *"Ai, Chihuahua!"*

"*And* the Chihuahuas! Look, we're just spitballing here. We've got a lot to prove and a lot of work to do, so let's start doing, Renfield."

"I am ever your servant, Master. But first, just a couple of things . . ."

Taking notes furiously, Wally peppered me with questions. I reminded him again that Janet Carter had insisted that Roma *never* asked for a cut of her two-thousand-dollar-a-pop fee. So the way it stacked up for me, after interviewing Janet, was that Roma was probably just currying favor with some grizzled old power player, gifting him with a succulent young hottie the way she gifts friends with drugs and champagne. Janet had absolutely no idea who this old geezer was or even where he lived. She said a chauffeured limo with blacked-out rear windows would pick her up, and the chauffeur would make her wear a blindfold. They'd drive for about forty minutes to an hour and she'd be led into a magnificent mansion—still in her blindfold.

"A servant would usher her into a huge, darkened bedroom. The blindfold would come off and she'd see this old geezer—and she emphasized he was really, really old—lounging on a huge bed with black silk sheets. For the next two or three hours, she'd be directed to strike various poses until he was sufficiently aroused, commit specific sex acts until he was satisfied, then she'd be driven home. And paid, in cash, by the chauffeur.

"It's just another sordid Hollywood story. Nothing really illegal going on. Janet Carter was involved in consensual sex with a man she couldn't identify, and no pimp was profiting from the arrangement—so it's a run-of-the-mill tale about a young girl from Hicksville falling on her ass, then opting to turn said ass into a money-maker. I felt sorry for her, and Darren's been a great undercover source of mine for years, so I had payroll send Janet a check for the interview—seven hundred and fifty dollars. End of story. *Until* she was found dead in her bed.

"The cops traced her movements the night of her death back to Phantom, another new club on La Cienega. It was the last place she visited. And it's one of Roma's regular hangouts. Somebody told the cops they'd seen Janet, and—here's what my senile brain *just* coughed up—the cops' source told them she'd had an argument with Scummy Bear, then left alone. The cops asked if Scummy had followed her out, but witnesses said he'd stuck around for another couple of hours.

"Later, the club called Scummy a cab. The driver told the cops he'd dropped him off at his place. Now what I *don't* know, Renfield, is whether

Roma was at the club that night. But what if she *was*? My gut tells me she and Scummy look dirty on this, but I've got nothing to back it up, so . . ."

I noticed Wally's eyes had suddenly rolled back up into his head. I'd seen him like this before. He'd go off into a trance—then come up with right-on shit that'd shame a psychic. If ever a guy was born to be a vampire . . . hey, who knows? Maybe I'll accommodate his conversion request someday.

"So," he muttered, "Scummy *didn't* off Janet Carter. Or so it seems, but . . . "

His eyes snapped open. "Boss, I've gotta make a call, okay?"

He punched in a number. I called the waitress over and asked for a coffee refill. When I focused back on Renfield, suddenly realizing who he was calling—and *why*—I marveled again at his hyperacute reportorial instincts. The guy's a natural born killer.

A moment later, he handed me the phone, and I said what needed to be said. He took back the phone, clicked off and asked, "Want me to take it from here, boss, or do you . . ."

I shook my head. "Get on it. Now. I'll take care of the check. Call me the minute you know something new."

He split. I sat there for a minute, chuckling—at myself. I'd just come up with another stupid gag for my vampire comedy act.

". . . So, folks, has this ever happened to you? I'm rummaging around in my coffin the other night, looking for something—and suddenly thought, I can't remember what the *hell* I was looking for . . . I must be getting *old*!" *(Rim shot!)*

Come on, admit that's a funny line for a vampire—I must be getting *old*? Fucking *hilarious*. Even more hilarious was me asking Wally to find something "new"—barely giving him time to breathe after the astounding discovery he'd just handed me on a plate: Scummy *had* murdered Janet! I just knew it! But how? And could I prove it?

As we vampires like to say, time will tell!

Chapter Twenty-Four

"He did *what*?"

Back in my cramped office at *The Revealer*, Elspeth took notes as I got her up to speed about what I had the team working on. Elspeth had to know everything. She was the spider at the center of our web. Once I put the heavy mob on a fast-breaking story, things can get very confusing, very fast. Even though I was the spearhead, passing out the assignments, I was also functioning as a reporter. I couldn't keep *my* shit and everyone else's together without Elspeth.

She emitted her trademark barking laugh. "Wally cracks me up! Just like that, he cut you off and suddenly phoned *our* payroll office?"

I spread my hands and rolled my eyes like the money-changer in *Merchant of Venice*.

"Yeah, just like that. He asked them who'd deposited our seven hundred and fifty dollar check to Jane Carter. I had to jump on the phone to give payroll authorization to release that info to him, but in just a few minutes, Wally had answered the question I'd never thought of asking. Turns out our check had been deposited into the account of Phantom, the nightclub Janet hung out at the night she died. You know what that tells us, right?"

Just to be clear here, Elspeth is *not* my secretary, although I often force her to function like one. She's an editor, a damn good one, and always gets on game quick.

"Well," she said, "either Janet was stupid or so fucked up she didn't know what a dangerous game she was playing. She probably needed to cash the check for money to pay her bar bill—even though she knew tongues would wag when club staffers saw it was a *Revealer* check. Right away, they'd figure she'd sold *The Revealer* some gossip on celebrities. Word like that travels fast. And that'd put her in big trouble with Roma and Scummy."

I nodded. "Right. Anyway, after Janet turned up dead, even though it looked like an overdose with no foul play, the cops did a quick investigation. They found nothing, except a waitress saying she saw Scummy Bear and the girl having an argument. The cops checked that out, but Scummy definitely had not left with Janet. He'd stayed at Phantom for hours. Anyway, the coroner's report that she'd died of an overdose ended police inquiries. My hunch? It's a good bet somebody told Scummy that Janet had cashed a *National Revealer* check. The cops say another witness saw him giving her a hard time about something. And we've since learned from our other sources that Roma was there that night.

"Okay . . . I've got Wally out hitting all this, and I'm hitting the phones. I've left a message for Dane Riggins, the owner of Phantom. Put him through fast when he calls back."

Elspeth nodded, rose to leave, then turned and asked, "So did you take my tip?"

"Oh, yeah. First time I've ever had waffles with fruit crap. Damn good."

Elspeth got a big, melty smile on her face. Like she really *was* my mom. Goddam, Renfield, right again!

Ten minutes later, I had the owner of Phantom on line one.

"Dane, thanks for getting back to me."

"Sure. And thank you, Clark, for mentioning Phantom in your column twice since we opened. What can I do for you?"

I laughed. "Ah, counting mentions, huh? Look, Dane, I need your memory of something that happened there a couple months ago. You remember the cops coming around asking about that girl who OD'd after leaving your club? Janet Carter, her name was."

"Oh, yeah, Clark. Not that I talked to the cops, but my employees told me they'd been around asking questions. So . . . reporters are kinda like cops, right? What do you want to know?"

"Dane, do you remember one of your bartenders or waitresses asking you if it was okay to let Janet Carter sign over a check she'd gotten from the *National Revealer*—to pay her bar bill, I guess? The check was for seven hundred and fifty dollars. I assume they'd need to clear accepting a third party check with you or with a manager authorized to do things like that."

Slight pause. "Yeah . . . yeah, Clark, I do remember. I okayed the check, figuring the *National Revealer* was good for the dough, with all the millions you guys make. Why? It cleared okay, as I remember."

"Who brought you that check, Dane?"

"Oh, sorry, it was my chief bartender that night. Sharp kid named Jimmy Whelan. So sharp he wrangled himself a new job as an assistant manager over at Beacher's Madhouse a few days after that. Always happens in this business. Get somebody good, you lose them. Fucking guy didn't even ask me for a raise, just up and quit."

"Dane, did he tell you about anything unusual that went on with Janet Carter and anyone else in the club? Like her having an argument with someone?"

"No. I was back in my office most of that night. Jimmy just brought the check, I signed it, and he went back to work. Never heard another thing about it, or the girl. What are you aiming at here, Clark?"

I laughed. "Hey, we're just like cops, right? We ask questions, but we don't give answers. Basically, I'm wondering if anybody at your club that night wanted to harm Janet Carter. Got any information like that?"

"No."

Slight pause, then, "But if you want, I'll ask around."

"Thanks, Dane. I'd appreciate that. And when I talk to Jimmy Whelan, I'll be sure to tell him he should go back to work for you. By the way, don't bother warning him I'm going to call. I've just been told he's already on the other line waiting to talk to me."

Dane laughed. "You're a pistol, Clark. But a good gossip columnist is always a step ahead of the news, right?"

"Well, like I told the students in a lecture I did at the Columbia School of Journalism: Gossip is just another word for news. Hey, thanks, Dane. You'll be counting another mention before you know it."

"Great. Drop in, let me buy you a drink, Clark."

Clicking off, I hit the intercom. "Elspeth . . . Jimmy Whelan?"

"Just called in. Got him on the line."

Ha! Thought I was lying, didn't you?

Chapter Twenty-Five

"Jimmy?"

"Hello, Mr. Kelly. Wow, big fan, sir. Read your column all the time. You wouldn't remember, but I was your busboy once at Spago—Wolfgang Puck's place?—and you gave me your autograph."

Goddam. I actually did remember.

"It's Clark, Jimmy. Yeah, I remember. The Spago host reamed you out for talking to me?"

"Yes, sir . . . uh, Clark. It was really embarrassing. I think he would've fired me if you hadn't said something to Wolfgang."

"Power of the press, Jimmy. So the way it stands now, you owe me one, right?"

"Right."

"Just kidding, Jimmy. Lighten up. How you been?"

"Fine, Mister . . . uh, Clark."

"Cool! So here's how you can help me, Jimmy. Do you remember taking a check drawn on the *National Revealer* from a girl named Janet Carter a couple months ago? The check was for seven hundred and fifty dollars. I think you took it to your boss, Dane Riggins, and he approved it. You remember that?"

"Sure do. That was the girl who died, right?"

"Right on, my friend. Now, you probably heard—even though you left the club right after for new employment—that the cops showed up at Phantom and asked the staff questions. But let me be sure of one thing, Jimmy—the cops never tracked *you* down, correct?"

"No. They never talked to me."

I pressed a button on my digital phone recorder. "Jimmy, the law requires that I tell you that as of this moment I'm tape-recording this conversation. You okay with that? Nothing sinister, my friend, it's just a hell of a lot easier than taking notes. You cool?"

Jimmy chuckled. He was digging this.

He said, "Yeah, I'm cool. I know I'm in good hands, Clark. You're a straight-up guy. I've watched you on TV and listened to you on radio for years. I'm just hoping I can help you."

So far, so good. "You're a total pro, Jimmy. I know because I've talked to people about you—including your old boss, Dane Riggins. He'd really like to get you back. Anyway . . . can you tell me what happened from the moment Janet Carter sat down at the bar that night?"

The kid was good. I stopped him once or twice to amplify details, but he really covered it—starting from the moment Janet ordered a dirty martini. Four drinks later, she was pretty fucked up. He asked if she wanted him to call her a cab. She told him she wanted to drink, but needed a favor. She had almost no cash, and her credit card was maxed. She pulled out a check, asking if she could endorse it over to pay for the drinks, get the rest in cash. It was for seven fifty, drawn on *The Revealer*.

"She was a good customer, Clark. She came in about twice a week since we'd opened, always tipped great. And she was one of Roma Kane's posse, so I wanted to treat her right. Plus, she was a cute chick. I liked her. Sexy, not stuck up. So I took the check back to the boss, told him I thought it was cool, and he agreed. I walked back out, put the check in the register, deducted what she owed—gave her the rest in cash. End of story . . . but later, she joined some guy at a table and kept on drinking.

"Then Scummy Bear walked in, sat at the bar. Things were quiet, we started talking about the Lakers, and sports shit. What happened then was, my assistant bartender went into the cash register and saw the check. He started joking around, saying I must've sold some scandal story to the tabloids. Scummy looked at me kind of funny, and I said Janet had asked me to cash it. That was it. But later, I heard voices raised out at the tables. I looked over and saw Scummy was giving Janet shit. And he gets really scary when he's pissed.

"I started paying attention, gave a heads-up to the bouncer. But after a couple of minutes, Scummy seemed to calm down. He walked away and sat down with Roma Kane, who'd just arrived with a couple of girlfriends. They started talking . . . sort of intense. I had a hunch Scummy might be telling Roma about Janet having that check from your newspaper. I mean, I'm not stupid. These celebs are always suspicious, even of friends and their own inner circle. They know someone's always blabbing to the press about what they're doing. Or tipping the paparazzi off when they're about to leave, or that they're drunk, or whatever. I've watched Roma a lot. She's like a stage performer, always on. Always laughing, smiling. But when she's pissed, she gets a really cold look, stops talking. Shuts down.

"Like I said, Clark, it wasn't very busy right then, so I was taking this all in—and I suddenly see Roma reach below the table into her purse, like she's trying to hide the action. And she fishes out a little white envelope she passes to Scummy. A minute later, Scummy gets up and—"

I stopped him. "Jimmy, you should be a reporter yourself, you're doing this so well, but let me ask you right here if you had any impression about what was going down. What did you think was happening?"

A pause.

"Jimmy, don't overthink it," I told him. "Just tell me the first thing that came into your head."

"Well, I don't know, but . . . I've seen *that* kind of action before. Anyone who works in clubs would look at that and say dope was being passed. A baggie in an envelope? Come on! I mean, I can't be sure, but . . ."

"Jimmy, of course you can't. I'm just asking a guy who knows his stuff what he thought might be happening. Trust me, Jimmy. You're not going to suddenly be quoted saying Roma passed Scummy Bear dope. I'm cooler than that!"

"I trust you completely, Clark. I really do."

"Okay, Jimmy, what happened next?"

"Well, Scummy got up and walked over to Janet. She was sitting alone at that point. The guy she'd been sitting with was standing a few feet away talking to some friends at another table. She looked all scared, but Scummy held up his hands, like, 'hey, it's okay.' He called the waitress, ordered Janet a drink on him, started talking to her. He was all smiles, so I was just about to look away and start cleaning up the bar—and then I noticed him lean forward, whisper something to her, and at the same time push that little envelope he'd gotten from Roma over to her. She smiled, palmed it and dropped it in her purse.

"I mean, it was nothing to me, Clark. Drugs are passed around like it's nothing, so once I saw that their beef—whatever it was—was over, I went back to work. Maybe ten minutes later, I noticed Janet had split. Scummy was back sitting with Roma—who was all smiles again."

This kid was good. Thorough. I had just one question. "How long was it before Scummy left the club? Do you remember?"

"Oh yeah. It was hours later, around three. I remember because I was watching the clock. We were past closing already, and there were still hangers-on, but he left alone. Roma and her girlfriends were still there, making potty runs. They left about fifteen minutes later."

"Just one thing, Jimmy. When did you hear Janet Carter had kicked? Was it the next day?"

"No. I guess they didn't find her body until the next afternoon, so the *LA Times* didn't have a story until the day after that. So we were talking about it at the club two nights later. Nobody was too surprised. Janet was a big user. Always fucked up."

"So you weren't around when the cops dropped by Phantom a few days later, right, Jimmy? You'd been hired away by Beacher's Madhouse. And the cops never came by to see you, because they'd heard what went down from others working at the club. Correct?"

"Yeah."

I paused, then told him, "Jimmy, I just turned off my recorder. Now let me ask you . . . anything else you want to tell me?"

He took a breath, thinking it over.

Finally, he said, "No, not really. If you're asking me if the thought crossed my mind that maybe she overdosed on the shit Scummy passed her —if it really *was* shit—yeah, I thought about it. But, so what? Janet took dope all the time. I think it was just a bad accident. Poor kid."

Good. Not great, but definitely good. Because I don't believe in fucking accidents. Not when it comes to evil pricks like Scummy.

"Jimmy, good luck in your new job. Stay on the line when I hang up. Elspeth will give you my personal cell phone number and personal e-mail so you can always contact me directly. Hoping to hear some tips from you, my man. You're in a good place to see and hear things. And remember, I pay fat bucks. You'd be surprised how many bartenders are on my payroll."

Jimmy laughed. "No, I wouldn't, Clark. You lay down the best gossip in town, man. So drop by the club and let me buy you a drink."

I chuckled. "No, Jimmy, I think we're going to be talking a lot in the future—so let's be discreet, play strangers in public. Stay on the line now."

I clicked off. Goddam, I loved working the phone. It's intimate, and actually can be better than a face-to-face if you know what you're doing. Which, after a few lifetimes, I actually do.

I punched the intercom.

"Get me Wally, Elspeth. And send Jimmy a check, the usual tip fee."

Chapter Twenty-Six

Always throw reporters at stories. It works, trust me.

Too many cooks spoil the broth? Uh-uh! Not when you're deep-digging for news no one wants to give up; or, "conducting investigative journalism," as the poufy-haired network television jagoffs ponderously put it. Today, I'd assigned three reporters to back Wally and/or me. And if we didn't get a break in the next twenty-four hours, I'd assign three more.

Or six.

Or fucking *ten*!

Elspeth yelled, "Clark, I'm leaving!"

"Clark left an hour ago, ma'am."

"Ha, ha! Bye."

"Bye."

I got up from my desk, stretched, walked to the window. Watched the sun bounce on the horizon. Time for a recharge, I thought. Get out of the office, channel Julie Andrews, enjoy a few of my favorite things.

Dusk dropped a veil over the City of Angels as I hopped a cab, headed for legendary Dan Tana's in West Hollywood, ready to savor one of the planet's finest steaks and enjoy the company of *my* favorite vampire—while grilling him relentlessly about his drag-racing/drinking buddy Taylor Logan, of course.

Not to mention his more *intimate* friend, Roma Kane.

Say *whaat*? TayLo *drag racing*?

Now that I have your attention, gossip fans, let me explain a couple of things: First, my "favorite vampire" isn't a vampire at all—he just plays one on television. He's Damon Strutt, the moodily handsome twenty-three-year-old Brit who's addicted to stunt airplanes and screaming race engines attached to four wheels or two. Strutt, as you know, reigns as TV vampire idol Kragen on the smash series, *Bold Blood*.

Damon and I are brand-new buddies, but he and TayLo are very close friends—"without benefits," as they're always quick to inform romance-sniffing journalists. United in their prurient love of hell-raising, TayLo and Damon often team up between romances to dance, drink, slam around in super-fast cars; occasionally getting arrested, and constantly generating lurid headlines.

TayLo and Damon triggered a truly fabulous tabloid rat-fuck one evening weeks back when Mexican gang-bangers in a '59 Caddy low-rider illegally crossed the double-yellow line on trendy Robertson Boulevard, attempting to rocket past Vampire Boy in his '69 Shelby Cobra sports car. TayLo was riding shotgun.

But as the *cholos* charged past in their guacamole-colored whip, wildly jeering insult shit like *"maricon"* and *"pendejo,"* Strutt suddenly floored it. His supercharged Ford hemi coughed and howled, and the gang-bangers were instant *fokking* toast, choking on fumes blown back from the Cobra's smokin' pipes as Damon's partner-in-crime yelled,*"YAAaaaaaayyyyyy!"*

Ass snugly nestled in the passenger seat, a stoked TayLo kept howling triumphantly, pumping her fist as the oft-photographed Kragen car —"Vampire Fire" written in flames on its hood—rocketed past The Ivy, Robertson's famed see-and-be-seen heavy-hitter patio restaurant. Showbiz types dining *al fresco* shrieked and waved in excitement as they recognized the two stars! But at that instant, a drunk ran a red light at the next cross-street, clipping the Cobra's rear bumper and sending it spinning into the display window of a high-end fashion boutique—which had, fortunately, closed for the evening.

Now, at any given moment on Robertson, where stars and wannabes flock endlessly to shop Hollywood's primo girlie-boutique block, paparazzi lurk like crocodiles, hoping to snap the celebrity shot of a lifetime. Suddenly, there it was: tabloid gold dropping right into their greedy laps. Two major stars—dazed, banged-up but, amazingly, alive—crawling out of the crashed Kragen-mobile as flashbulbs *pop-pop-popped . . .* naughtily revealing that TayLo, her plaid schoolgirl miniskirt askew, had made the fashion choice to go commando that evening.

WOW! The whole street was screaming!

And guess who happened to stroll past, purely by chance, at that *precise* moment?

"You, ya bloody bastard!" roared Damon Strutt, convulsing with laughter as we sat reminiscing about that crazy night over cocktails at Dan Tana's. "I just couldn't fucking *believe* it, mate. Here TayLo and me go crashing into the display window of this fucking chichi girlie shop, glass smashing, mannequin limbs flyin' every direction, and suddenly up *you* stroll, cool as fuck, asking if we'd like to join you for dinner across the street at bloody fucking Ivy."

I shook my head.

"Not quite true, my benighted Brit chum. First, I asked if you were okay. Then I mentioned that Cedars-Sinai Hospital was conveniently right around the corner. And you bellowed, 'Wot the fuck are *you* doing 'ere, mate?' And I explained that I live just two blocks down the street. I politely thanked you for conveniently staging a major 'drunk-stars-in-car-crash' story right in my neighborhood, asshole, and then—"

Strutt interrupted, as he often does.

"Yeah, you tabloid fuckers were all over that one—even me mum in Liverpool mailed me a copy of the shitbag *Daily Mail*'s photo spread of the mayhem. The old dear wanted me and TayLo to autograph it."

He chortled, knocking back his second Pimm's Cup—that curious gin-based booze the Brits swear is not cough medicine but an *aperitif*—as we awaited the arrival of our bloody-red-on-the-inside, charred-on-the-outside steaks.

"That's why I always tell these whining-poofter Hollywood types that nothing will ever kill the tabloids—because it's yer own mums wot's keepin' 'em in business, right? Fuckin' scary, it is."

I raised my Jack Daniels Old Fashioned in mock salute and intoned, "We who will *never* die salute ye, Mum!"

Ah, suddenly tonight felt good. Ensconced with a congenial buddy in a red leather booth with straw-wrapped wine bottles dangling from the ceiling over our heads, experiencing the red-meat-and-whiskey ambience of Hollywood's ancient-but-trendy Dan Tana's, which serves real Italian food —spaghetti and meat balls, lasagna, steaks, chops—and other no-frills man food.

More cozy private club than restaurant, Dan Tana's has been a treasured spot to hang cheek-to-jowl with Hollywood bigfoots—if you could afford the prices—for nearly fifty years. Adorable Drew Barrymore loves telling people, "I had my diapers changed here," while publicity-shy types like Bob Dylan loved the joint because they could easily disappear in the shadows of its dimly lit interior.

Brad Pitt, Cameron Diaz, George Clooney—the list of regulars goes on and on. It's a piece of Old Hollywood that New Hollywood still frequents.

"One of the most faithful customers over the years was Phil Spector," I told Damon. "On the night his troubles started, Phil had dinner here, left a five hundred dollar tip on a fifty-five dollar check—then went to over to the House of Blues, picked up that poor little B-actress, took her back to his so-called 'castle' in Alhambra and blew her fucking brains out."

"Another Hollywood asshole," grunted Strutt.

He waved his glass for a refill. I laughed.

"Man, you're raining hellfire on Hollywood types tonight. Which reminds me—did you read that spectacular ass-roasting you TV vampires got in the *LA Times* from the screenwriter who's working on the script for that new Dracula movie? What's his name . . . uh, McGreevy? It was *scathing*, old buddy, and I memorized it so I could quote him then watch you weep like a bitch. You ready, bitch?"

He waved a middle finger, so I socked it to him.

Mike Walker

"Okay! McGreevy says that today's TV Draculas, present company included, have . . . uh, 'taken the romantic vampire and cut off his balls, leaving a pallid, emo-pansy with the gaseous pretentiousness of a perfume commercial!' "

Damon rolled his eyes, started to open his mouth. I beat him to it.

"Wait! Dude then *doubles down* on the dis! He calls you guys '*castrati* vampires!' As in, no *balls*! Eat that, *emo pansy*!"

Strutt shrugged, and snatched up the drink the waiter had just put down.

"I'd kick your arse, Clark, but since you're paying for dinner . . . ah, *finally*, here's our waiter friend with our frickin' steaks. Burnt black on the outside, as ordered, hopefully bloody bright red when cut."

He took a pull on his drink. I discreetly drew my ever-present hideout Emerson knife—sharpened discreetly in the kitchen when I'd popped by to high-five my chef pals—and snicked through my meat in a clean slice. A lovely crimson spurted. Strutt nodded approvingly.

"A sight to gladden any bloody vampire's heart, *emo fucking pansy* or not. Right, let's dig in, then."

We got down to the serious business of eating a fine meal, making no conversation beyond the occasional approving grunt—especially for the pinot noir we'd chosen. Happy lads, we were. As teeth crushed meat and blood exploded in my mouth, I thought back to the first time I'd met young Damon Strutt. It was on the set of *Bold Blood*, the eighth episode they'd shot after the show debuted through the ratings' roof.

I was there because the head writer, Ronnie Fallone, was an old pal—and a secret source. I'd known Ronnie for years, and he knew from our endless boozy nights out that I was knowledgeable about vampire lore. So he'd begged me to drop by—not just for a mention in my column, but for any "atmospheric hints" I could impart. It was Ronnie who'd introduced me to Damon, a young British actor recognized as brilliant but a true *enfant terrible*—blacklisted by the BBC for his headline-making hijinks. Strutt's despairing agents had shipped him off to America, where he'd promptly blown away the *Bold Blood* casting director. After the pilot was shot, Hollywood buzz correctly predicted the show would be a major hit, "mainly because of Strutt's charisma in the lead role as scary-but-sensitive Kragen," raved *The Hollywood Reporter*.

Strutt endeared himself to me immediately that day when Ronnie introduced us.

"Oi," he barked. "You're that ink-stained wretch wot wrote about how I shagged Roma Kane while dressed up as scary old Kragen. Great story, mate. Love to know how you found out, but I'm guessing you won't be telling me anytime soon, right?"

Astounding. Unprecedented.

Stars either whine and deny scandalous stories or refuse to acknowledge them. But here was a guy who not only confirmed he'd fang-banged Roma in full Kragen drag, he actually *congratulated* me for breaking the story.

Later, we took a coffee break together at the crafts table, and Strutt totally got my attention when he mentioned he owned a Ducati motorcycle: the legendary Italian screamer dubbed, "Diavel."

How fast is a Diavel? Quick test: Imagine you're sitting at a red light. Get set to drop the hammer the *instant* you start reciting the following famous verse at its normal rhythm. And . . . GO!

"'Twas the night before Christmas, and all through the house . . . "
POW!

You just hit sixty miles an hour, freak . . . in 2.6 *seconds*!

Wonder why I'm so excited? Because next to the vampire gift of flight, nothing amps me up more than slamming my ass down on a cycle saddle, igniting thunder and lightning between my thighs and burning off a strip of smoking black rubber.

Biker bros bond fast! When I tipped Strutt that I own a legendary Vincent Black Lightning—so valuable it usually stays in the garage—and blast around SoCal on my Buell Superbike, or my workhorse BMW R1100RS, we immediately made plans for a run to 'Dago that very weekend.

Ah, Jimmy . . . Jimmy Dean . . . if only you could join us, bro. If only I'd known you were gonna wipe out in that Porsche, I would've converted you to vampire-hood, and we'd still be in the wind together, old friend.

I'd hung out on the *Bold Blood* set that whole day. Gave Ronnie a couple of script ideas he'd liked. In fact, they just shot the one about vampires that aren't mere hundreds of years old, but were alive a thousand, even two thousand years ago—in the time of the Pharoahs. And on that same day, even though no one had realized it, I'd helped Damon nail a key scene for the episode they were taping—where Kragen feasts for the first time on the human girl who's made him feel true love. They'd tried shooting the scene several ways, but it just wasn't working. Damon looked at the director, who seemed unsure of what he wanted.

"Fuck! NO!"

Damon, still standing on his mark with fists tightly balled, had looked like he was coming unglued.

"Damon, what's wrong? It worked . . . you looked scary as hell!"

The director glanced around at cast and crew. Everyone quickly nodded agreement.

"But that's not . . . not what I . . . *oh, fuck!*"

Instantly, I slipped into Damon's mind. I flashed him an image of how a feeding vampire looks at the moment of incision, and whispered of what emotions he'd be feeling . . .

. . . Damon, you're not supposed to look like the Hollywood cliché scary vampire. A vampire about to feed on a loved one is in the throes of ecstasy . . . he's a kid about to bite into a quarter-pounder . . . But even subtler emotions are in play . . . the fear of getting caught drinking forbidden human essence . . . the defiant thrill of knowing nothing can stop you . . . and finally, the sheer joy of your gnawing hunger richly

satisfied . . . now, let me show you what that looks like. Locked in his trance, Damon turned, looked at me, then faced the director and said:

"One last take."

The director shrugged, clapped his hands and barked, "Camera? Okay . . . we're rolling . . . anytime, Damon . . ."

And he nailed it!

There was silence for a moment, then wild applause. Cast and crew clustered to congratulate Damon. His eyes caught mine.

I did the most human thing I could think of. I gave him a thumbs-up.

Chapter Twenty-Seven

"Come on, then, Clark. Cut to the chase, mate, as we say in Hollywood."

As the waiter cleared our plates, Damon stared at me over the top of his glass, which now contained single malt Scotch whisky. Lagavulin, to be precise.

Jerking a chin at it, I said, "Prince Charles's dram, right?"

"You bloody well know it is, after me tellin' ya exactly that not a month ago. So come on! Get on with it, then!"

"Get on with what, cycle buddy?"

"Clark, don't shit me. You're in hunting mode. You brought me here to find out something. I've seen you go all mega-reporter before, mate, so get on with it."

"Look, Damon, here's the thing. When TayLo talked you into participating in Roma's get-fucked-by-Kragen fantasy, what did you think? Other than the fact you'd be getting a free piece of ass, I mean."

He laughed abruptly.

"For a big-shot reporter, you're not much at framing a proper question, are you? Spit it fucking out, man."

"I mean, was it *really* for Roma, or was TayLo getting off on it, too, somehow?"

"TayLo? No, not that one. Look, if she wanted a bit of fantasy mischief, she'd just come right out and say it. Makes no sense. And TayLo will do girls now and again, but she's not got the hots for Roma, that's for bloody sure. Nor, sadly, for me. I'd do TayLo in a heartbeat, if she'd have me. But she won't. We're mates, she says. Doing the old push-push would ruin it, she says. And she's right. Honestly, mate, TayLo can be tough as old boot leather, but she's a real softie for her friends. It was a favor for Roma, that's all it was. I mean, she never even asked to *watch*. She just knew vampire-shagging is Roma's big fantasy, knew she could get me to do the dirty deed, so she arranged it, the sweetie. Even told Roma it was her early birthday present, did you know that? Quite sweet, actually. So it was all, to put it simply, what you see is what you get. But why, pray tell, are you asking?"

I shrugged. "I think it's asked and answered. You're saying they're just real close and sweet to each other. End of story, I guess."

"Like bloody *fuck*!" He belted the last of his Lagavulin, waved desperately for a waiter, looked at me like I was daft . . . then actually told me so to my face.

"Are ya fuckin' DAFT, man? Christ, do reporters just *ask* questions or do they ever bloody *listen*? I told you, TayLo's a good friend to Roma. I *never* said that fucking cunt Roma is a good friend to TayLo. Why? Well, pardon me for playing reporter, mate, but allow me to just ask meself me own question: '*I say, Damon, why do you think that's true?*'

"Answer: 'I just BLOODY FUCKING *DO*, THAT'S ALL!' "

Instantly, Marco—one of Dan Tana's tough old bird waiters—materialized at my side, leaned over and murmured, "Everything okay, Mr. Kelly?"

"Yes, Marco, I think we *are* ready for another round. Damon?"

"Thought you'd never ask," he growled.

In an instant, fresh drinks arrived. We started blowing off steam quite happily then until I blurted, rather stupidly, "So . . . ready to ride again?"

His eyes flashed, went opaque. Instantly, I put myself inside his head. Not that I needed to, I knew the image he was seeing—and suddenly, I saw it, too . . .

. . . *the pair of us on motorcycles on our last trip, charging hard up the twisty Kanan Dume canyon road above Malibu, cranked way, way over for a sweeping left-hander, solid rock wall on one side, the cliff's edge and a sharp drop-off into deep space on the other . . . his Ducati Diavel in the lead, me bringing up the rear on my BMW, wind smashing us as we topped the rise and saw a tricked-out Mustang muscle car racing down the hill toward us much too fast . . . swinging wide, drifting over the white line and taking far, far too much of our road, barreling straight at us! SHIT! We're cranked over too far to safely hit the brakes hard . . . got to try to ride it out, hope we won't slide . . . but Damon jabs the brakes, the Diavel instantly highsides, flips. He flies over the handlebars, hurtling off the cliff into outer space . . .*

Across the table, I watched his face contort as his mind exploded in churning images of impending death. In my mind's eye, I picked up the action . . . In that terrifying split second, I'd aimed my bike at a clump of trees, let it crash as I launched into the air, flying after Damon. Rocketing down a second later, approaching from behind so he wouldn't see me, I grabbed him a heartbeat before he hit the lower slope. Instantly, I got into his mind, forcing him into unconsciousness while I saved his life.

His next memory was coming to and hearing me call his name.

"I'm over here," he'd yelled.

Slipping and sliding, I headed back down to where I'd dumped him just moments ago in a clump of brush. He was scratched up, but intact.

"You okay?" I'd asked him.

"Yeah . . . but I can't bloody believe it, because—"

"Well, believe it, old buddy. I was afraid you'd splattered on the rocks . . ."

Damn. I never did know when to shut up. He'd immediately gotten a haunted, suspicious look on his face.

He'd said, "Yeah, I was headed straight at some rocks, so how—"

"Damon, shut the fuck up, man," I'd told him. "You made it, that's what counts. Now let's go scramble up that slope. Your bike's about a hundred feet down, wrecked to shit. I got lucky and bailed a second before I hit some trees, then rolled over the side, and the brush broke my fall. Let's go, I'll help you back up to the road and we'll call a tow truck . . ."

Now he was eyeing me across the table. Wearing the same suspicious look he'd had that day. I took a belt of Kelt and smoothly (I hoped) picked up where we'd left it before taking our eyeblink trip down memory lane.

"Hey, Damon, sorry. Didn't mean to hit you with that 'you ready to ride' shit. I just—"

He waved a hand sharply. "Mate, I'm not afraid to ride again—nor am I afraid of you *thinking* I'm afraid. Walking away from a wreck like that is a bonus from heaven, as TayLo put it. But I still wonder how the hell I *did* walk away. I was falling straight at rocks, I swear, but the next thing I know, you . . ."

"*Woah.* TayLo? You've seen her? When?"

"I visited her the day after she went into Miracles. You know she's back there after her Vegas fuckup. I told her all about it. And she told me you two had quite a night on the town. Said you'd saved her life from some paparazzi."

"Saved her . . . life?"

Shit. What had she told him?

"Well, so to speak. She said there was a mob at Fury on opening night, and you cracked a head or two whisking her out of there. And I told her about my cycle crash, and how you'd come down the slope to save me. Told her I knew I was going to hit rocks, that I was a fucking dead man. But when I woke up, there you were. And I think you saved me somehow."

He smiled. "I told her I think you're a fucking vampire."

"And what did she say to that, you mad fucker?"

"That it wouldn't surprise her one bit."

"Really? Ah, she's a funny girl."

We both paused, sipped. Then he said, "She told me you two went out for drinks after your bit of bother at Fury. Got to know each other a bit."

Now I spotted it. The jealousy pulsing behind his eye. Good. Anything to divert his budding suspicion that his buddy was a vampire.

"Yeah, we hung out—I'd never really talked much to TayLo, outside of a word or two at press junkets," I lied.

He smiled thinly. "So I asked her if she'd fucked you."

Sip of Kelt.

"Did you, now? You always were a class act, Damon. And what did she say?"

"Her exact words were, 'No, Daddy . . . I was a *good* girl!'"

We both cracked up.

He said, "Don't you just love her?"

Sip of Kelt.

"Thought you'd never ask, Strutt."

"What's the answer, then, Kelly?"

Chapter Twenty-Eight

Don't ask me why it happened right at that moment. But it washed over me like napalm, a searing realization.

I was . . . insanely . . . in love.

Just like that. Caught me totally by surprise, stupid as that sounds. I'd known it on some level, I suppose, but I'd avoided dwelling on why I was suddenly fixated on this doomed young star. I'd allowed myself to be deflected by the shocking reemergence of Ludmilla, not to mention my mad-dog *modus operandi* of putting the pursuit of news ahead of literally everything else. Now—to extend my "napalm" metaphor *ad nauseum*—I suddenly discover that I'm *burning* for her. I'd spent centuries yearning for this feeling . . . and *WHAMMO!* Here it was: the dizzying, indescribable emotion that defines first love.

TayLo.

I love you.

I will love you forever.

For one startling moment, suddenly aware that Damon was eyeing me strangely, I thought I'd blurted it aloud. Was he sensing the intensity of what I was feeling? Perhaps. And I'd be telling him all about it someday, no doubt. But not now. My psyche had just crashed and undergone a massive, fundamental reset. Existence in the netherworld I inhabit would never be the same again. I was in love. And when a vampire pledges love, it's forever. TayLo was now a part of me. And I would protect her, at any cost, from any force in the universe.

Carefully casual, I smiled and asked, "Why the sudden interest in my feelings for TayLo, Damon?"

Not caring for casual chat, he lobbed a high, hard one.

"Because I love her, too, Clark. And she loves me."

I fixed him with a level stare. He chuckled.

"Not to worry, mate . . . she'll never be *in* love with me. Not the way she is with you."

Jolted, I cast my eyes down, contemplated the rich ruddiness of my cognac. But did not sip.

"She tell you that?"

"No, mate. But she didn't have to, did she? I know the girl well, you see. No words were exchanged. I just gave her a hug and said, 'Well, we've all got to have a drink together soon.' And she said, 'Dude, I'm in fucking rehab!' And we laughed. Ah, she's a special girl, Clark. And we've got to keep her safe. So let's consider this Roma thing. The bitch is a cunt, no question—even though, I must admit, she's hot in the sack. Don't quote me, but I almost dressed back up to have another go with her, you know? And you'd never believe how many times she begged *me* for another go! I would've done her, but I just felt too bloody stupid playing dress-up for the twisted bitch, who far prefers the kinky Kragen to dullard Damon."

I laughed. "Well, fuck *her* then, you sensitive girlie-man!"

He flicked his middle digit, but his tone was serious.

"That aside, Clark, you really think Roma's out to *harm* our girl? Why, pray tell?"

Now I sipped. And sipped again, polishing off the snifter.

"I have unleashed the hounds of hell to get that question answered, my friend. Once I have it, actions will be taken. And it won't be pretty, I promise you. Look, I can't tell you exactly what I'm working on. It might be a story, might not. So without getting specific about disturbing things I've heard, let's just say I'm looking for any indication that someone might be trying to sabotage TayLo's career—beyond the usual bullshit everyone in Hollywood pulls to sabotage everyone else's career. And I'm not talking about passive sabotage, like what she gets from her mother and father. I'm talking truly evil stuff."

"Like?"

"Like feeding her drugs."

Damon laughed, looked at me like I'd grown another head.

"Drugs? Be fair! The girl's hardly a stranger in that area. And what do you mean, '*feeding* her drugs'? She's been known to score drugs without anybody's help. And why would that *kill* her, barring a massive overdose?"

Ah. Now we'd arrived at one of those tricky moments that inevitably arise in the gathering of information; when you weigh the pros and cons of giving a little to get a little. Reporters want to know what *you* know, but hate divulging what *they* know. And it's more than playing dog in the manger. Once people know what you're after, they'll often start spouting what they *think* you want to hear—either purposely or subconsciously. But I trusted Damon Strutt. He'd become, in just months, my closest male buddy in the world. The human world, anyway; Jimmy Dean's still my best buddy ever, end of story.

"No, I'm thinking more about dirty drugs, the kind that *can* kill you, no overdose necessary," I told him.

Damon shook his head. "Mate, now that I think of it, you've got a real short memory. Or maybe you just fucking ignore me. Don't you remember that time down in Baja, us talking about TayLo's sudden string of arrests on traffic beefs? In just . . . what, a year? And I said it's almost like someone's engineering all this shit? We know she can get into trouble all by herself. But it's starting to feel like a pattern, is what I said. Remember?"

I did. It was foremost in my mind when I'd set up our boys' night out. But I said:

"Oh, right, now I remember. Sorry. Guess I do ignore you, pal. So, any thoughts?"

His attention was suddenly wandering. When you hang with a screen-ready stud like Damon Strutt, star of a hot television show, you start noticing how females keep looking your way. And you start suspecting that all those longing glances aren't aimed at you.

Damon's eyes were bouncing between a hot blonde sitting solo at the bar, and a nearby table where three attractive ladies were ignoring the glares of their visibly annoyed dates.

"Damon!"

Making an effort, he wiped the bad-boy grin and turned back to me.

"Sorry, mate, me attention wandered. But now that I think about it, I know TayLo's circle pretty damn well, and from what I've seen, she scores her stuff mostly from Roma. Thing is, though, TayLo's cut way, way back on the sniffy. Likes her booze, that girl. And she's pretty good at holding it, for a lass. So it's hard to believe the bit of drugs she's taking nowadays would fuck her up so bad she's blowing off work, plus getting into traffic accidents and club brawls—like when she kicked those security guards outside Beacher's Madhouse. And remember her slapping that huge black trannie at The Abbey? Now that was truly weird!"

"So?"

"You know, I'm starting to remember bits of shit—like how Roma started pushing Cara Prescott on me to costar in that big vampire movie at Universal that ended up not happening. I said to her, 'Why would I want vapid little Cara, when I can get our fireball friend TayLo?' I mean, Cara's a sweetie, but Roma knows TayLo's the best young actress in America. *And* my good mate. So why would she push Cara, especially when TayLo's supposed to be one of Roma's best girlfriends? Strange, I thought. And even after TayLo kindly arranged that fuck-date with me alter ego, Kragen, Roma kept digging at her behind her back, saying shit like, 'Oh, she just did it to prove I can't get a date by myself.' I ignored it like I do most mean-girl shit, but it was fucking odd, now that one thinks on it."

He started to speak, then stopped.

"What?"

"Christ, I just flashed on something that happened. One night a few weeks back when a bunch of us were partying up at Roma's pad. Well . . . I remember TayLo giving Roma the high sign she wanted a hit of naughty old sniffy. So Roma high-signs fucking Scummy Bear, as she often does when pals hit it her up. He always holds the stuff. And I remember him reaching into his fanny-pack . . . then . . ."

"Then? Spit it out, pal."

"Roma sort of . . . well, she shook her head at him—gave him the bloody old stink-eye, she did—and kind of jerked her chin like she was motioning him to go somewhere else . . . like, back toward where the bedrooms are, and . . ."

"Take your time, pal, just visualize it. Imagine you're viewing a videotape replay of how it went down, and just describe what you're seeing."

"Yeah, okay . . . so Scummy went off toward the bedrooms, then came back a few minutes later. When Roma looked up at him, still quite annoyed, he gave her a big wink, as if to say, 'It's all cool.' Roma smiled, looked happy. Thrilled, more like. Then she suddenly cocks her chin in TayLo's direction. And Scummy walks over and slips TayLo a little white packet. TayLo rolls her eyes like a happy cartoon character, then runs over and gives Roma a kiss."

Goddam.

Paydirt.

Comes just like that, sometimes.

I said, "To sum up here, dude—and stop me if I get anything wrong—it looked to you like Scummy wanted to give our girl the usual whatever, but Roma got quite angry and eyeballed him to go get some 'special' stuff, or whatever, right?"

"That's what it looked like, mate, yes."

"And did it look like, if you had to guess, that Roma was directing Scummy to bring back something even *more* yummy—or *less* yummy?"

The second I said it, Damon got a look like he'd suddenly seen Jesus. Or Satan. Murder burned in his eye.

"That fucking *cunt!*"

I smiled. "Don't let's jump to conclusions or contemplate doing anything rash just yet, milord. Be a pro. First, we look for patterns. And from patterns, pictures emerge."

"And then?"

"And then, my *faux nosferatu*, it's 'Attack of the Killer Vampires' time."

Chapter Twenty-Nine

Two hours later . . . 5:09 a.m.

Propped up on the master bed in my Four Seasons suite, curtains drawn, staring into the dark.

My cell phone rings.

"Wally?"

"I'm outside the apartment where Janet Carter died. Need you here, boss."

He told me why, briefly. I cut the connection, hopped out of bed and yanked the drapes. My first impulse was to leap off the balcony and fly across town, the fastest way. But dawn was breaking. Sightings of vampires in flight tend to unsettle the citizenry, even here in seen-it-all Follywood. So I exited the suite unseen, slipped down the stairwell, eased into the corridor two floors down, and caught an elevator to the lobby.

Three minutes later, I was in a cab and reconnected to Wally, listening to how he'd ended up at the murder site. I marveled again at how his mind worked. Seems that after I'd run down my conversation with Jimmy Whelan, the bartender at Phantom, Wally sat solo in a soundproof "rubber room" at *The Revealer* office, turned on a tape recorder and began narrating every random memory of Scummy Bear he could conjure up—especially all those times he'd witnessed the creep glued to Roma Kane at red carpet events or out on the nightclub scene. And then he recalled the night he'd witnessed the sadistic prick bullying a drunk who looked like a high school kid out partying on a fake ID.

"Just before stepping in to pound on this kid, Scummy suddenly stuck his fingers in his mouth, dug out the gummy bear he was chewing on—and tossed it," Wally recalled. "I remembered there was a security videotape of the fight because paparazzi had come in later and tried to buy it from the club—that joint, The Burn Box, way out on Sunset. So I went there last night, spread some bucks around, and got the head of security to show me the video, just to check my memory. And I'd remembered right! Scummy Bear had chucked his gummy bear right before going postal on that kid. And the way he did it sort of evoked the feeling of a ritual, like it was a habit."

Wally then started making phone calls. He contacted our lovely and effervescent Vanillo to ask if she'd ever seen Scummy spit out his chewy, gooey candy in public.

Paydirt *encore*!

Vanillo immediately recalled *two* incidents—both occurring when he got involved in screaming confrontations that had verged on getting physical. Wally got even more confirmation from a photog who'd seen Scummy expel his candy cud after a too-big-to-fuck-with bouncer ran him out of an after-hours poker game at Night Train over on La Cienega. Scummy loved his gambling.

Fifteen minutes later, I paid off my cab and walked up to the run-down, two-story apartment building where Janet Carter had lived and died. Set well back from the sidewalk, surrounded by old juniper trees and untrimmed bushes, the shabby complex looked like it had been there forever. Wally had five guys with him. Three were my reporters. The other two I didn't recognize. One had a gang of high-tech cameras swinging from his neck. The instant Wally spotted me, he held up a cautioning hand, walked over quickly and said, "Step softly from here on, boss."

Have I mentioned that Wally's a goddam genius?

Approaching the last door Janet Carter had walked through on Earth, we kept to the concrete walkway until we reached the single step leading up to its door. Mounting the step, Wally reached to his right and picked up a wooden yardstick leaning beside the door. He started thrusting it, swiftly but delicately, into clumps of low-lying plants bordering the apartment's outer wall.

"Ah, here we go," he said. Bending back the leaves of a plant slightly taller than the rest, he said, "I know you've got hawk eyes, boss, but look sharp."

I'd already guessed what I was looking for. And there it was. Right where that murdering cocksucker had spit it out. Dusted with a light coating of sand, a well-chewed gummy bear bearing a killer's teeth marks.

"Son of a bitch, he *did* murder her. Knew it. Wally, we'll need a DNA or dental test to prove it—assuming we're right. But how the hell else do you explain a gummy bear under the window of a girl who died an hour or so after running afoul of a guy named Scummy Bear who is famously addicted to . . . gummy bears? You've photographed the gooey thing, I assume?"

Wally nodded. "Thirty-six frames, all pin-sharp. And before you ask, none of us touched it or stepped on the ground around it. We've been super-careful. And we've shot every inch of the property. Every blade of grass, the trees, overlapping close-ups of the whole building wall. Plus I had a video guy here, shooting time-stamped footage of us as we approached the scene. We'll need to convince the cops we didn't stomp all over the place and compromise potential evidence, like . . . this!"

Wally parted more plants with the yardstick, exposing the dirt beneath them. Right away, I saw faint footprints. No way of telling if they were Scummy Bear's, but they were exactly where you'd stand if you were trying to peek into Janet Carter's apartment.

"So, boss, you think we've got enough for the district attorney to reopen the case?"

"Fuck, no—and neither do you."

"Well, if the DNA—"

I shut him down. "Let me spell it out. First . . . they've got an autopsy report that says the girl died of drugs, right? So even if we prove it's Scummy Bear's DNA, I doubt that forensics can pinpoint *when* he spat that gummy bear out? Look, he knew Janet Carter. So he could've visited her at any time *prior* to the murder. And before using the word 'murder,' we need to refute the coroner's report. That means digging up the body. You seriously think the DA will admit they were wrong and exhume her based on *this*? Dream on, pal."

Wally shook his head. "There's got to be a way, boss!"

I smiled. "Oh, there is. Leave that to me. You stay here and finish up, whatever."

I heard a door open. A stocky old guy wearing dingy gray coveralls shuffled toward us, big grin on his face. Looked like the janitor.

"The owner," said Wally. "He's smiling because he just scored a pocketful of *Revealer* moolah. I'm going to ask him more questions."

I whipped out my cell phone, punched in the number of the Yellow Cab that had brought me. The driver had said he'd catch a coffee and wait.

"Ready to roll," I said into the phone.

Then I murmured to Wally as the scruffy owner approached, "I presume he didn't see Scummy Bear hanging around on the night in question?"

Wally shot me a pained look.

I grinned. "Sorry, I imagine you *probably* did think to ask him that, right? Hey, I'll call you later."

I started walking back down the sidewalk. The cab rolled up before I got there. The cabbie asked, "Back to the Four Seasons, sir?"

"No. Take me to Forest Lawn cemetery."

Chapter Thirty

Still Living Her Dream.

That inscription on Janet Carter's gravestone reflected what Darren had told me.

Rather than inter their beloved only child in her Idaho hometown, Janet's bereaved mother and father had come to town and laid her to rest in fabled Forest Lawn, Hollywood's legendary cemetery to the stars, where she could dream eternally of the silver screen beauties she'd fantasized about since childhood, like Turner, Gardner, Taylor; perhaps even commune with their spirits.

A touching, romantic gesture. What child doesn't deserve parents like that? So unlike the bottom-feeders who'd done their best to doom their only child, TayLo. How I looked forward to meeting *them*!

I stood for a long moment peering down, and *through*, the earth that covered Janet Carter. And then . . . I was in the grave with her.

Closerthanthis.

"Closerthanthis," BTW, is a cutesy phrase coined by legendary gossip columnist Walter Winchell to describe romantic snuggling. And indeed, my proximity to Janet Carter was now as close as any real-life lover. But don't get ahead of me here, folks. Vampires can never be necrophiliacs, for obvious reasons. I prefer my gals hot-blooded, alive and kicking.

As I lay next to Janet, examining her up close and personal, I marveled that her body looked amazingly fresh and whole, which is not as unusual as you might think. A famous example was Medgar Evers, the iconic civil rights leader murdered in 1963. Medgar was dug up after thirty years, and when they opened the coffin, the corpse looked as fresh as the day it was buried, according to famed forensic pathologist Dr. William Baden. That's right, live friends; contrary to popular belief, the deceased do not decompose hideously the instant that first shovelful of dirt plops down on the coffin lid. Janet still looked fresh as a daisy . . . relatively speaking.

Just to be *absolutely* clear about my abrupt transition from aboveground: I was now lying beneath the lady's coffin lid. And to spare you a Vampire 101 on how I accomplished this, let's just say I dissolved into a cloud of mist and seeped into the earth. Technically, it's a bit more complex than that, but who cares? You get the picture, so let's skip the jargon and get on with it!

I desperately needed to know exactly how Janet had died. Her autopsy report had cited: "Drug Overdose, Cocaine." She'd suffered no wounds, no broken bones, no suspicious bruising, no indication of assault, but . . .

Time to test *my* theory.

Gently and respectfully, I pulled the poor girl's loose-fitting, silken burial gown down to her waist, exposing her bosom. Instantly, I saw what I was looking for—but only *because* I was looking for it. On her breastbone were two tiny marks, or impressions, quite faint and indistinct, hardly discolored enough to count as bruises, which is precisely why these subtle, but damning indicators—so difficult to spot unless you're expecting to find them—are often overlooked by autopsy docs, especially when deaths are deemed not suspicious.

Button impressions, that's what they were. No question.

They'd been pressed into the delicate skin between poor Janet's breasts by a great weight crushing down on the chest cage and compressing the lungs, slowly and painfully cutting off her breath. To confirm my diagnosis, I gently rolled back her eyelids and saw the telltale petechial hemorrhages that are indicative of suffocation.

Suspicions confirmed.

Janet Carter had been *burked*—murdered in diabolically deceptive fashion, by a technique cleverly conceived to deceive.

Its infamous creator? The arch-fiend William Burke, who, in early 1800s Scotland, hit upon a low-overhead, high-profit scheme to supply doctors with well-preserved, but illegal, human specimens for anatomy courses. To circumvent the messy business of digging up graves and retrieving inferior, rotted bodies, he and an accomplice simply murdered random victims. And to avoid leaving marks of violence on a corpse, which made it less valuable, William Burke pioneered his infamous, unique suffocation technique—sitting on the victim's chest and clamping his hands over nostrils and mouth.

Burke was hanged for his crimes in 1829, but his ground-breaking, difficult-to-detect contribution to the art of surreptitious murder lives on in crimes committed by modern copycats. So why did the coroner miss the petechial hemorrhages in her eyeballs? Because he'd stopped looking after finding the balls-out evidence that she'd ingested a massive drug overdose.

Gently, I closed poor Janet's eyelids. But before I pulled the burial shroud up to cover her, I looked again at that delicate chest and imagined Scummy Bear's bony knees pressing down on it, grinding the plastic buttons of the nightgown she'd worn that night into her skin as he crouched atop her like some great predator beast, one hand clamping her mouth, the other pinching her nostrils shut. Bastard!

Covering her up again and restoring her modesty, I whispered in Janet's ear:

"It was hard to believe a subhuman pig like that would know about burking. It's the kind of thing one usually discovers in books, unless you're a medical student. But an astute reporter of mine—I'm a journalist, by the way—remembered your two-hundred-and-fifty-pound assailant's habit of spitting out his gummy-bear candy pacifier when facing stressful situations, and said it looked like . . . a ritual. That's when I remembered Scummy Bear's well-known affinity for gambling in high-stakes poker games. And I realized that his candy-tossing was one of those subconscious, knee-jerk habits that professional gamblers call a 'tell'—an action a player might be unaware of, but that others identify as a hint as to how he'll bet.

"So, my dear Janet, Scummy's interest in gambling was another sort of tell and I finally deduced how he'd heard of 'burking.' I don't suppose you ever read newspaper accounts about the sensational Binion murder case in Las Vegas a few years back? It involved a casino owner, murdered for a buried fortune of seven million dollars in silver bars by his cheating girlfriend and her vicious lover. Well, just as in your case, death was ascribed to a supposedly self-administered overdose of drugs. But based on expert testimony, prosecutors contended that Mr. Binion was force-fed the drugs, then burked. Every gambler followed that news story, and that's how Scummy Bear heard about burking."

Okay. Why the hell am I talking to a corpse? For a vampire, it's not strange at all. And before you ask: Yes! Janet Carter *was* hearing me . . . on some level.

No! I was *not* expecting her to answer. Not directly, anyway.

Understand this: The dead are never as dead to *us*, the undead, as they are to you, the living. And never doubt that communication exists, no matter how rudimentary, among *all* souls, no matter their status. So I was simply engaged in what might be called, for lack of a better term, "socializing."

I was in the poor girl's coffin, right? So how could a little conversation . . . or a monologue . . . hurt? I was deriving great comfort from it. And maybe, just maybe, the dear dead lady was, too. Can you understand that? Stop viewing phenomena through the distorting prism of superstitious fear. Being "closerthanthis" in a grave with a soul who's passed over should be neither frightening nor unsettling, especially for one who's undead and already halfway there, so to speak. *Capisce?* Am I making sense here, people?

I muttered on and on—telling Janet of events triggered by her death, how we were tracking her killer, my fears for TayLo, etc.—until even I smiled at the thought that I might be *boring a corpse to death . . . (Rim shot!)*

Let's add *that* gem to my vampire comedy act!

Then I drifted into deep, plangent vampire sleep. My psyche began to sing, and then . . . I actually heard Janet, as if from a great distance, take voice herself and speak to me . . . mostly of love, and how it is the great constant of our universe, yearned for by even the most fearsome beasts of Earth, and every far-flung planet.

She said: "*. . . you must act, Dragomir, even before pressing forward with your quest. You must go to TayLo, and tell her that you love her more than your amaranthine immortality itself, because life without her means eternal torture. Listen to your soul, hear it sing, and rise on its music to claim the love you've sought for centuries . . .*"

Was it Janet speaking? Or my dreams? What did it matter?

I chuckled softly when I heard the dearly departed say:

"*Okay, Clark, I know I'm suddenly sounding all fancy-schmancy. Guess it goes along with being dead. One just tends to get all serious and all-knowing—because being dead is, like, heavy, dude! But you know what, Clark? I am a lot wiser dead than I ever was alive. I just see things more clearly. Like, I know that missing out on love was my big mistake. But you? You haven't crossed the Big Divide yet. You're kinda-sorta alive. So get on your horse and go nail TayLo. And I mean NAIL the bitch! Tell her you love her first, of course. Girls need verbal before physical, because that's how we roll—but the payoff's worth the price.*

"*Don't blow it, Vampire Boy. The sun's starting to set over Hollywood, so haul ass and get to it! Buh-bye, Clark. Drop in sometime and tell me the gossip. That's what I really miss!*"

And I was out of there, rocketing full-tilt through the darkening skies of La-La-Land.

Chapter Thirty-One

Deadline.

Sacred moment of truth.

It rolls around fast on a daily. On a weekly like *The Revealer*, you've got more time to develop stories, flesh them out. But there's a scary flip side: If another daily paper, wire service or website suddenly catches up and nails your story just as you hit the streets—or even shortly after—your weekly sits rotting on newsstands, its headlines screaming of days-old crap.

Time: 8:14 p.m.

En route: Forest Lawn to Beverly Hills via Air Vampire.

I phoned Wally moments before descending from the night sky to the balcony of my Four Seasons hideaway and told him to assemble our team for a working dinner at nine fifteen. We had less than forty-eight hours to lock up my column and last-minute story candidates for *The Revealer*'s front page.

Quickly, I freshened up in the suite, and checked my e-mail, phone messages. Nothing pressing.

Nothing from TayLo.

Focus, I warned myself.

Deadline, dammit!

Thirty minutes later, I launched into the night again, soaring over the hills of Beverly and Hollywood to the San Fernando Valley. Landing in a quiet neighborhood just off Ventura Boulevard, the main drag, I slipped into a dark alley behind a quiet row of upper-middle-class houses and rapped sharply on the back door of a commercial building.

The knob turned instantly. Light and sound flooded the alley as the door swung wide, revealing Wally and six of my heavy-mob reporters seated around a dining table already copiously stocked with wine bottles, beer steins, and cocktail glasses. Who says a working dinner can't be fun?

"Welcome to the Valley Inn, Master," said Wally. "Your Jack Daniels Old

Fashioned is on the way."

I bowed. "Thank you, Renfield."

I stepped through into my favorite hideaway, the fabled back room of the Valley Inn restaurant, a decades-old landmark of fine dining fronted by an atmospheric pub that can be entered from the street side. Back here, however—unbeknownst to all but Valley Inn regulars and tuned-in celebrities who use it for discreet trysts—was this hidden dining room, secretly accessible from the alley, where one can drink, dine and carouse in total privacy with as many as ten people. And no customer in the restaurant proper is ever the wiser.

I got a muted cheer as I sat. The team raised glasses as my favorite waiter, Jeff, entered from the restaurant side carrying my freshly made Jack Daniels Old Fashioned.

"Great to see you again, Clark."

"Good to be here, Jeff."

"The usual, Clark?"

"Absolutely, Jeff."

He left. I raised my glass, offered my usual toast.

"To even greater stories."

"Hail, hail!"

Everyone took a healthy pull. General chitchat ensued as Wally sat down beside me and began his debriefing, flipping open his iPad to a sequence of photos.

"First the good news, boss. Last night we got these photos of a very tiny dog, a Chihuahua, tied to a wooden stake out behind Roma's pad. You see it being killed and eaten by a coyote. Gruesome stuff. The photos are lowlight, of course, but the production department tells me they're perfectly usable for publication. Now take a look at this."

He wiped the iPad to a grainy shot that appeared to be a balcony occupied by half a dozen folks with fuzzy, out-of-focus faces.

"Our photo department pushed the exposure as far as possible, but it won't get any better than this. It's tough to get detail when you're shooting in the dark toward light that's coming from behind the subject. We *think* it looks like Scummy Bear and a few guys we've sorta half ID'd, but we're not sure enough to publish. We also tried for a video shoot, but there wasn't enough light. Here . . ."

He punched up a video. Looked like footage of the fucking Milky Way, spots of light flickering in a gray-black fog.

"Jesus!"

Wally shrugged. "I know. We've got a technical guy we pay under the table over at Paramount, and he's secretly working in their state-of-the-art studio to enhance the tape, but don't hold your breath. Meanwhile, I've hired another videographer totally experienced in lowlight work. He owns special equipment and he'll be staked on the hill behind Roma's from tonight on—if he's not nailed by her security. Trouble is, they'll go on high alert once you call her for comment on the photos. You still plan on doing that tonight?"

"Definitely. If we can't write that this dog-slaughter occurred on celebutante Roma Kane's property, what's the point? Otherwise, it's just a ho-hum, coyote-snacks-on-Chihuahua scene for Animal Planet! And if we're going to say the vicious abuse happened behind Roma's house, we need to give her the chance to comment, or we'll be dogmeat for her coyote lawyers in LA Superior Court."

"Okay, boss. Maybe it doesn't matter, anyway. Who knows if or when Scummy Bear will sacrifice another dog to the coyotes for the delight and profit of his gambling pals—and Roma. As for a DNA test on that actual chewed-on gummy bear he presumably tossed at the vic's apartment, you told me to hold off. We left it at the scene, untouched, as you instructed by phone after you left us this morning. I think you're right, by the way. If we do the test, defense lawyers will swear we contaminated it. And if the cops wanted to fuck with us, they could charge us with contaminating a crime scene."

I nodded. "Not to worry. That little gummy bear, whenever anyone's ready to test it, will positively come back positive. What I learned after I left you proves that Scummy Bear's guilty, no question. Trust me on that."

Wally paused, looked around at our chattering team to make sure no one was in earshot, then took a quick swallow of his drink and eyed me strangely. Knowing what I am, and what my kind are capable of, he made an educated guess—something he's uncannily good at, as you know.

"You went . . . uh, direct to the source, Master? And checked it out?"

I nodded abruptly. "Ever heard of 'burking,' Renfield?"

"Yeah . . . yeah, I have. *Damn!* And doesn't *that* make sense. Wow!"

I grinned. "Fun, huh? Anyway, we're not in a position to prove murder by burking in a court of law unless we can persuade the cops to dig up Janet's body. And you know how long that could take. No, we stay away from the cops for now. They'll just slow us down. But henceforth, for our purposes, we will consider piece-of-shit Scummy guilty. Okay. Now, anything new on Roma pimping out young girls? Or proof positive she's dealing drugs to pals?"

Wally shook his head. "Nothing on the pimping yet. But we've established, with hundreds of surveillance photos we started taking the other night, that she's often seen handing out little white envelopes, or packets, to friends—usually after Scummy Bear hands them over to her. I suggest we nail down exactly when Roma's carrying, tip off one of our friendly cops and get her busted. It's pushing the . . . uh, envelope a bit, but —"

I held up a hand. "That might be crossing the line, Wally. Entrapment. Don't do that without consulting with me first. Okay? Also, once she's busted, she's out of our control. I want her nervous and where we can get at her, not stuck in a jail cell."

He nodded. "No question, boss. Now let me ask you, do you think the dog-slaughter story is ready to roll? No one at the paper outside of our team knows we've got it yet. What do you want to do? I think it should be a Clark Kelly byline story for the front page lockup tomorrow night."

I leaned back in my chair, lipping my excellent Old Fashioned as I thought about it.

"Yeah . . . okay! The headline's something like, 'Dog Abuse Horror: Roma Kane's Tiny Pooch Sacrificed To Killer Coyote!' That'll work. But as for revealing that Janet Carter didn't die of a dope overdose and was actually murdered, we don't have enough yet to publish. And we can't even *hint* that Scummy Bear did the deed—or that Roma herself might be an accomplice because she passed drugs to him."

Wally hesitated. "The only problem—but you say it's *not* a problem—is that Roma and Scummy Bear will know we're eating at their asses once you call her for comment on the dog-killing story."

I smiled. "That's exactly what I want—those little sweeties *sweating*. Look, I'm not interested in truth, beauty and the pursuit of American justice here. What do I care if those nasty fuckers get convicted in a court of law? I'm not a prosecutor. What I want is great stories about scandalous shit. Absolutely, we'll proceed in a legal, careful way. But our job is stories that sell. We just missed guaranteeing a guilty verdict on O.J., that piece of shit, but it was a story that kept on giving. Newsbreaks . . . new angles . . . shocking unseen photos . . . the secret diary . . . or sex tapes that suddenly come to light. That's what we're after, pal. Leave justice to the justice system."

My voice had been rising. The guys were silent now, eyes riveted on me. So I stood, rather theatrically, and intoned:

"Let the cops and the DA issue their usual fence-straddling press releases. There's a reason the public holds its breath until they hear from us— because we deliver all the news they *really* need to know. We're not just journalists, my friends. We are *tabloid* journalists, carrying on a proud tradition of terrifying the rich and powerful—rooting out and exposing pustulent corruption wherever we find it."

A raucous cheer went up.

I hoisted my Old Fashioned. "Raise your glasses, gentlemen . . . to even *greater* stories! Now, here's our food. Let's eat."

Jeff and two other waiters swept in, laying down hot, fragrant plates.

"Rib-eye, black and blue for you, Clark."

"Thank you, Jeff."

The food was excellent, as usual. Everyone was hungry after a lot of hard work. We got through the meal quickly. I ordered a single-shot espresso and a snifter of the Kelt cognac they keep stocked just for me. Boris, a huge bear of a Russian man who owns the joint with homegal-wife Sophia, sent word he'd be buying an after-dinner round for all. I sat back, sipped and enjoyed the company of men drinking companionably.

After about ten minutes, Wally gently nudged me back into action.

"You got a minute for Tony, boss? He's got the skinny on this bizarro drug we've been hearing about. Or he could e-mail you later?"

"No. Now, Renfield."

He beckoned. Tony Giambalvo slid up a chair and sat between us. Tony's a born and bred Brooklyn "street" guy. Tough. Takes no prisoners. You couldn't ask for a more aggressive reporter. Once, after a bouncer at West Hollywood's most happening gay club, The Abbey, refused to comment about a fight involving a closeted male star and an underage boy, Tony slid a 9mm pistol between the guy's lips and snarled, *"Speak before I say 'three,' motherfucker. One . . . TWO . . ."*

He got his comment.

Tony had been a heroin junkie from his teens into his twenties. He'd kicked drugs after falling for a beautiful, ball-busting, neighborhood Italian girl, who told him he would never get in her pants unless he cleaned up. Today, she's his wife. But Tony knows drugs. And he knows the network that supplies them.

"Clark, this stuff is scary shit. It's called Oxi. Short for *oxidado*, which is Spanish for 'rust'. It's a cocaine derivative, like crack, but way more powerful. And dangerous. They beef it up with gasoline or kerosene, acetone, battery fluid and fucking quicklime. You start taking it regularly, in a year you're dead. Super addictive. They say you're hooked if you use it more than once. What's really scary is the stuff's so fucking *cheap*. It's not up here in the States much yet, but in Brazil one rock of Oxi costs two bucks. Cocaine? One lousy rock costs sixty bucks."

I held up a hand. "So . . . the drug gangs can't be behind it?"

Tony laughed. "Hell, no. I'll get to that in a minute. Basically, Oxi got started about ten years ago when lowlife, depraved fucking junkies down in Bolivia started collecting the stinking sludge left over from cocaine production, then added chemicals and crap. Produced poor man's crack. Big punch, plus cheaper than shit. And it slowly started to spread. In Brazil, they're going fucking nuts because all of a sudden they've got whole colonies of filthy Oxi addicts living on the streets. There's a section of downtown São Paulo called *Cracolandia*, 'The Oxi Disneyland.' Literally hundreds of human rag bags littering the sidewalks."

I waved to Jeff for a refill. "So, Tony, this shit *is* available in America?"

"Clark, let me tell you something. You know that *I* know a lot of connected people up in Brooklyn, people who know a lot about what goes on in *that* world, right? When I mentioned this Oxi shit to them, they got so fucking pissed off I thought I was gonna get whacked. They got the idea I might know people bringing this stuff into the country. Once I got them calmed down, I told them I was asking around because of a story we're doing. They wanted to know *what* story. I told them, but without using any names.

"You know what they told me? They said they've put the word out everywhere that anyone who brings this Oxi shit into this country will die like no one should ever die. And they told me that whoever our guy is that we're investigating, who's maybe bringing in a tiny quantity just to fuck with somebody . . . is a dead man."

Tony paused. Then he said it.

"They want his name, Clark."

He recoiled at the look in my eye.

"What the *fuck* did you . . . just . . . say?"

He spread his hands, looking very Italian. "They're not going to put any pressure on us right away, Clark. I can handle this, don't worry. But these are serious people. I told them this has nothing to do with drug business, and they understand. If they didn't, Scummy Bear would be iced right now. But they're serious. They don't want even *one dose* of this Oxi crap in America. So . . ."

"So cut the crap, Tony! What the fuck did you *really* say to make them hold off, these *serious* people?"

Wally tensed. The room had gone dead quiet.

Tony's last name could have been Soprano at that moment. He smiled thinly.

"Well, boss, I told them if *we* didn't ice him, we'd let them know."

I hunched my shoulders, dipped my chin, stared at him like Don Corleone.

"Great work, Tony. I ask you to Google a fucking drug—and you get us into a fucking mob war. *Che cosa?*"

The whole room collapsed in laughter. Guys were getting up, walking around with hunched shoulders, posing like wiseguys, saying stuff like,

"You talkin' to *me*?"

"Fuhgeddaboudit!"

And what was I doing amid all this hilarity, you might ask? The guy who bills himself as Mr. Funny Vampire Guy, who aspires to launch an undead comedy act? Was I cracking Mafia jokes? Or doing my *killer* Joe Pesci impression for the guys? Hell, no.

I was checking e-mail. Like a pussy.

Nothing.

Goddammit. You may well ask why, if I was so upset that she wasn't calling, I didn't simply call her. If you have to ask the question, you don't understand much about how to keep women fascinated, okay?

The phone jumped in my hand. Caller ID said: *Miracles.*

My psyche lit up like *JACKPOT!!* on a slot!

"Hello?"

"Mr. Kelly?"

"Yes."

"The patient just approved giving you information. The patient instructed us to tell you she has checked out."

"And where did she go?"

"That's all I'm authorized to say. Good-bye, sir."

Fuck.

Wally said, "Clark, I'm going to send everyone home after another round. They're pretty beat. Okay?"

"Fine. Everyone on deck in the morning. My dog-killer story will be written and on Elspeth's desk first thing, ready to move through the system. I'll leave a message with Phil that it's coming."

Phil Calder, the Managing Editor.

"Okay."

"Want another Kelt, boss?"

"No."

"Everything okay?"

Goddam it, I needed to feed.

Bad.

The Hunger.

Can't explain it to you, really. A week without food or water doesn't even touch the agony of the wrenching need a vampire experiences . . . and ignores at his peril. Immortality is not a pain-free state.

The Hunger.

I stood quickly before it took me over. It's not a pretty sight when it hits. I animated my face quickly to cover up, wrenching it from sudden grimace to twisted smile. Waving my arms like a happy camper, I headed for the door, yelling above the noise, "Thanks, guys. Tomorrow."

They yelled back as I lurched into the alley, slamming the door behind me. I cursed myself for ignoring this too long, but . . . distracted. Just fucking crept up on me. The phone call from Miracles had triggered the danger stage, I knew, but . . .

Goddam, *why doesn't she call?*

The Hunger.

Her not calling just made it even worse, silly as that sounds. But it's like getting doubly pissed about an annoyance just because you missed breakfast. *Aaarrrgh!* Why did I say *breakfast?*

Feed. *Now!*

I walked quickly through back streets to Ventura Boulevard. Turned west toward what looked like a restaurant still open. Walked a block. Yeah, open. Good. I veered into an alley that led to a parking lot behind it, stepped into shadows and started watching. Just five minutes later, I got lucky. A twenty-ish girl walked out to her car alone, juggling takeout boxes.

Quick hit. She never heard or saw me. My hand snaked over her mouth. I jerked her neck toward me, exposing the succulent white throat. *Control,* I told myself, dragging her behind parked cars.

Don't hurt her.

Just feed.

The Hunger.

Ah, ah . . . aaahhh . . .

Her body bucked and spasmed. Life essence spurted, hot.

I fed . . . and fed.

After a while, I put her down, gently resting her head on a still-warm takeout box. I reached in my wallet, took out an alcohol pad and swabbed her neck. Then I slipped ten one hundred dollar bills into her purse. Not for payment. I take what I want. *Never* get sentimental over food. But a girl can always use a little boutique money, right?

Voices.

The back door of the restaurant opened . . .

I shot up into the night sky.

Buh-bye, Hunger.

Appeased.

Yeah.

Feelin' *GOOD*!

Chapter Thirty-Two

"Vanillo?"

"Omigod, *Clark*! Where are you?"

Music blasted in her background. Live, lots of bass presence.

"Home. And you? Just a guess, but . . . Aqua Lounge, BevHills?"

"You got it first try! How'd you do that?"

I laughed. "Guy rule number one: *Never* tell a girl how you do tricks—but you're not a girl, Vanillo, you're news staff, so . . . I happen to be blessed with perfect musical pitch. I heard the bass player bending notes slightly flat in the upper registers, as he tends to do."

"Wow, amazing! Hey, Clark, come on out. It's *so* fun tonight. Blake Lively's here, and I just overheard Khloe Kardashian say that Special K might show up, and . . ."

"Can't. I'm on deadline. And I need your help, kiddo. Can you find out where Roma Kane is right now? She home in bed, you think, or still out?"

"It's not even one a.m. yet . . . *der!*"

"Okay, so where?"

"I can find that bitch in two phone calls."

"You tell me Roma's 20 in less than ten, and there'll be two bottles of Cristal with your name on them tomorrow at John & Pete's Liquors on La Cienega."

"*Cristal*? Omigod, yeah! Gotta get busy. Hang up, Clark."

"Go, girl."

Eight minutes later, my cell phone vibrated on the coffee table. I snatched it up and walked out to the terrace.

"Talk to me, Vanillo."

"Clark, she's at SLS Hotel on La Cienega. In their club, The Bazaar. No boys, just two girlfriends. They're not celebs. Roma's into the desserts there. And the cocktails, of course."

"Good work. Enjoy your Cristal."

"Clark, I . . . someday, my dream is . . . I wanna join your gossip team. The heavy mob."

"Cute little girl like you?"

"I'm one smart, tough bitch. Try me."

"I just did. And will again. Thanks, Vanill'."

I punched my iPhone contacts, containing, among other fun things, private cell phone numbers of just about any major showbiz star you can name. Plus many more fun secrets. Punch the listing under "POTUS: Mobile," for example, and you connect—quickerthanthis—to the President.

Yeah, *that* President.

Click.

"Hello?"

"Hello there!"

"Who the hell *is* this?"

"Hi, Roma Kane! What a pleasure. Having fun at The Bazaar? I'm crazy about their chocolate flan, aren't you?"

"Hey, I asked who—"

"Roma, it's Clark Kelly, *National Revealer*. I write the paper's gossip column. We were introduced once at that Warner Bros. wrap party for—"

"I *know* who you are. Everybody knows who you are. How interesting that you would call me tonight . . . uh, why are you calling me tonight?"

My reporter antennae quivered. Odd thing to say, unless . . .

"Why is it 'interesting,' as you put it, that I would call tonight?"

She stammered. "Er . . . no, no . . . I just meant it's interesting . . . that you would call me. You're a very famous man in this town. So what can I do for you?"

Experience has taught me that charm and small talk are superfluous in situations which need to be no-nonsense. Better to move straight ahead and be businesslike. In this case especially, because I was about to pull the trigger on what we newsboys call "legal shit."

"I know you're out socializing, Ms. Kane, but it's important that I tell you this in a timely fashion. The *National Revealer* is publishing a story that says a Chihuahua owned by you was purposely tied out to a stake at the back of your property as bait for coyotes that inhabit the canyons that back onto your home property above the Sunset Strip—and we are currently in possession of photos showing said adorable Chihuahua under savage attack, to wit, ripped apart by a coyote and carried off in its jaws to be eaten alive. Let me be clear: You have twenty-four hours to respond to the story and photos before we publish, giving us any comment you care to make— but I'm hoping you'll respond to me right now."

Silence.

Then, background female voices chattering, "Roma, what's *wrong*?" . . . "What is it, girl?" . . . "*Omigod*, what's up?"

Don't hang up, I prayed.

As *if*!

Then she spoke.

"Kelly, just who the *fuck* do you think you're dealing with here? You put that story in your fucking rag and you'll be sued into oblivion. How dare you make up such horrible, *horrible* lies."

I chuckled. Warmly, I hoped.

"In our business, Ms. Kane, we say that one picture is worth ten thousand words. And there will be, in addition to the dog-kill pics, a photo showing you with what looks like that same tiny dog peeking out of your Prada purse as you exited the Kitson boutique on Robertson Boulevard a couple of weeks ago. Was it the same dog?"

"Fuck you, Clark Kelly!"

She screamed it.

She took a moment . . . then, tense and tight, said: *"Listen to me.* I am a well-known animal lover. I contribute to animal charities. I have a huge, state-of-the-art doghouse on my property fabricated by a famous designer. My dogs live in luxury. Now, you son of a bitch, let me ask *you* the big question: Do you have a picture of me staking out that little dog? Or watching some fucking coyote attack it? Well, DO you?"

"No, I do not, Roma Kane. And we do not, in the story we are publishing, accuse you of staking out that dog. But I find it curious that nowhere in the notes I'm taking as we speak do I see *any* remarks reflecting the shock or grief one would most certainly expect from such a renowned animal lover. Does it not upset you that one of your dogs has been mercilessly killed by a coyote that crept down from the wooded canyons behind your home? Have you no tears for your pet, Roma?"

Ramming it home just a bit hard, aren't you, Kelly?

Nope. Just showing her the cards I'm intending to play. It's required, legally. Journalistically? I needed this bitch spooked! Because sometimes, when people realize you've got the goods on them, they'll babble facts not yet in evidence or suddenly start making the story even better by cooperating, either in fear or hopes of a fat payoff from us.

My assessment in this case?

Never gonna happen.

This world-famous billion-heiress, born with a platinum spoon in her mouth, wouldn't even know *how* to run fucking scared, not after a lifetime cocooned by downy-soft layers of power-generated protection. People like the Kane Klan own police, courts, politicians—and literally believe that, in the end, they'll beat it all, death included.

"Fuck you . . . and *fuck*, fuck, FUCK the *National Revealer*," Roma shrieked, voice rising as she played to her peanut gallery of brain-dead skanks.

"And are you *also* aware, Ms. Kane," I said, going on as if she hadn't spoken, "that a member of your entourage stakes out those defenseless dogs and viciously sacrifices them for the sake of a *gambling* game, with winnings going to whichever player comes closest to estimating what time the coyote will actually strike. *Have* you heard that, Roma?"

"Kelly, you son of a bitch, I'm hanging up now. But you'll be hearing from me soon. Very soon. And I'm warning you—don't print this stupid story, or any phony fucking photos, or I'll *own The Revealer*. My lawyers will *kill* you on this."

I laughed. "We know your lawyers. They're pretty sharp guys. And you know what question I predict they're going to be asking you? Why, pray tell, Ms. Kane, when you were speaking with Clark Kelly, didn't you think to ask, '*Which one* of my poor little dogs was killed?'

"Considering that you're a self-described *renowned animal lover*, you seem strangely unconcerned about *which* beloved pet might be missing, Roma. Or are you just *too* overcome with emotion to deal with it all right now, perhaps?"

"*You prick*," she hissed.

"Forgive me, Ms. Kane, but once more, for the record: Do you deny that a tiny dog belonging to you was deliberately staked out and used as bait for vicious coyotes that inhabit the canyon behind your property? And do you also deny that a member of your entourage regularly commits this vicious abuse to amuse your pathetic hangers-on?"

I paused, then triggered my stealth missile. "And do you also, Ms. Kane, deny any knowledge that Janet Carter was murdered?"

"*WHAT?*"

She screamed this too.

"You *motherfucker*—what did you just say?"

"I withdraw the question, Ms. Kane. Thank you for your time. Enjoy the delicious flan, and the rest of your evening."

"*You listen to me*," she hissed. "You are fucking with the *wrong* girl. Bad things are going to happen to you. Soon. And when they do, be sure to think of me."

"I never stop thinking of you, Wild Thang. You and your . . . *Scummy Bear.*"

Dead silence. Even the sluts were struck dumb. She howled like a slaughtered animal and killed the connection.

I laughed.

"That's for that poor, helpless little dog, cunt. Sweet dreams."

I stood, kicked back the chair I'd been sitting on, smiled into the mirror above my fireplace. Oh, yes, I look into mirrors. Don't believe that Bram Stoker shit.

I clicked Elspeth's line at the office, got her machine and said:

"Hi, while it's fresh in my mind at 12:53 a.m., let me dictate the gist of the conversation I just had with Roma Kane for the edification of our very fine lawyers. I have just now afforded Ms. Kane ample opportunity to comment on the dog-killing story, which I'll dictate to you after I complete this. I reached Ms. Kane while she was out with friends at the SLS Hotel, and their club, The Bazaar. After identifying myself, I began by saying . . ."

An hour later, I'd filed my front-page story. (Correction: Front-page story *if* Phil Calder deemed it so. But he would.) Headline: ROMA KANE'S TINY POOCH SACRIFICED TO KILLER COYOTE!

Would *you* put that on Page One?

You bet your ass you would!

I poured a snifter of Kelt, wishing I felt better . . . or worse. Either would have been preferable to the way I *was* feeling.

Dead.

You'll pardon the expression.

Hating the schoolboy-ish angst that was possessing me, I checked my e-mail for the fiftieth time.

Nothing.

GOD . . . DAM . . . IT!

Suddenly, I wanted . . . to *kill*! The new blood roiled up in me and sang its power. Swiftly walking to the balcony rail, I threw back my head, exposed whetted fangs and howled madly at the moon, muscles clenching and flexing.

I waited.

And waited.

Nothing.

Until . . . a querulous yowl rose from the streets fourteen stories down. I peered over the rail, vampire eyes penetrating the dark. *There!* A beast! Darting out of an alley off Doheny Drive, it sensed my presence, and peered up at me malevolently. YEAH! Bring it on, lupine motherfucker! Yelping a challenge, the thing skulked out of the dark and onto the dimly lit sidewalk then scampered off down the street.

I howled again—this time in utter frustration.

My "beast" was a mangy, stray dog.

Where's a fucking werewolf in this town when you need one?

Only in LA, I thought. It's like a Seth Rogen movie.

I shook my head and chuckled. It *was* kinda funny, I had to admit. Shaking off my drama-queen angst, I went inside and willed myself to sleep.

Chapter Thirty-Three

Deadline day minus one.

In the newsroom, it was the usual panicky rat-fuck. But for sick, depraved news junkies, the unrelenting pressure of a thousand last-minute fact checks and fixes can be quite tolerable, even exciting, when you know you're on the way to locking up a genuine blockbuster; not some stretched-to-the-limit "Angie catches Brad texting Jen" dog shit.

Late that afternoon, Phil Calder—a bear of a guy who looks like Irish actor Brendan Gleeson in *The Guard*—banged into my office moments after *The Revealer* lawyers had completed their endless interrogations regarding my story's sourcing and, visibly exhausted, finally trooped out.

"Man, when I see shysters sweating like that, I *know* I've got a great story," Phil boomed. "Christ, they spent half the day raking you over the fucking coals. But they couldn't lay a glove on ya, right, baby? Because that story's solid."

I shook my head. "Never resent lawyers, Phil. Polls show they're the one group that people actually rate lower than journalists."

"Yeah," he barked. "And we both rank somewhere south of dentists, right? Anyway, I just laid out the front page. It's a great story, Clark *and* photos to match. Man, the goddam animal lovers will go *insane* when they see that little puppy torn to bits. They'll demand Roma Kane's head on a fucking stick. My gut tells me we're about to sell some papers, big time."

He threw himself down on my couch.

"Okay! Now . . . the way I see it, Clark, from what Wally's told me anyway, your team's working three possible page ones for next week, right? You've got the Scummy Bear murder, the South American killer drug Roma Kane's pushing to TayLo and her in-crowd, and Roma pimping out her hot young Hollywood girlfriends to rich old geezers. Any chance you can pull in one of those for tomorrow's lockup?"

I laughed. "Never quit, do you, Phil? Just gave you one front-pager, you're already hungry for more."

"Hey, Clark, guess no one told you, but—the presses roll *every* fucking week, man. I'll be here, will you?"

I stood up and stretched. "That's a date, Phil. In the meantime, I'm outta here."

He nodded. "If you're not doing anything for dinner, drop by Musso & Frank's later. I'll be buying a few rounds."

"I might have something going, but who knows? Thanks."

Phil exited; Elspeth entered.

"You look like shit," she said.

"Thanks. That must mean I've been working hard."

She glared. "Clark, you have no earthly reason to be here. Your story's laid out, so it's time to blow off steam. The next lockup's a week away. You've released Wally and the guys, so *go!*"

"You're *not* my mom, Elspeth."

"Look, why don't you hit that taco shack above Santa Monica beach you're always raving about and have a couple of beers."

Suddenly, that seemed like an awfully good idea.

"I wish you *were* my mom, Elspeth."

"Yeah, that's me to a tee—everybody's mom! Even my damn husband says that."

"Don't believe him. He told me he married you strictly for the hot sex."

"Get out of here, Clark. Now!"

"Yes, Mom . . . uh, Ma'am."

Two hours and three beers later, I sat peering through the slats of a ramshackle beachside hut that serves the finest tacos south of El Cholo, the fabled Mexican restaurant on Wilshire. Now there's a thought; maybe run up to El Cholo, snack on a big helping of their to-die-for green corn tamales now that the sun's sinking in the West? While I'd been sipping my beer and vacantly watching El Sol's killer rays bake the beach—all the while endlessly, fruitlessly checking e-mail—I'd been sorely tempted to stroll out on those burning sands and . . . uh, work on my suntan. Yeah, I know. Vampires don't sunbathe. Not unless they're looking for a surefire way to end their misery forever.

Oh, goddam. Listen to my fucking whining—or rather, *don't*! Truly, I'm so sick of my own asinine, lovesick mopery I'm ready to order the Vampire Suicide Tacos . . . which come with *extra garlic*! Ha, *haaaa.*

Hey, I thought, not a bad book title: "Vampires Don't Sunbathe!"

I ordered another beer, checked e-mail again. And again—NOTHING! Where is she? Why isn't she . . . goddammit! I'd just locked a hot front-page story, so where was the usual thrill? Why was I feeling like crap? Hating myself for ducking the obvious answer, I faced up to what was obviously driving my angst—I was suddenly so *not* in control, and it scared me. Now that I knew I was in love, her sudden lack of contact had me crazy! Why? Because, I reminded myself, she was a wildly impulsive, live-for-the-moment ball of fire with a gnawing yen for drugs, partying and . . . sex. But why, godammit, are you escalating this irrational fear that she's already dumped you. And wouldn't she just fucking tell you if she had?

Not wanting to answer my sorry-ass self, I paid my check and walked down to the beach parking lot. I'd snap myself out of my mood by joining Phil and other assorted tabloid riffraff at the always-soothing Musso & Frank's on Hollywood Boulevard. I got to my car just as dusk crept into the nearly empty lot, and paused.

Drive . . . or fly? Rush hour wasn't officially over yet, so . . . Air Vampire it was.

I hate to drink and drive, and was primed to get seriously drunk, so I launched skyward and flew north up the beach, not banking east until I'd passed over the gaily lit Santa Monica pier. I'm such a sucker for that neon-splashed nighttime view, especially with all those screaming, excited kids on the giant Ferris wheel. What would it be like to have a kid, I wondered? With you-know-who? *Prrretty* cool, as Miley Cyrus would say.

I'd barely passed Third St. Promenade when my cell phone burped. A text.

I fished out the iPhone. And there it was, at last!

A *TayLo-gram*!

What *pun*!

(*Hey!* A dumb joke! Which means, hopefully, that I'm suddenly my normal, obnoxious self again—as opposed to the whiny, love-struck wimp I'd been over the last few days.)

Her text said: **MISS U! Friend loaned me her cool pad. 9211 Mandeville Canyon Rd. I'm alone. Come now, pleez.**

I texted: **Will drop in.**

Hit *Send*.

Kicking in the after-burner, I banked north and poured on the horses. Could I beat my own text there? Checked GPS . . . and five minutes later, there it was below: a two-story brick house on nearly two acres, ringed by shrubs and trees. Nice. Fulfilling my promise, I "dropped in," landing neatly on the patio between the house and a huge, illuminated pool.

Peering through closed, French doors that led into the house, I spied her seated at a chic, well-stocked bar in what appeared to be the Great Room.

Feelings emanated from me like radioactivity. She sensed my presence. Turning, face aglow, she spotted me. In five quick strides I was through the French doors. She slid off the barstool, and buried herself in my arms.

I held her tightly. Now that I was here, holding her close, what to say? Then she said it all.

"You know, I've got a theory. I think you really care about me . . . you're not just a gossip columnist after a hot story. I feel like . . . you're trying to, like, *protect* me, sort of. Crazy, huh? Tell me I'm just a silly, romantic girl."

I inhaled the scent of her hair. "You're a silly, romantic girl. But you're absolutely right on about the protection thing. Even I missed that at first.

Just proves you can't judge a girl's brain by the size of her breasts. Uh, I mean, it's not in inverse proportion, is it?"

WTF?

Did I just *say* that? Nice move, Clark. Bit nervous, are you, asshole?

She laughed, stepped back out of my arms.

"So . . . you've been thinking about my breasts?"

Okay. Here comes the big save . . . watch this, ladies!

Softly, right into those beautiful eyes, I said, "Not as much as I think about how . . . how I *feel* when I'm with you."

Sha-*ZAM!*

She nodded. "Nice one." But she *was* smiling.

She walked behind the bar and produced a bottle, theatrically, like a magician inviting applause.

"Got you a bottle of Louis XIII. Surprise, surprise."

I sat down on a barstool. She poured my nectar of choice into crystal snifters for us and said:

"To life . . . in *all* its forms."

Still wondering why I'm in thrall to this smart, tantalizing creature?

"Hear, hear!"

We sipped.

"You have just the right amount of grey in your hair," she said.

Stupidly missing my cue, I answered, "Beautiful place, this. Your girlfriend must be very rich."

A beat. Then she said, "Well, her family is. Actually, she's more my mom's girlfriend than mine. But she's closer to my age. We know the family from New York. Old friends."

I nodded. "Uh-huh. So what happened? You left Miracles. Why?"

"Because I think I can achieve recovery better with you. You want to protect me, so . . . *protect* already." Then she held up a hand, sharply. "But, *whoa* . . . don't do that creepy, disappearing-behind-me shtick again. It's not necessary."

Wow! Reading my mind. She walked from behind the bar, stood in front of me and cocked her head to one side—offering up that dainty neck. Was the bitch toying with me? Or did she really think that drug-detecting was the aphrodisiac that fired up my fangs?

"You may sample when ready, Dr. Vampire. And thank you, by the way, for not leaving even the tiniest mark last time."

I nodded. "I pride myself on the precision of my bite. And I can henceforth withdraw from other places on your body, if you like."

"Sounds like fun. If there is a 'henceforth.' But right now, let's stick with the neck."

I stood, drew her close, unsheathed my fangs and broke skin so delicately she didn't even flinch. The temptation to feed was surprisingly powerful still, but I resisted. Good thing I'd found food. Taking only what was needed for analysis, I stepped back and stood facing her, sampling her

familiar essence, and . . .
Ah! Blood never lies.

Chapter Thirty-Four

Instantly, in one loud, wailing scream, blood sang its truth.

Corruption triggered my receptors: No question about it, she *had* ingested fucking Oxi!

I detected faint but unmistakable traces of kerosene, gasoline, acetone . . . and dreaded quicklime—which is a toxic, fertilizer-like substance often dumped into graves to accelerate the decomposition of corpses. Centuries ago in Europe, when millions died of the plague, bodies were stacked like cordwood in mass graves, then sprinkled with quicklime to atomize them efficiently and quickly. Be assured that no vampires ever rose aborning from those fetid pits.

Oscar Wilde vividly immortalized the horror of quicklime in a bit of doggerel:

And all the time the burning lime
Eats flesh and bone away . . .
It eats the flesh and bones by turns,
But it eats the heart away.

Her eyes, impatient, were riveted to mine.

"So . . . verdict?"

"Guilty as hell," I told her. "You've used at least once since you departed Miracles, right?"

She nodded.

"Who gave it to you?"

She shrugged. "What difference does it make?"

"So it *was* Roma."

She started to speak, but I cut her off.

"Don't bother denying it. We're way past that now. I'm goddam worried about you, lady. So I'm guessing you indulged early yesterday morning, or was it the night before? And how did you react to it? Was it different in any way from whatever you've had before?"

Her eyes narrowed slightly. "What are you getting at?"

"The truth, apparently—judging from your reaction. Stop the bullshit. Just tell me, Taylor."

Her face lit up.

"You called me . . . Taylor."

"It's your name."

"But it sounds so wonderful when you say it. Don't ever call me TayLo again, Clark. Please?"

"Done—except in my gossip column, of course."

"Bastard!"

I grinned. "That sounds *so wonderful* when you say it. Now answer the question—what did the drug make you feel like?"

She knocked back Louis XIII, shuddered visibly.

"It felt incredible at first. All I could think was, 'I want more . . . give me more.' But then, I just . . . went to pieces. After a while I actually started vomiting—and worse. For hours, I felt like I wanted to die. I was alone here, and finally I tried to call someone, but I couldn't get a cell phone signal. And when I tried the landline, it wasn't working. Then I passed out, woke up twelve hours later. When I finally did get a hold of . . . someone, I was told I was just having a reaction to all the trauma I've been through. That, and the fear of leaving Miracles. I didn't know what to think. I haven't touched a thing since then, but . . . why are you asking me this? And how did you know I had a bad reaction?"

I shrugged. "I didn't. Just an educated guess. One more question: Ever had a reaction like that before?"

She thought about it. "Well . . . I guess it's happened two or three times in the last year or so, but . . . I never noticed the effect as much because I was drinking booze big-time, back in the day. So I'd just pass out before the pain got too bad, then forget all about it."

"You never complained to your . . . supplier?"

"Well, yeah, but it didn't happen often. Usually, I'd get these wonderful highs. What are you suggesting? I mean, every once in a while you get a bad dose, right? Luck of the draw."

I shrugged again. "You're the expert. How do you like that Louis Trez, by the way?"

She smiled, lighting up those limpid green eyes. "Very nice. And how do you like me, by the way?"

Before I could answer, she walked across the room to a leather sofa facing a fireplace. She sat, gestured at me to join her. Ah, I thought, that's better. I smiled at her, seductively I hoped, walked over and sat. She looked at me, raised an eyebrow. I raised an eyebrow—an attractive look for me, I've been told. She looked annoyed. Visibly.

"What?"

"I asked a question," she said. "You didn't answer."

Whoops.

"Oh, sorry. I . . . uh, lost my train of thought. The answer, of course, is that I like you very much."

"Yes, I make good copy for your column, don't I? What's not to like?"

"No . . . I mean, *what* are you talking about? You're all I think about now. Let me tell you how much . . ."

As I spoke, I started to slide across the sofa toward her again. She drew back, fixed me with a baleful glare.

"I'm *all* you think about? No, all *you* think about are those stories about my friends that you're cranking out for your goddamed gossip column. Fuck you, Clark Kelly. You really do think I'm a stupid actress bimbo, don't you?"

Women truly are confusing creatures. Here we were, two star-crossed beings who'd been crazily attracted to each other at first sight, alone at last in a cozy, private place—but suddenly, she was holding me, angrily, at arm's length. What had happened to the maddeningly sexy, brilliant-but-doomed creature who'd begged me from the start, over and over, to possess her?

"Look, Taylor . . ."

I slid toward her again. She recoiled, moving to the end of the sofa.

"Don't you 'Taylor' me, *and don't you come near me*. In fact, I think you should leave!"

"WHAT?"

The fear that flashed instantly in her eyes made me realize that I'd inadvertently roared at her in my vampire voice, and that she'd be seeing my eyes, lit by inhuman fury, glowing red as burning coals. I hadn't intended to lose control, of course, but her inexplicable hostility had suddenly affected me in a way it would not have days ago. *Why* wasn't I acting like myself? Then it hit me; the simple answer. Because I *wasn't* myself anymore. So that must be why *she* suddenly wasn't acting like herself, because . . .

I know, I know, you're way ahead of me. You're wondering how anyone —alive *or* dead—could be so excruciatingly stupid, correct? How could I not have divined the simple truth that was driving this insanely circular conversation between two intelligent creatures? *Why* were we suddenly acting like hostile strangers? Shout it out, people! Vampires can handle the truth! All together, now . . .

"Because you're in love with her, schmuck! And she's in love with you!"

I burst out laughing. Just couldn't stop. Her jaw dropped. She sat staring in shock for a long moment . . . until I finally regained control enough to gasp the words coherently.

"Taylor . . . forgive me, but . . . I . . . *love* you!"

Instantly, her eyes flashed with emotion so pure, so vivid, that speech was superfluous. In that split second, I felt her soul rush across the space separating us and merge with my own. Unspoken words resonated from her like the cacophonous tolling of temple bells, telling me over and over, "I am yours forever, my love . . . forever!"

Then it all just . . . exploded.

Driven by desire stoked too long, I pulled her into my arms, felt her hot breath on my face. Our bodies and lips meshed in dizzying intensity as I fought to control the surging power triggered when my kind are aroused; wanting her desperately, yet desperate not to hurt her. Ethereal music welled up inside me. It had begun. The vampiric phenomenon of blood singing out to blood, a mounting crescendo of heart-pounding excitement more powerful even than The Hunger. Yet this blood song does not derive its power from the impulse to feed; it's a wrenching, gut-felt yearning that occurs when a vampire encounters a human essence so uniquely compatible that he must possess it, at all cost, and forever.

Suddenly, as if from a distance, I heard her voice keening, "Master . . . Dragomir, *take me!*"

Still in locked embrace, I levitated us straight up from the sofa, and we wafted up the staircase to the master bedroom. Blowing open the closed door via mind power, I made a soft landing on a thick, goose-down comforter covering the bigger-than-king-size bed. Good. We'd need some room tonight.

Next thought: Do not go "full vampire." Do *not* hurt her.

Mentally, I dialed in "half vampire," and hoped for the best.

As if reading my mind once more, my beloved spoke softly.

"I know you might hurt me . . . but I don't care . . . and *don't* stop!"

She swung her legs over the side of the bed suddenly and stood, facing me. And she smiled the most beautiful smile.

"I know this sounds stupidly romantic," she said shyly. "But I want to . . . offer myself to you."

Slowly, she began removing her clothes. Not acting sexy or seductive, simply stripping away the utilitarian layer that covered her magnificent breasts, hips, thighs. Then, naked, she stood still as a statue.

What I did then felt all at once totally natural, yet eerily strange. Going to her, I dropped to one knee, and I bowed my head. Respectfully. Then I reached up, took her hand and kissed it.

"I love you . . . now and forever."

I rose, kissed her impossibly soft lips and ran worshipping hands over that vibrant skin, feeling heat rise wherever my fingers touched. No vampire woman could ever feel so soft, nor offer the emotionality, the sweetness one experiences with a human female.

Suddenly, she laughed huskily, leaped into my arms, wrapped her legs around my torso and whispered in my ear.

"Please . . . now . . . *take my blood*. And then . . . love me. Just love me, please."

Turning, I flipped back the huge down comforter, sank onto the soft bed with her in my arms, then covered us both. She burrowed deeper, insistently pulling me down under the comforter with her until even our heads were covered.

Her eyes sought mine in the darkness, and she said, "I want to imagine we're buried together . . . for eternity."

And then . . .

I could bear it no longer. Until this moment, I'd avoided unsheathing and baring my fangs, following an impulse I'd never before experienced. I somehow had the strange urge to appear normal, like a human boyfriend, if you will, not a vampire.

In a thunderclap of irony, the next words she uttered were, "I want to be one with you, join you forever. Make me *vampir*, Dragomir . . . now."

Incredible. I yearn to be human; she aspires to the vampire state. So weird, even funny. Perverse, and so . . . human. It all felt right, somehow.

A wave of indescribable peace and warmth flooded through me. I rolled her gently onto her back. Instantly, she threw back her head and lifted her neck, poised and waiting eagerly. I shrugged out of my shirt, dropped my pants and felt, for the first time, her soft, naked breasts pressed against my chest. My fangs grazed her skin. Then my tongue found the tiny openings I'd made before. I pleasured the wound. She moaned deeply. I popped the skin, letting the fangs penetrate gradually until she gasped in sudden, mortal fear. She struggled, then subsided abruptly and lay still as she surrendered to the powerful suction . . . feeling her blood rush out of her body as it entered mine.

I drank deeply, fighting not to lose control as the heady sensuality of her perfect essence triggered sexual desire that could not be denied. Now she was aroused. Her heels drummed madly on the bed, beating out a tattoo of passion desperately seeking release. I sucked harder, reveling in her blood, its hot red taste. We were at the threshold of danger. Stop now, I told myself. Think of the even greater pleasure that can be taken. And take it . . . *now*!

Retracting my fangs, I licked away all traces of blood. My tongue pleasured the wound insistently. She came alive then, twisted to kiss me hungrily, and we were a coiling, twisting maelstrom of lips, limbs, hands as the comforter exploded off our naked bodies and we writhed through a perfect storm of lust and love.

She screamed, a power-shout of pure pleasure. Seeking me with her hands, she adeptly transformed us, at last, into one being . . . *Iamyouyouareme* . . .

Chapter Thirty-Five

I think we dozed a while, or slept, in some kind of wonderful lassitude.

"Please get the comforter, Clark," she said finally. "We're naked. And I want to talk."

"Uh-oh, the talk thing."

"Shut up."

"I thought you wanted me to talk?"

"*Funny* vampire!"

"Thank you."

"*Not* a compliment."

"Honey, we're having our first fight."

"Bite me," she smiled.

Arranging the comforter, I lay down beside her. Once again, she pulled it totally over our heads, encasing us in a cozy cocoon, or, in her imagery, a grave.

"I like being like this with you," she said.

Yep. She wanted to do the talk thing. I kissed her, taking my time, figuring it would be my last chance for a while. And it was. But ignore these curmudgeonly asides. I won't pretend that I wasn't enjoying every minute of this intimate world she had created. When I finally let her come up for air, she snuggled even closer and commanded sweetly, "Now tell me the story of your life . . . or lives."

"Not much to tell," I said. "The first three-hundred years kinda zipped by. Then I met you."

She shot me a warning look. I'd apparently hit my kidding-around limit.

"Tell me about Ludmilla," she said.

Yeah, I sighed inwardly, let's cut right to the chase. And why not? It was actually a good place to begin, right at the dawning of my identity as a fully formed young man getting the first inkling that loving someone can actually shape your destiny. In moments, I was surprised to find myself speaking quite easily of things I had never revealed.

Only once had I ever felt the urge to tell anyone of my human life or the centuries that unfolded after I entered the world of the undead. I had actually been on the verge of revealing what I am to my best friend of all time, Jimmy Dean, but left it too long. I'd endlessly cursed my hesitation after he died in that stupid car crash. There's no question that had the adventurous, mystical Jimmy known who and what I was, he would have begged for conversion and become my motorcycle-riding buddy for all eternity. And, yes, it had been a lonely old world without him. How good it would have been to share my secrets, my very existence, with someone I cared deeply about.

How good it felt now.

Knowing where Taylor's query about Ludmilla was going, I answered her unspoken question and confirmed what Ludmilla had already told her—that we'd never consummated our love. And when I mentioned the shocking revelation Ludmilla had made about her father on that warm, sunny afternoon in Romania, she wept.

"It is the worst thing that can happen to a girl," she sobbed. "Believe me, I know."

I held her tight, not asking the question yet. Suppressing my fury.

After a while, she said, "When I met Ludmilla that night on the beach, I knew I had fallen in love with you. She was so beautiful, and I was so jealous. I wanted to hurt you, and it would have been easy because I was attracted to her. When we disappeared up the beach in the darkness, I was absolutely going to do her. I knew it would make you crazy.

"But then . . . I couldn't. I just couldn't. For once in my life, I did the right thing. And it felt good. I mean, I don't feel I'm as wicked or evil as people make me out to be. But I can't blame that perception on anyone but myself, I guess. Ever since my mother shoved me into show business when I was little girl, I learned that so-called 'stars' can get away with almost any awful behavior. So I just started doing whatever the fuck I felt like doing—no matter who got hurt. I got an itch, I scratched it. That's why I was always in trouble. But I usually got away with it, because of what I am . . . a boldface name, a fucking celebrity! But believe it or not, sometimes I'd feel really awful about it."

Tears started flowing again.

I told her, "That's what originally steered me to you. You were always wrecking cars, getting fucked up on drugs and booze, throwing glasses in clubs. But people in the know kept telling me you were more than you appeared to be—that if you made it to the set, you worked hard and were terrific to everybody, not just the big shots. But then, you'd have these mega-death meltdowns. The consensus around town was that you were doomed. And I sensed a story . . . a tabloid tale of a Hollywood dream gone to hell."

She laughed through her tears then. "How the hell do you *write* that crap?

But it's true . . . that's why people love it, I guess."

I kissed her closed eyelids.

She looked up at me and said, "You know how it works. The older you get, the harder it gets to change. You just don't feel as awful about the shit you do. But then you came along with your siren song, plucking at a young girl's heartstrings by playing white knight. And you finally made me do, for once, the right thing. I should have been inspired to do that long ago, by the people who supposedly love me. But it's hard to believe your mother really loves you after you catch her fucking your young boyfriends *twice*. Not to mention my piece-of-shit father who molested me. No, no . . . it wasn't them, it was *you* who made me feel like I can be a decent person, not a pathetic egomaniac, so self-centered she doesn't get how painfully alone she is."

Before I knew it, I was hugging her so hard she gasped. I eased off, making up for it with a soft but impassioned kiss that was all about love, not sex. We came up for air and stared into each other's eyes.

"But that night," she said, "I did it right, for once. I stopped to consider *you* before carrying out my evil little seduction plan. And that's when I knew I'd fallen in love . . . with a vampire. Not the boy next door, of course, but now I don't feel alone anymore."

We got in some really good kissing then. No sex. Not for the moment, anyway. She still wanted to talk about feelings and shit. But that was okay, because . . .

So did I.

Good thing, too.

There'd be little time for talk later, as it turned out.

Chapter Thirty-Six

Glowing shafts of sunlight filtered through shuttered French doors that opened onto the balcony. I opened my eyes. Taylor was a pretty picture, lying naked beside me, one arm thrown back over her head, breasts rising and falling with each breath. First thought: Initiate further pleasurable contact; never can have too much of a good thing. Second thought: Where the hell's that damn comforter?

I reached out a hand, groped around the mattress but encountered nothing. Reluctantly opening both eyes, I spotted it on the carpet next to my side of the bed. Snatching it up, I spread it over us both again, smiling at the memory of how—in the midst of our second bout of lovemaking—Taylor had suddenly turned sexual aggressor, throwing off the comforter and straddling me like a cowgirl busting a bronco. Most amazing memory: She did what women rarely do if you give them even a second to think about it—left the lights on during sex.

YEE-HAA!

Oh, what a visual! To quote Frankie Valli, *"Oh, what a night . . . hypnotizing, mesmerizing . . . sweet surrender, what a night!"*

The third time, we *took* our time, ramping up slowly, then getting wildly physical and adventurous, not to mention sweaty. Finally exploding off a towering peak high enough to trigger nosebleed, we slowly and happily slid back down the slippery slope of desire, drifting into what seemed an endless sleep of the kind enjoyed by . . . my kind.

Now I contemplated kissing her awake, but my cell phone suddenly buzzed in my pants—which were ten feet away on the carpet. I slid off the bed quietly, padded over and yanked it from a pocket, glad I'd silenced the ringer last night.

"Hello?"

"Boss, can you talk?"

"If need be, Renfield."

"I figured you'd want to know right away. That tail we had on little Miss You-Know-Who just paid off."

Cara Prescott. Had a private dick dogging her for two days.

"So you've tracked her to the Mystery Geezer's door? Who is it?"

Wally chuckled. Rare, for him. I knew this was going to be good.

And it was.

"The perp is her pimp's grandfather!"

Wow! If this was for my column, I'd write: My eyelids shot up like busted window shades.

"Am I hearing you right, Renfield? First name rhymes with boo-hoo-hoo?"

Never say names on the phone.

"Right on, boss."

Montague Kane!

Goddam. It really *was* him! And I'd pooh-poohed the idea. Forgotten what I'd pounded into heads of journalism students at Columbia University and Berkeley—not to mention Howard Stern, Geraldo Rivera, Bill O'Reilly, Larry King, Nancy Grace, et. al., *and* my own reporters: *Truth is stranger than fiction!*

Roma Kane pimping out her young hottie girlfriends to her billionaire granddaddy, who's . . . what . . . eighty-eight years old?

Only in Hollywood, folks.

"Wally, I love this dirty town!"

"Well, we're really sniffing the sweet smell of success now, boss. So . . . what's our next move?"

I ruminated a second. "Ordinarily, I'd be ashamed to admit that intelligent thought eludes me, but this absolutely boggles. It's what one might call a headline-making revelation."

"You can say that again."

"I can—but I won't. Seriously, dear boy, I think I need to tear myself away from the . . . uh, business meeting I'm in right now, and meet you for waffles drenched in blueberry goo. That should shock my thought processes. Say, forty-five minutes?"

"Very goo, boss . . . uh, I mean, very good."

I chuckled. "My, aren't we in a *gooood* mood, Renfield?"

"I'm a sucker for a story that breaks funny—even if it's not 'funny ha-ha.' See you at Dupar's, Master."

I clicked off, snatched up my pants and slipped them on. A voice behind me said, "*Goo?*"

I turned, smiling. "Oh look, Baby's awake. Goo-goo to you, *too*, precious. And ga-gaa! Now give Daddy a big kiss."

"Okay, whip it back out."

I waggled a finger sternly. "*Bad* girl . . . gonna spank!"

"Promise? . . . OH! . . . Ow, ow . . . *OOOW!*"

"Okay, I'll stop."

"Don't you *dare!*"

After a moment of rolling around kissing, she said with a pout, "Do you *have* to leave?"

"It's work, babe. You catch another hour or so, grab a shower and coffee, and I'll pick you up here for brunch in Pacific Palisades."

She smiled lazily up at me. "Yeah, maybe I need a beauty nap. Don't know *what's* made me so tired. Hey, take my car. Keys are on that little table by the front door."

I threw on my clothes, kissed her again and was gone. Precisely at eight thirty, I strolled into Dupar's and joined Wally, who was firing on all cylinders.

"When my phone rang this morning, boss, the last thing I expected to hear was that Cara was getting a seven a.m. booty call," he began after I'd ordered my waffles *avec geu bleu.* "But it was just like our source said—a limo with blacked-out windows picked her up and took her to Kane's huge estate up above Mulholland Drive. It's gated, of course, so our PI's parked outside. There's a rear gate, but we've got another PI watching that. And I've got two of our photographers hidden up on slopes around the property with telephoto lenses and video cameras. No telling how long she'll stay up there. But don't you find it weird that the old guy would call for his little cutie at the crack of dawn?"

I grinned. "Many a man has awakened with dreams of a crack at dawn, Renfield. Our guy does seem a bit old to be developing morning wood, but who knows? Hey, how many movie moguls in this town get illegal stem cell or testosterone shots from that Swiss doc in Beverly Hills so they can keep banging teenagers? Anyway, we sit tight until the limo moves, then try to snatch pics as she exits the house."

I leaned back as the waitress laid my colorful breakfast plate down.

"Okay, Wally, let's run down the possibilities here. Even if we can manage to waylay Cara—say, after she exits the limo at her house—she's got no reason to talk to us. And we certainly can't offer her money for an interview when she's banging a guy who could easily outbid any offer *The Revealer* makes. As for directly contacting Kane, or trying to intimidate him in any way, it's not even worth thinking about. Agreed?"

"Agreed, boss. Unless we rattle his cage by threatening to tip off the cops?"

I shook my head. "This guy owns the cops—or the cops' bosses. And what's the charge? Being rich enough to attract young pussy? Although . . . hey, wouldn't it be a laugh to open fire by hitting Roma Kane with a *pimping* charge? But really, for the moment anyway, I suggest we simply let the pot simmer. From what I've heard about Kane's castle, there's not much chance of us slipping one of our guys in there, right?"

"No, the place is crawling with security. We've ID'd the old man's master suite. It's up on the third floor—actually, it's the *whole* third floor—but all the windows are shuttered, and overhung with low awnings. No chance of using a high-tech telephoto rig. We're working all the angles, like checking out whether he hires his household staff from one of the agencies where we've got the fix in to see if we can get a maid or housekeeper to talk. And after Cara's dropped off today, our PI will follow the limo, then tail the driver after he drops it wherever. There's always a good chance that the guy'll open up if we offer him a payday, like most drivers in this town. But what's he going to know, really?"

I wolfed down the last bit of waffle, savoring the blueberries. "Yeah, you're probably right, but you never know. Cara may start yapping to the guy. How many times have we gotten stories because even major Hollywood stars can't stop running off at the mouth once they get locked in a limo alone? Limo drivers are like bartenders. People just naturally start confiding in them. But let's not hold our breath on that one. Just keep doing what you're doing, and remember this—even with what we know right now, we could publish a story. Even without spelling out details, it's the fascinating tale of movie starlet Cara Prescott's mystery relationship with one of the world's top tycoons: 'Rich, Aging Recluse Secretly Romancing 20-Something Hollywood Hottie?' Even that would sell papers."

I peered over at Wally. He was furiously writing down my impromptu headline. I shook my head. The guy's maddeningly compulsive, just like the real Renfield. Glad I had him.

He looked at his watch and said, "I'd better get back to the team, set a few things in motion. We've got a few days to work on this, but still . . . you going to the office?"

I shook my head. "Not today. I'm meeting someone for brunch. While I'm here, I'll just walk around the Farmers Market and The Grove. Check out the Apple store and Barnes & Noble. You go ahead if you want to, and I'll catch the check."

He collected his stuff and started to leave the table. I stopped him with: "Hey, there's another upside to this already. We've got a hell of a bargaining chip if Roma Kane sics her lawyers on us over the dog-killer story we just put to bed!"

Wally not only smiled, he actually laughed his ass off all the way to the exit. He really lives for this shit. We all do.

But then, the laughter died.

Chapter Thirty-Seven

Here's how it all went down: I drove back to the house in Mandeville Canyon and picked up Taylor. We stopped at a Starbucks in Pacific Palisades, grabbing lattes to go. She wanted to unwind, go shopping on Robertson, so I drove her back to West Hollywood. And while I dutifully followed her in and out of trendy boutiques, our lives were invaded when a phone rang at a suite of offices in an old Art Deco building miles away on Hollywood Boulevard. A female voice answered.

"FangBanging.com, good afternoon . . ."

The female voice on the line said, "Hello . . . I'd like to speak to whoever is in charge, please."

"Well, that would be me, mostly. How can I help you?"

"I have something incredible for sale."

"Can you be more specific, please?"

"It's a sex tape, very hot."

"Does it have a vampire angle?"

"Yes."

"Well, we might be interested, of course, but—"

"It involves two famous people."

A pause. "Well, it depends on who—"

"*Very* famous people!"

"Okay, but you'll have to tell me who—"

"Look, let's cut to the chase here. I'm not going to tell you a damn thing until you send me a signed nondisclosure form. I presume you've done that before? Send it right now to the fax number that I've just sent to your e-mail address. My lawyer is sitting right here. If he's happy with the nondisclosure form, I'll come to your office now and we can get down to business. And when you see what I have, it will blow your fucking mind. I'm only ten minutes away from you. Okay?"

"Er, yes . . . of course. Okay, I see your fax number, and . . . give me a second, please . . . ah, here's the form . . . so . . . I'm sending you the form even as we speak, and . . . okay, there it goes . . . is your machine receiving it yet?"

"Yes, here it comes. Hold on . . ."

Linda Purcell, Senior VP of FangBanging.com—a wildly popular website specializing in kinky porn featuring pro and amateur freaks tarted up like vampires—felt a tiny tingle of excitement. The woman on the phone sounded so totally no-nonsense and businesslike. Linda hoped she was telling the truth about her sex vid featuring "two famous people." Because Linda's dream for FangBanging.com was to someday acquire star hardcore, like the Paris Hilton and Kim Kardashian sex tapes, but with a twist—tapes of real-life celebrities fucking in vampire drag. Rumor had it that such tapes actually existed, fueled by the current craze for vampire books and television shows. Probably bullshit, in the opinion of her boss, the website's owner, but maybe not.

"Hope springs eternal," he'd said, the last time they'd discussed it. "Imagine if there'd been tape rolling when Roma Kane got banged by Damon Strutt in his *Bold Blood* vampire costume."

"Hello?"

The phone voice shook Linda out of her reverie.

"Yes . . . yes, I'm here."

"Okay, we've got your signed nondisclosure form, barring you from ever revealing what you're going to see, even if we never do business. My lawyer's okay with it. Now I'll tell you what *I've* got, but I'm not saying names over the phone. Look at your e-mail again."

"I'm looking . . . okay, it's—"

HOLY SHIT!

Linda went into total mind-fuck. Speechless, she stared at the two names on the screen. The voice on the phone burbled, "Hello? . . . HELLO! . . . Are you there, or what?"

Linda fought for control, then said, "Yes . . . uh . . . sorry. My screen . . . uh, didn't come up right away."

"So? What do you think? Those names *famous* enough for you?"

"Yes . . . yes, they certainly are."

"Are you ready to do business now, or do I go somewhere else, like Vivid? They'd love this, but it's perfect for your site because of the vampire angle. And let me be clear—I want a *lot* of money."

Linda caught her breath, then said calmly, "Our owner will need to be present to evaluate your video and negotiate the price. Let me contact him and set up a meeting. I'll call you right back. What's your number?"

"*My* number? In your dreams. I'll call *you* back in fifteen minutes. Set up a meeting for three o'clock."

Click.

"Bitch," hissed Linda. She picked up her cell phone, speed-dialed.

"Hello?"

"Are you sitting down?"

"Hey, sis, what's—"

"Shut up and listen. A woman just called, wants to come in and show us video of two famous people having sex. Says there's a vampire angle. That's all she'll say, but she wants a meeting in an hour."

"Hey, can't you handle—"

"Shut UP! And look at your e-mail for the names of the two famous people."

"Okay, hold on . . . I'm looking and . . . WHOA!"

"That's what I thought you'd say. So . . ."

"Did the woman who called you ID herself? I'm assuming not."

"No. She's calling back in about five minutes. She wants to set a meeting for three o'clock. And she left no forwarding number, so . . ."

"Damn. Linda, set the meeting. Then call me right back."

"Okay."

Click.

Moments later, the phone rang. It was her, right on time.

"Okay, we will see you here at three," Linda told her. "Bring the video and—this is important—*all* copies that exist. If we decide to do business, you'll need to sign a legal document attesting that you've given us the original and *all* copies."

"Of course. At three, then."

Click.

Chapter Thirty-Eight

Two minutes before three o'clock, a manicured finger pressed the bell outside the always-locked door of the FangBanging.com office. Inside her private office, Linda checked her watch and hit the buzzer that unlocked the reception area door. An imperious female voice said:

"Hello? *Where* are you?"

Linda had sent the receptionist home. Through the half-open door of her office, she called out. "In here."

Linda's eyed widened as the stylishly dressed, perfectly coiffed woman walked through the door. Recognizing her instantly, she rose and said:

"Roma Kane. What a pleasure."

"And you are?"

"Linda Purcell, senior vice president. Are you alone? I thought your lawyer—"

"He's instantly available by phone. And your owner?"

"Just called to say he's been delayed a few minutes. But please sit down and we can begin. Before you show me what you have, does your lawyer feel that your ownership of this tape can't be challenged? Legally, I mean."

Roma smiled thinly. "Anything can be challenged. But there's no question it's legally mine. Even though the subjects were not aware they were being taped, they had no right to privacy, under its legal definition. Now . . . I have a DVD copy here. Shall we get on with it?"

Linda took the DVD to her desk, slipped it into the tray of her computer-projector. A screen dropped down on the opposite wall and the lights dimmed.

Roma took a seat. "Just a few seconds after the action begins, I'm going to ask you to hit the freeze-frame. You'll see why. Okay, here we go . . . our hero throws her down onto the bed and . . . here it comes . . . and . . . *freeze!* Okay, there you are, Linda. *That's* the money shot. That's what makes this tape so absolutely perfect for FangBanging! Check out those choppers!"

Linda, mesmerized, leaned forward intently, focusing on the scene. No question about it. The man—lips drawn back in sexual hunger so naked Linda felt an inner thigh twitch—was sporting a savage-looking set of vampire fangs.

"Look almost real, don't they?" said Roma. "I envy the girl."

She looked over at Linda, smiling a bit more warmly. "As you may have heard in the gossip columns a while back, the whole vampire thing turns me on—me and just about every other woman on the planet, it seems. But then, that's why you guys are in business, right? Okay, let's watch it now—or as much as you want to watch. It's irresistible. A world-famous movie star and one of Hollywood's most notorious players—fucking *vampire style!*"

Linda hit play and images exploded into motion. The man and woman embraced on the huge bed, then disappeared under its comforter. There was an abrupt edit. Suddenly, the woman was standing by the bed, stripping off her clothes. When she was naked, the man approached her almost reverently, kneeled, said something inaudible, then kissed her hand.

"The sound's not great," said Roma, "but you'll hear them grunting and groaning big-time in a second."

The couple disappeared under the comforter. After another abrupt jump cut in the video, the woman threw off the comforter and the couple's naked bodies joined passionately. The action became almost unbearably intense. Linda thought her head would explode. Like many women, she found most porn flicks were mechanical, unsexy. Not this one. Waves of guilt washed over her. Watching this man was . . .

She shuddered involuntarily, turned away from the screen and said, "Why did the lighting suddenly change? It's almost like there's daylight in the room."

Roma rolled her eyes. "We've got two famous people vampire fucking, and you're worried about the *lighting*? You can *see* it, can't you? Oh, look, he's going down, down, down—"

"You've made your point. I can see just fine. Kill the play-by-play, please!"

Nearly twenty minutes went by before the man and woman achieved obvious completion and fell back exhausted. Linda's body tingled as she hit *Off.*

"Wow!"

Roma looked over and smiled. "If a man even spoke to me right now, I'd probably come. Is that a great tape, or what? And speaking of men, where the hell is your boss?"

Linda shrugged. "Traffic. He'll be here."

The speakerphone on her desk rang.

"Hello? Oh, hi, we were just talking about you . . . yeah, I just viewed it. It's sensational . . . oh, yeah, the vampire angle's solid. He's wearing fangs when they begin. You don't see them after that. Probably fell out, or he removed them. But we can do a big close-up of his mouth with the fangs, and maybe keep coming back to that . . . no, it's great, really! . . . Oh, you want me to . . . okay, hold on."

Plucking the portable headset from its stand, she walked over to Roma and handed her the phone. "He wants to talk to you."

Exasperated, Roma took it and snapped, "Hello? To whom am I speaking, please? Uh, wait . . . hey, where are you going?"

Linda was walking out of the office. She mouthed "ladies' room" at Roma and exited.

Putting the phone back up to her ear, Roma said, "Hello? . . . Look, your girl just left the office and—"

She recoiled as hot breath bathed her opposite ear.

"YOU'RE ALL ALONE NOW, YOU FUCKING *BITCH*!"

Screaming as terror paralyzed her, Roma toppled from her chair and hit the floor, her body spasming. A foot roughly booted her onto her back. Half-blinded by tears of panic, she stared up into glowing, enraged red eyes and uttered a strangled cry.

"Nooo . . . *Nooooo*!"

"Yes, you dog killing CUNT. IT'S ME! YOUR WORST NIGHTMARE! Go on, say my name . . . NOW!"

Jaws trembling, teeth literally chattering, Roma gasped:

"Clark . . . Kelly . . .!"

Chapter Thirty-Nine

Crouched over Roma's jerking, twitching body, I fought a powerful urge to reach down and snap her scrawny neck. First, this vicious skank had slowly poisoned the woman I love; now she threatened to ruin Taylor's career with a sex video secretly shot while we'd rolled around on *her* bed, blissfully fucking . . . and blissfully fucking unaware that we were on *Candid Camera*.

I leaned close to the blubbering bitch's face and vampire-roared: "READY TO DIE, WHORE?"

I flashed my most sinister leer, being careful *not* to flash my fangs. That Roma hadn't made me as a real vampire was *the* luckiest break yet in this bizarre debacle. When I'd apprehensively viewed the tape in an editing booth as Linda rolled it simultaneously for Roma in the main FangBanging office, I quickly realized *why* she hadn't.

Lucky break: the tape did NOT show me *flying* into the bedroom with Taylor in my arms, because Roma's hidden videocam wasn't set to switch on until it was triggered by body weight *actually hitting the bed*. And while the videocam caught a flash glimpse of my fangs just an instant before Taylor had yanked that huge comforter over us, Roma no doubt figured I'd inserted a set of those fake choppers you can buy at any Goth freak shop on Hollywood Boulevard. So we were just another horny couple—like her and Damon "Kragen" Strutt—playing fuck-the-vampire. And later in the video, when I emerged from under the covers to romp nude and lewd, I'd already sheathed my choppers.

Mystifying questions remained, however. Like . . . why the hell hadn't Taylor told me that the house she'd "borrowed" belonged to Roma? Well, that was easy enough. She'd wanted access to that ideal hideaway for our first sexual encounter, but knew I'd nix the deal instantly if she admitted Roma owned it.

Another nagging question: Roma wouldn't keep her secret videotaping gear switched on 24-7, so how had she known exactly when I'd show up with dick in hand? Because Taylor had *told* her, of course! My weeping wench had ultimately confessed all of this to me—but not until *after* I got the shocking phone call about Roma secretly selling our sex tape to FangBanging.com.

Next question: Who'd tipped *me* off about her sordid sale?

I smiled at sobbing Roma. "Guess who *really* owns FangBanging.com?"

She shook her head, turning away.

Gripping the witch's pointy little chin, I twisted her head back, locked my gaze on those terror-filled eyes and snarled:

"You're *looking* at him, skank. *I* own FangBanging!"

Shock popped her eyes wide open.

"That's right, stupid bitch," I told her. "You played your ace at the wrong table. I started this business myself, with a partner, and we've done incredibly well. You wouldn't believe how many people get off on the fantasy of fucking vampires! Oops, excuse me . . . no surprise to *you*, of course."

Okay. Torture, as Dick Cheney likes to say, can be fun. But enough is enough. There'd be torture aplenty for Roma in just a bit. I fished out my cell phone and called Linda.

"Hi . . . can you come back over here, please?"

I reached a hand down to Roma, who flinched and mewled like a frightened kitty as I pulled her up off the floor and sat her back down in her chair. Linda walked into the office and I told her, "Take this one to the ladies' room, let her clean up a little. If she tries to run, yell."

Linda nodded, escorted her out of the room.

I wasn't worried about letting Roma out of my sight. Linda, a single mom who works hard for her money, is one tough cookie. She runs the business for me and my partner—who's her big brother, and a super-smart guy. With those two at my back, I don't do much except dream up marketing ideas for FangBanging.

But, honestly? Sex-plus-vampires is a business that sells itself, with a little help. That's why Linda gets a five percent profit rake-off, and a hefty salary—and I'd given her brother forty percent ownership, because he's the one guy I can trust in all things.

Big-time.

His name?

Wally Tate.

That's right . . . good old Renfield!

SURPRISE!

Chapter Forty

Now . . . let me *really* blow your mind—vampire-style!

Here's how it had all gone down.

I'd taken Wally's bombshell phone call three hours ago.

He'd told me urgently, "Linda just called, boss. Good news and bad news. Roma Kane's trying to peddle what she claims is a sex videotape of you and . . . Taylor Logan."

"What the fuck?"

"Yeah, sorry, boss. But here's the good news: She's contacted our very own FangBanging.com to negotiate. Says she wants two million for the tape. Linda hasn't seen the footage yet. Roma wants to set up a meeting today at three to show the video to 'the owner' of FangBanging. Linda's asking how you want her to handle it."

Ah, *shit*! The shock of it hit so hard it hurt physically. I cursed myself.

Why had I never thought to ask Taylor the identity of the "friend" who'd loaned her the house for our assignation? That fucking Roma. I sighed. How to handle it, indeed?

"I know you're dying to crack a 'handle *this*' joke, Renfield—but don't. Yeah, guilty as charged. We've been punk'd by that evil cunt. I'll explain it to you later. Right now, tell Linda to set up the meeting with Roma. Tell her we'll get back to her in a few minutes, after I figure out how to unravel this mess."

Shit!

As soon as I hung up on Wally, the thought hit me that Linda, his sister, was about to witness me doing the wild thang on video! Well, nothing you can do about that, I told myself. So stop thinking about it. Focus on damage control, and . . . AH! . . . I suddenly had it. Desperation often breeds inspiration. Fight fire with fire, that's the ticket! But fight *fast*.

Five minutes later, after interrupting our shopping interlude to tell Taylor I needed to leave suddenly, we had a rather intense exchange that left her standing on Robertson Boulevard about to burst into tears as I sped off in the car Renfield had sent over. In less than thirty minutes, the driver dropped me off in a neighborhood of exclusive, wooded estates just below Mulholland Drive, the twisty road that winds along the top of the mountain range that bisects Los Angeles and the San Fernando Valley. I told him to wait and quickly started walking up the hill.

Two minutes later, I turned a corner, slipped into a wooded area and launched into low-level flight just above the treetops. In less than a minute, I had reached my target unobserved. There it was, spread out below me, just as Wally had described it—the imposing mansion owned by Montague Kane set on ten wooded acres, fancy pool and pool house, meandering fishpond set in a copse of trees, huge guesthouse, the works.

I hovered overhead, carefully using the trees for cover. The property was surrounded by a high wall. There was a small gatehouse with a guard reading a newspaper. I raked the grounds for roaming security or guard dogs. Nothing. I'd been told there was a suite of apartments in the basement where extra security bunked, but they never emerged unless summoned. Concentrating then on the wide patio surrounding half of the third floor, I peered into the shadows created by awnings that swooped out and down from tightly shuttered windows, but saw nothing. Not one peephole chink in Kane's armor, dammit. But if I couldn't see him, he probably couldn't see me.

I suddenly shot out of the trees in an eyeblink, landing cat-silent on the patio. A moment later, bringing my acute hearing to bear, I heard voices inside: One male, one female. Good! Cara was still here.

Levitating about six inches off the patio deck, I floated silently along the perimeter of the huge patio. The voices faded as I moved. And when I suddenly heard them no more, I knew I'd passed the room they were in. Descending lightly to the deck, I quickly found what I'd been looking for— a door. I tried it. The knob turned easily. A second later, I was inside the magnificently decorated sitting room of Montague Kane's huge master suite.

Just off it, I spotted a book-lined study, a formal dining room and a kitchen. And behind glass-paned French doors, there was a well-equipped gym. Totally self-contained, I thought. The old man never has to leave the third floor if he doesn't want to. Cautiously, I flitted through the rooms, keeping an eye out for servants. As I expected, there were none. And never were, probably, whenever the old master was enjoying the company of prime young pussy supplied by his doting granddaughter.

Quietly, I approached massive mahogany double doors leading to the master bedroom. They were closed, of course. Instead of knobs, there were massive brass levers, the kind you push down to open. Locked from the inside? I had a strong feeling my luck would hold. But before trying to gain entrance, I wanted to know what I'd be facing on the other side of that door. I've explained what my kind call 'mind-rolling.' Projecting power through the wooden panel, I mind-rolled Cara Prescott, looking out through her eyes at a bizarre, unsettling scene.

Wrinkled, wizened Montague Kane, wearing diapers and a bib, was sitting in an adult-size baby's high chair. Face screwed up in a pout, the old man twisted his head side to side, making cranky baby noises as he ducked spoonsful of the mashed baby food Cara kept trying to push between his lips.

"Bad baby," she cried. "Bad, *bad* baby!"

Cara—naked except for an emerald necklace, Louboutin high heels, black sheer stockings and a garter belt—suddenly yanked the spoon away from the grimacing geezer, stuck it in a bowl on a side table and yelled:

"Baby must eat . . . you *must* eat, do you hear me? You need your strength, so *here!*"

Moving close to the adult-sized high chair, Cara grabbed Kane's head and thrust one naked breast into his mouth. Instantly, "Baby" stopped fighting and started suckling noisily.

That was my cue. Thoroughly engrossed, if that's the word, Kane and Cara never heard a slight click as I pushed down on the door's brass lever, opening it just wide enough to slip through, then quietly closing it behind me as I dropped to the floor and lay perfectly still.

But finally, after a moment of listening to Cara's squeals and Kane's enthusiastic grunts, I realized I probably could have marched past them at the head of a brass band, for all the notice they'd have taken. Kane's suckling noises were obscenely loud as Cara, chanting nonstop in a rhythmic rant of cooing approval, pulled his face ever tighter to her bountiful bosom.

"Good baby . . . good, good baby . . . Nanny *loves* feeding baby . . . oh, baby is feeding so *good* . . . Nanny is *sooo* excited!"

They were sideways to me, over against the opposite wall of the huge master bedroom. Taking in the layout, I spotted a closet ten feet to my right. Timing my move, I waited until Cara emitted what sounded like a loud squeal of pain, then slithered like a snake across the carpet, well below their sightline, and darted inside. It was a huge walk-in, lined with racks of hanging clothes. Perfect. Leaving the door slightly ajar, I reached into my jacket pocket and extracted the mini-videocam that I'd requisitioned on Robertson Boulevard—in exchange for a pocketful of cash—from one of the photogs who perennially patrols there, snapping gotcha's of celeb chicks out hitting boutiques.

Bringing the viewfinder to my eye, I fired up and began recording the weird, creepy scene unfolding before me. Even now, I find it almost impossible to describe. It played less like sex, more like psychodrama. And I wondered what roiling, deep-seated emotions would drive a brilliant man like Kane—who'd single-handedly built one of the world's greatest business empires—to seek sexual satisfaction as an adult baby in a highchair? I'll spare you the blow-by-blow, but the action suddenly notched up to frenzied intensity when Cara scrambled up and straddled the old perv, demanding:

"Are you hiding something big in your diaper, bad boy? Don't try to stop me from looking, you little monster . . . Nanny needs to see what's in your diaper *now!*"

Jesus.

I stuck it out as Cara truly began earning whatever sum Kane paid for her services. For her sake, I hoped it was obscenely high! Judging subjectively, by the way, I had to admit Cara was more than hot enough to arouse even an old dude like Kane. Looking like a teenager didn't hurt, either. But for me, the creepy context snuffed the stirring of even involuntary sexual arousal.

I concentrated on the job at hand, continued videotaping until the . . . uh, climax. I'd wondered if there'd be one, actually . . . until Kane suddenly started gasping, wheezing and crying out. He'd either hit his peak—or desperately needed an ambulance. Finally, after a minute or two, he subsided, leaned back in his high chair.

"*Good* baby," said Cara—rather perfunctorily, I thought. Then she flounced off toward the bathroom. Time to fly, I thought. Wait until they're both distracted and . . .

"Where's my *fucking* bathrobe, goddammit! What fucking good are you, Cara, if you can't do things right? Do I have to call my goddam maid, you lazy *bitch*?"

Kane's abrupt outburst startled me. Suddenly, this was no passive little old baby acting out his pathetic dream of sexual rebirth. This was an imperious, cranky old rich prick ordering the hired help around. Cara, who'd just closed the bathroom door, emerged like she'd been shot and rushed straight across the room toward the closet where I was hiding. Fading quickly into its depths, I hid behind a rack of hanging suits. Cara slammed open the door, reached inside, grabbed a wooly white Turkish robe hanging behind it, and was gone.

As the old prick started barking at her again, I opened the closet door a crack and resumed videotaping. Glad I did. But it was heart-rending. The old bastard kept haranguing Cara as she stood there, naked, obviously humiliated, looking like a bullied high school girl.

He finally dismissed her with a contemptuous wave of his gnarled hand, and she turned back toward the bathroom. The angle was perfect, and I caught a heart-rending close-up of Cara's tear-streaked face. As she walked out of frame, I did a smash-cut back to the old shit, capturing his expression of pure sadistic pleasure as he watched her retreat. I turned again swiftly and caught Cara, just for a split second in my viewfinder; I saw her tears stop abruptly as a foxy little smile creased her lips.

Jesus. So it was *all* girlie theater! Even for a hardened tabloid gossip bottom-feeder, this whole perverted tableaux ranked as one of the creepiest things I'd ever witnessed. But I now had it locked in the can, and that's my job. Period.

Time to fly. I slipped out of the closet and onto the patio, launched and went airborne over the woods above Mulholland Drive. Moments later, I hopped into my waiting car and blasted off toward Hollywood Boulevard and the FangBanging offices, checking my watch. Good. Even with traffic, I'd make the three o'clock meeting, no sweat. So . . .

Fight fire with fire.

Check.

Fight fast!

Check.

Hit 'em so hard they'll never rise again!

Chapter Forty-One

When Linda brought Roma back into the office from the ladies' room, she shot me a warning glance. Something had changed. Amazing what a splash of cold water in the kisser will do for a girl's spirits.

Roma's trademark sneer was pasted back on her face, and her lip curled as she planted herself in front of me and snarled defiantly.

"I'm leaving. *Unless* you hold me against my will, of course . . . and *that* would be kidnapping!"

I'd been holding onto her purse. Now I reached inside it, tossed over her cell phone. She caught it and looked at me, confused.

"Call *anyone* you want, bitch. Call the cops, call in the fucking Marines . . . or maybe your grandfather? He'll protect you, right? Or will he? But then, you don't really *need* protection right now . . . not from me, at least."

She gestured at her purse, still sitting in my lap. I tossed it to her.

"Look," she said impatiently, still acting like she was the smartest head in the room, "you can keep that fucking video of you and your little whore. I brought you *all* the copies, so you don't have to worry about me putting it out there."

I shot her a cold grin, held it. She started looking scared again.

"You know what your problem is, Roma? You never hang out with people smarter than you are. Ergo, you think everyone is stupid. Don't ever make the mistake of insulting my intelligence again. You really think I'm dumb enough to believe you haven't hidden away a copy of that video? So you can sell it to some other porn website if FangBanging.com screws you over or our check doesn't clear? You think I'm a moron, you lowlife parasite? Do you believe, knowing what I do for a living, that a vapid celebu-skank like you can *outsmart* me? You really believe you can *fuck me over*?"

Yeah, she was scared. Now for the finishing touch. I roared, with just a touch of vampire in my voice: "WELL? . . . DO YOU?"

She staggered back, terrified and cowed again.

(Aaaand, that's the way . . . uh-*huh*, uh-*huh* . . . I like it!)

Linda jerked Roma's arm, sat her down in a chair. The bitch immediately started babbling denials that she was holding a hideout tape.

I leaned in close and told her, "I don't care if you do or you don't! If you do, and it ever sees the light of day, you're a dead woman, period. But just before you die, you'll face the horror of witnessing *this* unspeakably pervy tape released on the Internet. Watch the monitor screen again, please."

I picked up the remote, hit *Play*. The screen flickered to life.

She gasped. Linda gasped. And I commenced a blow-by-blow narration.

"Look, Roma . . . isn't that Gramps in a baby's high chair? And in a *diaper*? WOW! . . . Oh, and there's your good friend, Cara . . . omigosh, the girl's naked, except for accessories! Fishnets, garter belt—and what *great* shoes, eh? Hey, want some popcorn?"

Linda buried her face in her hands. Roma screamed. Leaping up from her chair, she made a run for the door. It took her less than a second to get to it, but I was already there barring her way, arms crossed and shaking my head reprovingly as she broke down in panic and sobbed hysterically.

I smiled down at her. "Really, Miss Kane, I thought you were made of sterner stuff. Pull yourself together, please. Just sit down, and get one thing through your head—if you walk out of here, I'll release that video of Montague Kane playing kinky games in baby diapers with one of your best friends. A baby-doll YOU pimped to Gramps! I'd say that might be the death knell of the whole Kane dynasty, wouldn't you?"

Linda, looking shaky and pale, had paused the video. She grabbed Roma, shoved her back into her seat. Then she whispered to me, "Clark, I don't think I can watch this . . ."

I whispered back, "Linda, just sit, please. Avert your eyes if you have to, but I need a witness, *capisce*?"

She took a deep breath, nodded. "Sorry."

"Don't sweat it."

Turning to Roma, I said, "Let me make this as easy as possible. I'll show you the key elements of this disgusting video, and fast-forward through the rest. And may I add that your acting all sensitive is the height of hypocrisy, considering that this kinky production sprang from your diabolical decision to pimp for Grandpop! Oh, and we've got a socko ending, by the way. Very powerful! I particularly want you to see that."

I hit *Play* again.

Chapter Forty-Two

Sparing them the queasy ordeal I'd had to endure, I zipped through the tape in about ten minutes, but clicked out of fast-forward just before it ended.

"Now here's that powerful closing scene I promised, Roma. Watch closely, please. You should be very proud."

It was even more wrenching than I'd remembered; Cara, naked and vulnerable, hurrying away from the creepy, sadistic, wrinkled "baby." Then that close-up of the girl's tear-stained face . . .

I looked over at Linda. She was open-mouthed, eyes moist.

Roma? No goddam reaction, except maybe annoyance.

I hit *Stop.*

Roma snarled, "Are you really going to fuck with *me*? Do you know what I could do to you?"

I smiled. "Get real, rich bitch! In Hollywood, I'm referred to as 'the man who knows everything,' so I know exactly who I'm fucking with. And here's how it works, Ms. Kane—your stupid, rich-girl arrogance knows no bounds, so I imagine you'll call your powerful lawyers and order them to cook up criminal or civil complaints against FangBanging.com and me, personally. But, as I'm sure they'll tell you, the chances of you prevailing are slim to none. And all of that will pale in contrast to the shit-storm that will bury you, your mommy and daddy, creepy old Grandpa, and the meal ticket that sustains your evil empire should the world ever lay eyes on this filthy video.

"Here's my suggestion, however. I pledge here and now that I will never tell anyone about this tape. And, presumably you never will, right? Because once the cat's out of the bag, it's out. And don't ever tell anyone about the video you shot of me and Taylor, or you're toast."

She started to speak. I held up a hand.

"Here's the final thing to consider, Roma Kane. On *The Revealer* side, my reporters and I are tying up the final loose ends on a blockbuster story that ties you to the dog killing, plus feeding the Brazilian killer drug Oxi to various victims—including the now-deceased Janet Carter, supposed friends Taylor Logan, and Cara Prescott—*and* evidence tying you and your smelly slave-boy, Scummy Bear, to Janet's . . . *murder.*"

"WHAT?"

She sprang to her feet, eyes flashing with rage. I'd watched her carefully during my little speech.

Murder was the demon word that pulled her trigger.

"Now you've gone too far!" she shrieked. "I didn't murder anybody, and —"

"State it correctly, lady. You might not *know* you helped kill somebody, but Scummy Bear definitely did the deed, which will make you an accessory before the fact. Now here's the funny thing: I believe you maybe *didn't* know the end result of your Oxi mischief. Because you just don't think that deeply. Hell, you even give Oxi to your best girlfriends on occasion, putting them in harm's way. It's like you're still the queen bee in high school, and the girls are the usual needy, ass-kissing weaklings who suck up to you for reflected glory rather than find their own honorable place in the sun.

"You're a hateful fucking bully, whore. Now get the fuck out of my sight before I puke all over your Christian Louboutins!"

Linda stood up suddenly.

"Yay, boss!" Then she whirled, glaring at Roma. "On your feet and out the door, bitch. You know the way. Say another word, I'll slap the shit out of you."

The door slammed. Buh-bye, Roma.

Ding, dong, the witch is gone!

Chapter Forty-Three

Playing it low-profile, I strolled down Canon Drive in Beverly Hills, sipping a Peete's latte and window-shopping. Just a face in the crowd.

When I came to the sweeping brick courtyard of the mega-swanky Montage hotel, I paused, staring like I'd never seen anything like it back in Kansas, by golly. Tossing my latte cup into a trash receptacle, I casually walked toward the busy front entrance. Valets and doormen barely noticed me. Just another tourist.

Once inside the hotel, I rubber-necked the restaurant, the newsstand, then strolled past the elevator bank. When a descending car opened on the floor and stood empty, I slipped inside and punched eight. A quick ride later, I was punching the bell outside suite 809. The door swung wide, and there she was, looking sad and defeated.

Stepping inside and kicking the door shut, I gathered her in my arms and said, "How I've missed you."

Her body shook suddenly. She sobbed. "I'm sorry . . . I'm so, *so sorry*. Please forgive me!"

"Okay, stop it," I said. "Yes, you should have told me that the pad we were shacking up in was Roma's place—or, as I like to call it, Soundstage 69. Honey, you should see us on video. *So* friggin' hot! Especially the shot where you're on your knees and the camera's shooting right up your—"

"Stop!"

But now she was giggling a little. Looking up at me with that irresistible "I'm a naughty girl" pout, she said, "So . . . you're not really mad at me?"

I took that adorable face between my hands and covered her cheeks with kisses. She shivered in my arms. *Never* fails.

"Sweetheart, at least you didn't tell the bitch I'm a vampire. So come on, cheer up. I got cranky with you because Wally had just hit me with the news. Hey, your first hidden-camera sex tape is always a shocker—just ask Kim Kardashian, Paris Hilton or Pam Anderson!"

Then I laid one on those sweet, full lips. We stood there, kissing like horny teenagers for nearly five minutes, then came up for air.

I asked, "How do you like the suite?"

"Clark, I love it. I've always liked the Montage, but I've never stayed here. It rocks. What a great idea to book it."

"Well, I had to leave you on short notice earlier, babe, so it was the best idea I could come up with. Going back to Roma's pad was out of the question. And I knew you wouldn't want us to rendezvous at your Château Marmont suite. So, since you can't access my hidey-hole at the Four Seasons without me, I figured we needed a safe, neutral spot where we could chill and be together. The hotel staff knows you're here, of course, because you're a celebrity. But nobody made me downstairs, I'm certain, so now we're truly alone. I say we stay in, order up cocktails and dinner from room service, and then . . ."

I reached down and squeezed that gorgeous ass.

"And then *what*, mister?"

"And then . . . we stage our very first *off-screen* love scene!"

"God, you are one romantic vampire. Think we could spend eternity together, Dragomir?"

"Thought you'd never ask, girl."

Cue hugging and kissing, then . . . *wait for it!* The vampire speaks.

"You know what? I've got a sudden craving for a margarita. On the rocks, salt on the rim."

"Omigod, perfect. Out on the balcony."

"And then dinner in, and . . ."

" . . . And?"

We never got around to an actual dinner. I ordered a gang of appetizers with our drinks because margaritas always make me instantly ravenous. We just lazed around on the balcony, worked our way through the snacks, then cuddled up on a chaise lounge and gazed at the reddening sky as dusk chased the sun. Alive or dead, I have never spent happier moments. She talked; I looked at her adoringly.

My memory reeled back to that day in the haystack with Ludmilla, all those centuries ago. That's when it hit me: My dream was finally complete! I was experiencing that which I'd yearned for so desperately—the unique, giddy passion of first love. Unbelievably, it felt even more intense than it had when I was alive.

How inadequate words can be, I mused. I hadn't felt this alive when I *was* alive.

"Now that I've met you, I am not the person that I was."

For a split second, I thought I'd inadvertently blurted out what I'd been mulling. But it was she, not I, who had spoken.

"How strange," I said. "You just said exactly what I was thinking."

Her eyes, as she looked up at me, radiated a soft passion that resonated to the depths of my soul.

"Really?" she said. "Well . . . let me tell you what I mean, then you can tell me if it's what you were thinking. Okay . . . this may sound totally stupid, but right now, because of you, I don't feel . . . morally bankrupt, if that's the right term. I mean, I don't feel like taking a hit of coke, or getting wasted on booze, or hitting the nightclubs, or speeding like a fucking idiot in my car. I'm not angry, or anxious, or bored, or depressed. I mean, if I were still my old self—and you've written endlessly about my raging temper in your gossip column, right?—I'd be out prowling the clubs right now to find Roma, that fucking whore, so I could beat the shit out of her for videotaping us.

"But *look* at me. Clark! Look! I'm calm. Oh, I still hate the bitch and I'll get her eventually, but right now I'm totally chill. And it's all because of you, darling Dragomir. Loving you, and you loving me back, has . . . I don't know. It's just changed me, profoundly. Omigod, I must sound like some girl in a *Cosmo* article."

I laughed. "Funny how our most fundamental emotions are so . . . fundamental. Simple and moving. Yet when we experience them, we're confounded by how they transform us. Hey, all we can do is relax and enjoy, I guess."

She reached out for her margarita glass, took a sip, stayed silent for a moment.

"You said you were thinking *exactly* what was in my mind. So . . . *what?*"

I shrugged. "That I've finally experienced what I've wanted for centuries. That singular, giddy emotion we call first love."

Her answer was totally girlie-girl. "Aha, you've been thinking of Ludmilla, haven't you? Don't make me jealous, dude." Then she rolled her eyes and smiled slyly. "Just joking."

I kissed her and said, "Just for the record, lady, first love is even better the second time around. That's what I was thinking . . . and *now* who sounds like a *Cosmo* article?"

She snuggled even closer. "I just love that you love me . . . but enough with the love talk. Are we going to order dinner?"

"You hungry?"

"Not that much, really. Why don't we order another pitcher of margaritas, and more snacks? Do you like fried calamari? I hear they do it great here."

"Yeah, order a platter of that."

The food arrived and we picked at it, talking endlessly. It was fascinating to hear Taylor describe how she was thrust into the world of kiddie beauty pageants at age five by her ruthlessly ambitious mother, Alina, a not-unattractive blond model wannabe. Alina came from upstate New York, and had started her working life as a secretary at a Manhattan publicity firm that handled several movie star clients.

"My mom fell in love with showbiz and made it her life. Problem is, she made it my life, too, but I never got a choice. Honest to God, when I was a little girl and Mom taught me to dress and act like her, I used to think I actually *was* her—just a miniature version. I felt like there was no *me*. It didn't make me angry, really. But as I grew up, I started to feel . . . well, doomed, I guess. No, no, that's too dramatic a word. I just felt like I was being carried along on this wave that my mother had created, and when I actually began having some success and we came out to Hollywood, I started feeling soiled and stupid and all caught up in the celebrity lifestyle —easy money, freebie designer clothes, powerful old men hitting on you constantly—then the mind-blowing sex with hunky young stars, male and female, and fabulous, endless champagne and drugs.

"The worst part was my mom always wanting us to hang out and party together . . . and then catching her fucking my young boyfriends. That's how I got to be tight with Roma, actually. She caught Mom doing a guy I'd been doing—who's like almost twenty years younger than her—and ripped into her one night in front of everybody at Beacher's Madhouse. Mom was actually terrified of Roma because she was such a big deal on the Hollywood scene and she threatened to get her banned from all the nightclubs. And she could have done it, too. Mom calmed down a lot after that."

Wow.

"Where was your father in all this?"

The look of sadness that crossed her face beat anything on a soap opera.

"They got divorced when I was twelve. We'd had a pretty good life and I really loved my dad because he sort of protected me when my mom started working me too hard. He'd tried to break into the movie studio hierarchy as a low-level executive, but that didn't work. Then he tried managing schlock nightclub acts and strippers. He ended up as a salesman in stock market brokerages and did pretty good, but he was always getting fired. He drank too much, and he and Mom fought all the time. It was like he was jealous of her because, as my manager, she was suddenly making money from all the acting and modeling gigs I was getting, and he suddenly wanted his cut. He started fighting her about what jobs I should take. Anyway, it all blew up. The divorce was nasty, and that's when she told me he'd sexually abused me."

"Did she tell the courts?" I asked.

"No. She said it would hurt my reputation with agents and studios. She kept it quiet, and told me to never discuss it."

"Ever think she might be lying? Divorce makes people crazy, you know."

As in, crazy enough to risk letting her daughter believe she'd been molested by her own father?

She shrugged.

"Whatever. It's all in the past now."

"You knew Janet Carter, right? The girl who died?"

"Not very well. She wasn't really a part of our posse."

"And Cara Prescott?"

She sighed and took a long sip of margarita. "I tried hard to get along with Cara. But we were always up for the same parts, and jealousy makes friction, right?"

"Didn't having the same agent make things worse? What's his name?"

"Mark Olson. Yeah, I actually left Mark for a while, but we kissed and made up—not literally, of course. Although he did try to fuck me, back when I started with him, but it was no big deal. I just blew him off, and he was okay with it. He actually laughed when I told him I was saving myself for a studio head! Later, I found out Cara—who'd signed with Mark right after I'd left his agency—*was* fucking him. No big deal, happens all the time, and I wasn't really worried about favoritism, because Mark's a killer agent and knows better than to let his dick get in the way of business. But . . ."

"But what?"

"One time a major director . . . well, it was Martin Scorsese, told me he'd contacted Mark and insisted on signing me for a big starring role. Mark told him I'd read the script but just wasn't interested in the part. Then he got Scorsese to sign Cara. Thing is, I'd *never* seen the script. I found out later from someone who'd overheard Mark and Roma, while listening in on an extension, that Roma had lobbied really hard for Cara to get the part. The person who told me this remembers Roma saying to Mark a couple of times, 'Don't forget our business.' Whatever that means."

"Interesting," I said. "Hey, eat more of this calamari before I pig it all. And let me ply you with a bit more liquor, my darling. I've heard it makes women . . . loose."

Chapter Forty-Four

By the time the sun dipped into the Pacific an hour later, we were in bed. We made love in a whole new way, languorous and sensual, then dropped into deep sleep. A couple of hours later, my cell phone rang. I grabbed it quickly. She stirred, but didn't wake.

"Yeah, Wally . . . *What?* Hey, that's some great news. Is he a name or a nobody? . . . Uh-huh . . . yeah . . . okay, fine. Good work, man. Big story for the next issue. But don't tell anyone on the paper yet. Okay? And that other thing? . . . Oh, okay. Great."

Wally hung up. I kept right on like we were still talking. Never know who's listening. Girls are devious information gatherers, the sly little devils.

"Uh-huh. Right, Wally, I understand, but . . . Oh, come on, man, sounds like you've got it under control. Why do you need me there? . . . Oh, I see! Yeah, that does kinda change things. All right, give me a few minutes and I'm headed your way."

I hung up. My great acting job had been wasted. Taylor truly was out like a light. Comatose.

I dressed fast, left her a note:

You looked so at peace I didn't want to wake you. Got to meet up with my team for a couple of hours, then I'll be back under the covers. Sleep well, my love.

I launched straight up from the balcony into the night sky. In less than five minutes, I was descending toward ultra-swanky Bel Air Estates on the outskirts of Beverly Hills. Landing lightly on a third-floor balcony not unlike the one I'd just left, I strode through open French doors into the master bedroom suite of the mega-mansion owned by Hollywood super-agent Mark Olson, a good-looking guy in his late thirties who'd just emerged from the master bathroom dressed in chic silk pajamas.

He seemed quite surprised to see me. All he could manage was a strangled *"What the fuck!"* as I bore down on him, grabbed him by the throat and pinned him high up against a wall.

"Recognize me, Mark?" I asked him. "Well . . . DO YOU?"

I screamed it in his face as he froze, paralyzed by fear. And who could blame him? It's not every day a fucking vampire smashes into your privileged, protected world and terrorizes you.

He nodded, finally. I relaxed my grip, letting him slide down the wall until his elegantly slippered feet touched down on the carpet. But I kept my hand around his throat.

"Yes," I said. "It's me, Clark Kelly of the *National Revealer*, your friendly neighborhood gossip columnist, Mark. Aren't I lucky to find you at home this evening?"

Luck had nothing to do with it, of course. Wally had assigned, at my request, a reporter to follow Mark Olson. He'd phoned in when the agent had finally said good-bye to friends he'd met for dinner and started motoring toward the ocean along Sunset. Wally had called to tip me that our pigeon was winging back to its coop.

Still pinning said pigeon to the wall, I riveted him with vampire eyes.

"Listen to me as you've never listened to anyone, Mark. Your attention is crucial to your survival. First, the good news: I do not believe you are in any danger of dying here tonight, because I am sure you will see the wisdom of cooperating with me. You're a smart, tough agent and a power player. That's because you *understand* power, Mark. Your m.o. is to seek out those who have it, then control *them*. That's why you've latched on to Roma, knowing she's better than anyone at influencing her powerful grandpappy. But you're a long way away from true power, and you know what *that* is, don't you, Mark? It's when you don't really need *anyone* anymore . . . but *everyone needs you.*"

"And you're telling me this because..." he rasped.

The guy had balls. Big brass ones.

"Because right now, *I* need you, Mark. You have knowledge I want. Give it to me and you'll score big-time. Because even though I think I know what's going on, I've got no time to confirm my suspicions. So save me that precious time, Mark. Give it to me straight, and I'll give you info that'll make you the biggest power in Hollywood. Not just as an agent, Mark, but as a studio head. Wait . . . make that studio *owner!*"

Despite my chokehold, the guy's eyes lit up like spotlights.

"Good. Now here's the bad news, so listen carefully, Mark. I'm going to take my hand off your throat. Then I'm going to reveal myself to you. But if *you* ever reveal *my* true identity to anyone, you'll die screaming in an underground pit full of starving rats who'll strip your bones. And I mean that literally. You won't be alone, though. I'll be there to watch. Underground, you see, is where I'm most comfortable. In my own element, one might say. You know why that is, Mark? *Do* you?"

"No," he gasped. I squeezed his throat harder. His eyes rolled back in his head.

Moving close, I hissed in his ear. "I am vampire, Mark. *Nosferatu.* The undead!"

I released him. He opened his eyes . . . and was amazed to discover I had disappeared.

Poof!

He staggered away from the wall, stumbling, disoriented, eyes frantically searching the room.

"Right here," I said.

He whirled, found me suddenly behind him.

I smiled. "Hello, Mark."

He opened his mouth to speak, but uttered a strangled bark of terror.

I'd disappeared . . . again. He whirled again, expecting to find me behind him.

Nope.

He jumped a foot in the air when I tapped him on the shoulder. *Now* I was behind him. Recoiling, he turned to face me, his face a mask of fright.

"You'll never lose me, pal."

He shrieked like a girl as I suddenly lifted him up, bum-rushed him out to the balcony and threw him over the railing. He fell down, down into the night . . .

. . . and was still howling in terror when I caught him in my arms on the pool deck below.

"Having fun yet, Mark?"

Oops. He'd fainted.

Moments later, he regained consciousness, back upstairs and lying on his own bed. His eyes focused and he found me, standing at the well-stocked bar across the room. I raised a snifter of Louis XIII cognac, gesturing at his bedside table.

"You have good taste, Mark. Knock it back, relax, then let's talk a little business, shall we?"

He shook his head, blinked, reached for the snifter. Taking a pull, he sighed and said wryly, "I certainly hope we can be friends, sir."

I laughed. "Over and over, we hear word that there's no tougher, smarter agent in Hollywood than Mark Olson. And they're right. I'm impressed. You're not crying like a bitch and puking, so I think you've figured this situation out. First, you know I had to terrorize you, swiftly and completely, to make you realize what kind of power you're dealing with, and it worked —because right now you're thinking you'd really *like* to deal with a powerful dude like me, right?"

"You bet I would . . . pal."

He smiled and raised his snifter in a comradely toast.

"To power."

"Hear, hear."

We knocked one back. I sized him up, liking what I saw. I took a wild guess. "You Irish, Mark?"

"I am," he said. "From one of the last Irish bastions, South Boston."
I like Irish guys. We were going to get along, Mark and I.

Chapter Forty-Five

In just fifteen minutes, sitting out on the balcony under a full moon, this tightly focused super-agent told me how he'd wriggled his way into Montague Kane's inner circle. He started off by explaining that Roma—always quick to sense who's red-hot or who's so-not—had assiduously wooed Taylor as a BFF after *Girlie Girl* smashed box office records. Unfortunately, Montague Kane had also loved *Girlie Girl* and immediately demanded the pleasure of Taylor's company in his creepy lair. Without batting an eye, his granddaughter had put on her pimp hat and tried her damnedest to recruit Taylor for the old man's sexual pleasure. She never told Taylor his identity, just rhapsodized about scoring huge bucks from a powerful old man who had behind-the-scenes Hollywood power.

Roma's pimp move was stupid. She should have sensed that proud, ballsy TayLo would never bang anyone for bread. It just wasn't in her. And even if it had been, Roma's timing sucked. She'd tendered her sleazy proposition just when Taylor was sitting, at last, on top of the world. She had a hot flick, big bucks, and hadn't yet fallen into the drugs-booze binging cycle that later turned her into tabloid fodder.

"Mark, here's what I don't understand. What the hell does Roma get out of pimping girlfriends for dear old Grandpop? She already has a huge trust fund, so . . ."

Mark chuckled. "You still don't get Roma's ruthlessness, do you? Look, as simply as I can put it, she wants to ensure that when Montague dies, he does *not* leave his fortune and full control of his empire to his son, Roma's father. Despite her public image, Roma's way beyond worrying about keeping herself in Prada and Louboutins—*la chica wants the whole enchilada*. And, trust me, she stands a very good chance of pulling it off. Old Man Kane, first of all, thinks his son is a lightweight dunce who couldn't run a candy store. More than that, he knows his son's only ambition is to live like a rich guy. He's got no goals, zero drive. But the old monster's got to leave control of his beloved empire to somebody, so why not a tough little cookie like the sweet apple of his eye, Roma? He'll take care of all his grandkids in his will, but she'll be in control. It's no wonder she works hard to keep him . . . well, hard and happy with an endless supply of young hotties."

"Like Cara Prescott."

"Exactly. The old man's nuts about that girl. Wants to make her a 'huge movie star.' Those were his very words, in fact."

"Uh-huh. And that's where you come in, right, Mark?"

He shrugged. "It's a dirty job, but somebody's got to do it, Clark."

"But I don't see you doing all this *just* for your ten percent commission. What are you gunning for here, boyo?"

Mark hesitated. Just for a second. Then he saw me tense slightly, and his mouth got into gear fast.

"After Roma and I became . . . er, besties through our mutual goal of keeping her grandpa sweet, things went very well indeed. The old man's promised to buy a major studio for me to run. And that would be the answer to every prayer I've ever had in this business. It's what made it worth helping Roma. And she's helped me because even the future queen bee of Kane Industries can use a studio head in her back pocket."

I splashed a generous dollop of the Louis XIII I'd brought out into my snifter. "Is it worth it to help her commit murder?"

That rocked his world. "Whoa, just a damn minute! Who's she trying to murder?"

"Taylor."

"What? Look, I swear I don't know what the hell you're talking about!"

I shrugged. "I'm not sure whether you do or not, Mark, but before we go down that road, are you aware that Taylor and I are now an item?"

He hesitated.

I shot him a warning look.

He got it and said, "Sorry. Lying and obfuscating are tough habits to break when you do what I do, but believe me, I've totally got the message: I will *never* lie to you. So the answer is yes. I know that you and Taylor have become special to each other. And I know about Roma's ill-advised attempt to sell that sex tape. I swear to you I didn't know beforehand that she'd videotaped you surreptitiously, or that she was trying to sell it. When she finally came to me for advice, as she should have in the first place, she actually told me with a straight face that a sex tape would probably help Taylor's career, the way it had for Paris Hilton and Kim Kardashian. And she was absolutely serious! Such astounding stupidity. I told her that sex tapes had helped those lightweights precisely because they were no-talent, nonentities who desperately needed something that'd make them famous for being famous."

Incredible! Idiot Roma had actually assessed TayLo as a no-talent? How jealousy blinds lightweight females. I nodded, liking this guy's mind.

"So," I said, "you think Roma's essentially stupid. But she appears to have some control over you. Why is that, Mark?"

He shrugged. "Remember what you said about *real* power. In this town, that's called being a studio head, or as you put it, a studio owner. More than a year ago, Roma took me to meet Montague Kane. And that's when he told me, quite forcefully, that I should make Cara Prescott a major star. If I got the ball rolling on that, he promised he'd not only buy a studio and put me in charge—but, he'd also give me an ownership position. I've put a great deal of effort into promoting Cara, but it's not easy. She's beautiful and a good little actress, but she's no burning talent like Taylor Logan. And who is? That girl's the best around."

I gave him a hard look. "Don't drift down the road to Bullshitville, Mark. I thought we were having a straight up, man-to-vampire talk here. Don't con me with compliments about my girlfriend. If you think Taylor's so great, why did you tell Martin Scorsese she didn't like that script he sent her a few months back? And don't lie, buddy, I know all about it."

He looked nervous again, took a quick belt of the Louis XIII.

"Like I said, no lying, Clark. Look, I told Scorsese Taylor wasn't available only because Roma ordered me to, pure and simple. And I've already told you why I wasn't about to ignore her orders. I want that studio. Desperately." He took another nervous sip of the Louis XIII. "And while I'm in no-lying mode, let me remind you that Taylor is no easy sell these days—not because of her talent, but because she's become nearly uninsurable for obvious reasons. Insurance companies don't dare touch her. And, as you know, that's certain death in this town. But believe me when I say that from now on, Taylor will be my number one priority, *not* Montague Kane. I recognize and acknowledge that you are the new power in town. And I cannot tell a lie; I'll take that studio any way I can get it."

He paused, then said, "Look, can I ask a question here? You made the rather shocking statement that Roma is trying to murder Taylor. What does that mean?"

"Mark, you're aware that Roma often hands out little gifts of sniffy-sniffy to members of her skank 'ho posse, right?"

He hesitated . . . and then nodded.

"Yeah, I thought you would be. But are you aware that some of Roma's little gifts are more deadly than others? Have you ever heard of the South American drug called Oxi? No? Well, I didn't think so. Steady Oxi users usually die in a matter of months, Mark. Roma's slowly been feeding that drug to Taylor. To be honest, I'm pretty sure she never intended to kill her, but she's sure trying to slow her down dramatically while she pushes little Cara's career, for reasons that are now vividly obvious to all of us. And, by the way, Roma may have aided and abetted an actual murder by supplying the Oxi that killed a young woman recently."

I'd rocked him, but he stayed cool, assessing what I'd told him, eschewing reaction for contemplation. That's why the best Hollywood agents make sharks appear warm-blooded.

"So . . . are you getting the picture, Mark?"

Silly question. I knew my boy. And sure enough, he put down his glass, stuck out his hand and said, "The enemy of my friend is my enemy. Could we shake on that . . . friend?"

We shook. I poured fresh Louis XIII and we clinked snifters.

Mark made a little bow and said, "I await your orders, sir. But how will we handle Montague Kane the first time that I am inevitably forced to ignore Roma's orders because they supersede yours? Make no mistake, the man would be a formidable enemy to make."

I laughed. "Not for us, Mark. *Not* for us."

I clapped him on the shoulder, walked him off the balcony into the master suite.

"I brought something with me that I'd like to show you," I said. "It will answer *all* your questions. Point me at your DVD player!"

Chapter Forty-Six

I slipped into the Montage suite just after midnight. She awoke briefly, snuggled into my shoulder, then blinked out like a light. The girl was exhausted, drained in the wake of the whirlwind we'd suddenly gotten caught up in; not to mention the emotional hammer blow of falling in love at darn-near first sight. But she'd been sleeping deeply and well. And, best of all, she hadn't so much as whispered the word *drugs*. Okay, she'd downed a few margaritas. But then she'd gotten sleepy and nodded off like a normal person.

So far, so good.

I lay back, closed my eyes. I needed to dream, recharge the psyche. Vampires don't get tired in the normal sense. And as we don't have living organs to regenerate and refresh, human-style sleep is not necessary. But we are miraculously refreshed by our dreams, which—as I believe I mentioned early on—are not at all like those pale images that flitter through the human mind, so imprecise and surreal that they often cannot be recalled. No, vampire dreams are insanely rich and vivid, actually more "real" than what we experience via normal vision while walking the earth. And, happily, we can *share* our dreams. In certain states of consciousness, we can communicate with vampires all over the world.

I lay thinking about what Wally had told me on the phone. We'd scored an incredibly lucky break. Tony Giambalvo had turned a guy who'd told us he'd not only witnessed Scummy Bear staking out Roma's tiny dogs for coyote bait, he'd helped him clean up the killing ground. The guy was just a kid, a handsome wannabe actor who'd been casually cougar-banged by Roma then kicked to the curb. Suddenly banned from hanging with her cool posse, he admitted that he'd immediately dreamed of killing the bitch. Now he was willing to settle the score by ratting her and Scummy out for a mid-five figure *Revealer* payday.

It was fantastic news! If we could quickly top our own story about

Roma's dogs being staked out for slaughter by actually *naming* the killers, the public would go berserk.

Tony had the kid under guard by one of our private eyes at a West Hollywood hotel. He'd bring him into the office in the morning, make him spill his riveting story into a tape recorder. And I'd be there to monitor the interview. Ah, what a great day it had turned into after a shocking start.

And now, I needed to dream, have some vampire fun, let my mind run loose.

Instantly, I mind-rolled Ludmilla, who happened to be . . .

"I'm in Paris, my darling Dragomir. And you are? Hmmm, let me guess. Sleeping beside the enchanting Taylor Logan, perhaps?"

"Ludmilla . . ."

"Abandon that placating tone, please, you egomaniacal bastard. You don't need to soothe me. You are arrogantly assuming that I am jealous of your love for her, which I could see plainly even before *you* really knew what had hit you, by the way. That's how well I know you, still, Dragomir. You were my first love, and that's an enormous thing, for a girl. You were the entire, intense focus of my life for that sadly short, but sweetly seminal interlude in our human youth. That's why I know, as the Americans put it, what makes you tick.

"Therefore, trust me when I tell you that this girl is perfect for you. She's engaging, talented and tough, yet vulnerable in the most charming way. She worships you, and will shape herself to be exactly as you need her. By the way, I've finally seen several of her films. *Girlie Girl* was monumentally fantastic. All my friends here in Paris love it. You are a very lucky vampire, my dearest friend."

I sighed deeply. "Ludmilla, I—"

She laughed. "Do *not* wax maudlin, Dragomir. I sense that you now need to return to your earthly consciousness. This is not a night for you to dream with us. Another time, when you are more settled, I hope you'll allow me to introduce you to some very fun vampires here in Paris. Or perhaps you and Taylor could actually come to visit me in the City of Love. What fun to dine at Maxim's and toy with the delicious idea of a three-way, eh, *cheri*? And don't tell me that thought hasn't crossed your mind, you Romanian rakehell. It has certainly crossed mine. But for now . . . farewell, my Dragomir."

Ah, Ludmilla!

I lay still for several hours, got up quietly, showered and dressed. Ready for the day, I moved toward the bed to wake Taylor, then thought better of it. My girl was bone-tired. Let her sleep.

I wrote her a lover's note and split. Hit the office just after eight. Wally and Tony were already in the conference room with our kid snitch, who—like every hick-from-the-sticks Hollywood wannabe—had a made-up name. Called himself Teddy Bright, if you can believe that shit.

After stating the legal name he'd been born with in Chillicothe, Ohio—

Harold Knox—not-so-bright "Teddy" spilled his guts into Old Faithful, our vintage Ampex reel-to-reel tape recorder that we keep around for nostalgia, and because it still beats trendy digital devices for sound quality. Two *Revealer* lawyers were present, poised to whip out legal documents they'd force the kid to sign when he'd finished. And Martha Baker, a court stenographer we hired for crucial jobs like this, was here too. Martha sat typing stoically on her tiny stenography machine, tapping out every word the kid said into the recorder so we'd have an instant written copy. The kid would then be made to sign every page, verifying that this was a true representation of his testimony.

When I walked into the conference room, I sat out of the kid's line of sight and listened as Wally and Tony hit him with questions that needed to be answered.

"Was Roma Kane present while your pal Scummy Bear staked out these little dogs for the coyotes—or even later, when everyone was observing the actual killings? Think carefully before you answer."

After a moment, the kid responded, "No, she was never right there."

Wally pounced. "Why do you use the term '*right* there'?"

"Because . . . well, she was around. I mean, like in the house, you know? But I never saw her come outside or look through a window. I mean, she might have, but I never saw her. She'd be inside, hanging out with the girls, mostly. The girls never came out when Scummy was playing Dog-Gone."

"What?"

"Uh, 'Dog-*Gone*.' That's what he called the game."

The lawyers recoiled visibly. Wally and Tony went cold-eyed.

"How about the noise?" Tony asked the kid. "You said that when the coyotes finally hit the dog and killed it, there'd be a lot of yipping and howling. You think that racket could be heard in the house?"

Teddy-slash-Harold shrugged. "Maybe. But Roma always had music playing. And her fucking girl posse were always talking and screaming, so . . ."

At one point, Wally asked, "What was Scummy's manner during all this? Was he all business, acting like he was running a serious gambling game, or . . ."

"Hell, no. That motherfucker never stopped laughing his ass off. He'd be cracking jokes while those little dogs were getting ripped apart by those fucking coyotes."

It was painful testimony. At one point I noted tears in Martha's eyes, a woman who routinely transcribed, dry-eyed, the testimony of serial killers, sex predators and other assorted monsters in Los Angeles Superior Court. Animal cruelty always rips your heart out, and if it doesn't . . . you just might be a Scummy Bear.

I had one question. "I understand Scummy gave you the job of cleaning up the backyard in the morning every time a dog was killed the night before. He ever tell you why?"

The kid turned around, looked at me.

I held up a cautioning hand. "Take your time, okay? Really think about it."

He paused, then said, "Maybe the first time I did it, or maybe the second time, I'm not sure which, he said, 'Roma goes apeshit if she sees a mess.' "

"And when he said 'a mess,' did you know what was he referring to?"

"Uh . . . well, he was pointing at the blood and fur all over the grass."

Bingo.

One lawyer gave me a thumbs-up. Not that the kid's answer actually proved anything, but it told us what we'd wanted to know. Famous "dog-lover" Roma, who carried miniature pooches around like so many accessories, was an even sicker fuck than Scummy Bear, if that was possible.

I sat there for nearly an hour, monitoring the interview. Suddenly, Elspeth appeared at the conference room door, urgently beckoning. I joined her in the corridor.

"You are *not* going to believe what Photo just found. Can you break away from this?"

Elspeth never wasted my time. "Let's go," I said.

Chapter Forty-Seven

Jules Cooper, *The Revealer*'s esteemed Pulitzer Prize-winning photo editor, was standing over a light table peering down at color transparencies as Elspeth and I walked into his office.

"Total mind-blower just landed in my lap, Clark. You won't believe it," he said. "But just give me one second here . . . *aah*! That's the ticket!" He hit his intercom and barked, "Mindy, come grab this image I've picked for the Ashton Kutcher story. The layout desk needs it yesterday."

Cooper's assistant trotted in, grabbed the pic and trotted out. Mindy had the cutest ass in the office, but for the first time in memory, my eyes didn't track it all the way out the door.

That's how a guy realizes he's truly in love—glance at a female bottom, think of your girlfriend.

I wondered if Taylor was still asleep. I'd had the fleeting idea of lingering over breakfast in bed together this morning, but she really needed sleep. Tomorrow, I'll do it, for sure. I'll move her into my rarely used apartment on Robertson. She'll be safe there. Even I can barely remember where the hell it is.

Jules hit a dimmer switch. "Okay, Clark, let's direct your attention away from Mindy's butt and over to our giant viewing screen. You're not gonna believe this one, buddy!"

He tapped his computer.

A shocking image—videotape of a nude girl masturbating energetically on a bed—flashed up on the screen. Elspeth gasped. My first reaction was that Jules was roguishly showing off the bootleg celebrity film and photo images he loved collecting—inside stuff the public never sees—but he would never screen it in front of Elspeth unless it was business. Then my eyes focused on the girl's pretty face, and I got it.

"What the *hell*? That's . . . Janet Carter? Where'd you get this footage, Jules?"

"You know what Random Image Search is, right?"

"Yeah. It's when you photo guys search the Internet to find matches for an image, usually a photograph."

"Right. Every week, for instance, we feed in all the photos we're using in the issue and run a Random Image Search to see if exact matches come up. That's how we catch websites out there ripping off our copyrighted photos. We track them down and our lawyers make them pay up. So we fed in a picture of Janet Carter, describing her as one of Roma's posse who ended up dead of a drug overdose."

"Yes," said Elspeth. "It was an adorable picture we got from Janet's poor parents. It showed her in front of her apartment just after she moved out here from Idaho, planting flowers in a big wooden tub. Her parents said she loved gardening."

Jules nodded. "Well, nobody out in Internet-land ripped off that picture, but as often happens, the image search found *other* pictures of Janet—even a few Janet look-alikes with similar facial characteristics. But when this video popped up, and I saw it really was her, I tracked down where the footage had originated. Turns out it's a pay-to-peek porn site. So it looks like, to me anyway, that Janet did naughty vid-clips for money. And at first I thought, so what? So do a lotta wannabes who run out of dough in this town. But I knew you guys were working an angle on the Roma Kane story about young chicks being pimped to some rich old geezer, right? So I figured I'd better let you judge whether it's relevant."

My mind was racing a million miles a minute. "Jules, you sure it's porn? I mean, she wasn't just doing sex stuff for kicks while some boyfriend filmed her?"

"No, Clark. First, that camera's on a fixed angle. Nobody's holding it because it *never* moves. No, my guess is she was doing what a lot of young girls do in this town to earn money while they're waiting for that big Hollywood break—she produced at-home amateur porn using her own videocam. It's not a bad deal compared to stripping, hooking or doing hardcore porn movies that kill you for legit acting jobs. There are literally hundreds of thousands of websites featuring amateur girls. Even guys who get turned off watching pro porn chicks *love* seeing the girl next door getting herself off. It's simple enough even for a girl—uh, sorry, Elspeth—to do. You just set up an inexpensive videocam, aim it at your bed or sofa, then masturbate, play with sex toys, or even your boyfriend's dick. The money's not huge, but it pays the rent. And the best part is—it's safe. You're in your own home, with no danger of getting arrested, mugged, raped or killed."

"Interesting," I mused.

Elspeth, measuring my reaction, said, "It's shocking, of course, but probably no big deal as a follow-up for our story. So she did solo porn? So what, right? She's dead, poor girl. And, *omigod*, can you imagine how much seeing this would hurt her parents?"

Jules shrugged. "Just thought it might fit somehow, but—"

I held up my hand. "Guys, you're thinking I'm not interested, but I am. But now I need the magic ingredient that solves all problems—information. Jules, I can call that porn site, or get one of my guys to do it. But here's what I need to know: If she really did sell self-produced porn, was it always from that same location—her apartment—and was the camera always stationary? I think we need a photo expert who knows the technical side. Can you help?"

Most photo people on newspapers and magazines are frustrated reporters. Jules hit the bait right on cue.

"Tell me everything you need to know, Clark."

I briefed him, left his office and walked back to the conference room. Wally and Tony had just wound it up with Teddy Bright. The kid kept asking when he'd get his check. I nodded at the lawyers, and they ushered him out.

"How'd the interview go, guys?" I asked.

"Terrific. It's one of the creepiest cruelty stories I've ever heard," said Wally. "Well worth the money. It'll sell."

I nodded to Tony. "Good job."

"Thanks, boss."

"Wally, you got a minute?"

We walked into my office. I shut the door and told him what Jules had shown me. Wally got it, instantly. He always does.

"You thinking what I'm thinking, Master?"

"I don't know what you're thinking."

"Of course you do, boss. Shall I go get the key?"

I grinned. "Yes. Maybe we'll take a drive. It's a beautiful day."

"Just what I was thinking," he said.

Chapter Forty-Eight

Wally drove. Twenty minutes later, just as the apartment building where Janet Carter had lived and died came into view, my cell phone rang.

"Yeah."

"Oh, hi, Clark. It's me, Freddie. Just wanted to tell you that Mr. Jensen, the landlord, agreed to the interview with me, boss. I've just sat down with him. Hey, Mr. Jensen, it's the famous Clark Kelly on the phone! He says 'Hi,' Clark."

"Freddie, don't forget, we need forty-five undisturbed minutes in that apartment. Keep that guy on ice. Did he like the sight of those ten hundred-dollar bills?"

"Absolutely, Clark. And, yes, I've told Mr. Jensen we need his in-depth recollections of Janet's personality, her habits, who visited her. He'll be very thorough."

"And I'll be thoroughly pissed if you don't keep him in-depth and off our backs. Say 'good-bye,' Freddie boy."

"Good-bye, Clark."

Wally slowed, peering around intently as we entered the winding street leading to the apartments, then he said:

"Okay, Freddie's on the job, keeping the landlord occupied with his phony interview and . . . ah, good, there's my guy, Jack."

Jack Haley, one of our heavy mob, stood leaning against his parked car, smoking a cigarette. We didn't wave as we drove past. He didn't nod.

"Okay, Master, now we're ready to raid. The landlord's locked down. And if the girl who's now renting Janet's old apartment suddenly leaves the boutique she works at in Santa Monica, our girl who's staked out there, and ready to tail her, will alert Jack. He actually popped into the boutique earlier for a quick peek at the salesgirl . . . uh, her name's Thalia Gordon . . . so he'll recognize her if she decides to come back home unexpectedly. If that happens, he'll intercept her, and offer her five hundred for another phony interview about what it feels like to live where somebody's been murdered."

I chuckled. "Think she knows her predecessor died?"

"Probably. You can bet the landlord didn't tell her. He wants to rent his apartment. But you know how bigmouth neighbors are. Okay, here we are."

We parked, looked around. Not a soul in sight around the complex. We got out, walked quickly up to the apartment door. Wally produced a key we'd commissioned from our favorite locksmith, slipped it into the lock, and the door opened. Inside, I lowered the one open window shade before we walked into the bedroom.

Instantly, I pointed at the louvered air conditioning vents high up on the wall over the bed where Janet Carter had died.

"The angle's exact," said Wally.

"I agree. Down angle from one side only. Matches the videocam angle. Okay, I think I make a more convincing dead person than you, so I'll do the honors."

One side of the bed was pushed nearly up against the wall. I lay down flat on the other side, next to the nightstand.

"Shall I 'burk' you now, Master?"

"Funny! But what's *not* going to be funny is feeling like an asshole when I reach my hand way back toward the side of the headboard . . . like *this*, and feel around behind it . . . *like this*."

"Hey, boss, what if the landlord put in a new bed? Then he would've seen the thing. Shit! I didn't think of that."

"I did, but my answer was, 'Hell, no!' Does this look like the kind of joint that'd buy a new bed just because a dead body was . . . *goddam!* I think I just hit pay dirt!"

Instantly, Wally crouched beside the headboard, clicked on a small, powerful flashlight, followed my fingers with the beam and . . .

"*You were right, boss!* It's a tiny fucking *switch*! And a wire's still attached, so . . ."

"Yeah. So *don't* throw that switch, whatever you do."

I hopped off the bed and peered behind the headboard. "Okay, give me some more light. Let's follow this wire and . . . ah, it just disappears under the carpet. Figures. Now . . . let's look at those louvers up there on the wall."

We stood up. Wally shined his light up at the air conditioning vent.

"Holy shit, look at that. Two of the louver slats are actually pried apart. Not much, but just enough. *Bingo!* You nailed it, boss."

"Don't count your chickens."

I walked into the kitchen, found a foldaway stepladder. Wally produced a neat toolkit he'd concealed inside his jacket, climbed up and went to work. In a moment, he had the vent screwed off.

He pointed his flashlight inside and said softly, "*Now* can I call you a genius, Master?"

"Yes, Wally, you can, as a matter of fact. *WINNING* . . . as Charlie Sheen would say. Can you retrieve it? Is it all tied down?"

"Nope. In fact . . ."

He turned around on the ladder, faced me and handed it down.

A beautiful mini-videocam.

"It was hard-wired to the switch behind the headboard," said Wally.

I couldn't wait. Quickly but carefully, I inspected the camera. I already knew the model, Sony CX190, and how to work it. Less than an hour ago, Janet's parents had answered my request to check her credit card bills for any electronic devices she might have bought in the last year. We'd told them we were just playing a hunch that was probably wrong. I'd then downloaded the online manual for the videocam.

I pressed the appropriate button. Bingo! The batteries were still good. The camera's tiny screen lit up. I watched for a few seconds as Wally came back down the ladder, then hit *Off*. He raised his eyebrows questioningly.

"I can't breathe," I said.

I moved to the side of the bed, pointed the camera down at where Janet had lain in the last moments of her life. Wally stood just behind me, looking over my shoulder.

"Brace yourself, pal," I said. I pressed *On*.

The screen lit up. Suddenly, it felt like we'd been transported back to that fateful night. We were watching as hulking Scummy Bear overpowered desperately struggling Janet, kneeling on her chest, pinning her thrashing body, imprinting impressions of her buttons into her skin, then pressing lips and nostrils shut with his fingers as she fought for the precious air that would never again fill her lungs with life.

Janet Carter died fighting hard.

"Good girl," I said softly. "Now I can get him for you."

And I knew, absolutely, that she had heard me from across the void.

Back in the car minutes later, we rolled down the street as I phoned Freddie, told him we were out of the apartment and he should wind up his phony interview with the landlord. We passed Jack Haley, still standing by his car, still sucking on a weed. Wally gave him the Hollywood "cut" signal.

It was over. We'd done it.

"Never a word to anyone about this, Wally. Ever! We clear on that?"

He nodded. "One last question, boss. You going to the cops? Or is this, don't ask, don't tell?"

"Justice will work in its mysterious way, Wally."

He nodded, rubbed his neck briskly and said, "What gets me is that *you* figured it out, but our illustrious photo editor didn't."

I laughed. "You know what we say in our business, Wally. Photographers are just reporters with their brains knocked out. No, Jules is actually a very smart guy, but truly great reporters have great imagination. Like you, pal. After all, you figured it out, too, right?"

"Nah. I just read your mind, Master. I never go wrong when I do that."

But then he asked how I'd figured it out.

When had the hunch hit me?

"On that tape Jules showed us, I noticed her look up toward the ceiling like someone or something was watching her," I said. "She looked like some vulnerable little thing about to be sacrificed. And I thought of those tiny, terrified dogs, staked out for the nasty death they knew was coming . . . and my next thought was of that ugly fucking Scummy pig.

"Then I got inside her head and figured that in her desperation, at the very moment he was killing her, she might have looked up at the camera aimed at her and thought, how great it would be if she could somehow catch him on tape . . . throw the switch on the bastard, so to speak . . . and I thought, hell, why not?

"See, at first I'd figured she'd probably used a remote control she'd point up at the vents when she was filming herself, but Scummy would hardly let her grab a remote while he was offing her. And this morning, when Jules got those porn site managers to send him links to all the scenes she'd sold them, we saw one where she was giving a hand job to a guy who definitely did *not* look like he knew he was on *Candid Camera*. So how could she point a remote without him seeing it? I figured she must be controlling the camera with a switch and it had to be within easy reach.

"Sure enough, the porn guys told us that's exactly how they advise girls to set up their cameras—using a switch hard-wired to a hidden remote control, so they can just reach back and click it on. So when Scummy jumped poor Janet, she literally threw the switch on him. Neat, huh?"

"*Wow!*"

"You can say that again . . . uh, no, on second thought, please don't!"

We rolled into the *National Revealer* parking lot, got out.

I cautioned Wally. "Remember, no one knows the real reason we went back to toss Janet's apartment. So we tell nobody nothin', right? It was a fishing expedition, but we didn't catch a fish."

"You got it, boss."

"Good. You up for take-out pizza?"

Chapter Forty-Nine

I felt good. And I felt *hungry*. No, it wasn't The Hunger. I was jonesing for pizza, not blood.

How incredibly ghoulish, some might think, that I'd work up an appetite immediately after viewing the grisly murder of an acquaintance—which Janet Carter was, technically speaking, even though we hadn't met until *after* her death. But before you dismiss my seemingly unseemly urge for pizza as *vampiric*, let's not forget that human reporters—not to mention cops, EMTs, firefighters, soldiers, etc.—develop cast-iron stomachs and, despite frequent exposure to gruesome, gory scenes, manage to function quite normally.

I hit the intercom. "Elspeth, tell our gossip team I'm springing for pizza."

"Damn. I just ate my lunch."

"Tough ta-tas, brown-bagger."

"Well, I don't want to offend you, Clark, so I'll eat *one* piece."

"You sure? Twelve grams of fat . . . two hundred and ninety calories?"

"Also, the lovely Vanillo's hanging out with our team this morning. Something about *desperately* wanting to become one of us. I know you'll want to order for *her*."

"Do women ever outgrow their inborn jealousy of other females?"

"Stupid question. Why should we? Tearing each other apart is *fun*! Anyway, I should order the pies from Pomodoro, I presume."

"Where else?"

Wally knocked and walked into my office.

"Just ordered pizza for everyone," I told him. "My treat."

"Cool. Pomodoro again?"

I hit the intercom. "Elspeth, change that order to Domino's."

"Clark, stop buzzing. I've got work to do out here."

I sighed. My staff loves making fun of my devotion to Pomodoro, a tiny, but elegant Italian eatery I'd discovered just south of the UCLA campus off

Wilshire. It's no pizza joint, and actually serves gourmet sit-down dinners, but its super-thin crust pizza brings tears to the eyes.

"Okay, what's up, Renfield?"

"Just early warning that we'll catch hell about our budget if we don't chill a bit. Can I take the tail off Cara Prescott? We've got her limo driver paid off, so do we have to pay a private eye?"

I nodded. "It's good to be prudent. And you're right. We don't need a private dick now that we know where Cara gets herself off to, so to speak. But remember, this is a big, mother-humping story we're working, so I'm not going to penny-pinch either. Fuck the bean-counters. How are the early sales numbers looking, by the way?"

"The circulation guys are whooping to our glorious CEO, the money-hungry prick, that the issue's probably gonna sell out—thanks to the Clark Kelly gossip team's hot Roma Kane scoop."

"Not bad news."

Should I send a Pomodoro pizza to Taylor, I suddenly wondered?

I phoned the suite at Montage. No answer. Tried her cell phone, got zip. In the shower, maybe? Still sleeping? Try later.

"Okay, Wally, let's discuss Scummy Bear. Ordinarily, we'd pressure him to come clean about the dog cruelty by tipping him that one of his pals spilled his guts to us, and that we're breaking the story—with or without him. Then tell him he'll look a lot better if he cooperates with us, confesses his sins, makes a big *mea culpa* to *Revealer* animal lovers, then contributes money to the Support-Tiny-Fucking-Dogs Foundation, or whatever. And if Scummy cracks, that just might force Roma to admit all, exclusively, to us. Call that Plan A."

Wally chuckled. "I like it, Master. But you're already thinking of an even more sensational Plan B, right?"

"How you do read my mind, Renfield? You're absolutely right, because now that we've got that sensational murder tape, we're playing in a whole new ballgame. The paper's biggest bang for the buck might be to publish photos from the tape in the paper with a headline in the order of: 'Vicious Dog-Killer Murdered Roma Kane BFF!' And then run that horrifying tape on *The Revealer* website, of course. Ordinarily, the cops would go apeshit and threaten us for using murder evidence to sell papers, but I think they'll play ball if we secretly agree to give them the tape *first* so they can make a highly publicized arrest of Scummy before we hit the streets. That's Plan B."

Wally grinned. "Don't make me beg, boss."

"Okay, to really milk this baby and get a few more weeks out of it, we initiate Plan C. We secretly tip Scummy *before* we tip the cops. He'll almost certainly panic and go on the run. We could then mount a nationwide 'manhunt' and 'catch' him a few weeks later. We could do that very easily, of course, because what Scummy wouldn't know is that we'd put private dicks on his ass, ready to track him the second he started his run. *Eh*, Renfield?"

"I bow to your consummate wickedness, Master. Plan C is evil on a fucking stick."

"How kind of you to say so, my faithful Renfield. Okay, let's chew it over, you and me, and make a decision by tomorrow. Then we'll bring our esteemed managing editor into the mix. Agreed?"

"Yeah, boss. But one more thing: You showed Roma the tape of Old Man Kane with Cara Prescott. I know you did it to back the bitch off, but what if she tells the old man about it? He's a powerful, mean bastard. He could probably get the Pentagon to launch Scud missiles and blow us all to hell if he wanted to—and I'm not exaggerating."

I shook my head. "I think Roma knows that could backfire on her. She's not that stupid—but the precise danger of Roma is that she's not all that smart either. We'll just have to keep an eye on her. I haven't told you about it yet, and I will later, but I've lined up someone to watch every move she makes. So I'm on it, cowboy."

Wally nodded, went back out to the newsroom. I checked my watch. Just after one o'clock. I tried Taylor again, got no answer. I thought for a minute then hit the intercom.

"Elspeth, would you ask Vanillo to come in, please?"

"Ah, they told you about the miniskirt, huh?"

I sighed. Then smiled when Vanillo tapped on the door and walked in. Wow! Thigh-yai-*yaii*!

"Hi, Clark. I hear you're buying me pizza!"

"Well, it's for everyone, actually, but, uh . . . sit down."

Or maybe better *not*, I thought instantly, but . . . too late. Vanillo sat, and suddenly her legendary legs were the Highway to Heaven. And, heaven knows, I needed to raise my sinful eyes. I did, but then they tracked right up to her bountiful chest and . . . *whammo!* For the second time that day, Taylor's face suddenly materialized, blocking Vanillo's naughty girl parts.

No doubt about it, gossip fans—this vampire's in *love*!

I said, "Look, Vanillo, you're always nailing great inside-lowdown from the Montage hotel for my column. What I need, fast, is a *very* discreet inquiry about an off-the-books guest. Anyone there you can call for me?"

Her megawatt smile amped up so fast I thought her face would break.

"OMIGOD, Clark . . . you're giving me an *assignment*! Oh, yes, absolutely, I am super-tight with the head doorman *and* the chief valet— even though neither of them knows I'm tight with the other. So what can I find out for you?"

I wiped all traces of friendliness from my face and intoned the ritual initiation speech: "You know that you must *never* repeat anything I tell you not to repeat, right?"

Her smile disappeared. Not like she was scared, but like she wanted to get serious. Good.

"Okay, my mystery guest is . . . Taylor Logan."

I watched her face. No reaction. Did she know we'd become an item? Probably. In fact, almost certainly. No Hollywood secret stays secret long. I said:

"She's at the Montage, but not registered under her name. I've been trying to reach her there, and on her cell phone, but she doesn't answer. Can you find out if she left the hotel or not?"

She nodded, pulled out her iPhone and hit a "favorite." She got an answer, asked the question. Nodded a couple of times and clicked off.

"Taylor left about forty minutes ago, Clark. She asked them to slip her out a side entrance to avoid the paparazzi that are always prowling outside the front entrance. She told them she was just going to walk around Beverly Hills and go shopping. She didn't say where, exactly. That's it."

Goddammit! I should have told her not to leave, no matter what!

My intercom blinked.

"Yeah, Elspeth."

"Pizza time!"

"Good! Bring it in."

"Vanillo's, too?"

Bitch.

"No, Elspeth, Vanillo's just leaving."

Vanillo, being a girl, caught the byplay, but kept a straight face.

"Thanks for your help, kiddo."

"Clark, if you need more help finding Taylor . . ."

I shrugged. "She'll turn up. Thanks, Vanillo. And even though you get spoiled by great food on the club circuit, I think you're gonna love this Pomodoro pizza."

"Thanks, Clark."

She got up to leave and I almost, but not quite, kept my eyes off those sky-high legs topped by that pert ass. And, yes . . . there was Taylor's face *again*.

Man, talk about P-whipped. This vampire's been vamped!

Chapter Fifty

The crunch of crisp, thin-crust Pomodoro pizza resonated in my head as I chewed, when a sudden thought struck me. Why not ask Hollywood's celebrity CIA to find Taylor for me? I punched the intercom.

"Elspeth, get me our favorite *paparazzo*, Randy Cooper."

"You just like him because he's one of the last ones who still speak English," she cracked.

"Yeah, but it's nostalgia, not racism."

A moment later, line one buzzed.

"Randy, it's Clark. Need a quick favor. You tied up?"

"I wish, bitch!"

That's right, gossip fans. A *gay* paparazzo!

"Actually, Clark, I'm staked out in front of that high-end—or should I say *low*-end—bikini wax joint just off Rodeo Drive. Got a tip that Selena Gomez is in there now for her first-ever Brazilian. It's probably bullshit, but I've got nothing better to cover right now."

"Good, you're in Beverly Hills. Look, we're trying to find Taylor Logan for . . . uh, a comment on a story. We heard she's walking around there somewhere, shopping. Can you get me a fix on her location?"

"What's going down? You're the second person to ask for her 20 in the last twenty minutes."

Alarm bells!

"Oh? Who was the first?"

"That asshole Scummy Bear. I told him I'd call if I saw her, but claimed I was staked out on a real important job. I've gotta be a little bit nice to the slimeball because of his access to Roma Kane and her celebrity posse. So—hey, wait a minute! Has this got anything to do with that story about Roma's little dogs being staked out for coyotes to kill we're hearing you guys are going to run? You know, when I heard that I thought right away it sounds like something Scummy would do."

Shit. But why was I surprised? In our business, everybody hears everything. We're always trading information. But smarty-pants Randy needs to be slowed down before he gets *too* interested—and gets in our way.

"Look, Randy, Taylor's involved in a story we're working about a possible new film deal for her. So if you could tell me where she is, I'll shoot you a fee. But tell you what, dude, we've been chasing Scummy for comment on our coyote story, so locate him for me as well and I'll double your money."

"Great. Back in a few."

He clicked off. My mind was screaming that old reporter's adage:

There are no coincidences!

Why the hell does Scummy want to know where Taylor is *right now*?

Better question: Why am I so stupid? Scummy almost certainly knows by now that we're gunning for him as the probable dog-killer. He might even have heard that Teddy Bright had ratted him out to *The Revealer*, and . . . then it hit me: Why hadn't I anticipated that Roma would tell him her hot new secret—that Taylor and I are lovers! Knowing that, he might threaten her to get me to back off our upcoming story. Or even . . .

Jesus!

What was the matter with me? I was thinking behind the curve. I'd just proved Scummy was a dangerous motherfucker, a killer. Would he hesitate to kill me if it kept his name out of the paper? Or to *control* me by—

The intercom buzzed.

"Clark, it's Randy calling back. Putting him through."

I snatched line one and said, "You find her?"

"Yeah. She's just walked into Van Cleef & Arpels on Rodeo Drive."

"She with anybody?"

"No, she's alone."

"Good. I'll send a reporter over there. Hey, any Scummy news?"

"No. I've got calls out. I'll get right back if we spot him."

"Randy, take my cell phone number and call me direct."

I gave it to him, hung up, told Elspeth to hail a BevHills Cab, chop-chop. Five minutes later, I was on my way to Rodeo.

Calm down, I told myself. She was spotted alone, walking into the elegant quiet of Van Cleef & Arpels, one of the world's toniest jewelry stores. You're only ten minutes away, so chill. Five minutes later, Randy called again. My heart jumped in my chest.

"Yeah, Clark, we just spotted Scummy. It's weird, because my guy saw Taylor come back out of Van Cleef & Arpels, then start walking down Rodeo toward the Beverly Wilshire Hotel and, and Scummy's walking right behind her. My guy says . . . oh, hold on, Clark, I've got him on my other phone . . . *What? . . . Huh, that's weird!*"

He came back to me. "Hey, Clark, you can kill two birds with one stone. They're not twenty feet apart. Funny thing, though, Scummy's not even trying to catch up. Just following along behind. She's got her back to him, so maybe he hasn't seen her yet."

Keeping my voice even, I said, "Great work. Tell your guy he can go buy himself a great dinner at Mastro's or Wolfgang's tonight and send me the bill. And you haven't forgotten how to send an invoice, right, Randy? Hey, I'm being called into an editorial meeting, so . . ."

"Okay, thanks, Clark!"

"You got it."

I punched off the phone and told the driver, "Floor it for dollars, pal."

Two minutes later, we rolled past Van Cleef & Arpels and I spotted her, just dawdling along through the light street traffic, eyeballing window displays. No sign of Scummy Bear.

"Pull over," I told the driver. Handing him a hundred dollar bill, I told him to stay put, but leave if I didn't return in five minutes. I got out of the cab, keeping my head down, just in case. Then I spotted the fucking punk. Emerging from a recessed store entrance. Keeping *his* head down. Taylor kept strolling. He was definitely following her, a man on a mission sinister. If not, why not simply walk up and say hi?

In a heartbeat, I'd joined the parade, keeping ten feet behind him, pretending to mutter into my phone, keeping my face averted.

And suddenly, I sensed what was about to go down. I saw Scummy turn his head and make eye contact with the driver of a panel van that was just pulling even with us, chugging slowly along our side of the street like it was looking for a parking space. The driver nodded slightly as he idled past, and Scummy cocked his chin at Taylor, clearly signaling that she was their target.

Unbelievable. Snatching a movie star in broad daylight? In Beverly Hills?

But it could work, I realized. The van suddenly accelerated, took off down Rodeo and turned left at Dayton. Scummy picked up his pace, got closer to Taylor.

Now I knew the drill. The van would circle the block, and on its next pass down Rodeo, Scummy would strike. He'd walk up and stop her with a friendly hello. Her natural reaction would be to stop and respond. Scummy would subtly herd her toward the curb, as if stepping aside for passing pedestrians. The van, its panel door already open, would pull up alongside them. Scummy would grab Taylor and jump into the van's cargo area, pulling her inside with him. The panel door would slam shut, and the van would take off.

Simple.

I was pissed. And trust me, human pals, the last thing you ever want to face is a pissed-off vampire. I'd been pondering Scummy's fate, now that I held it in my hands. The video showing his brutal murder of Janet Carter was a first-class ticket to the gas chamber. I'd considered handing him over to the cops, but now that he'd set out to kidnap—and, no doubt, rape and murder my girl—I was entertaining thoughts of burying him alive or ripping his limbs slowly from his body.

Then I remembered what I'd said to Wally as we'd walked out of Janet's apartment with rock-solid proof that this pig had committed murder most foul. Deciding to keep our reason for tossing Janet's apartment a secret, I had Wally tell our team: "It was a fishing expedition, and we didn't catch a fish."

I'd been an avid fisherman as a boy in Romania. For centuries, I'd indulged my hobby during sojourns above the soil. And just like Scummy, I'd learned that having a killer of a good time fishing depends very much on procuring primo bait.

Suddenly, it was *showtime*!

Chapter Fifty-One

The van reappeared, slowing as it drew even with Scummy, who stepped up his pace as he walked behind still-oblivious, window-shopping Taylor. Then the van passed me and braked abruptly, right alongside her.

Scummy struck fast; he didn't waste time pretending to have a conversation with Taylor like I thought he would. As the driver slid open the van's panel door, Scummy bear-hugged and hoisted her into its cargo bay before she could react.

Me? I'd made my plan, and I was sticking to it!

Remember, if vampires are famous for anything besides fangs, it's speed. In an eyeblink, I flew into the van right behind Scummy, instantly cold-cocked the driver with a massive head shot, then opened his door and shoved him into the gutter, making sure his head popped hard on the curbstone. Scummy, still struggling with Taylor, never saw the hammer blow that hit him so hard he'd stay iced until I got around to hitting him again.

Hopping into the driver's seat, I shot a glance into the street. It had gone down in a heartbeat, but . . .

Not a single eye cocked our way.

I turned to face my shocked, gasping sweetheart and said, "Hi, honey! You didn't tell me you were going shopping."

I patted the passenger seat.

"Please join me up here, my love."

Mouth open, eyes wide, she was hyperventilating. And who wouldn't be? I helped her into the seat.

"Look, babe," I told her urgently. "Calm down and we'll catch up with all the explanations, kisses and hugs later. Right now, we've gotta move before someone spots our friend in the gutter."

As I accelerated into the light midafternoon traffic, I shot a quick glance back at our guttersnipe lying motionless in the gutter. I know dead bodies, and this guy was a corpse. Mission accomplished. Apparently, there'd been no witnesses to the swift, abortive kidnapping that I'd so neatly turned into an abduction of the abductor. We were ticking like a fine Swiss timepiece. So far, anyway.

We got away clean. I turned the van into Dayton Way, rolled up to Canon, pulled over a block or so from the Montage. Taking my darling's face in my hands, I kissed her and said, "Go back to the hotel. Don't leave. Don't answer any calls. Keep your cell phone on for me, but don't talk to *anyone else*. You've got to chill until I sound the all-clear, babe. These are nasty people. Stay in the room until I get back this evening, okay? Now *promise me!*"

I felt her shiver as she nodded. "Okay, but what are you—"

I kissed her again. "No time for chitchat. Now go straight to the Montage and disappear."

She nodded, calmer now but looking glum. "I just keep fucking up, don't I?"

I laughed. "Yes. But only because you've never played this game before. Starting to get the hang of it?"

She nodded. Kissed me again, quickly, desperately, then hopped out. I headed up Canon, crossed Santa Monica, caught Sunset and gunned it toward the beach. I needed to be there while the sun still shone.

My cell phone buzzed. Wally.

"You left in a big hurry, Master. Is all well? What's up?"

I leaned back in the driver's seat and smiled.

"Everything's fine. I'm going on another fishing expedition."

"Good luck. Hope they're biting."

"Count on it, Wally."

Chapter Fifty-Two

The sun played hide-and-seek with a bank of cumulus clouds building ahead of a marine front just reported on KABC Radio. Perfect conditions.

I pulled off the highway just north of Malibu, parked the van and sat idly watching the Pacific panorama unfold. My prey, sprawled on the rear floor of the cargo bay, stirred and groaned. Instead of knocking him cold again, I allowed him to revive. He opened his eyes slowly, tried to focus on me peering down at him from the driver's seat.

"Hey, Scummy. How many fingers am I holding up?"

He stared, bleary-eyed.

"None, asshole!"

I laughed.

He didn't. Go figure.

"Wake up, Scummy, it's a beautiful day. Let's go take a walk on the beach. Come on, stand up. You're a big, strong guy, right? Word is you scare the hell out of girls and puppy dogs. That true, Scummy Boy?"

Pushing himself up on one elbow, he said, "What are you doing? Why are you fucking with me?"

I laughed. "You ask great questions, dude. But stop talking. Get on your feet. You need to get out in the fresh air. Hey, you like fishing? I do. Perfect weather for it! Clouds over the water, sun dropping into the horizon. The big ones are biting out there right now, I can smell it!"

Painfully, my prey pulled himself up onto hands and knees. He stared at me again, eyes finally focusing.

I stared back. Saw the fear.

Smiled.

"Look," he said, "all I was doing before was . . . it was just a thing where —"

I held up a hand. "Don't worry about it. We'll square the whole deal. But right now, let's get you on your feet."

I pushed back the side panel door, stepped out of the van. Reaching into the open bay, I grabbed the pudgy slob by the arm, nearly gagging at his sweaty stench.

"Come on, brace yourself on me and pull up. That's it . . . good, now just crawl over here and put your right leg out the door. Good, now the left leg, and . . . okay, you're on the ground, and you're standing up. Don't try to move, just get your bearings. You need to be wakey-wakey for all the fun we're gonna have."

I'd parked in a clearing behind a line of dunes overlooking the Pacific just north of Malibu Beach. Letting Scummy stand on his own, I walked to the van and leaned inside, hovering over the driver seat like I was rummaging for something. I heard his feet move, and smiled. Just like I'd figured, turning my back had triggered his survival instinct, made him think about escaping. Good. It meant he was waking up, and that's what I wanted.

Abruptly, I walked back and faced him. "Feeling okay now, Scummy?"

He dropped his eyes. "Yeah. Uh, hey, can we work this out? My uncle's got money, so if you let me call my mom, she'll . . ."

I chuckled. "You want your mommy? Was your mommy good to you when you were growing up, huh? Was she?"

"Uh, yeah?"

"Well, that's great! Scummy had a nice mummy. You're lucky, dude. Not like mine. She wasn't that nice. But actually, she made me what I am today. And do you *know* what I am today, Scummy? What I've been for *centuries*? Take a real good look, dude."

He looked at me again and screamed like a wild creature, jolted by coal-red eyes staring back at him, pointed fangs and a sudden sense of death's chill presence.

Getting up in his ugly face, I roared:

"Mommy and her best girlfriend made me into a *VAMPIRE*!"

He staggered, started to fall. I grabbed him by the throat, slammed him against the van. Reaching through the open panel door, I felt around under the driver's seat and pulled out what I'd spotted while he'd been out cold: a coil of rope. Shaking it in his face, I snarled.

"You brought the rope along to tie her up, right? Just like you tied up Roma's little dogs! Were you going to stake Taylor out for the coyotes, Scummy? Or just take her somewhere and rape her? Before you killed her, I mean."

Now sobs shook him. He blubbered, begged for his life.

Good.

Not that I had any sadistic interest in listening to that shit, believe me. I just wanted him shaken up and alert. And now he was—totally. Shaking out the coil of rope, I hog-tied his upper body, leaving his feet free. I wanted this piggy alive and kicking.

"Please," he sobbed. "What are you doing with me? I don't understand."

Yanking up the slack and tightening knots as I trussed him up, I said, "You're lucky, you know that? My original plan was to bury you alive and let you die in slow, excruciating panic in a coffin, right below Janet Carter's grave, you piece of shit. But then I thought, let the punishment fit the crime. Janet's death was, after all, relatively swift. Those tiny dogs, however, died a thousand deaths as they smelled the coyotes creeping slowly down from the canyons with saliva dripping off their fangs. And then, thanks to you, they were torn to bloody shreds—while you and your posse laughed your asses off. That's the horror I want you to experience on this beautiful California day, Scummy."

I tied the last knot, yanked hard. He was now secured for the purpose at hand. The rope harness crisscrossed his chest, went under his armpits and was tied off at his back, leaving him attached to twenty-odd feet of line. I coiled a loop in my right hand, and jerked him around.

"Vampires, as I'm sure you've heard, can do all manner of magical things. In a moment, any lingering doubt you may have had about whether I really *am* a vampire will be dispelled when you suddenly experience, for the last time ever, the sensation of your feet leaving the ground. And at that precise moment, I want you ponder this chilling fact, Scummy Dummy:

"Your feet will *never, ever* touch Mother Earth again."

Punctuating my little speech were gasps and moans of, "No . . . oh no, please . . . don't . . . I'll pay you! My family is rich! No, oh GOD . . . no, PLEASE!"

It was so pathetic I was actually amused. Can't blame a guy for trying, though, albeit ineptly. Grasping the harness at his chest, I hefted the rope coil and said:

"Now, let's go fishing, shall we? But we need to be very clear about each of our roles in this exciting piscatorial adventure, and here's how it's going down: *I* will be the fisherman, while *you*, Scummy Bear . . ."

Jerking his harness, I suddenly rocketed straight out toward the horizon, his endless screams trailing in our wake. Soaring to an altitude of about fifty feet, dangling him below me, I looked down on his upturned, terror-stricken face and roared:

". . . you will be the *BAIT*!"

Laughing quite insanely, I bellowed, "Think those tiny dogs you staked out were as terrified as you are right now? No, they were *more* terrified because their keen little noses had sniffed what was coming to feed on their flesh. But I'm quite certain you haven't guessed your predator *du jour*, so let's take a gander and size up the coyote 'surrogates' you'll be facing."

Swooping closer to the sea's glassy surface, I spotted swirling dark shapes I'd been searching for a mere eight hundred feet offshore. Hovering above the massive shadow shapes, I pointed down dramatically, like an avenging angel. God, how I was enjoying this.

"Behold your hunters, *prey*!"

Shrieking and jerking in spasmodic panic, Scummy Bear stared down at the roiling pack of huge, man-killing sharks swarming just below the surface.

"No, NO, NO," he kept screaming. "Don't drop me! DON'T!"

I laughed again. "*Drop* you? I'm not going to drop you, Scummy. Like I told you, we've got some serious fishing to do, boy. And it's going to be exciting, I promise."

Staring into his tear-streaked face, eager to savor his terror, I purred: "We're going trolling, pal—for *great white shark*!"

Chapter Fifty-Three

Circling slowly over the sea and keeping a sharp eye out for fins cutting the surface, I waited for his screams to subside to whimpers, then began talking idly, to myself as much as to him.

"If you ever saw the movie *Jaws*, Scummy, you should be cognizant of what most Americans learned for the very first time with that movie: the great white shark is one of the most fearsome killing machines on this planet. Up to twenty feet long, they weigh about five thousand pounds, attack prey at speeds of forty miles an hour. And it's always the same m.o. They charge straight up like an express train, shoot fifteen feet out of the water, then slam those massive jaws and *three thousand* razor-sharp teeth into their prey, aka *you*, Scummy Bear."

I grinned down at him companionably. "Or should I say . . . 'Scummy *Bait*!'

"Oh, and here's a fascinating fact, you murdering fuck—a great white can smell even *one drop* of blood in the water from a hundred yards away. So with that in mind, it's time for me to prepare the bait . . . *you* . . . for surface trolling."

Yanking him up close to me, I shot my fangs out to the max, letting him get a really good look as I opened my mouth wide, *à la* Christopher Lee in those classic English horror flicks from Hammer Films. Swiftly raking his neck, I slashed two shallow, six-inch cuts that yielded modest trickles of bright red blood.

"Perfect," I exulted. "Not *too* much, because we don't want you bleeding to death on us, do we? But more than enough to trigger the olfactory glands in the shark's nostrils. Oh, yes, sharks have nostrils for smelling things, Scummy, just as we do. But they don't *breathe* through their nostrils. They take in oxygen through their gills. Amazing creatures. Although I imagine you're not terribly interested in all this shark lore, are you, Scummy? No? Didn't think so, really. Because why have a lecture when you're about to experience the real thing, eh? So I'll just stop talking, and let's get on with it, shall we?"

He never stopped screaming. "No . . . nooo! *Noooooo!*"

I descended toward the sea's surface. I'd finally spotted just the right great white, a huge bastard, cruising idly in the waves and keeping apart from other smaller predators lurking in the area; bull and tiger sharks, mostly. Now I played out the rope until Scummy was dangling fifteen feet below me. I slowly lost altitude until he splashed down abruptly and started bouncing along the surface of the water, panicked and shrieking, dreading immersion, sensing that it signaled the endgame. He thrashed desperately until I yelled down at him.

"Good job, Scummy, keep jerking and splashing. Sharks sense vibrations even more acutely than they smell blood."

Instantly, he froze.

Fat lot of good it'd do him.

I increased my airspeed to about eight knots, perfect for shark trolling. My bait was bouncing along nicely as I dragged him out toward the horizon, moving roughly parallel to the lurking great white I'd eyeballed, not crowding the beast even though it *was* feeding time. "Presenting the meal boldly," as I'd once heard Wolfgang Puck put it.

Now it was a waiting game. You cannot force fish to bite. The great mystery of whether they will or will not rise to hit your bait has lured fishermen to stream and sea since the dawn of time. It's hard to explain the lure of sport fishing to the uninitiated, but at the heart of its thrill is the stoic anticipation, pure and simple.

God, how I was loving this day. Vengeance for Janet Carter and Roma's tiny pets aside, I was about to witness the swift and frightening death of a marginal subhuman who had plotted to murder my beloved Taylor. It was a scene even great-white-guru Spielberg would be thrilled to film. I'd replay and savor it forever.

A swift shadow flashed in the wake behind my bouncing bait. I jerked the rope up sharply, a millisecond too late. Scummy shrieked, this time in genuine, visceral pain. Damn! A smaller shark, a tiger, had darted up and nipped him while I'd been checking out the great white.

"HE BIT ME! Please . . . stop! *PLEASE!*"

Scummy was thrashing insanely now. A bright red trail threaded the white froth spewing behind him. Vibration, plus blood. Irresistible. My eyes flicked back to where ol' Great Whitey had been cruising.

Nothing. He was gone.

Now you've done it, Scummy, I thought. Triggered the perfect storm. And it's headed right at you.

I could actually sense the awful energy coiling in the depths. Smaller sharks strike from just beneath the water's surface, but the killer king of the seas attacks after making a deep descent, then barreling straight upward, smashing into its prey and erupting out of the water in the great leap known as a "breach."

A microsecond later, the sea exploded in a paralyzing thunderclap!

The great white burst ferociously out of the water—every inch of its seventeen-foot long, torpedolike body exposed and glowing in the sunlight —with Scummy's writhing, blood-spattered body gripped in its massive jaws.

In one split millisecond, at the peak of the monster's arc, I saw the doomed killer-creep's terrified eyes staring into mine. With no conscious thought, I flipped ol' Scummy the bird as he, and the monster eating him alive, crashed back into the sea and disappeared.

A split second later, I disappeared right after them.

SHIT!

The fucking rope had coiled around my wrist!

It was so goddam absurd, I actually laughed. A moment later, I shot out of the sea in full flight. Clothes soaked, but . . . hey, you fly, you dry, right?

I just hoped the damn saltwater hadn't ruined my silk cape.

Chapter Fifty-Four

She ran into my arms as I walked into the suite.

"I've been so goddam scared. I even cried and I *never* cry," she said all in a rush. "But then I thought, what the fuck am I crying about? You'll always protect me. But it was just so . . . scary."

I kissed her gently, held her for a long moment and did the "there, there" thing. Then I said, "Look, Taylor, I understand. You kept it together until you got back here and had a moment to think, then it hit you all at once, right?"

She nodded. "Clark, do you . . . was Scummy actually going to *kill* me? I know he's a mean prick, but I never thought he'd *literally* murder me."

I led her over to the sofa. There was a pitcher of iced tea on the table. "Just what the doctor ordered," I said, pouring a glass. Then she started looking me over the way women do, and frowned.

"You look kinda rumpled. Your clothes, I mean, and . . ." She sniffed the air. "Is that *gasoline* I smell?"

"Bingo!" I responded. "But don't ask."

Yep. I'd torched the van at the beach. For two reasons: to obliterate DNA, fingerprints and other forensic traces, and to ramp up the mystery of Scummy Bear's disappearance once the van was traced back to his deceased buddy—who'd probably be reclassified as a murder victim. That'd sell a few extra copies of the paper *and* slow down the cops.

"Sweetheart, let me start at the beginning and I'll catch up to all of . . . well, most of your questions. But first, and most importantly, you must *never* tell anyone what happened today in Beverly Hills. You haven't said anything so far, right?"

She shook her head. "Look, I know I've screwed things up too many times with my big mouth, Clark. But I've learned my lesson. Really! Just tell me what happened."

"Okay. In a word, I fed that scumbag to a seventeen-foot great white shark off Zuma Beach. I trolled him as bait and it got very bloody."

I didn't know quite what to expect from my volatile minx. Would she laugh? Cry? She said nothing for a moment and I sensed her visualizing it all. Even savoring it. My little sweetheart didn't disappoint.

"*Fuck him.* He tried to kill me."

I suppressed a chuckle and said, "The murdering son of a bitch was a sociopathic sadist who liked torturing small animals as well. Animal torturers routinely turn into sadistic killers of human beings. And that's not just opinion, my love. I have proof, absolute photographic proof, that he killed Janet Carter in cold blood. And look what I found in his pockets after I left you in Beverly Hills."

I opened a Starbucks Coffee bag he'd been carrying, took out a small package and extracted several small white packets.

"Look familiar?"

"Yes! They look like the, you know . . ."

"Yeah. Like the dope packets he and Roma would pass out like candy to the posse. *You* included. But this batch is special. I've already taste-tested it, babe. It's that fucking killer shit Oxi that Roma kept slipping you. And, although I can't absolutely prove it, this is what Roma passed to Scummy the night Janet died of a sudden, massive overdose . . . helped along by the murdering bastard, who followed her home, sat on her chest and suffocated her to death."

She stared at me, taking it in. "You think Roma is actually . . ."

"I *absolutely* do. I might not be able to prove in a court of law that she's a murderer. I'm not convinced myself that she knew that Oxi shit might kill you. It might also be hard to prove legally that she knew Scummy was staking her pets out for the savage amusement of her vicious, ass-kissing pals and his buddies, but how could she not know what was going on right under her nose—that little dogs were being ripped apart by coyotes for fun? No, she's guilty in the Court of Clark. And she's going down."

I looked at Taylor, grinning. "You gotta problem wid dat, girlfriend?"

She didn't crack even a small smile.

"No, I don't. Listen, you haven't asked, but I want you to know that I haven't been near drugs since that first night we made love. You are the sole reason for my sudden sobriety. My love for you, and hating that horrible fucking bitch, will make me even stronger. It makes me sick that I used to think she and her wannabe douchebags were worth hanging out with. Yeah, *Dragomir*, do us all a favor. Throw Roma off a fucking cliff— only don't be there to catch her ass like you caught me when I jumped off that balcony!"

"Wow! Listen to my little *killer*."

"Kill or be killed, right, vampire man? The worst part, and you made me realize it, is that I was killing myself. But that shit's over for good—as long as you don't stop loving me, of course. But . . . didn't you say something about 'all eternity,' or something to that effect?"

That rocked me. I sensed that my little minx wasn't simply joking around this time. Had she just proposed marriage to a vampire and becoming . . . Mrs. Vampire?

I took her in my arms, kissed her quite thoroughly and said: "I believe I did use those very words, yes."

My cell phone buzzed.

"Wally?"

"You okay, boss?"

"Tip-top, sport. Why do you ask?"

"Oh, no reason. Funny, though, Beverly Hills cops fished a dead guy out of the gutter right near where some paparazzi spotted you today."

"No kidding. What did the poor fella die of?"

"Cops say he apparently fell and hit his head on the curb. No witnesses."

"Imagine that. Even in Beverly Hills, a person's just not safe anymore."

"Guess not. Well, then, if you have nothing else to tell me, I'm calling it a day, Master. See you tomorrow?"

"Yes. But I won't be in early. Need to chill. Too much going on lately."

"You got that right. Bye."

I clicked off. My adored one was smiling, big-time.

"Did you say it's time to *chill*? Does Big Guy need to calm down, relax, get . . . loose?"

"Yes, I do. Think you can help me with that?"

"Oh, I've got a few ideas you might like. In fact, I have three or four. Shall we start with a nice sit-down dinner here in the suite? I mean, a *real* meal, not snacks. First, a frosty margarita, then Cristal champagne . . . and you can chase that with an *early* nightcap of Kelt. I emphasize the 'early' part because I want to maximize beddy-bye time with you, you irresistible creature."

"Please—don't call me a *creature*."

"OMIGOD! . . . I'm sorry . . . I . . . I didn't mean . . ."

She looked so horrified, I burst out laughing.

"Girl, I'm yankin' yo' chain. I know you ain't prejudiced against us otherworldly minorities. Don't be so politically correct, you Hollywood liberal. My only beef with 'creature' is that it sounds wimp-ass. Call me beast or monster! Or better yet . . . WILD THANG!"

How to describe that wonderful evening? The meal from the Montage kitchens was exquisite. I had lamb chops, done the French way. Bloody. *(Der!)* She loved the lobster; damn near had an orgasm, then insisted on baby-feeding me a piece with her fingers. I dutifully aaah-ed over it, but I'm *so* not a fish guy. (Again, *der!*) Love catching them, but that's about it.

We shared dessert, something pink and cold. Again, she kept feeding me spoonsful, and I actually . . . well, call me a girlie-man, but I really enjoyed it. I was just nuts in love with this funny, flame-haired, voluptuous creature with the laughing eyes, and made sure she knew it.

On the sofa, and on the table. Afterward, she called room service to deliver decaf cappuccino and clear the dishes, then poured a snifter of Kelt with her own dainty little hands and gently pushed me out toward the patio.

"Let me get organized and I'll join you outside, darling."

Time passed. I watched the moon, thought for a moment I'd heard a werewolf howl. More howls. Ah, coyotes. Above Sunset Boulevard. Pining for their tiny dog *hors d'oeuvres à la Roma*, no doubt. And I thought of Scummy Bear. Dead. *No* grave to mark his passing. Just meaty chunks dissolving in the acid slime of a great white's belly.

It made me smile.

"Sorry, my love," I heard her trill a moment later. I turned and—just as the little minx had calculated—thrilled instantly to the silhouette of her born-for-sin body, outlined through her sheer nightie by back-lighting. She sauntered out of the sitting room and onto the darkened balcony.

"Well, now, look at you!"

"That's the *idea*, mister. And I've got a few more ideas! Just remember one thing . . . tonight is *my* night. So you just relax and leave the seduction stuff to Momma, okay?"

The next sound heard in the still night was . . . a zipper.

Unzipping.

Mine, as it turned out.

Again?

She smiled up into my eyes, then bobbed in an elegant curtsy, just like a little princess—although "bobbed" is not *quite* the right word, as it implies she'd bounced right back up. She did not. Actually, she sank gracefully to her knees. Surprise followed surprise . . . and when we finally made our way to bed, she asked:

"Beginning to relax, darling?"

I played it smart, of course. "Sorry to be a bore, my love, but I'm *still* experiencing just a tiny bit of tension."

She smiled lazily. "Luckily for you, my dear, I know the secret to dissipating that tension, once and for all. The trick is to vigorously massage all that tightness down toward one area, centering it. Then you concentrate on generating *good* vibrations in that area and . . . *poof* . . . tension released."

Her hands were everywhere then. And so were mine. I hummed that old Beach Boys favorite, "You're givin' me good vibrations!", and she *giggled*. See why I worship this girl? I have never been happier, dead or alive, than I was in that moment. And gradually, I actually did feel my tension centering in that one area until . . .

Poof!

Just as advertised, one relaxed and happy vampire.

Chapter Fifty-Five

Blinding headlights, squealing tires. The Ducati's front wheel abruptly crossed up, ejecting me over the handlebars and into space. I hit the road helmet-first, bodysurfing the tarmac at eighty miles an hour.

The nightmare ripped me out of sleep. I jerked upright in bed. Knew instantly, as vampires do, that this hadn't been a dream, but a vision. Knew what it meant. Hated that the contact had come too late to stop it. I just hoped it wasn't too late, period! Had to move fast. Slipping out of bed quietly without waking Taylor, I threw on clothes, ran for the balcony and leaped straight out into the night sky.

I spotted the Trauma Hawk's running lights instantly. It was a mile out, coming fast toward Beverly Hills. No need to intercept it. I flew straight to its inevitable destination: Cedars-Sinai Hospital, North Tower. Moments later, the chopper landed on the roof's helipad. I touched down behind it, keeping to the shadows as a team of EMT medics erupted from the building, pushing a gurney and a medical equipment cart. Trauma Hawk medics were deplaning. As the two teams met to offload their patient, I heard the words, "motorcycle accident."

No one noticed as I slipped through the shadows and strolled into the building's receiving area, waving casually as I passed some guy at a desk talking into a phone. I walked over to the elevator and pressed the *Down* button. The guy looked at me curiously as he talked into his phone. But I had to be with the chopper guys, right? How else would I have suddenly landed on the roof? Could be I was the patient's doctor, still dressed in civvies after a hurried house call turned into a Trauma Hawk emergency? Hell, I sure didn't *fly* up here to the fifteenth floor, right?

A second later, the medics came rushing in from the roof, pushing the gurney with their unconscious patient and shouting stuff like, "keep the pressure up!" and "we still okay on that pulse?"

I stood off to the side, started mock-talking on my iPhone. No one paid any attention to me. My plan had been to hang back and watch for which floor they'd stop at, but when the elevator came and I kept talking on the phone, one guy actually held the door and said, "Hey, chop-chop if you're going down, buddy! We've got a head injury here."

It was that simple. When we hit their floor, they rushed off down the hall. I dawdled along behind, noted the number of the room they'd put the patient in, then ducked into a men's room halfway down the long corridor and waited a while. When there was no hue and cry, I strolled back out.

It was the middle of the night, dead quiet. Hospital quiet. Keeping my eyes open as I passed empty rooms, offices and a supply closet, I found a set of green medical scrubs and put them on over my clothes. They made me effectively invisible. The clipboard I'd picked up in my travels didn't hurt either.

As I explored the floor, I watched doctors and nurses hustle in and out of the room they'd put my patient in. My vampire ears overheard conversations that put me in the picture.

"He's banged up, not one broken bone, but it's the usual motorcycle shit —traumatic brain injury caused by rotational acceleration. Dr. Phillips thinks it's probably permanent damage, fatal if his brain stem shuts down. We've got him set up on a monitor now. Dr. Phillips wants Dr. Carney to see him. They're calling him in."

Ah, yes. Rotational acceleration. After initial impact, the head keeps turning, or rolling back, creating devastating damage to the soft tissue and blood vessels. Even a well-engineered helmet and a thick skull can't always save your life.

A young blond nurse came running up. "Omigod, you guys, they just checked his ID and he's a celebrity—he's Damon Strutt, that cute British guy who plays a vampire on TV! How's he doing, anyway?"

"Bad! Touch-and-go. Might not make it through the night. They've located Dr. Carney and he's due any second."

About ten minutes later, Dr. Carney, all dolled up in a fancy suit with a few drinks under his belt after dinner on the town, walked onto the floor. I joined the scurry of nurses and orderlies who eddied in his wake as he headed for Damon's room. After a brief examination of his patient, he walked back out again, shaking his head.

"Do you hold out any hope, doctor?"

His eyes flicked to me. I shot back a boyish grin, shrugged. "I'm a huge Kragen fan. I think a lot of us are . . ."

The nurses tittered. A male orderly fist-bumped me. Dr. Carney said, "Even if he makes it through the night, the brain damage . . ."

He shrugged, asked the head nurse, "Any luck on locating his family yet?"

"It's just his mother in England, doctor. His agents will call us as soon as they make contact."

"Right. Call me if there's any change. Good night."

"Good night, doctor," we chorused.

Things got quiet on the floor then. Corridor lights dimmed, personnel departed. A matronly woman at the nurses' station was now in sole charge of the floor. She'd glanced at me earlier, not showing much interest, but now that I was the only non-patient in her bailiwick, I suddenly became the focus of her attention. I walked up to her, smiling.

"Hi," I said. "Bill Franklin, Engineering."

She nodded, looking a bit puzzled; engineering guys didn't wear scrubs here, I guess. But she said, "Hope you're here about the thermostats. They're still not working right. Cold one moment, and hot the next . . . OH!"

She stared blankly at where I'd been.

"Just relax," I said from behind her, pressing a nerve in her neck until her head flopped forward. I eased her gently down onto the desk, then ran to Damon's room. He was lying on his back in the bed, tubes stuck in his body and connected to a bank of monitoring equipment. I pulled a chair up, put my mouth to his ear and spoke his name loudly several times.

No response.

I mind-rolled him, but . . . nobody home. Nothing. Not a flicker of mental activity, conscious or subconscious. Now what? I'm a vampire, not a doctor. I'd hoped to make contact with Damon's psyche, even on an elemental level, so I could ask my good pal the crucial question. With his life in the balance, would he opt for conversion to an undead state? Or would he rather die?

Goddammit! I'd missed my chance with Jimmy. Had I left it too late again? I got up close to Damon's ear and said aloud:

"Look, old buddy, you're a heartbeat away from lights out. Question is, do you want to survive as a vampire . . . like me? Or do I make that decision for you? I think I know what you'd opt for, but it's now or never because—"

His body twitched. For a moment, I thought he'd heard me. My eyes flicked to the oscilloscope screen, and saw the squiggly green lines suddenly flatten. Instantly, the monitor alarm began braying. Moving vampire-fast, I hit a switch and killed it, then sprang for Damon's neck, biting hard and drinking deeply, simultaneously slicing a vein in my wrist. Blood welled up and I pressed the gushing wound tightly to his mouth, praying I was not too late as I pounded on his chest to generate enough airflow to trigger a gag reflex. Then I heard a gasp, felt his body jerk. I looked up at him, blood dripping from my fangs, and cheered him on.

"Yeah, buddy . . . You can do it, Damon!"

I forced my blood into his mouth. And then I felt him start to suck hungrily at the force that could give him life. As he consumed my essence, my ears were cocked for any noise of visitors. I wasn't worried about the nurse at the station. She'd be out for an hour, at least. But somewhere in this vast, high-tech hospital, there had to be a monitor that monitored all the other monitors, so . . . it could have heard that instantly stifled alarm.

Minutes ticked by. Damon sucked at my wound more noisily now. Concentrating my physical force, I made my heart pump harder. And then, abruptly, he sat up straight, eyes blinking as he wiped his mouth and said:

"What's all the bloody noise, mate? Fuck, you're bloody, as well! Where are we? In *hell*?"

Before I could even ask him to try to stand, he stood. Effortlessly. Tough bastard, I thought. No wonder they'd cast him as a star vampire.

"Okay," Damon said. "I remember pranging my bike, so I guess this is a hospital. Am I going to live, mate?"

I grinned and winked. "Uh . . . yes, in a manner of speaking. Here, take this cloth and wipe your face while I bandage up my wrist. Okay, pal, here's the situation."

I heard voices heading our way.

"Damn, no time to explain now. We've got to move fast. The docs might try to stop us, so—"

"Wot? Stop us? Why?"

"Told you there's no time to explain, you thick-headed git. They'll want to hold you for observation and we cannot allow that . . . so don't fret, follow my lead, and Bob's yer uncle, mate!"

I hustled him out the door and down the corridor toward the elevator I'd used.

Somebody yelled, "Hey, hold on! Where are you going with that patient?"

I turned. A doctor I'd spotted earlier was hustling up behind us, two nurses in his wake.

Before I could answer, Damon turned and declaimed in his actor's voice. "Wrong, Doctor—it's *your patient* who's taking himself somewhere. Good work, by the way, old chap. I'm feeling GREAT, thanks! Send the bill, and I'll be enclosing a big donation for the hospital! You know who I am, right?"

Doc wasn't buying it. He broke into a trot, and barked at the nurses. "Call Security, *stat*!"

Now we were running flat out. In a moment, we'd skidded up to the elevator and punched the button. It must have been set to stay in place, because the door slid open instantly. A moment later, it closed in our pursuers' faces.

Faintly, I heard someone yell, "Look . . . they're going UP!"

In a second, we were out of the elevator. We trotted through the now-empty receiving area that led to the roof. The guy I'd seen before wasn't there. His phone was ringing furiously. Then we were out on the deserted North Tower roof of Cedars-Sinai, a huge complex that dominates the nexus of West Hollywood and Beverly Hills. Damon followed me as I walked toward the ledge overlooking Beverly Boulevard.

"I know you're as sharp as they fucking come, Clark," he said, somewhat anxiously. "I'm sure you've got a brilliant plan for escaping those mad medics when they come piling out of the elevator. Yes? So, uh . . . care to share it with me, mate?"

We'd reached the roof's ledge.

He peered over and said, "Crikey, must be sixteen stories down, at least. And I just heard the elevator bell tinkle, did you?"

I looked him square in the eye. "Damon, two things you've got to absorb *fast*: One, you're a real vampire now—not just playing one on TV. Two, vampire-wise, you already know how to talk the talk. Now it's time to walk the walk. You want a *plan*, Damon? Here's the fucking plan, mate."

And I shoved him off the roof.

Chapter Fifty-Six

Power-diving after Damon at warp speed, I instantly cursed myself; *not* for tossing him off the building, but for tossing him off on the Beverly Boulevard side. Beverly's a busy main drag, so at any given moment, eyeballs could flick skyward and spot indiscreet vampires indulging in aerial antics.

The good news? It was late, well after one a.m., and LA's an early town. The bad news? It was Saturday night, dammit. Club night! Still a fair amount of vehicle traffic, but . . . *c'est la vie*. I rocketed down after Damon, shot past him, and was waiting smugly in place to catch him in my arms, but . . . surprise, surprise! When I looked up to locate him, he wasn't falling toward me. He was suddenly rising up, up, UP!

Dude was fucking *FLYING*!

Stunned, I watched my newbie vamp snap off several sharp turns and rolls, like a test pilot wringing out a new fighter jet, and damn near cheered when the euphoric wacko suddenly executed a full somersault! *OMFG*, as we say in Hollywood. Why did I not anticipate that ever-fearless Damon Strutt, licensed stunt pilot, motorcycle nut and daredevil *extraordinaire*, would *instantly* intuit how to employ the exciting new tools suddenly at his command—and, being Damon, would unhesitatingly, recklessly, fly off like a vampire bat outta hell? A positive sign that his sudden conversion hasn't totally freaked him.

WHAT THE HELL?

Damon suddenly shot straight up to the top floors of Cedars-Sinai and was hovering in thin air outside the windows of patients, waving cheerily, executing aerial stunts like a bloody circus performer!

Oh, fuck . . . *MOVE, Dragomir!*

Rocketing up behind him at Mach 3, I groaned as I spotted an orderly and at least two patients waving at our boy through the windows, wide-eyed with fright and delight. Grabbing an ankle, I flipped Damon upside down, dragged him in my wake as I flew into the quiet backstreets behind the hospital, finally landing in the darkest corner of its huge parking lot. Glaring at him through smoldering red eyes, I blinked in disbelief as he ignored my baleful stare and started laughing. Giggling really, like a goddam fool.

"You fucking *wanker*," I began.

Now he *was* in hysterics! "Sorry, mate, but it's right fuckin' hilarious whenever you launch into the old Limey slang!"

Well, at least he was laughing. I told myself it was time to help him deal with his staggering transformation from living human being to undead, blood-drinking vampire; I could always rip into him later for his indiscretion.

I threw an arm around my old pal, dragged him down to sit beside me in the parking lot.

"Let's keep a low profile here, mate," I said. "Look, I'm amazed at how calmly you're taking all this. I don't know if you remember anything, but you were knocked out at the hospital and almost certainly a goner, the doc said. You were running out of time, and you couldn't hear me when I asked if you wanted eternal bloody life, to convert . . . to be . . ."

"Like *you* are," he said. "And I am now, right?"

"Well, yeah, but did you know that I was . . ."

He grinned that lopsided grin of his and said, "Look, mate, I always knew you were bloody unique. Like, I damn well *know* you saved my life in that bloody crash in the canyons. I absolutely sensed your presence in my mind. Not like a vision or anything, but you were there. Angel or devil, I wasn't sure what you were, really—and I actually did think 'vampire' at one point. But then I noticed how much you liked your drinks and steaks, and I kept hearing from vampire experts that vamps can't actually taste anything except blood, so . . ."

I laughed. "Yeah, the fucking so-called experts! Some of whom will swear that vampires *cannot* fly. Of course, other 'experts' insist that they absolutely *can*. So in light of your recent experiences, what's the truth, mate? Wasn't that *you* swooping around the sky, playing silly buggers with the whole fucking hospital?"

He went silent, like he'd suddenly got it. How to do this right, I asked myself?

"Look, Damon, you are a vampire now and that's that. But, mate, I'm here to guide you until you get the hang of it. Ask me questions, I'll give you straight answers. I am now your official mentor. And we have an obligation to each other that I'll explain later. But more than that, you're my buddy, man! I've got your back, just like always. And here's what I learned, right off the bat, after I was converted: When you're above ground, just play it like you're still human. Remember, nobody knows what's happened tonight, so you can go back to your own pad, sleep in your own bed, wear your own clothes, drive your own car, and still play a vampire on

TV—which is quite a mind-blower, actually. You have no wife or even a steady girl, so no complications there. And your only close family is your English mummy back home in Bumfuck-on-Avon or wherever. Right? So you just play it like who you are! Because you *are* still Damon Strutt, world-famous poofter . . . uh, actor."

That got a smile out of him.

Then he asked, "How about the hospital people. Won't they—

I held up a hand sharply. "Damon, don't disappoint me, mate! Where *are* you now, this minute? In Hollywood, right? And what is Damon Strutt in Hollywood? The star of a hit TV series, right? And as you fucking well know, nobody in Hollywood fucks with stars. If you had turned into the Wolf Man before their very eyes back there, they'd still shut the fuck up and deny everything if your agent or manager told them to. And, by the way, doctors and nurses at Cedars-Sinai treat Hollywood megastars day in and day out. They'll just figure you for another arrogant star too rude to hang around and grant autographs after your miraculous recovery. Right? Even if they had *videotape* of me biting your neck, cutting my vein and feeding you blood—which they *don't*, by the way."

I reached in a pocket, dramatically fished out the videocassette that I'd ripped from the recorder attached to the nursing station monitor after knocking out Florence Nightingale, and waved it under his nose.

"Even if they *did* get to screen this videotape, do you *really* believe Cedars-Sinai would ever admit to Hollywood, and the world, that stars under their care might somehow become vampires? Like, George Clooney goes in . . . and walks out with *fangs*?"

Now he was laughing like the Damon of old.

I said, "You know what you need, mate? Not old Dragomir—that's my birth name—philosophizing and boring us both to bloody death. You need to mellow out with a few stiff ones, and—"

"And stick my stiff one in a human girl, right, Clark? I mean, Drago-what-the-fuck? Bloody hell, what *do* I call you now, mate?

"Call me *Ishmael*, motherfucker!"

Now I had him shaking with laughter, and . . . *wow*, he'd actually used the term, "human girl." Talk about embracing your inner vampire in a heartbeat! But, hey, I got it. When you're still human, girls are sexy creatures, of course. But the second you're undead, the lust for human female flesh can drive you insane. Literally. Ask a man . . . uh, a vampire who knows!

We walked back toward Beverly Boulevard. I had the perfect destination in mind: a joint called Dominick's, one of my favorite watering holes, where they make the best spaghetti and meatballs in the city. Ask anyone. Best part, they stay open late.

"So," I said as we strolled, "can't wait to try out your new vampire . . . uh, equipment, eh? Well, I just *might* be able to help you out there, horny creature."

He looked at me sharply in mock horror.

"Not in a gay way, of course," I said.

We cracked up. Ah, yes, old jokes are best. And this was a happy occasion.

In *so* many ways.

I slugged him on the shoulder.

"Happy birthday, Damon!"

Chapter Fifty-Seven

We sat at the bar, looking up at the shelf that ran from one end of Dominick's to the other, festooned with rare, collectible whiskey bottles. And when we tired of that, we zeroed in on the female bartender's fecund ass. For whatever reason, Taylor gave me a pass this time.

"Now I see why you hang out here, mate!" leered Damon and he kicked back a healthy belt of Pimm's Cup.

"So, me old darlin' Damon," I said, "does your libation of choice taste just as good as it always did?"

He nodded thoughtfully, swirling it in his glass. "It does, Clark, it does. So why do they say vampires can't taste food or drink if it's not true?"

"Vampires are hot in Hollywood. Do I have to tell you that, *Kragen*? Didn't you just get mobbed when we walked in here until I warned the proprietor to back everyone off if he didn't want his joint slagged in my column? Anyway, *every* vampire fan thinks they're a goddam expert nowadays. But, *you're* the expert now, my friend! Man, if the fans only knew that their favorite TV vampire had suddenly transmogrified into the real thing. What a great story!"

I swung around on my barstool and faced the room. Diners at their tables, people along the bar . . . all eyes were on The Vampire Kragen. God, how I wanted to tell them the truth. And in a moment of party-guy euphoria, triggered by my soul-shaking relief at snatching my pal from the jaws of death, I damn near did.

"Ladies and gentlemen," I bellowed over the chitchat, bowing from my barstool. "Thank you for giving this great star his space—and in appreciation, Kragen will now treat you to that which few on Earth have experienced: the mind-stopping roar of a rutting vampire who's just spotted the female of his choice!"

Swinging halfway round to face him, I made a courtly bow and said stagily, "Most illustrious and awe-inspiring Kragen, we beg you! If you please, Maestro?"

He fired back a penetrating stare that actually frightened me, then rocked on his barstool, leaped to the floor, threw back his handsome, leonine head and emitted an explosive basso profundo bellow, topped by sharp, keening overtones, that literally froze the room. The mind-blasting roar of a vampire male in full rut was underscored by the subharmonics of silverware crashing to the floor. Two women instantly fainted dead away. One man, in tears, rushed up and dropped to his knees before Mighty Kragen in abject supplication.

Stifling an overpowering impulse to burst out laughing, I looked over at Damon, who was damn near pissing himself. The crowd came to its feet, cheering and applauding. Damon blessed them with upraised palms, then shut them up brilliantly with: "Drinks all around, barmaid—ON ME!"

The joint exploded. Cheers, applause, laughter. Damon nudged me. "Pretty good roar, wasn't it, mate? Authentic, eh?"

I shook my head in genuine admiration. "Couldn't have done it better myself, dear boy. Now I *know* you're fucking horny!"

We clinked glasses, then toasted the crowd. Now it really was a goddam party—people up on their feet raising glasses, girls dancing with wild abandon, several encroaching, or should I say *en-crotching*, on Damon's space. I knew it was time to implement the *coup de grace*, the diabolical endgame that had sprung full-blown into my mind at the moment of the dream triggered by Damon's near-death experience.

On cue, he asked, "Didn't you mention that you might be able to help a horny new vampire get a bit of the old, bit-of-the-old? Eh? *Wink, wink, nudge, nudge* . . . eh?"

I held up a finger, pulled out my cell phone and punched in Vanillo's number.

"Clark! Hi, where are you? Sounds noisy."

"Dominick's."

"Omigod. I love that place. It's got a real guy vibe. You know who hangs there a lot? Your favorite metrosexual, Ryan Seacrest. He says the spaghetti and meatballs are awesome."

"They are. Look, Vanillo, I need you to pinpoint Roma Kane again. I want to—"

"Clark, I'm looking at her, *right now*."

"Where?"

"The Roosevelt."

"She with anyone special?"

"No. Just her skanks. Nobody around tonight. She looks not so happy."

"Great. Thanks, Vanill' . . . love ya. Mean it!"

"Clar—"

I clicked off, punched another number. "Roma," I told Damon.

His eyes lit up.

Covering the mouthpiece, I whispered, "One thing—she'll be your first, so you'll probably want to go full vampire on her ass. Try not to kill her, okay? I want the bitch alive."

We traded grins. Then she was on the line.

"Hello?"

In my best concierge voice, I intoned, "Please hold for Mr. Damon Strutt, Ms. Kane."

I thrust the phone at him.

Smooth bastard never missed a beat, dropping his voice two octaves.

"Roma. My need is great. I told you I would return for you. *This is the moment.*"

He listened, then said, "Speak to my man. He will bring me to you. *Be ready!*"

Grinning, Damon handed me the phone. We fist-bumped as I intoned pompously, "Ms. Kane, please go home immediately, prepare yourself, then wait in your bedroom for my phone call. I will deliver Mr. Strutt at precisely three a.m."

"Yes, I understand," she said, in a hot, wet voice that told me she was already under his spell.

I clicked off. "The game's afoot, dear boy. She awaits your pleasure."

We dissolved into helpless laughter, damn near giggling like girls.

Damon raised his glass. "You've been a great mentor, mate. You teach me to fly, you get me laid—and I've only been on the vampire game for what? A fucking hour? This beats so-called real life, doesn't it? So far, at any rate. Oh, I say, your glass is bloody near empty."

He turned away, called the barmaid over and instantly started flirting, asking her if she was free this weekend. I smiled, remembering how I'd felt after my conversion three centuries ago. Far from being frightened, I'd been absolutely euphoric, feeling mysterious new powers coursing through me, even though I had yet to experience their potential. Imagine *knowing* you can fly before you've even tried. It's a state of mind impossible to describe; a confident, innate knowledge of newfound physical and mental strength, and a liberating release of all the fears you'd harbored as a human being.

And even though you know you've crossed the boundaries of life itself, it feels no more disturbing or disorienting than, say, leaving Los Angeles to take up residence in Honolulu—as evidenced by Damon, who certainly wasn't wasting a bloody minute bemoaning the "life" he'd left behind. Immortal now, he'd move endlessly through many lifetimes. And many women, by the looks of it.

I unlimbered my cell phone again, and made a call to my favorite paparazzo, Randy Cooper.

"Hey, Clark, what's up?"

"I need something special, Randy, and I know you've got everything photographic and electronic in that new Range Rover of yours. Here's what I need . . ."

After hearing my laundry list, Randy chuckled. "I'm not even going to ask what you're up to, Clark—not that you'd tell me. You need it right now?"

"Yeah. I'm at Dominick's. And I'm with people."

"No problemo. I'll swing by and my guy will run it in to you. In a plain, brown wrapper, of course."

"You're my man. Bill me."

"Duh!"

I chuckled. "Randy, hip people say *Der!*"

"Excuse me, *muchacho*, but I am a gay man. In West Hollywood, we're using *duh* again. *Comprendo?*"

"Duh!"

I clicked off. Damon was ordering the spaghetti and meatballs. I asked for the fried calamari appetizer. Ten minutes later, Randy's guy walked into the bar, slipped me my package and left. Damon, eyes locked halfway down the barmaid's cleavage, didn't even notice. Good. Baby vamp's all fired up and well fed.

"Damon, listen, I've got one of my reporters right next door at Jerry's Deli. He needs to talk to me about a story he's covering. Can you just hang here about fifteen minutes?"

He barely glanced at me. "Cool, Daddy-O," he said. "Plant you now, dig you later."

"Wow," I said. "How does a Brit learn to talk sixties hipster talk so friggin' fast? Do NOT move. I'll be right back."

I walked outside, slipped into an alley behind Jerry's Deli, and shot up into the friendly skies.

Six minutes later, I'd jimmied open the French doors on the balcony outside Roma Kane's bedroom. Four minutes after that, I'd done the deed I'd come to do and was outta there. Electronic device planted. Mission accomplished. Back again with Damon at Dominick's in just under twenty minutes, I ordered us one each for the road. We knocked them back, slipped out to the alley and got in the wind.

Showtime.

Chapter Fifty-Eight

Down we flew, landing lightly on Roma Kane's bedroom balcony. Damon adjusted the billowing opera cape he'd thrown on during our brief stop-off at his pad. He hadn't wanted to wear it, but I'd insisted.

"Clothes make the man, and the vampire," I told him. "Plus, girls love to play dress-up. Capes make them *nuts!*"

It was time. I threw him a thumbs-up, stepped back into the balcony's deep shadow, and punched up her number on my cell phone.

"Hel—"

"Miss Kane, hang up *immediately*, then walk to your balcony door and open it . . . *NOW!*"

I'd positioned Damon so he'd be standing directly in front of the French double-doors. She pushed them open, gasping as he loomed out of the dark, sinister and handsome in his dashing cape; every inch her fantasy vampire. She breathed his name:

"Kragen."

Her hands flew to her cheeks like pretty little birds as he moved toward her. She retreated, face flushed in sheer sexual excitement, confronted at last by the beast who stalked her dreams. Kragen stepped through the doors. Knowing what was coming, I braced. He roared. She stiffened in shocked reaction. I crouched, moving swiftly toward the still-open doors. Roma's eyes were riveted on Kragen. She never saw me as I carefully aimed a tiny electronic remote control at the device I'd planted. Craning my neck at just the right angle, I saw a red pinprick blink back at me.

Perfect.

I slid back into the shadows, played voyeur for a moment, watching through the partially opened doors. He'd already ripped off her négligée. Gripping her blond hair and twisting her head back violently, he forced her to her knees, snarling in her ear. Her tiny hands fluttered. Suddenly, she was holding his rampant beasthood, trying to control him as he rammed haphazardly, pounding cheeks, lips, eyes. He was hurting her now, and she gasped and panted, knowing she had no control but sounding like she loved having no idea of what would please him, no way to restrain the dangerous, haphazard thrusts.

He stopped suddenly then, tore off his clothes and yanked her up savagely by the neck. Emitting the vampire rutting howl, he threw her on the bed and ripped off her wispy panties. Now she was facedown. His hands slid back to her ankles, and he forced her apart, pushing her forward until she slammed violently into the headboard. Her throat opened in endless, ecstatic barks of pleasure modulated by shrieks of pain. Word on the street was that Roma liked it fast and hard. Just the way Damon was dishing it. But he *was* heeding my advice, holding a little something back. Otherwise, he'd have killed the bitch already. Three-quarter vampire, so to speak. She'd live.

I turned and leaped back out into the night. Climbing to about six hundred feet, I cruised over Beverly Hills, enjoying the brisk buffeting of wind. I fished out my iPhone, dialed the number of the tricked-out Android cell phone I'd also tossed under Roma's nightstand earlier. Back in her bedroom, it rang silently, answered on autodial . . . and suddenly I could hear it all: the shrieks and the begging; the bestial grunts and the pounding of furniture as it slammed against floors and walls. I smiled. Then I laughed out loud into the wind. *Justice at last, goddammit*, for my damaged Taylor. Not to mention poor, dead Janet Carter.

Call it revenge if you like, I don't give a shit. Bottom line: Damage was being done, through me, on behalf of Roma Kane's victims. As for Roma, she'd survive this night—and her aches and scars. Me? Despite my earlier warning to Damon, I honestly wouldn't care if Kragen's love bites killed her. I was like the old Hasidic Jew who is taken to a strip club, returns home horny and decides to bang the wife, even though they'd already done their once-a-month, and says philosophically: "Hey . . . if the bitch dies, she *dies!*"

I kept the cell phone on, a perfect soundtrack thrumming under the murderous thoughts swirling through my soul. *Fuck you, Roma!* Sure, you're technically not quite a murderer, but you're a borderline criminal at best; an archetype of all the overprivileged, self-centered narcissistic scum who swirl and flourish in Hollywood's glamorous sewers, mindlessly hurting and infecting everything you touch while finding it all so *gloriously* fucking funny.

I chuckled at the crash of furniture breaking. Not that I needed to hear it all, but I listened to the entire digital recording as it spooled into an audio file linked to my Dropbox, making sure it was, uh . . . suitable for playback to Taylor. Should she hear it? Hadn't decided yet, couldn't think about it now.

So much more to be accomplished this night, which I would pattern after one of the greatest movie sequences ever; the so-called Night of the Vespers in *The Godfather*, when Mafia patriarch Don Corleone strikes back at all his family's enemies in one ruthless night of vengeance. Tonight, the Vampire Vespers had commenced. This was my Judgment Day, when Taylor's slate would finally be wiped clean.

The audio from Roma's pad subsided to grunts and whimpers. I clicked off my phone, turning the night back to silence. I hovered just above that swanky enclave known as Brentwood, and pinpointing my target, dropped out of the sky onto the back lawn of a walled estate. I had checked the layout some time ago, knew there were no dogs or security guards. Piece of cake, even if my prey had dragged home a weightlifter or freestyle karate fighter to warm her bed, which was Cougar Lady's m.o. if she couldn't snag any late-teen, early-twenties boy stuff.

The house was dark and quiet. I projected through the walls and quickly mind-rolled Alina. She was asleep. No one beside her in the bed. Good.

"Can you feel me?"

She stirred. Then . . .

"Yes, yes, I can feel you . . . I . . . *OMIGOD!*"

"Good. Be very calm. Do not be afraid. Now, listen carefully. I want you to leave your bed and walk slowly to the front door. Then open it. I will be waiting for you there. Do you understand?"

"Yes. I understand. I am not afraid. I want to see your face . . . know you . . ."

A moment later, the door opened. She stood motionless, facing me, her stare blank under the power of my mind. And as I looked at her, it suddenly struck me how affected I was by this meeting—a reaction I had not anticipated. What the hell?

And then it hit me. This woman was, after all, the mother of my one true love. As I looked at Alina Logan intently, I realized she was nothing more than a cheap knockoff of her daughter. She was well stacked, conventionally pretty, but lacked Taylor's beauty, fire, and fierce intelligence.

I moved toward her. She stepped back into the room as I closed the door behind me.

"You know who I am, yes?"

"You are the one who commands."

"But you know my identity. You recognize me."

She nodded. "You are Clark Kelly, *The Revealer* columnist. I have seen you before, and I read your column."

I guided her across the room to a low table surrounded by four chairs, sat her down facing me, and said, "Make no mistake. I am inside your mind, anticipating your every thought. If I were not, you would be deathly afraid, yes? You understand that I am a powerful being, answerable to no one. So be aware that you must never lie when I ask you a question. Do you understand?"

She nodded.

"Are your breasts real?"

Something flickered behind her eyes. "Yes," she answered.

In an eyeblink, she slammed back in her chair, writhing in agony, limbs twisting and locking.

"Stop!" she screamed.

I leaned forward, transfixing her with eyes that now glowed red.

"Do you want the pain to stop?"

"Please, *please* . . ."

I snapped my fingers like a cheap magician and intoned theatrically, "All your pain is now gone, yes?"

A look of sheer relief transfixed her. "Yes, Master."

"*Never* lie to me again." I looked at her intently. "In your present state, Alina, you will be able to absorb what I'm about to tell you. Now, listen carefully. Your daughter Taylor and I are deeply in love and we will be together for all eternity. I am now her protector. She's had serious problems in her young life, as you know, but I have eradicated most of them, just as I will eradicate you, Alina, or anyone who stands in the way of her eternal peace of mind."

I knew she felt my mind gripping hers as I probed deeply, finally confirming my suspicions—there was a dark, writhing, suppurating lie lodged deep in her soul. It was all I could do *not* to break this woman's neck for what she did to her daughter.

"Now, I can feel your inner agitation. Because you *know* of what I speak . . . but tonight, all of that changes forever. Your stupidity and pettiness during the divorce from your husband drove you to conjure up an unspeakable lie that still causes your daughter pain. And you are going to *admit that lie* to her—tonight! This is your moment of truth, Alina. Embrace it, I urge you. And remember, the pain you felt moments ago will be as nothing compared to what you will suffer if you *dare* speak anything other than the truth. So . . . listen carefully, and answer carefully."

I looked down at her. Her mouth hung open. So terrified she was all but drooling.

Riveting her with blood-red eyes, I commanded, "Admit right here and now that you convinced Taylor, when she was still a very young girl, that one of the reasons you'd divorced the father she'd always loved was because he molested her when she was a child—even though *she* had no memory of that alleged abuse."

Her eyes widened. My fangs had exposed themselves, involuntarily. Damn.

Retracting them, I hissed. "Your accusation of sexual abuse was a lie, Alina, wasn't it? And again, may your God have mercy on your soul if you answer me with yet another lie!"

Her body began to shake, and not by my doing. Inside her churning mind, I felt a powerful urge to deny her sin warring against her fear of me, and the pain she knew I would inflict with no mercy. But finally, tears running down her cheeks, Alina expelled the filthy secret she'd locked in her soul so long ago.

"Yes . . . yes . . . I *lied*! God help me, I lied to my little girl. And I know it was wrong, so wrong—*but I hated him so much*. I hated him for leaving me, so I wanted to drive him away forever. But I knew he'd never stay away unless she hated him, too—and told him that she did. So I told . . . the lie. And she stopped acting like his adoring little girl. God help me, I loved seeing him in pain. I knew it was wrong, but I always thought that someday . . . someday I'd tell her the truth. But I just . . . I was afraid to show her how cruel and awful I'd been. I wanted her to love me, so I tried never to think about the lie. I just took it inside myself."

As she rocked back and forth in pain, my sudden empathy for this stupid woman took me by surprise. Even though her cowardice had shattered the core of her child's soul, I hoped she'd find forgiveness. Sure, she was a weak fool who did the expedient thing, rather than face life bravely. She was barely fit to be a mother. But here's the reality: She'd given birth to the world's most wonderful woman. And I knew Taylor needed her mother made whole again.

Well . . . cue the violins, people. Getting sentimental in my old age? Could that be a good thing? Oh, *puhleeez*, Clark!

Get on with it, boyo!

"Alina, hear what I'm about to say *very* carefully. Tonight, before I leave, I'm going to relinquish control of your mind completely. Then you're going to tell your daughter what you've done, and ask for her forgiveness. Look, I'll even support you. You're practically my mother-in-law, so we'll have to get along, I guess. Hopefully, that'll all go well—but right now, let's clear the decks and wash away the lifelong pain your awful lie has brought down on your daughter."

I fixed her with calm eyes. "Okay . . . feel your mind expanding outward, feel your freewill growing as I release you, feel your mind coming back . . ."

She expelled a deep sigh, blinked and looked at me strangely.

"Who . . . what . . . are you? How can you?"

"How can I make you do what you're about to do? Because I persuaded *you* to confront the evil your lie caused, which is something *you've* wanted to do for a very long time. Sadly, you just didn't have the courage. But now that you've got me to confide in, your future son-in-law, you've realized it's the right thing to do. But *I'm* not doing it, Alina. *You're* doing it."

She nodded. A small smile surfaced through the tears.

"Tell me what to do? What to say? Please!"

Then we got down to it.

Chapter Fifty-Nine

The Montage.

Touched down on the balcony outside the suite exactly ten minutes after four in the morning. I moved quietly, not wanting to wake Adored One.

Instantly, a light flicked on. I walked in. She was sitting up in bed, glaring.

"Where have you been? Why didn't you tell me you were going out?"

I flashed my best naughty-boy grin. "Aw, honey, you're busting my balls —and we're not even *married* yet!"

That got a faint smile. Girls *love* the M-word. And I knew she'd picked up on the "yet."

"No, seriously, Clark, this is bullshit. *Another* night you just disappear on me with no warning. Why?"

"Bitch, I'm a *vampire!*"

The hint of a grin tugged her lips. She looked so pretty in the soft light cast by the bedside lamp. Nightie about to slip off her nips. Damn. I really wanted to slip in beside her, catch some sleepy-time nuzzles, then nod off into black dreams before recounting all my adventures, but what the hell— there could be *no* cancelling of The Vampire Vespers.

"Okay, I didn't want to wake you, babe, but a couple of things came up."

"Like what?"

Lots of ground to cover. So I made the mistake of trying to compress.

"Okay. Um . . . first, Damon woke me . . . well, his mind did, actually . . . and he was dying after a motorcycle crash over at Cedars, so I converted him. Or 'sired' him, as we vamps put it. Just in time, too. So, anyway, Kragen's a real vampire now . . . and, wouldn't you know, first thing on our newly undead's mind? He's itching to bang a live chick. So I took him over to Roma's house, told him to go full vampire on the bitch without killing her, if possible. Not that I care if he does, but . . . oh, by the way, I stopped off at your mom's and—"

"WHAT THE FUCK ARE YOU TALKING ABOUT? ARE YOU *CRAZY*? YOU . . ."

Suddenly she was all over me, clawing and scratching like a Tasmanian devil, screaming nonstop that she hated me for toying with her, that I was a sadistic prick playing her for cheap laughs. In other words, her insight was unerring, except for the motive she'd wrongly ascribed. I wasn't being sadistic. It was just that in my attempt to encapsulate all the shit that had happened I'd tried to be cute and, as often happens, I came off like an asshole. Now I was in *really* deep shit with this Mommy Dearest thing.

Still unsure how to play it, I whipped out my cell phone, and clicked to *Video.*

"Honey, stop . . . STOP! Calm down . . . I'm sorry, but look. *Look!*"

Within five seconds, my darling was sitting perfectly still, staring wide-eyed into that tiny screen as Alina spoke directly to her daughter's heart.

". . . So I know you'll probably hate me forever now, and that's just killing me, but it doesn't matter, honey. All that matters is that you finally know Mommy told you a horrible lie all those years ago. It's no excuse, but honest to God, I was in pain so bad I wanted to kill myself—which I probably should have done—after your father left me. I nearly went insane because I saw how much you missed and loved your daddy, and I swore that he'd never have your love again because only I deserved that. I know now how sick and weird that sounds, sweetheart. But that's when I . . . when I . . ."

The screen froze on Alina's agonized face for a few seconds. I had paused the camera while recording her because she'd totally lost it at that moment, simply couldn't speak and started sobbing uncontrollably. I'd swiftly seized her mind again, calmed her down, then let her continue after suggesting she shouldn't screw up a noble moment like this up with narcissistic reflections about how *she* felt.

"*Fuck* how you feel! That's your daughter looking back at you," I'd barked, pointing at the blinking red eye. "Speak right to her soul and end the torment you've put her through. Do this right, or I'll make sure she hates you forever . . . *I'll tell her myself what you did to her!* It won't be pretty!"

Alina's face came alive again on the screen. "Taylor, baby . . . when you were still a child, I told you the awful lie that . . . that Daddy had sexually molested you . . . and that you didn't remember him ever doing that because you were just a baby when I caught him with his . . . *oh, GOD!* . . . Taylor, please forgive Mommy! Even if you don't, I'll love you forever, which sounds so stupid to say, because what kind of so-called love makes a mother do such a . . . a . . . soul-destroying thing to her own child? I'm saying this all so badly, but never mind . . . what's important is this: I ruined your love for your father with my mean, vicious lie! And I've hated myself for being too weak and afraid to tell you this before, because I know that the pain I caused has driven you to make awful mistakes in your life. Oh, baby, I am so, so, so, so sorry! Nothing matters now except somehow making you understand that having a monster like me for a mother is not your fault, and your Daddy was always good and loving to you, even though I still hate the asshole."

Onscreen, Alina's face streaked with tears as she wrapped up her two-minute confession. The camera blinked off. Beside me, Taylor shook with deep, racking sobs. Oh boy, I thought. This was going to take some time. But she surprised me, as always. In a moment, she sat up, checked her watch, picked up her cell phone and speed-dialed.

"Daddy? Hi, sorry to call so late, or so early. No, don't bother talking, I'm sure you're drunk . . . and please apologize to whatever cheap little whore you've got beside you for waking her up, but I want to make a lunch date for tomorrow—or, today, I guess—about one o'clock on the Polo Lounge patio? I MUST see you, Daddy, because I miss you and I . . . I love you. And, Daddy, there's somebody I desperately want you to meet . . . so go back to sleep now, Daddy. I'll give you another wake-up call just before noon. Nighty-night!"

Jesus.

She looked at me with a smile that made me feel . . . well, alive again.

"You've had a busy day, Vampire Boy. Anything else you need to tell me? I sense there's still something you want to get off your chest. But if it's a downer, save it, okay? I want to stay happy right now. Because I really am SO happy, Clark. I never stopped loving my Daddy, but I had to act like I did all these years, treating him badly, blowing off his advice. Now I don't have to, because even though he's kind of an obnoxious jerk sometimes, at least he's not a piece of crap who abused his own daughter. And, as you know, I have a certain affinity for obnoxious jerks. And, by the way, thank you so much, darling."

I couldn't remember ever feeling so happy.

I said, "Okay. Now let's lighten up and have some fun, fun, fun! I've recorded something you've just got to hear, my love. It's audio, no video. It all went down less than an hour ago—and it's still going on, no doubt. But this will give you the flavor of a moment I think you'll want to . . . savor."

I clicked Dropbox on my iPhone and cranked up the audio of Kragen on the rampage at Roma's. Just as I'd hoped, Taylor immediately started laughing hysterically.

"Tonight on *Funny or Die* . . . Roma fucks her favorite vampire!" she screamed.

When the audio finally ended, and our sadistic giggles subsided, we snuggled under the covers and she said:

"Uhh . . . NOT right now, because we've got lunch with Daddy in a few hours, but one of these days, darling Dragomir, I want you to go full vampire . . . with *me*!"

That's my girl, folks.

Chapter Sixty

10:30 a.m.: Arose, splashed happily in our outsized marble bathtub, nibbling on a fruit plate and, occasionally, each other.

12:45 p.m.: Hopped a limo, drove to the fabled Beverly Hills Hotel.

1:04 p.m.: Greeted the maître d' at the Polo Lounge, who fawned over Taylor, winked conspiratorially at me, and led us to a power booth facing the bar.

"Daddy!"

"Ah, there's my beautiful girl!"

Snarky mutter as we passed tables: *"Look, it's that fucking gossip columnist! And why's she with him?"*

"Got a hug for Dad?"

Brian Logan, tall and muscular, stood arms outstretched as Taylor rushed into his embrace. More muttering from the Polo Lounge lunch brigade, an older crowd of movers-and-shakers, sprinkled with faded celebrities of the "Oh, wasn't that so and so?" ilk. The room got pin-drop quiet as they strained to eavesdrop. Taylor said:

"Daddy, I want you to meet my very good friend, Clark Kelly. He's—"

"Oh, I know who Clark Kelly is—and so does everyone else here. They're all watching him—and you—like hawks," said her dad, flashing me a big, friendly salesman's grin. That's what Brian Logan is, folks, a salesman: stocks, bonds, hedge funds, commodities . . . strippers. "Actually, honey, Clark and I met once in New York years ago at The Rainbow Room, before it went out of business. You may not remember, Clark. Someone introduced us briefly."

Oh, I remembered, all right. We had indeed occupied The Rainbow Room at the same moment one evening. But no one had introduced us. Typical salesman bullshit. For my darling's sake, I smiled warmly and said, "Of course I remember, Brian. Who could forget a Logan?"

He flashed a million-megawatt grin. Invariably described in the press as a devilishly charming womanizer with a volatile temper, Brian Logan made decent money, but wasn't rich. He worked hard, but played harder. And he'd been photographed more than once being marched off to jail after bar brawls. His most notorious arrest occurred when he leaped onstage at the Manhattan titty joint, Scores, one night, started stripping with the strippers —then drunkenly demanded tips from jeering male patrons before security tackled him.

We sat and ordered as Taylor, absolutely glowing, chattered nonstop to Daddy-O, compulsively reaching out to touch his hand after every other sentence. He smiled and responded, yet I sensed he was somewhat taken aback by his daughter's unbridled affection.

Our drinks arrived. Brian Logan stood suddenly.

"Just need to make a pit stop," he said.

He walked across the Polo Lounge, stopping briefly to chat with acquaintances who were jerking chins in our direction, obviously agog over his movie star daughter.

Taylor reached over and squeezed my hand. "Do you know how incredibly happy I am?" she asked.

"That's quite apparent," I said. "And I'm happy for you, sweet thing."

"You don't know what a great weight's been lifted from me—and it's all thanks to you," she said, blinking back tears. "Every day of my life, especially just before I'd fall asleep, I'd think about how much I still loved my daddy, even though I thought he'd betrayed me. I just refused to stop loving him, but at the same time, I cursed myself for being stupid. God, I was fucked up! I even felt guilty for hating my mother because she'd told me what he'd done. I always wished she'd never told me. And I never quite forgave her for it."

Aware of the all the eyes on her, she flashed a practiced star smile that didn't match her mood.

"But now that I know it was all an awful lie she'd told me, I'm . . . I don't know, I'm . . . okay with it now. I'm just so, so happy to know he didn't do anything awful. And I'll forgive my idiot mother because she's weak, and she never stopped being scared that he'd figure out a way to take me from her. Dad's a scary guy, in many ways. He can be a complete asshole. And if that all sounds fucked up, well . . . it is. Now I understand why *I've* been fucked up. And I can kind of forgive myself for all my crazy shit. So, thank you, Clark. I feel like my life's been given back to me."

I wanted desperately to take her in my arms. But knowing it would hit every gossip column and website in the world, I resisted.

"So . . . when will you tell Daddy that Mom finally came clean?" I asked.

Taylor looked at me blankly. "What?"

Jesus.

I'd *never* felt more stupid.

"You mean . . . neither of you *ever* told him about the disgusting accusation she made?"

Her mouth literally dropped open. "Omigod, you thought . . ."

"Well, I just assumed . . . you mean, he *still* doesn't know your mother told you that he'd molested you as a child? *Goddam!*"

"What?"

"So through all those years of press reports about bad blood between you, your dad never knew *why* you'd were always blowing him off, or blowing up at him? He just assumed you had a chip on your shoulder *simply because he'd left your mom*? Christ! No wonder he looks like he can't fathom why you're suddenly being so fucking nice!"

Under control now, no tears, she said, "Look, I wasn't *always* mean to Daddy. So, now . . . well, he'll just think I've grown up a bit."

Suddenly, she laughed.

"What?"

"I'll make him believe it's *you* who's mellowed me out, darling. That you've stopped me being such a little bitch. And he'll love you for that, so we'll all live happily ever after."

Now we both were laughing.

My cell phone beeped. A text. I glanced at it. The phone buzzed.

"Yes, Wally."

"Major shit-storm just hit the fan here at ground zero, Master. They want you at HQ, pronto."

"Don't tease, godammit. Report!"

"Don't know the story yet, sire. Word is the paper's been sold. New owner's in the building, demanding a meeting with all management in thirty minutes."

"New *owner*? Who?"

"Don't know. Strange security goons are surrounding our conference room. What shall I tell the Powers-That-Be?"

"I'm at the BevHills Hotel. Be there in twenty minutes."

I clicked off.

Brian Logan rejoined us just as the appetizers arrived.

"I'm sorry," I said to Taylor. "Just got a call from the paper. They need me right away."

"Godammit, Clark!"

"Honey, I'm sorry. It's deadline, or the breadline. Good news is you get to eat all my calamari, *and* spend quality time with your dad. I'll catch the bill on the way out."

I stood. Brian Logan stood and held out his hand. "Good to see you, Clark. And judging by my daughter's disappointment, I'm sure you're a guy I'll be seeing again soon."

"Count on it, Brian."

I looked down at my love, who hated me at the moment. I knew how to handle that. Leaning down, I whispered in her ear:

"My phone text was from our newly undead Damon, inviting us to a private screening. Turns out he's got the Roma sex-fest on videotape!"

She gasped, giggled, and actually kissed me on the cheek.

"Can't wait for *that*. How long will you be?"

"I'll call you. Gotta run. I'll send the car back for you."

"Wait!"

She scooped up a succulent, warm calamari and popped it in my mouth.

Three minutes later, I was hauling ass up Sunset Boulevard to *The Revealer* office.

New *owner*?

I suddenly had a very unsettling suspicion.

Chapter Sixty-One

Blood in the water.

Paparazzi were swarming outside *The Revealer* building on Sunset. The news had hit the street. I swung past the pack, headed for the underground garage. Two camera-toting werewolves made sudden eye contact, discreetly baring their teeth and aiming their Nikons at me. Now this was weird. Werewolves here? They'd never come to my workplace before, not even for a story. Not that I feared these menaces in a fight. No self-respecting vampire does. But why, suddenly, were they everywhere I turned? Winking and waving like we were all old pals, I rocketed down the ramp, parked and caught the elevator to the newsroom.

The doors slid open and there stood Wally. As we headed for my office, I noted that the newsroom was all but empty. Weird. The next lockup was just twenty-seven hours away.

Elspeth wasn't at her desk outside my door.

"Wally . . . ?"

"Master, please, they're waiting for you in the conference room. And Elspeth's *fine*. Bottom line: No one's been fired. Not yet, anyway . . . except for our beloved editor-in-chief and a few execs on the business side. But thirty minutes ago the new owners ordered all editorial staff to go home until further notice, except for a skeleton crew on the production desk. So next up for a face-to-face with our new overlords are you and Phil Calder. That's all I know . . ."

He flinched as I glared at him, my eyes glowing red. Fighting for self-control, I said evenly, "What question should a good reporter like me be asking you right now, Wally?"

He exhaled sharply and said, "Uh . . . I guess it would be, 'Who's on the other side of that fucking conference room door?' "

"Precisely."

"Thought you'd never ask."

He told me.

Suspicions confirmed.

"Stick around," I said.

I continued down the corridor to the conference room. Blocking the closed door like they absolutely-no-shit meant business were two massively built security thugs. Deadpan, they opened up and stepped aside. The door clicked shut behind me as I paused to survey the room.

Surprise: Seated around a table designed for twenty were . . . four people.

Phil Calder: Deadpan, too.

Two expensively dressed, tight-lipped middle-aged guys. Yep, deadpan. One I knew by sight; a *very* high-priced Hollywood lawyer. And . . . coiled like a snake at the head of the table, and in no way deadpan, was my worst nightmare. She was wearing what looked like extra pancake to cover telltale vampire hickeys, and hissed before I was even seated.

"It's about *time!*"

I slid into the chair next to Phil Calder, and said cheerily to my new "boss": "Well, hello to *you*, Roma Kane! What a surprise to find Ms. Shopaholic playing Working Girl—even though Kitson's boutique on Robertson is running their annual, to-die-for one-day-only sale. What up, girlfriend? Hey, introduce me to your two laddies-in-waiting."

"GODDAM YOU! Shut up, you fucking piece of SHIT!"

She shrieked it like a street whore. High-Priced Lawyer put out a hand to calm her as she rose, fists clenched. Goddam, is the bitch going to attack me physically?

The conference room door burst open with a bang and the gorilla guards charged in, running dead at me. Suppressing my vampire reflexes, I dialed my metabolism down to a reaction time just a notch north of Navy Seal, and cautioned myself. *Don't tip your hand just yet, Vampire Boy.*

I stayed seated, unmoving. The first guy to reach me instantly screamed like a bitch, doubled over and crashed to the floor, clawing wildly at his crotch. My move had been dead simple. Sliding my left foot sideways as he'd charged me full-speed, I'd slammed the chair beside me into his nuts. His buddy, coming up fast behind him, made a crucial error, throwing a punch at my head as he charged. Still seated, I ducked the fist, nudged my shoulder into his armpit, grabbed his wrist, abruptly stood up and let his momentum flip him down hard on the conference table, where he shuddered once and lay still.

Over Roma's shrill shrieks and the lawyers' howls, I heard more heavy feet pounding down the corridor. A second later, five thug-clones burst into the room. Three had guns drawn. Okay, I thought, time to go full vampire. But—

"STOP!"

A quavering, but commanding voice cut through the bullshit, freezing everyone cold.

"Back off and back out, you idiots! Roma, *shut up*! Remember who you

ARE, goddammit!"

The room had gone freeze-frame. Where had that voice come from?

Above our heads, lights flickered as the ceiling-mounted, giant-screen television monitor we used for video-conferencing came to life. And suddenly, there he was, hawk-faced and wizened in his old-guy scooter, far away and untouchable in his fortresslike lair.

The legendary, ancient, yet ever-fearsome Montague Kane.

The old man leaned forward, staring down at the room, glittering eyes a prism focusing a still-potent life force. "Get *out*, you monkeys!" he rasped.

Obedience was instant. Holstering guns, the thugs faded without a peep, lugging their unconscious colleague. As the door closed behind them, Kane chuckled dryly. He started to speak, was racked abruptly by a spasmodic cough, recovered and said:

"Let's bring Clark Kelly, our star gossip columnist, up to speed. Sound like a good idea, Mr. Kelly?"

"It's your party, and pretty exciting so far," I said. "I'll just sit here and enjoy myself, if that's all right, Mr. Kane. And call me Clark, please."

"And you call me Monty, Clark. Nobody else does anymore. Even though it's how I prefer to be addressed."

I smiled. "People fear Montague Kane. Most wouldn't dare address you so casually."

"Do *you* fear me, Clark?"

"Not even a little bit, Monty."

"Good. Now let's listen to the in-house counsel for Kane Industries, George Brewster. Briefly now, George, tell Mr. Kelly where we're at."

Brewster pursed his lips, leaned back slightly in his chair and began. "At midday yesterday, Kane Industries concluded the purchase of *The Revealer* from the Barton Group, the investment conglomerate that's owned the paper since the death of its founder a decade ago. Despite the paper's incredible success, in a time when print publications are under serious assault from Internet-based news, we felt a few changes needed to be made on both the editorial and corporate sides."

Brewster cleared his throat, looked down at some notes, and continued.

"Before your arrival here today, Mr. Kelly, we informed all *Revealer* employees of the sale and announced that the only major change on the editorial side would be the dismissal of the editor-in-chief, Joel Claussen— who has accepted our very generous severance offer. There were several dismissals on the corporate side, as would be expected with a new company taking over management. But we are pleased to announce that Managing Editor Phil Calder will run editorial until further notice.

"The other key player is you, Mr. Kelly. Reader polls show that you're *The Revealer*'s most-read feature by a wide margin, in all age groups. Your contribution to our circulation is unquestioned. We want you to stay with *The Revealer*, and will meet with you in due course about the conditions of your employment, including compensation."

Again, Montague Kane's voice cut through the bullshit. Everyone peered up at the screen as he snapped, "You exceed the limits of 'briefly,' George. Now here's your question, Clark. Do you accept my authority as *The Revealer*'s new owner?"

I shrugged. "If that means taking orders from your callow, inexperienced granddaughter, I think not, Monty."

Kane chuckled. "Roma's just dying to learn the news business from you fellas, Clark. Callow and inexperienced she is, I'll grant you, but—"

"*Granddad*! You can't—"

"Roma, shut the goddam hell UP! Listen, LEARN! Evaluate. Be patient!" He chuckled like the indulgent granddad he was.

"Please forgive her, Clark. She's a smart girl and I trust her entirely. But she's young and needs to learn this complex business. Please help her. And as for her giving you orders, who on this paper ever gives *you* orders? You run a world-class gossip column; an art that's insanely entertaining when done well, and embarrassingly dreadful when it's not. Now let's cut to the goddam chase. Question: Do you concede that I am now in charge?"

I took a deep breath. Fun time.

"Monty, the front-page story that just locked-up under my byline, is headlined: 'Roma Kane's Dogs Fed To Coyotes By Her Vicious Pal'. Subhead: 'Did Roma Know About Cruel Gambling Game?' It's on the presses now! How do *you* feel about that?"

The old man's lips curled. "I just stopped the presses and destroyed all copies. How do *you* feel about *that*? Your story, hinting that my beautiful granddaughter was a participant in the disgusting sacrifice of her own dogs as food for coyotes, is now 'spiked,' as you news guys put it. It's a false story, Clark. This paper will print only the truth, the whole truth, and nothing but the truth."

Even he twitched when I barked, "*Bullshit!* Nothing could be *further* from the truth, Monty. That story *will* run, like it or not. To put it succinctly, you can own this damn paper, but only if you understand that *I'm* in control —editorially, and every other way. Understand *that*, pal—and damn quick!"

I whirled on Roma, who recoiled as I bellowed, "You've *told* him, right? About the Kane Family Sex Tapes—you doing the Dirty Vampire with Damon Strutt in full Kragen costume, and Granddaddy in his high chair, playing adult baby with young girls pimped and paid for by you?"

She stared back like a stricken animal. Speechless. For all her in-your-face bravado, Roma Kane suddenly was just another scared little Hollywood bimbo.

Holding up my cell phone, I told Kane, "Even if your thugs come charging back through that door, they won't stop me from pressing a pre-programmed button on this phone that will transmit your sex tapes to the Internet and viral infamy—instantly. Won't that play hell with the Kane family image, eh, Monty?"

I glanced over at Phil Calder and winked. Our newly crowned editor-in-chief was apparently fighting to hold back unseemly giggles in front of his new Supreme Leader. I looked up at the giant screen.

The old man sank back in his wheelchair. His eyes closed. He started to shake. For a panicky second, I thought: *"Shit . . . heart attack!"*

Then I realized that the old bastard was laughing.

Hard.

Dumbstruck, I tried to comprehend . . . and then he *floored* me.

"Hit that goddam button, boy. Let those babies *fly to the sky!"*

Erupting out of her chair, Roma wailed, "Granddad! What are you saying?"

The old man was shaking with laughter. *"Who gives a fuck,* Roma? Sex tapes sure didn't hurt Kim Kardashian or Paris Hilton . . . Pamela Anderson, and the rest. They made millions and became huge Hollywood stars, right? You always wanted to be a star, didn't you, honey? Well, hallelujah, along comes genius Clark, and he's just handed us a huge opportunity, girl . . . don't you get it?"

Roma, completely unglued and hopelessly confused, started sobbing—just as it suddenly hit *me* where the crafty old shark was going with all this. Before I could speak, he spelled it out:

"Reality! That's the hottest word in showbiz today, Roma. *And that's what we've got here*—a made-to-order platform for a can't-miss reality television show. Built around a cute blond heiress, plus her weird Hollywood posse of hot baby dolls, wild gay-boys, star pals like TayLo, plus her hot MILF mom, handsome loser dad . . . AND . . . in his very first starring role, the heiress's crazy old billionaire grandpappy—who loves playing adult baby with the young, sexy, half-dressed nursemaids that *she* pimps for him . . . all while she and his other heirs count the goddam days until the old bastard kicks the bucket!

"Hell, reality fans will think you are all probably plotting to poison my Pablum, right?! Now I ask you—who the hell *wouldn't* watch a sicko psychodrama like that? We'll call it . . . *Raising Kane.* How's that for a title, Clark? Think a network would buy *that* show?"

I was struck dumb. Not to mention awestruck. This brilliant old prick had just alchemized a PR disaster into a billion-dollar idea! But was he kidding, or what?

Sourpuss lawyer Brewster was on his feet, huffing, blowing and barking. "Now, just a minute here, Montague . . . this is *insane!* Why, a man in your position—"

Eyes ablaze with sudden fire, Kane cut him off. "The only *position* that counts is my position in Forbes magazine's ranking of the world's richest men. Godammit, Brewster, sex tapes are *proven* career launchers. *Everybody* loves them. So just imagine how a man in my position will be able to exploit the massive worldwide publicity resulting from what will go down in history as Hollywood's greatest TV reality show *of all time!* Here's a series you can sell even to foreign TV; one that chronicles three generations of one of the world's richest families, plus Hollywood hotties, kinky sex—and a horny old nut case who's fascinating because he's filthy goddam rich. It just *cannot* fucking miss, Brewster. Scenes from *Raising Kane* are already running in my brain—it's a *winner!*"

I stared up at the television screen and said, "What will *really* make this a winner, Monty, is if you buy Monolith Studios. That'll make you an instant Hollywood mega-player, able to produce your own show."

"DONE," bellowed the old swashbuckler. "Get that fucking agent, what's-his-name . . . Olson . . . on the phone!"

Shyster Brewster, shaking his head in disbelief, sat back down. I glanced at his cohort, Hollywood Lawyer. He grinned at me, winked, and started dialing his BlackBerry.

Even Roma suddenly smiled through her tears.

Goddam. This was suddenly exciting. *Hey, kids* . . . we're gonna put on a SHOW! Hooray for Hollywood, right?

Wrong!

You want a happy ending?

Book a massage.

You want to *win*?

Watch the vampire, kids!

Chapter Sixty-Two

Back in my office, Wally Tate shook his head in disbelief as I recounted what had occurred in the conference room. "So what's our next move, Master?"

"Wally, not ten minutes ago I asked myself that very question. Then I did what I always do when I hit the damn wall—I asked the question that must always be asked: 'What is the nature of the beast?' Immediately, of course, I had my answer."

"Which was?"

"Sorry, Wally." I chuckled. "Can't explain right now. But I know exactly where we're going, so trust me."

He rolled his eyes. "Well," he said, standing and heading for the door. "Knowing that, I'll sleep a lot better."

"Don't pout, Renfield," I called after him. "I think you'll fall head-over-heels for the devastating plan I'm putting into action. I'd tell you details, but I'm still working shit out in my fevered brain . . . oh, and by the way, here's a high priority: Assign someone to keep close track of the lovely Cara Prescott until further notice. I need to know where she is every minute. Okay?"

He waved over his shoulder and kept on truckin'. Pissed. He'd get over it.

Now . . . vampire work to be done. My first call was to my one true love.

"Where are you, adorable creature?"

"After dealing with the problem men in my life—namely, you and Daddy—I decided that I needed to blow off some steam."

"So you're shopping?"

"How *ever* did you know?"

"Look, I've got a few things to do here at the office. How about we meet at Wolfgang's, six o'clock; cold martinis, hot steaks? And you can tell me how it went with your father. Did you do what I suggested? Did you tell him what your mother—"

"Yes."

"And?"

"He cried."

"Wow! Can't wait."

"Bye," she said.

Okay! Move, move, move, I told myself.

Next must-call: Good old Brit buddy Damon Strutt, the world's only real-life vampire who plays one on television. (Please, don't quibble about the semantics of "real-life" vampire. You know what I mean! It's not as if I said "real, live" vampire.)

Damon came on the line.

"Oi, Clark-o!"

"Damon, the game's afoot, old bean. Happy to inform you we'll be doing crazy shit again this evening, baby vamp. Be available after nine o'clock or thereabouts, okay? Your Master commands you, et cetera, et cetera!"

I explained what was on the agenda. He gave a low, appreciative whistle. "You can actually *do* that?"

"And so will you be able to do *that*, my newly formed vampiric sidekick, after just a bit of instruction that I'll give you tonight in a live demonstration. So, meet you at Bar One just before nine o'clock, okay?"

I clicked off and punched a new number.

"Mark Olson's office."

"Clark Kelly. It's urgent."

"He's on a—"

"Get him *off*, and on with me . . . NOW! And trust me, he'll fire you if you don't. This isn't some fucking actor you're talking to!"

"I know who you are, Mr. Kelly. Hold on, I'll do my best . . ."

Click.

"Yes, Clark? What's up?"

"Mark, I was present when Montague Kane phoned earlier and ordered you to snatch up Monolith Studios. Did he later call and tell you to hold off on that order?"

"*What?* . . . Uh, no . . . no, of course not."

Liar.

"Thanks for taking my call, Mark. I'm going to hang up, and when I do, you'll hear my voice briefly. So listen . . . and obey."

"Wait, I—"

Click.

Damn. Mark just got added to my to-do list.

Then, I dialed a number for the first time. Where did I get it? Vampire 411, of course. She picked up on the second ring, purring:

"Well . . . my first-ever phone call from my girlhood lover boy! If I actually had a heart, it would definitely be beating faster. What a surprise, Clark. Does Taylor know you're calling?"

"Ludmilla, you just proved that girls are always girls—even when they're undead, right?"

"As in, 'we're all jealous little bitches?' If you say so, darling."

"Look, I need you tonight . . ."

Her tinkling laugh was infectious. "Why, Clark, this is so *sudden!*"

I chuckled. She'd matured intriguingly, my Romanian country lass.

"Seriously, there's a lot going down tonight. I need your help, Ludmilla." I explained briefly.

"Ah, serious business, indeed," she said. "But it won't be my first time, you know. You absolutely can count on me, Clark."

Done.

The mischief was afoot.

An hour later, I parked my car on a quiet street near Bel Air Estates and strolled a few blocks, nodding to Mexican maids out walking rich-bitch pooches. I paused in a street that ran along the rear wall of Mark Olson's to-die-for estate, looked around. Not a soul in sight.

Abruptly, I flew straight up and swooped down onto that now-familiar third-floor balcony-patio. Strolling inside, I spotted Mark mixing himself a martini at his bar. He looked up, flinched slightly, then smiled. I flinched also. Damned frightening sight, a Hollywood agent's smile.

"Can I pour you one?" he asked.

"One can't hurt."

"Well, now I know why I felt so compelled to leave the office earlier than usual. I swear I actually heard your voice in my head."

"Don't say I didn't warn you. Hey, this vodka's great. Grey Goose?"

"It's one you've never heard of, called 'Boru.' Irish. Named after their ancient king, Brian Boru. It's cheap. Runs about thirteen bucks at Ralph's Market. One of my junior agents, who's always out drinking the best stuff at Hollywood events, can't afford the best on his salary, but he damn sure knows what the best tastes like. He talked me into trying this cheapie, and it's been my favorite ever since. Brad Pitt tried some at a party I threw at last Christmas; now he and Angie order it for their French château direct from Dublin. Clooney's drinking it, too, of course."

I nodded, sipped appreciatively, then said, "Mark, from those to whom much is given, much is required. You lied to me earlier—don't bother to deny it—when I asked if old man Kane had called to slow down the Monolith deal. So . . ."

He opened his mouth to speak. I raised my hand sharply, unsheathing my fangs.

His mouth stayed open. No sound emerged.

"So even though I honored our pact, and shared the secret of who and what I really am at our last meeting, you've now disrespected me with a blatant lie. Oh, I know, 'liar' is an agent's job description. What the hell did I expect, right? But I held out my hand in friendship, Mark, and you spit on it. Well, I'm a forgiving soul, so there may yet be big times ahead for you, but only if I know your loyalty is beyond question. You've proven that it's not, so now I need to put you under my exclusive control. Hey, wanna knock back your drink before I begin?"

He froze.

I lunged, sank my fangs into his neck, choking off his rising scream with fingers clamped to his Adam's apple. Silently, I counted off four seconds, withdrew my fangs and eased him back down into his chair.

"Christ!" he gasped. As conscious thought returned, horror crossed his face like a cloud from hell. Staring out through panicked eyes, he croaked:

"Am I . . . a . . . a . . ."

I chuckled. "A vampire? Mark, you should be so lucky! No, you are still human and normal in every way, except that . . . well, now I'm able to control you whenever necessary. Even when I'm not anywhere near you. But don't worry yourself about how it all works. It's no big deal, really. We're on the same side, anyway, right? You want to own a studio, and I want TayLo to be a big, big movie star, so . . ."

"You mean . . . you mean I'm . . ."

I nodded. "Mark, you are now a vampire slave. *My* slave. But it's no big deal, really. You'll hardly notice it, as I said. Unless you resist me, of course. Then it can get . . . well, quite painful. But honestly, nothing has changed. You'll sleep, eat, work, get laid, etc., just as before."

"Except," he said with a rueful smile, "I'm . . . your bitch."

"You got that right, girlfriend," I roared.

Suddenly, we were both laughing. Mark's not known as Hollywood's toughest agent for nothing. Even a monstrous creature like myself pales in comparison to the megalomaniac moguls he deals with daily; *except* for the old fangs-in-neck thing, of course. I mixed another round of martinis. We chatted sociably for a while about what great fun we'd have producing that insanely funny new reality television show, *Raising Kane*.

Then I told him, "You'll get a call from Montague Kane tomorrow, empowering you to go full speed ahead with the Monolith deal. Trust me."

"Oh, I trust you . . . er, *Master*? Is that the correct terminology?"

"Yes, *slave*."

We chuckled companionably and sipped our martinis. Abruptly, Mark dropped to the floor and started doing pushups. As he strained through his twelfth, arms shaking, his breath a tortured wheeze, I asked quietly, "What are you doing, Mark?"

"Pushups," he gasped.

"And why, pray tell, are you suddenly doing pushups?"

"Because you have willed it, Master!"

"Ah, so I did. And I never even spoke a word. Remember this little lesson, Mark. Now, on your feet, and show me out, please."

He was still wheezing at the front door. I said, "Mark, you're too young to be so out of shape. How about I program you to drop and give me thirty every morning when you fall out of bed?"

He looked at me in naked fear. I laughed.

"Okay, okay, you're on your own."

Chapter Sixty-Three

Twenty minutes later I rolled down Beverly Boulevard, handed my car off to the valet at Wolfgang Puck's, hustled inside . . . and there she was, that exquisite creature; this girl of my dreams. I'd arranged for an isolated table in the main room, right around the corner from the bar. In a courtly mood, I took her hand and kissed it, sat down across from her, gazed into those mesmerizing eyes and said with Old World flourish:

"Your image reigns eternal in the forefront of my mind's eye, yet I am eternally shocked at how much more beautiful you appear each time I see you."

Her cheeks colored, tears formed in her eyes.

She said, "This is the happiest moment of my life . . . literally."

"I'm honored to be sharing it with you," I said. "Is this happiness something you care to talk about . . . or are some things better left unsaid?"

She shook her head. "No, I want to talk about it. I want to *shout* about it. I've never, ever felt anything like this. Every time I see you, every time you speak, or smile, I fall more and more and more in love with you. It's so unlike anything I've ever experienced that I wonder if you're, like . . . well, you know . . . if you're hypnotizing me somehow?"

I rolled my eyes in mock dismay. "So the very *idea* of falling in love with me is so totally weird and unthinkable that I must be *making* you do it by casting mysterious vampire spells? Gee, thanks loads."

She giggled. "Admit you *could* do it!"

"Well, yes," I conceded. "But the technique's so damn difficult it's hardly worth doing."

Oops.

"In your case, it definitely *would* be worth doing, of course," I quickly averred. "And just for the record, I swear that I am *not* employing black magic. And now that I think of it, please confirm that you are in love with me of your own free will."

Her eyes flashed a message: Passion.

"Yes, Master," she purred. "You is my man, Porgy."

God, this girl.

The waiter arrived and took our order for vodka martinis. "Do you have Boru?" I asked.

He looked at me blankly. "I've never heard of that one. Shall I check?"

"Never mind," I said. "Grey Goose is fine."

He turned to go. "Wait," Taylor told him. She turned to me. "Let's order now," she said. "That way, we won't be interrupted. I have tales to tell."

We ordered filet steaks. Mine, black and blue; hers, medium rare.

"So," I said as the waiter left, "went well with Daddy, did it?"

"It went perfectly," she said. "I still can't believe it. Years of misery wiped away in one day. Sure, my father's still a loudmouth asshole, and my mother's a monster bitch, but I can deal with that. What I had never been able to deal with was the horror of believing that my father had . . . you know. They're both idiots, sure, but I still love them. And I know they love me. We're a family, and whose fucking family is perfect?"

"Hear, hear!"

"Which reminds me . . . you've never told me about your family."

"Another time, my love. Today is *your* day."

The martinis arrived. We sipped, settled, smiled. I said:

"So . . . you showed Daddy-O the video?"

"You mean, 'Confessions of Alina'? Oh, did I! What a nerve-racking moment *that* was. I had no idea what he'd do. Daddy's got a flaming temper, you know, and there we were—right in the middle of the Polo Lounge. I had to keep the volume on my iPhone very low, but he leaned close to the screen and stared right into Mommy's eyes as she told the scary truth about how she'd betrayed him with his own daughter. I waited for him to explode, but he just looked at me and said, '*It must have been awful for you.*' Then, very quietly, he began to cry.

"Clark, I nearly fainted. He took my hand and asked, '*Can you forgive her? Your mother just didn't stop to think that it was you she was hurting, so much more than me. Please, honey, don't hate her.*' I just couldn't take it all in, at first. Here he was, standing up and apologizing for a woman who'd used him badly, like some part of him still loved her. I started crying, and couldn't stop. So there we were, both bawling our eyes out, but *very* discreetly because we were in the la-de-da fucking Polo Lounge. Can you believe it?"

I shook my head. "It's a movie scene. And I want to write the movie. But it all ended well, right? You dried your tears . . . and had dessert?"

She nodded, giggling. "Sinful Polo Lounge chocolate fudge sundae. Daddy had one, too." We sat quietly for a moment, then she said, "Just weeks ago, I was living in tabloid hell. Wasn't it your paper . . . no, it was *The Enquirer* . . . that front-paged that awful photo of me emerging glassy-eyed from some club . . . Tru Hollywood, I think. And the headline was,

'Taylo: Death Wish?' And I remember thinking, 'Maybe they're right!' I was living a very fucked-up, scary life until you came along and made me see how I was destroying myself—and casually allowing others to destroy *me*!"

She took a deep sip of her martini. "So, after I left Daddy, I stopped by Neiman Marcus to do a little shopping, then walked down to the Beverly Wilshire Hotel, went into the bar and ran into a few of my so-called girlfriends; assorted rich hos and models who live in Beverly Hills. I joined them for a drink. Then one suggested a trip to the john. Everybody giggled, and several girls jumped up, all like, *'We are so not going for a pee!'* But I didn't move, even when one whispered that Jenelle was holding real puro stuff she got from her music producer boyfriend that was 'killer'. I didn't go. I stayed put, waited until they came back from tooting their snoots, all glowy and glassy-eyed, then finished my drink and said, 'Girls, gotta run.' "

She paused, looking at me. "And I didn't lay back because I was afraid you might do one of your blood 'fang-spections.' *I just did not want to*—not even a little bit. And that's what you've done, Vampire Man. You've made me respect myself too much to keep fucking myself up with funny powder."

Suddenly, she came around the table and was in my arms, kissing me like it might be our last. After a long, thrilling moment on my lap, she leaned her head against mine and purred, "I am yours for eternity, Clark—and that's not just a Hallmark message. I mean it . . ." Her gaze held mine. ". . . and *you* can make that happen. Right?"

I leaned back, started to speak, but was interrupted by a familiar voice.

"Well, well . . . looks like our gossip king is creating a little gossip of his own, *ja*? And hello to you, Taylor, you look so very beautiful, as always."

Yes, gossip fans, it was celebrity chef Wolfgang Puck himself, bowing playfully from the waist as TayLo hopped off my lap and curtsied prettily. A real charmer, our Puck; loved unreservedly by Hollywood for his legendary culinary skills—but even more for his total discretion. Wolfgang sees and hears lots of juicy stuff, secrets gleaned from his catering forays into the homes of the rich and famous, but keeps it strictly to himself. The guy *never* gossips. Believe me, I'd know. Wolfie's a Sphinx. And Hollywood power players appreciate that. So, starting with a tiny, cozy, fine-dining joint that literally hung off a canyon wall over Sunset Strip, Wolfgang Puck had built an empire stretching coast to coast, opening eateries and expanding so quickly I'd dubbed him "WhizBang Puck" in my column.

TayLo was babbling. ". . . so, you see, I was giving Clark a big kiss for the wonderful mention he gave my new film in his column!"

My embarrassed girl was trying overly hard to explain the sizzling smackeroo Wolfgang had witnessed. I rolled my eyes as he looked at me, winked and said, "Please, allow me to select dessert for the both of you, yes?"

"Oh, how sweet," said my adored one.

"Exactly," said Wolfgang. And off he bustled.

"Omigod, do you think he'll tell *TMZ* or *Radar Online*, or—"

"Chill, doll. Wolfgang's old school cool. Now here comes our steak, so let's enjoy. Another martini, m'dear?"

She calmed down, we tucked in and enjoyed our perfect meal. And as we chatted, I filled her in on the dramatic events at *The Revealer*. She was shocked at first, even worried for me, but I told her, "There's nothing to worry about, or discuss. Tonight, all events—including our future—will be ordained. And I will tell you everything when this night is over. So let's enjoy this wonderful moment, as we will enjoy many more, I promise you. Isn't this steak wonderful?"

After a busboy cleared the table, our waiter brought two demi-goblets of Cristal champagne. "A palate-cleanser, compliments of Wolfgang," he said. "And the best is yet to come."

Moments later, Herr Puck himself bustled up and laid a small silver platter on the table.

"Omigod," said my Hollywood honey.

"Freshly baked to celebrate fresh new beginnings," said Wolfgang.

It was a round layer cake . . . its white frosting festooned with two red hearts.

"To match your glowing cheeks, my dear," he said to Taylor.

"Exquisite," I said. "Thank you."

Bowing, Wolfgang withdrew.

"Omigod, he's treating us like new lovers!"

"He's a discerning man, Wolfgang. And that cake looks great."

I picked up the pastry knife from the platter.

"Have a heart, my dear? . . . *HEY!*"

Behind us, a camera flash popped. Taylor shrieked. I whirled to see a retreating paparazzo who'd snuck up on us for a grab shot. He was already halfway to the door. Diners turned to focus on the commotion. Too many witnesses for me to pull any vampire shit, dammit . . . so I quickly yelled at the guy's back:

"FIVE THOUSAND DOLLARS . . . RIGHT *NOW!*"

He turned instantly, looked back at me, and that was it—he'd surrendered his eyes. Idiot. Hit 'em where they live, I thought. Keeping my gaze locked on his, I mind-rolled him, forcing him to walk back to our table while I kept up a cheery chatter for the sake of the curious crowd.

". . . and you know, pal, you might not sell that pic to an agency, because what have you got, really? Just a movie star enjoying dessert at Wolfgang Puck's with a journalist, right? Clark Kelly interviewing Taylor Logan. So what? And those hearts on that cake don't really add up to a romance, right? Might sell. Might not. But five grand in the hand's better than zip in the bush, right? Now let's see if I like your shot, okay?"

He marched up to me like a *Night of the Living Dead* zombie. Stopped, held out his camera, showed me the viewing screen.

"*Click on the exposure, fool,*" I commanded in his brain. "*Now . . . look down at it and repeat these words exactly . . .*"

"DAMMIT!" he suddenly yelped. "I overexposed."

I threw back my head, laughed and said loudly, "Serves you right, sneaky devil. That shot's not worth a nickel, much less five big ones."

I looked roguishly at the watching diners. They burst into jeering laughter.

"Get lost, paparazzi," yelled a woman.

Waiters and Wolfgang's security guys came rushing forward to eject the guy as I howled inside his frazzled mind, "Delete that shot . . . NOW!"

His finger came down on the *Delete* button. Electrons dissipated into digital oblivion. The photo was no more. In a moment, El Pap-o was ejected by Puck's posse. Wolfgang bustled up and said, "Sorry, Clark, one of my waiters probably blabbed about the cake . . ."

"Or a customer," I said. 'Everybody's a gossip reporter these days. Don't worry about it, pal. No harm done. Anyway, it was such a lousy photo the guy deleted it."

Wolfgang looked at me sharply, then shrugged and walked away, telling our waiter, "More Cristal for Mr. Kelly's table."

Taylor smiled, quite lewdly. "So that's how you make me crazy to fuck you—mind-melding!"

"Hey, whatever works, babe. Want me to stop?"

"Never."

I smiled as my mind worked furiously, thinking, *WTF?*

When I'd mind-rolled that pushy pap, a signal had pulsed back loud and clear: WEREWOLF!

Chapter Sixty-Four

We lingered over our heart-y dessert for a bit, thanked Wolfgang again and left the restaurant. Outside, fans who'd been tipped TayLo was on the premises surged around us, begging for her autograph. A few even asked for mine.

Moments later, a paparazzi ringleader sidled up, glaring at me with murder in his eyes.

Werewolf. No question. WTF? Suddenly, werewolves were in my face everywhere I turned. Menace? Or mere coincidence?

He said, "Once again, you have harassed and humiliated one of my brothers."

"Oh," I said. "So was that one of your brothers who . . . uh, *lost his head* outside Fury? After he rather stupidly attacked me? When will you guys learn that the best way to avoid trouble with me is to stay completely away from me? Beware, wolf! Get it? Be *were*wolf!"

I flashed my fangs, turned away laughing as he growled like a fucking rottweiler. The valet pulled my car up to the curb. I rescued TayLo from the crowd. Minutes later, we pulled into the Montage. I told her I'd be occupied for the next three hours on the business that would set our future in motion.

She said, "Don't worry about me, darling. I'm going to take a lovely nap. I'll be waiting."

I escorted her from the car and saw her into the elevator. A minute later, I was driving north.

Made my first stop on Sunset: Bar One. Damon was just getting out of a cab.

Before my wheels stopped rolling, he yelled, "Got delayed on the set. One drink before we go, mate?"

I shook my head. "No time, Damon. There's vampire work afoot."

He sighed and got in. I flicked on the car's Bluetooth and told my iPhone, "Call Wally Tate." When he answered, I said, "Where can I find Cara

Prescott right now, Renfield?"

"She arrived at her apartment in Pacific Palisades about forty minutes ago. Where are you, boss?"

"About twenty minutes away. You've got the exact address?"

He gave it to me and I clicked off. Looked over at Damon. He was grinning hugely.

"What?"

He laughed. "I've never had so much fun in my life—or death, or whatever you call this state we're in. And to think that it will never end. I am greatly in your debt, m'lord."

I nodded. "Pay close attention to what I will teach you tonight. It is an invaluable technique."

We rolled down Sunset, catching up on showbiz gossip. I told him about the run-in with the werewolf paparazzo and his stupid threats. Twenty minutes later, I found Cara Prescott's apartment building in Pacific Palisades and knocked on her door. When she opened up, I pushed past her and sat on her couch. She was outraged.

"Just because you're a big, famous fucking gossip columnist doesn't mean you can just come barging into someone's apartment—this goes way beyond freedom of the press, okay? And what are you doing here, Damon? I don't get this. It's beyond weird. What do you and your TV vampire want, Clark Kelly?"

I smiled. "Let me correct your sentence, Cara. It's, 'What do you *two* vampires want?' "

She looked suddenly uneasy. "What's going on?"

"Let me make it simple, Cara. I am a vampire. A *real* vampire. And tonight I will make you my slave forever. But don't worry, it's not going to hurt or anything. And life will go on just as before. It'll be better, really, because Montague Kane is totally devoted to you, so you'll never have to worry—especially now that he's bought Monolith Studios. You'll be a star, kiddo."

Her eyes were darting around in her head. She looked at Damon in confusion and said, "But . . . *you're* not a vampire. I mean, not a real one."

Damon grinned. "That was true just days ago, but this formerly made-for-TV vampire is now a proud member of the undead, my darling. And I'm here to watch Clark demonstrate the technique that will turn a human being —you—into a vampire slave. Then it's off to Roma's house, where I'll use the technique he's taught me. Which is quite odd, really, because Roma's my slave already, so to speak; one never wants to instill *too* much subservience in a woman, wouldn't you agree?"

Cara suddenly made a break for it, sprinting toward the back door of the apartment. I leaped before she'd run two steps, brought her to the floor and ripped off her hoodie sweatshirt.

Exposing her neck, I unsheathed my fangs and told Damon, "Watch closely now. First thing is, you don't want to go in too deep. You're not feeding, you're simply injecting saliva, but in just the proper amount. It will enter her system forever, but will not convert her to a full vampire. It will simply be dormant, always ready to control her. And, as it is my saliva, she will be *my* slave. That's how it works. Okay, here we go . . ."

My fangs popped her skin, sank half an inch into her flesh. Probing delicately, I detected a vein and slowly infused it with an emission of hot saliva. She writhed and mewled beneath my weight. Experience told me she needed just another teeny *soupçon* of spit. I oozed it out. She shuddered and was still. Good.

"That's all there is to it, really," I told Damon. "Let's lift her up onto the couch and let her rest for couple of minutes while my mighty juice spreads its magical warmth through her bloodstream and possesses her completely. Now, mate, let me give you a quick lesson in saliva control."

Leaving Cara on the couch, I led Damon into the kitchen, scrounged around until I found what I was looking for and said, "Okay, here's an orange—I find they're the perfect thing to practice on. I'll cut it in half . . . like so . . . and now, observe closely. When I sink my fangs into my half, you should be able to detect dark saliva oozing through the lighter orange membranes. Okay, watch!"

I bit down, released saliva. He nodded eagerly.

"Yes, yes, I can see it. Amazing!"

I showed him the exact amount of saliva that need to be released, then he practiced with his orange while I critiqued. At first, as expected, he overflowed, drooling on Cara's clean kitchen floor.

"Bugger," he said, frustrated. He tried again, did a little better, finally achieving precise control after four or five tries.

"Good," I said. "Now let's abandon the fruit for a real, live person. You told Roma to meet you at her place, yes?"

He nodded. We went back into the living room. "Now," I said, "let's see if my newborn slave is ready to respond to commands."

Cara was sitting up, eyes wide open. I focused on her dilated pupils and said, "Cara, stand up, please, drop your skirt and give me twenty high kicks —Radio City Rockette style." I clapped my hands. "Quickly, now. Hop to it, like a good little girl."

She jumped up off the couch, wriggled out of her skirt and started kicking her quite excellent legs high in the air, hands on hips.

"*Brava,*" I yelled.

Damon joined in with, "Love the thong, love."

After her final kick, Cara folded her hands in front of her demurely. I stepped up and whispered in her ear. She nodded, picked up her skirt, walked back to her bedroom and closed the door.

"I ordered her to change clothes," I told Damon. "She's coming with us."

He looked at the closed door suspiciously. "Aren't you worried she might climb out a window and run off?"

I chuckled. "She can run anywhere on Earth, but she will always hear my commands. Otherwise, she can live her life quite normally."

"Heavy, dude," said Damon.

Moments later, we were back in the car and tooling along Sunset, headed for Roma's pad. Cara sat in the back, humming happily to herself.

Chapter Sixty-Five

Roma opened her front door, did a double take when she saw me, and screamed at Damon:

"What the fuck is *HE* doing here?"

Damon grinned lazily, reached behind her neck, twined fingers in her blond tresses and yanked her head back. Quite ferociously.

"Steady on, little titmouse, give us a kiss first, luv."

Then he laid one on her. Lots of over-the-top tongue. She melted in his arms.

Releasing her hair, he flashed an evil grin and said, "My dear friend Clark is here to teach me how to transform you into much more than my mere love slave, my darling. Tonight, you will fulfill your destiny and become, quite literally, my slave girl . . . forever! Exciting stuff, eh?"

Roma's evil little brain started signaling urgently that something was terribly amiss. Her eyes darted from him to me, then back again as she strained to comprehend the weird resonance she sensed. Then she got it, sort of.

"But how? Why would *he* be teaching *you*? You're the vamp—"

I locked her mind down, not wanting to hear her scream again. Unsheathing my fangs as her eyes widened, I completed the unspoken thought I'd interrupted.

"Yes, Roma . . . Damon is 'the vampire.' But your Damon was sired by . . . me."

She gasped.

Damon chortled. "Strange but true, old girl . . . Clark's me daddy!"

"Please," I groaned. "That sounds *so* fucking gay!"

"OMIGOD!"

Roma was retreating back into the house, shrieking, twitching and shaking. Damon reached an arm out to steady her, but she scrabbled away, tripped, fell backward over an ottoman. He ran to pick her up, trying to calm her down before she woke the servants, but she was inconsolable, terrified.

Damon rasped, "Mate, what do I do?"

Reaching out with my mind, I screwed hers down tightly and said, "I'd been hoping we might all sit down to a lovely cup of tea, dear boy, but let's get on with it. Take her into the bedroom and lay her ass down."

I followed him in. He arranged her on the bed and said, "What the hell's got into her?"

I shrugged. "Think about it. She opens the door for the vampire lad she's fucking, only to suddenly discover that he's brought along her worst fucking enemy—who, it turns out, is a vampire himself. And, even worse, *her* vampire's best buddy. Then she senses we're backing her toward the bedroom. Her girlie-warning system starts sending out alarms. Who knows? Anyway, let's get this show on the road. Expose her neck . . . that's right. Now, take a minute to compose yourself. *Really* think about what you're doing. *Never* be sloppy about saliva control, pal. It's the key to good vampire technique."

"Stop," he said. "You're making me bloody laugh. Anyway, as you Yanks say, what's the worst that could happen?"

"The worst that could happen, my friend, is that you over-deliver and send her over the edge—you actually *convert* her, making her a vampire. Then she's your responsibility. Question is, do you really want a nagging vampire girlfriend who can follow you *anywhere*? From whom you can never escape?"

He pursed his lips, nodded, got all serious.

"Like you said, mate, saliva control—it's bloody crucial."

Actually, Damon ended up doing a damn good job. I monitored his technique, coaching minimally, but in the end he did it on his own. Amazing. Creating a slave's a far more delicate undertaking than converting a new vampire.

"Now you can wake her up, pal, explain her new existence to her, just as we did with Cara," I told him. "Better she doesn't see me right away until she calms down. I'll be out at the bar. Don't be long."

Five minutes later, he emerged from the bedroom with Roma. She looked dazed, but okay. Damon, eyeing the frozen vodka shot in my hand, glared accusingly. "Didn't somebody say there's no time for a fucking drink, eh, mate?"

"Why, whoever gave you that idea, dear fellow? Step up to the bar and help yourself. Roma, sit and relax a bit. Care for a belt of something settling?"

She shook her head. From behind the bar, Damon whooped. "Sweet leaping Christ, she's got Pimm's Cup back here . . . and No. 4, at that. My favorite."

"Brit girlie swill," I muttered.

"For God and country," he bellowed, throwing back a mouthful. "Long live the Queen, that wonderful chap!"

A minute later, he splashed out another full measure of Pimm's.

"Come on, Damon, we have to go," I said.

"Easy on, laddie, I'll just toss this back and we're on our way, aren't we?"

Leaning across the bar, he leered at Roma and barked, "All right, love, up on your feet and all your clothes off—chop-chop, please. Let's show Clark your smokin' hot bod, my little crumpet."

Jesus.

"Strip NOW, slave girl," he whooped.

I looked at Roma. She rose to her feet, and as I watched her face, the characteristic blank look of a slave was warring with deep emotion struggling to emerge. Was it defiance? It looked like she was actually fighting command-and-control. Amazing! I'd never seen a slave resist a master's order, no matter how repugnant. I looked over at Damon, marveling at what a game-playing prick he was. But admittedly, that was what I loved most about him. The guy never let up. What he was doing now was excruciatingly obvious. He knew that the last person on earth Roma would flash boobs, cooze and booty to—even under pain of death—was me, the hated Clark Kelly. But death is not an option for a slave, only unquestioning obedience. Ordering her to get naked in my presence was Damon's way of showing off, proving to me—and, I suppose, to Roma— that she was his to command.

Abruptly, she stood, her face finally blank of emotion. Then she stripped and stood naked facing me . . . us. I wanted to turn away, but did not.

"Hot little piece of ass, ain't she, mate?"

She was, actually, I had to admit. I'd never thought of Roma as a sexual being because I hated her so much. But . . . how do you hate a slave? Now she was one of us, forever connected. Truly.

"You are a beautiful woman, Roma."

I said it, and I meant it. She bowed her head respectfully. I felt the bitter hatred sloughing off my soul. But could I ever forgive her for all the evil she'd committed against Taylor? It was a question that didn't need answering just yet.

"Tell her to put her clothes back on, Damon. Time to get in the wind."

Chapter Sixty-Six

Five minutes later we rocketed up into the night sky, Roma cradled in Damon's arms, Cara in mine. The girls shrieked a bit at first, then started enjoying the ride.

"Omigod, look at that beautiful full moon," gasped Cara. "It's like I can reach out and touch it. My friends and I go to the beach on nights like this."

Now there was a thought. It triggered the most wonderful idea.

Then she asked, "Where are we going?"

I smiled. "To a magical place. All our dreams for the future will be on track to come true after tonight."

She twisted in my arms and peered downward. "Where are we?"

"That road you see directly below is Beverly Glen. We're headed toward Mulholland Drive."

"You mean . . ."

"You guessed it, Cara. But you won't be babysitting tonight. We're going to have a little business meeting, so there won't be a baby highchair in sight —at least, I hope not."

Moments later I started to descend. Damon was right behind me. I heard Roma bleat, "Why are we *here*?"

And there it was below me once again, the mansion owned by Montague Kane. Lights dotted the high wall surrounding the property. I eyeballed the security post next to the massive wrought iron gates at the front. I could see a single guard sitting in the gatehouse, reading a newspaper. Just as on my first visit, I swooped down and landed lightly on the patio encircling Monty's floor. I walked up to the door I'd entered before and tried the knob, but this time it was locked. I turned to Roma:

"I know your grandfather doesn't scare easily, but perhaps it's best that he hears your voice first. Go ahead, knock."

The instant her knuckles rapped on the door, the old man barked, "Who the hell is out there? I've got a gun and I've just buzzed my security guards!"

Roma yelped, "Granddad, it's me . . . Roma. Cara's with me, and—" I shook my head sharply. She nodded, then yelled through the door, "It's *okay*, Granddad. Let us in, please."

Grumbling, cursing, then the faint sound of an electric motor. The door opened. I felt a sting of apprehension as Montague Kane, astride his scooter, emerged brandishing what looked to be a .44 Magnum Smith & Wesson—the Dirty Harry pistol. Roma went in first, then Cara.

"Just how the hell did you get up here on the third floor balcony?" barked Kane—then he caught sight of me and Damon. The gun came up, pointed at me.

I raised my hands, smiled and said, "Hold your fire, Monty. It's me, Clark Kelly, your faithful employee. And the fellow behind me should be a familiar face if you watch vampires on TV. It's Damon Strutt, the star of *Bold Blood*. Better be nice to him. Damon could really help our little reality TV enterprise, don't you think?"

Kane, quick on the uptake as always, flashed Damon a megawatt grin and said, "I thought you looked familiar, young fella. You're the one that's sweet on my granddaughter, right? Are you up here to ask my permission to marry her? That would technically be my son's prerogative, of course, but he's off in Europe somewhere as usual with that bimbo he married, both of them drunk on their asses in some nightclub, no doubt."

"Granddad!" chided Roma. She knelt by his scooter and kissed him on the cheek. Cara followed suit.

Kane muttered into the Bluetooth transceiver screwed into his ear. "Just a false alarm, Charlie. Stay at your post." Then he boomed good-naturedly:

"Well, my two *favorite* girls. I'm a lucky man. But will somebody tell me, real quick-like, how in the hell you got up here to my floor from outside. Stepladders? Or did you parachute in?"

Looking right at me, of course. He knew who to blame, the canny old coot.

I said, "Monty, while the ladies are freshening up and getting themselves a drink, could I have a few minutes of your valuable time to discuss pressing business?"

Eyes drilling me, he nodded. Roma said brightly, "Come on, Cara, I'm dying for a martini. And Damon, Granddad *does* stock your disgusting Pimm's Cup, too."

They moved away, and Kane motioned me into his study off the main room.

"There's another bar in here, Clark. Want anything?"

I shook my head. "Maybe later, Monty. If later we're still good pals."

He nodded. "So, speak up, Clark."

"Monty, you're one of the most brilliant minds on earth today. You can look at the most complicated business deal and spot golden opportunity where others see only disaster. But you've got another great gift—you're a master negotiator. Case in point, when threatened with the release of truly shocking sex tapes—both yours and Roma's—you quickly divined how they could spawn the greatest, wackiest reality TV show in history. And when I suggested you should buy Monolith Studios, you immediately agreed and put in a call to Mark Olson—telling him to start negotiations immediately. Ignoring the nature of the beast I'm dealing with, I naively took that as a done deal, not realizing that a deal with Montague Kane is never done until you've studied every angle, turned it upside down, then inside out."

Monty smiled thinly as he popped the .44 into a drawer. "Brilliant summation. And you've arrived at some breathtaking, tabloidesque conclusion, no doubt?"

I nodded. "Fortunately, Monty, I possess an almost supernatural talent for detecting lies. And to be fair, I shouldn't call your agreement to buy Monolith Studios a lie—you meant what you said, but you knew from my interest in a studio acquisition that you now had leverage over me. And you wanted that leverage because I'm a key player at your newest acquisition, *The Revealer*, and I know you're a power player, Monty. So it took me no time to divine that you'd order Mark Olson to drag his feet on the Monolith deal."

Monty grinned and threw me a thumbs-up sign. He seemed genuinely pleased that I'd put two and two together—me, the dumbest kid in class.

Fighting the urge to flash fang, I smiled.

"But here's a late-breaking bulletin, pal. When it comes to *The Revealer*, I *am* the big dog, because my gossip column is far and away its most popular feature. That's why the paper is going to be run my way—and so is Monolith Studios after you buy it, which will be immediately. No more foot dragging, okay?"

I looked at him and grinned, glad—as I faced the glare in those feral eyes —that he'd put his cannon away. Vampires can't be killed easily, but flesh wounds are annoying, and slow to heal.

Then I told him, "You have just run up against a power you do not comprehend—and cannot control. Time now for you to know who you've been fucking with—and we're looking each other right in the eye, Monty, so here it is: I'm a vampire."

No reaction. Nothing.

He looked at me levelly and said, "I can sense you really believe your own bullshit, but are you prepared to *prove* that, Clark?"

Instantly, I performed my favorite parlor trick.

"I most certainly *am*, Monty," I whispered in his ear. "Hey, look, I'm not sitting in front of you anymore, am I?"

I strolled out from behind his scooter chair and stood facing him. His face had gone white.

"Hypnosis," he barked. "I've seen it done before. You put me under, walk away from where you've been, then pop me out of my trance."

"Monty—"

"Show me your damn fangs, then, *vampire*," he sneered. "*If* you've got 'em, of course."

I unsheathed the choppers. He grinned, then pressed a button on his intercom and barked:

"Roma!"

"Yes, Granddad?"

"Come into my study—and bring Cara."

A moment later the girls walked in. Monty said to Roma, "I'm going to ask again—how did you get up here tonight without going through the front gate and coming up the stairs or the elevator?"

Damon walked into the room just in time to hear Monty's question.

He looked at me, then his eyes flicked to Roma.

"Answer your grandfather's question, truthfully."

Monty shot him a "*Who the hell are you, boy?*" look, but before he could say a word, Roma—like a good little slave—answered forthrightly.

"We flew here, Granddad."

"*FLEW* here? I didn't hear no goddam helicopter or jet outside my window! What the hell are you telling me, girl?"

I sent Cara a silent slave command. Calmly, she took Roma's hand in hers and walked over to Montague Kane. She leaned over, turning her head to the side so he could see her neck—and those telltale fang holes. Stepping back, Cara took Roma's face in her hands and showed the old man the telltale punctures on his granddaughter's neck.

I said gently, "Just take it easy and try to take it all in, Monty. Roma, tell your grandfather what Damon and I are."

"They're vampires," she said. "They can fly. That's how we got here, Granddad."

Montague Kane sat perfectly still, staring into space. It was a lot to absorb, but his mighty old brain was processing it. I turned to Damon and the girls.

"Okay, gang, enjoy your libations out at the bar. Monty and I need to talk now."

They left the study. I sat, saying nothing until the old man's eyes regained focus. Then:

"Understand this, Monty. I'm not a world-class genius, nor am I totally ruthless, as you so famously are. I'm a sharp enough guy and a world-class talent in my own field, yet I couldn't begin to compete with the likes of you if all things were equal. But they are *not* equal, Monty. I *am* a vampire. The real deal. I have supernatural powers. So I can easily impose my will on you, but there's really no need for that. Why? Because you and I are natural allies. Each of us has something the other wants.

"I want to control *The Revealer* and help turn the woman I love into the Hollywood star she deserves to be. And you? You want desperately what only I can give you—a need I'm betting you can't even articulate. Do you know of what I speak, Monty?"

The old man growled, "What the hell *are* you babbling about? What do *you* have that I want—*fangs*?"

I leaned back in my chair, smiled and shook my head. "Forgive me, I don't mean to play games, so let's cut to the chase: You will give *me* everything I want . . . and I will give *you* eternal life. Even if you've never admitted it to yourself in your conscious mind, that's what you really yearn for, Monty—to live forever. And why wouldn't you? Because you know that—given enough time—with your formidable talents, the day would inevitably come when a sign erected at the top of our planet would read, 'MONTY'S WORLD.'

"You've conquered life on Earth as few men ever have. And you love the game because you're a winner. You love the power plays, the acquisition of precious toys. Even now, trapped in a progressively aging body, you stoke your libido relentlessly with endless sex play because you refuse to surrender the pleasures of the flesh. So even if you've never articulated what's truly driving your heart and mind, admit it to yourself now, Monty. Just say what's burning in your mind . . . '*I want to live forever!*' "

I had him. His eyes were dancing. "You mean you can . . ."

"YES! I *can*, Monty. Just like in the vampire movies—a flash of the fangs, one swift, deep bite, a quick exchange of blood and you'll be inducted into the legions of the living dead. Speaking from experience, I can tell you it's a state of existence that might not be palatable for everyone, but I believe it's your perfect place in the universe. Just as it has been for me, these three hundred years. Trust me, pal, it's a blast. And if you think you had an active libido in life, you ain't felt nothin' yet, Mr. Kane. Not to be crude, but if you enjoyed Cara before, wait until you test-drive lovely Cara Mia *after* conversion. Your new theme song's gonna be, 'Feelings.' "

Monty opened his mouth to speak. No words came out.

I said, "Monty, I'll bet you're a Jack Daniels man. Got any of that fine Tennessee whiskey in that bar behind your desk?"

He nodded.

"Let's have a quick belt, then," I said, walking over and locating the bottle. "JD has an uncanny way of settling the mind. Straight, I presume? Water on the side?"

He nodded. I served him, then sat and raised my glass. "To . . . long life!"

He grinned. We knocked it back.

"So am I right?" I asked.

"Clark, I swear to you, I have never said the words, 'I want to live forever.' But you *are* right on the money, dammit—it's been percolating in my subconscious. Which is understandable, right? Even now, faced with what you're telling me, it's hard to believe it's possible. And . . . *is it*? Is what you're telling me true? Or is all this some elaborate scam to get a hold of my money?"

I laughed. You could feel him suddenly wanting desperately to believe everything I'd told him. Like a kid who'd just met the "real" Santa Claus. Looking around the room, I got up and walked to the huge natural stone fireplace set into one wall.

Picking up a thick brass poker, I faced Monty—bent the thing in half and said, "I can fly. I can bend metal bars. I can disappear at will. And if I wanted your money, I'd rob one of your banks. It would be a hell of a lot easier. But you and I, Monty, are about to be partners in a new venture that'll become a major part of your financial empire of manufacturing groups, airlines, hotels, shipping lines, whatever. We're going to control Hollywood and it's going to be *fabulous*! Why? Because we're all going to be reality stars on *Raising Kane*—you, me, Elspeth, Wally, my reporters, Damon, Cara, Taylor Logan, your society son, your fashion-plate daughter-in-law, plus Roma, her hot sisters, and her posse of wild and crazy night-crawlers who make this town jump.

"And the icing on the cake? Taylor Logan, a genuine mega-talent, will become a huge movie star and the face of Monolith Studios. But that's just the beginning. Like it so far?"

I straightened the bent poker and sat back down. He stayed silent for a while.

I said, "You're a man who usually makes lightning-fast decisions, Monty. So maybe I was wrong—maybe you don't want eternal life. If that's the case, let's end this discussion."

He cut me off sharply. "Thought you said you weren't ruthless, boy? Okay, look, it's just that . . . well, is there any other way to do this, other than with your goddam fangs biting me?"

I laughed. "What's the matter, you old pussy. Afraid of a little pain in the neck?"

Suddenly, he couldn't meet my eyes. "No, hell no, it's just . . . well, I saw that movie *Interview with the Vampire*, and it was . . . well, dammit, it was gay as hell! You know, the part where . . . uh, what's his name?"

"Tom Cruise?"

"Yeah, that guy, when he goes to bite into the neck of Brad Pitt, right? And Brad Pitt ain't too happy about it all—he's acting like he's being raped. The idea of a guy biting my neck makes me queasy."

I laughed. "Can't blame you, Monty. I know how you feel, of course. A vampire leaping on you is kind of a rape. And if it's a male vampire, well . . . okay, I got it! Excuse me a moment."

It was just too fucking funny. Fishing out my cell phone, I punched a number and got an instant, "Hello?"

I said, "Where are you now?"

"Hovering right overhead . . . I think. These estates all look alike from up here!"

Chapter Sixty-Seven

I walked to the French doors opening onto the balcony and stepped outside. Peering up into the night sky, I smiled, then waved while muttering instructions into the phone. Clicking off, I walked back into the study.

"This is your lucky night, my friend. Drive your scooter out onto the patio, please."

He shrugged and chugged outside. Standing next to him, I pointed up into the night sky and said, "One of my vampire friends is dropping in, Monty. Try not to be too obvious about peeking up her dress while she comes in for a landing . . . ah, there she is! *Skirts ahoy!*"

Ludmilla performed her entrance perfectly. Slowly fluttering down for a landing, her dress blew up and swirled around her spectacular thighs. We could hear her giggling as she tried to cover up, failing prettily. Then she landed, smoothed her skirt. She curtsied to Montague Kane and rushed to me for a hug.

"Clark, darling, so sorry I'm late. My, what a beautiful place."

"Ludmilla, allow me to introduce you to the famous Montague Kane."

Her lips parted in a dazzling smile. She sashayed over to the scooter and took his hand in hers. "I have heard so much about you, Mr. Kane. What a pleasure."

Dazzled speechless, Monty flashed a smile and kissed her hand.

Ludmilla giggled. Again.

Jesus.

"So, Monty," I said, "I've revealed that Ludmilla is one of our kind. And I brought her here tonight hoping that if you did wish to become one of us, she would be the perfect choice to escort you across the abyss. So . . . how do you feel about submitting to a 'vampire's kiss' delivered by *this* lovely lady, Brad? . . . I mean, Monty."

He still looked a bit uneasy, and who wouldn't be, but he smiled and said, "Thanks. Ready when you are, ma'am."

We repaired to the study.

I walked to the door and yelled, "Hey, everybody, we need witnesses for this ceremony."

Damon, Roma, and Cara walked in.

I said to Roma, "Your grandfather has made the decision to convert and join us in eternity. Now I want you all to meet Ludmilla, a dear friend—and my first love when we were teens, as a matter of fact. From what Ludmilla's told me, she's probably had more experience in conversion than I have. Also, she's indisputably more beautiful and sexier than I am, so your grandfather says he'd prefer her. I am not, however, offended."

I walked over to Monty, lifted him out of the scooter and said, "You won't need this little rocket ship after the ride you're taking tonight, pal. I'll have the Jack Daniels ready for a birthday toast. Bon voyage."

I laid him on a deep, leather couch, stepped back and nodded to Ludmilla. Instantly, her fangs snapped out like daggers. One-time teen angel transformed into adult demoness, eyes glowing red. Then, lunging too swiftly for any but vampire eyes to track, she pounced, covering her prey like a feeding leopard. Baring her fangs, she slashed open a vein on her wrist, then bit into Monty's neck. His mouth yawned wide and he groaned, emitting a tiny choking sound as Ludmilla forced her coursing blood down his throat. Monty thrashed furiously for a long moment under the viselike grip of those powerful jaws, then shuddered and lay still. Gradually, the awful sucking sounds subsided, and I monitored that which human ears cannot detect: the urgent whisper of saliva rushing into veins newly thick and rich with undead blood.

Ludmilla finally pulled back from her newborn vampire and sat quietly beside him, gathering strength. I knew the feeling. Conversions can really take it out of you sometimes. After a long moment, she stood gracefully and smoothed her dress.

"No matter how many times I do this," she said, "I am always in awe of the power we possess. He'll recover in a few minutes. Now, Clark, darling, I'd love some tea. Lots of sugar, please."

I walked into the kitchen, put a pot on to boil, then phoned Taylor at the Montage.

"Hey . . . hope I didn't wake you."

"No, I actually woke up about ten minutes ago after the most refreshing nap. I feel wonderful. How's it all going?"

"Missions accomplished, my sweet. Wait'll I tell you. It's like the greatest gossip item of all time—if only I could publish it. Anyway, still got a bit of mop-up left, then I'll be with you."

She said, "I'm out on our patio. Have you looked at this magnificent moon tonight? It's given me an intriguing idea."

I smiled. "You thought it might be exciting to rendezvous, encore, on the beach above Zuma?"

"Wow. Now you *are* reading my mind!"

"No, my love. It's just that you and I are of *one* mind. Hold on a minute, okay?"

I speed-dialed the concierge at the Montage, had them put a limo on standby.

"Hi, I'm back. Okay, there's a limo downstairs at your beck and call. You can make the beach in an hour, easily. Just park and sit. I'll find you."

I walked back into the study and escorted Roma, Damon and Cara to the bar in the other room, leaving Ludmilla with Monty to walk him through the initial shock of waking up undead.

"*Omigod*, it's too weird . . . my grandfather's a *vampire*," said Roma.

"There goes the neighborhood," sighed Damon. "Although I've heard that some of these bloodsucking bastards can be quite nice, really."

Roma swatted him. "You are *not* funny," she giggled.

Ludmilla, totally composed, joined us about fifteen minutes later.

"He's doing very nicely," she said. "Keeps saying he feels wonderful and will be out here shortly. Meanwhile, he'd like you to join him, Cara."

Roma did a double take, rolled her eyes. Pouted. *"Whatever!"*

Cara's smile betrayed the slightest hint of apprehension as she rose and walked into the study, closing the door behind her. Her instinct was unerring. Mere moments had passed when muffled moans and shrieks filtered faintly through the walls. Instinctively, we all started chatting a bit more loudly, but it was obvious to all that Cara was . . . well, getting her brains fucked out.

Ludmilla, Damon and I desperately held our laughter, but it burst out spontaneously when Roma abruptly wrinkled her kisser and went, *"Eeewwww!"*

En masse, we all stood and, drinks in hand, walked out onto the balcony to escape the sounds of wild rut . . . but it was hopeless. Finally, even Roma lost it, cracking up when we heard a keening cry of, "*Bad* baby!"

Things quieted down a bit after that, and I said, "I'm afraid I'll have to admit some responsibility for all this—I told Monty that conversion beats Viagra a hundred to one. I'm afraid I also mentioned that girls who become vampire slaves are imbued with a mega-increase in libido."

Damon looked archly at Roma. "Fuck like bunny rabbits, do they?"

Roma giggled abruptly. "Now that I think of it, that's *so* true!"

Shit, I thought, so much for my dreams of Roma suffering horribly from her almost full-vampire assault.

Damon offered to whip up a fresh pitcher of martinis.

"Nothing for me," I grumbled. "I've got to fly. Meeting Taylor on the beach for a spot of moon viewing."

"And moon-*ing*?" quipped Ludmilla.

Roma reached out, touched me on the arm, and shyly said, "Clark, you're the chief vampire, master of all you survey, so I want to ask you . . . is my grandfather going to be okay? I mean, do you have to teach him stuff, or what? Because, he's, like, an old man."

Well, well! A humbled Roma. Were we bonding like family now, or what?

"Don't worry, Roma, even though he'll still *look* like an old man, he's now got the strength of fifty men. And Ludmilla has taught him everything he needs to know for the moment—although I'd like Damon to help Monty with his flying."

"How long does it take to learn?" asked Roma.

Damon snorted. "No time at all, if you follow Clark's method," he said. "Just fucking minutes after I was converted, he threw me off the roof of a sixteen-story building. But I was flying before I hit the ground."

We heard the study door slam open.

"WHERE'S THE PARTY?" bellowed Montague Kane, Billionaire Vampire.

Time to fly.

I turned to Damon, whispered a few instructions. He laughed. I lifted off and shot straight up into the moonlight. At about one-hundred-and-twenty feet, I stopped ascending, hovered and looked back down as Monty, feisty as hell, swaggered out onto the patio, instantly planting a kiss on Ludmilla's lips just before Roma charged into Grandpa's arms and jealously elbowed her away.

Then Damon walked up to the newly minted vampire with a big smile on his face and held out his hand. Monty took it—and was instantly jerked off his feet and sent flying over the patio railing. Even I held my breath, wondering if I'd miscalculated how quickly a newborn vamp can adapt; after all, Damon had had the time it takes to fall ten stories in which to trigger his aviation skills. Monty had to do it in just *three* stories, or about four heartbeats.

But a second later, I joined in the cheers that wafted up as Monty suddenly arrested his fall and, displaying great *élan*, swooped back up to the level of the patio and executed a flashy barrel roll for his awed, applauding audience.

Damon looked up at me, pumped a fist and yelled, "Vampires rule!"

I waved, fired up the afterburners, and powered north for the beaches, channeling my inner Frankie Avalon, on the prowl for beach blanket bingo with my sweet surf bunny. Following the coastline up past Malibu, I finally spotted a limo, lights on and engine idling, parked along the Pacific Coast Highway just above Zuma. Just to be sure it was her, I reached for my cell phone to call, but . . . what the hell?

Gone-zo!

I must have left the damn thing back at the mansion. Damn! Well, I'd use Taylor's phone to call Damon, ask him to hold it for me until tomorrow. Assuming, of course, that he hadn't left yet. But no way was I going back there tonight.

I touched down a few feet behind the limo, walked up and tapped the rear passenger window. The door opened instantly and my darling stepped out.

We kissed. The driver exited, stood looking at us expectantly.

I walked around, handed him a twenty and said, "Thanks, we won't be needing you anymore tonight."

He looked at Taylor, who nodded and asked, "Could you open the trunk, please?"

Chapter Sixty-Eight

Moments later, we were trudging happily toward the ocean, me schlepping the small picnic hamper she'd ordered from the Montage. Now we had the beach to ourselves. The sands shimmered silver in the moonlight, stretching to the limits of vision.

"It's just . . . magical," she said, squeezing my hand excitedly. I took the cue, leaned over and kissed her.

We reached the spot where we'd partied before. "Wasn't that a night," she said. "I can hardly wait to work on that screenplay."

"What screenplay?"

"Omigod, you don't remember! You came up with that great title . . . '*Vampire Surfers from Hell!*' It sounded so Tarantino."

I watched as she reached into the basket, pulled out a woven throw and spread it on the sand. God, women! How do they do it? She knelt on the throw, pulled out a plastic container filled with edibles, plus two bottles of Cristal.

She patted a spot next to her and said, "Sit. It's not a meal, just gourmet munchies the chefs whipped up fast. God, I love living in hotels. Okay. Let's start with your favorite . . . fried calamari. Still warm, too."

Now we were in heaven. The sighing surf, the fresh and salty night air, the moonlight. For fifteen minutes we noshed and sloshed champagne, then lay back and stared at the stars. After a while, she said:

"Let's make love."

I raised up on one elbow and looked at her, aghast.

"In the dead of night? Under a full moon?"

"Why not?"

"Too creepy!"

"*Creepy?* You're a fucking *vampire*!"

We laughed 'til we cried.

Eventually, I said, "You're right. A romantic beach . . . beautiful moonlight . . . shall we make love, my darling?"

"Bite me," she said.

And we laughed 'til we cried again.

"Omigod, I've *got* to pee," she eventually gasped. Bent over, she rushed back into the grassy dunes. Moments later, she emerged and walked back toward me, rearranging her skirt.

"You need a refill," I said.

She rolled her eyes, then stretched lazily, gazing up at the moon. I poured more champagne. Then, over the soughing sounds of surf and the offshore breeze, my ears picked up a faint howl in the distance. Coyote. How the moon stirs lupine creatures, I thought.

The howl came again, this time raising hairs on the back of my neck.

Just a coyote, I thought, and far away at that, but . . . my gaze drifted down the dark line of sand dunes and . . . *there!* . . . a fleeting shape, then another, nearly invisible, moving swiftly through the darkness and . . . *JESUS!*

I should have seen this coming.

Werewolves!

Howling insanely, the pack of hellhounds exploded out of the dunes, nearly a dozen strong, bounding swiftly up the beach toward us; hairy, muscular beasts, jaws agape, gnashing razor-sharp teeth. Taylor's screams rang in my ears as I pushed her behind me. Bracing for what would surely be a fight to the death, I mind-rolled desperately, firing off a distress call to my newly created slave-girl:

"CARA! Alert Damon and Ludmilla . . . werewolves attacking at Zuma!"

It was probably too little, too late. Even assuming my distress call had resonated. No time to think about it now.

As the werewolves pounded toward us, I focused on their leader, that now-transmogrified paparazzo who'd threatened me outside Wolfgang's, and tried to lock my eyes on his . . . until I sensed he was staring just past me. I whirled and—

Goddammit!

One of the beasts had sneaked up behind Taylor! Hairy, clawed paws reached out for her head. Launching at vampire speed, I flew at the monster. My hands shot out, connected, twisted, and I ripped off his head. Blood geysered out of the gaping hole between his shoulders. Whipping back around to face the charging horde, I pushed Taylor behind me, raised my bloody trophy high, and roared at the suddenly wide-eyed leader of the pack:

"IS *THIS* THE HEAD YOU WANTED? . . . HERE IT IS, WOLF MAN!"

I flung it hard. The head bounced through the ranks, shocking evidence of their comrade's decapitation. And it broke momentum; their charge slowed momentarily. Quickly turning to scoop Taylor up and fly us out of danger, I realized, too late, that my grandstanding with the werewolf's skull had probably sealed our fate. Yet *another* beast had sneaked up behind us and now stood facing me defiantly—with Taylor's neck hammer-locked tightly in his powerful bicep.

Stalemate!

If I charged, no matter how swiftly, he'd simply twist and snap her neck. My beloved's eyes, bulging and terror-stricken, locked on mine. I mind-rolled her, yelling my message aloud for good measure:

"I must go fight them, my love. I know you're frightened, but . . . TRUST ME!"

I turned and ran.

In seconds, the charging beasts had me surrounded. Using my superior speed, I rained blows as we closed, even drew blood, but there were just too many of them. I feinted, ducked, threw kicks and punches—even played my "whoops-I'm-behind-you-now" trick. Each time they turned and discovered me. I sprinted down the beach, screaming like I was totally panic-stricken, even though I could have outrun them easily. But I was praying they'd all follow me—especially their leader. If he stayed behind with Taylor and her captor, he might just threaten to kill her unless I surrendered. At best, my ploy was weak.

But, no . . . these were werewolves; not the brightest of supernatural beings!

Incredibly, every man-jack of the stupid wolfen-swine, the leader included, came racing after me, caught up in the blood-heat of running down escaping prey. Now, if I could just keep their turgid brains confused long enough to lure them well away from Taylor, I'd simply go airborne, swoop back down the beach, snatch her away from her captor—then fly off through the air with the greatest of ease! A perfect plan, but . . .

"UNH!"

Pain exploded as something heavy slammed into my back, knocking me flat. My face smashed down on the sand and an object landed just in front of me—a camera tripod! They'd thrown it like a spear; a paparazzi trick I'd actually witnessed one night outside the Comedy Store on Sunset, when cuckoo comedian Andy Dick—who'd inexplicably snatched a stunned *foe-tog's* camera, then run off laughing—was brought down like a speared wildebeest on the African plain.

Now I was well and truly fucked.

Stunned, not hurt. But before I could bounce back up, the pack swarmed all over me. For the first time in three centuries, I felt the icy grip of incipient doom. Vampires are notoriously hard to kill, short of total decapitation or a stake through the heart—but tearing me limb from limb would do the trick nicely. Wolf paws clutched and clawed at every part of my body as I fought back savagely, bucking and biting. But suddenly, I had no chance. My limbs were finally immobilized. I braced for the unthinkable: total obliteration. Even for vampires, death can be cheated, but never denied . . . and now . . . my only thought was of my love . . .

"NO . . . NO, NO, *NO!*"

What the hell?

The Leader of the Pack was suddenly howling at his underlings, raging through them and yanking them away from me, one by one. Finally, I sat crouched alone on the sand, encircled by werewolves roaring my death song. Advancing and pointing a clawed finger, the leader snarled at me, "No . . . NO! You *cannot* die so easily, *Dracul*!"

Instantly, I felt alive.

This dim-witted wolf man, stupidly wanting to prance, swagger and threaten me with death by torture, should have killed me quickly when he had the chance. Oh, I was still surrounded—but now the idiot had given me breathing space, or, more precisely . . .

Flying space!

I braced for vertical blastoff . . . then heard Taylor screaming my name. The circle parted as the werewolf who'd been holding her captive down the beach dragged her forward. Now he faced me, grinning evilly, and slowly flexed his huge bicep. Taylor's screams choked off abruptly, her eyes bulged, her tongue lolled sickeningly from her mouth.

Leering at me, the leader barked, "Do you think I'm stupid, vampire? Go ahead—fly away! But Taylor Logan will die instantly—and that's probably not a good career move, right?"

He threw back his head, roaring with laughter. The werewolf pack joined in. My mind raced furiously, searching for a slick way to roll before they laid paws on me again. Then I heard a voice say, "*Just sit tight . . . be ready to grab TayLo. Then hit the dirt, stay down, and enjoy the show!*"

Damon?

Or my tortured brain playing tricks?

The werewolf leader ranted, "Your unnatural life will end in great pain, Clark Kelly, you vampire prick, because we're going to pluck your limbs from your body, one after another and very slowly, while your girlfriend watches—then I will deliver the *coup de grace* by ripping your fucking head off your body, just like you did with my brother. And if you resist me in the slightest degree, you'll get to see Taylor Logan's head ripped off— right after I rip off her *tits*!"

My mind exploded, flashed: *Kill this fucking wolf man NOW!*

But before I could hit my physical trigger, I heard that inner voice say urgently, "*No, Clark! CHILL!*"

Raising my eyes slightly, I looked up at the night sky, saw a figure barreling down at vampire speed. I looked over at Taylor, smiled . . . and winked. Her eyes widened and stared back, saying, "Are you *insane*?" Holding my smile, but careful not to move a muscle, I braced internally.

And then, it happened . . .

In an eyeblink, the werewolf holding Taylor wilted like the air had gone out of him and he collapsed to the sand, a hairy pile of lifeless trash. And standing atop the pile? Undead-and-loving-it Damon Strutt, grinning wildly like the slightly mad television vampire character teenage girls—and not a few of their mothers—lust after. Taylor, suddenly free and somewhat dumbstruck, sat rubbing her neck, unharmed, thanks to Damon's swift execution of the killing blow known to all vampires. Sinking his fangs into the base of her captor's skull, he'd neatly severed the brain stem, instantly cutting off all motor control, not allowing even an involuntary death twitch that could have snapped Taylor's neck.

Action exploded. The leader threw back his head, howling in rage as Damon threw him a big, fat middle digit and bellowed:

"INCOMING!"

I looked up at the moon, its glowing surface dotted with black silhouettes of vampires rocketing down toward us at warp speed.

But who . . .

And then I got it: Ludmilla had quickly summoned her European Mob, aka . . . *Vampire Surfers From Hell!*

They attacked, swarming out of the sky like dive-bombing killer hawks!

POW!

The first werewolf to die took a devastating direct hit, literally disintegrating in a spray of body parts. One down, ten to go, by my count. I held Taylor in my arms, but disobeyed Damon's plea to stay put and stay down. I had just one thing to do—and I did it fast.

Pouncing on the attack-distracted leader, I landed hard on his chest and roared: "GREET YOUR BROTHER FOR ME . . . IN *HELL!*"

Then I ripped his head from his shoulders.

Shrieking like an Indian brave and laughing madly, I executed a quick war-dance and boogalooed back over to Taylor. Instead of terror and screams, my dream girl shot me a double thumbs-up and whooped a *Woo-Hoo!* just like I was her high school quarterback squeeze. She even laughed when we got slapped with a fetid spray of wolf's blood a second later.

Red mist filled the air as twenty-odd raging vampires tore into the demoralized werewolf pack, ripping off limbs, whooping and roaring. Slaughter raged unabated for less than five minutes—until every last werewolf was torn into bloody bits and pieces. Watching the last one die, I burst out laughing as the vampire straddling his kill caught my eye with a sly wink.

"Not bad for the world's *youngest* vampire, eh, Clark?"

Goddam! It was re-vamped old codger Montague Kane, drenched in blood and loving the afterlife.

"You *rock*, Monty!" I yelled back. "How you likin' Eternity so far?"

Damon swooped overhead, yelling down at the milling, war-whooping vampires, "Let's keep these lovely beaches clean, clan! Throw all bloody bits against that dune over there and we'll torch up a bloody big bonfire. I'm betting nothing burns brighter than bloody werewolf flesh!"

"Bloody good idea, mate," roared feisty old Monty.

In moments, our fire was crackling merrily.

Party time!

Chapter Sixty-Nine

We sat around our impromptu campfire like boy and girl scouts, chatting animatedly and renewing acquaintance with our European rescuers. One of the French vampires, who was vacationing at a Malibu timeshare, offered to fly down to the village and buy booze. We all pitched bills into a hat, and off he went with a pal to help him lug the stuff back.

"Omigod, Clark, listen to this," said Taylor, who was being hugged and comforted by Ludmilla as they compared notes on the night's adventures. "We could have died out here tonight, but—"

"Yes," said Ludmilla, smiling at me warmly. "I was just telling your princess how we found out you were in trouble. You know that you left your cell phone behind at the mansion, yes? Well, it rang, so Damon answered, thinking it could be you. But instead, it was . . . *merde!* Damon, what was the man's name?"

Sitting to my left, Damon told me, "It was your trusty sidekick, Wally Tate. When we told the lad that you'd left without your phone, and Taylor was not with you, he got nervous. He said he'd been hacking into paparazzi phones and heard some kind of message about them keeping eyes on Taylor around the clock tonight, no matter what. He said it didn't make sense, and it worried him—especially when he found out you weren't keeping an eye on her. He asked if you'd said where you were going. We told him you were meeting Taylor at the beach."

Damon shook his head. "Now, here's the funny thing. I didn't think much of it until I remembered that just before Wally called, Cara told me she'd gotten a weird feeling, like maybe you'd tried to communicate with her. She didn't know if it was you, because she'd never had a slave communication before. I asked her if she'd gotten any message at all. She said it wasn't anything she could understand, but she'd felt scared. Heard kind of a roaring sound. So I went back and asked if the sound could have been water—like, the ocean. And she said that was it, exactly. So . . . fear plus ocean, plus TayLo being stalked by paparazzi, *plus* that threat at Wolfgang's from a paparazzi who's a known werewolf, plus the full moon —it all added up.

"We felt sure you were under attack by werewolves and got in the wind immediately as Ludmilla phoned the Vampire Surfers. I'm dying to actually watch them surf, by the way. Wish we had boards here."

A happy cry went up. The French guys were back with a big cooler of booze. Everyone rushed it. I looked at Taylor, who shook her head. Moments later, we finished saying our thank yous and good-byes. Everyone understood.

"Dodging death can be *so* exhausting," quipped Damon. "To bed with you, then."

"And *right* to sleep, of course," purred Ludmilla.

"Oh, I *swear*," Taylor purred back.

Girls.

Gotta love 'em, right?

We walked up the beach toward Pacific Coast Highway. My phone, returned to me by Damon, rang.

"Hi, Wally! . . . Yeah, I heard all about it. Hey, thanks for being concerned about Taylor. Tell you all about it tomorrow. You'll be at the office, right? . . . No, I'm going to sleep in, but I'll probably catch up with you after lunch, okay? . . . Right. See ya!"

Instantly, I scooped Taylor up in my arms and zoomed skyward. Moments later, she smiled and said, "Let's get out of this moonlight as fast as we can."

"Why?"

"Too *creepy!*"

We laughed even harder this time.

Then she whispered two words in my ear. A command. We both turned instantly sober. A moment later, I made a mid-flight course correction. Bedding down at Montage tonight was now out of the question. Our new destination: my Four Seasons hideaway. Why? Better sound-proofing.

And why was *that* suddenly so important?

Those two words she'd whispered:

"Full vampire!"

Chapter Seventy

The Olson Agency, Beverly Hills, California

ACTION MEMO

To: Montague Kane, Clark Kelly, Roma Kane, Damon Strutt, Taylor Logan, Cara Prescott . . .
Fm: Mark Olson
Date: May 19
Re: Phoenix Channel post-season evaluation meeting

Hi everyone,
Hard to believe it's only a year since we sold our show to the Phoenix Channel. I'm dashing off this note just moments after the network gave me *its* notes as we close out our first smash season, and I won't keep you in suspense—they love, love, LOVE *Raising Kane*!

CEO Frank Jacobs called it "the greatest reality show since *The Kardashians*—but with even greater ratings." You've already seen the numbers—and our sensational viewer demographics—in the formal memo we sent out an hour ago. Watch tomorrow's *Hollywood Reporter* front page.

Cutting right to the chase: Our most sensational segment is the one Phoenix Channel had really worried about—"*Raising Baby Kane*"! Well, guess what? Turns out America is not only ready to see a "billionaire geezer" (Monty's words, not mine) playing an adult baby, he's actually inspired that major movement started by college girls who show up in scanty outfits to "baby" lonely older fellas in nursing homes, or wherever.

It was a great boost for our show when that adorable NYU co-ed who kicked it all off on the Internet told Barbara Walters on *The View* that "God invented poon-tang to make men happy, and my eighty-seven-year-old grandpappy is still a man—so what's the harm if a couple of my girlfriends dress sexy and play adult-baby with him? And why shouldn't I then put on naughty lingerie and go spoon-feed *their* old geezer grandpops! We should all think more about helping the elderly, right?" (Cara Prescott, you're a role model!) The network's going insane over these girls, and I think we've sold it as our first spinoff show.

Frank Jacobs says his wife and daughters are crazy about Kragen/Damon's appearances to seduce Roma, and vampire clubs around the country now follow the show avidly.

And it's no surprise that Taylor Logan's drop-bys really spike our ratings —her new flick *Desire Kills* just broke this year's box office records. Also, they're crazy about the plot twist of romance brewing between Taylor and Clark Kelly. The network guys find the pairing of a movie star and a gossip columnist—traditional enemies—sin-sational! Frank showed me one letter from a lady who wondered if they're just into "grudge-fucking!" WAIT! Is that another spinoff? (Just kidding . . . or am I?)

And three cheers for Roma and her posse of what Clark called in his column "her oh-so-hotties, and *abs*-urdly hunky boy toys"—eye candy for both male and female viewers. And Wally Tate with his hilarious suspicion that Kragen is a *real* vampire! Not to mention the twist about arranging vampire porn shoots for FangBanging.com—pure GENIUS!

I could go on and on, but the point is: We're winners! . . . BIG, *BIG* WINNERS!

It's my privilege to be associated with this breakout TV series, and the resources of The Olson Agency are already working on unique ways to exploit our momentum—and make damn sure we keep on "*Raising Kane*"!

Thanks, all . . .

Mark
From the desk of: Mark Olson
President
Cc: Executive Only

The End . . . ?

About the Author

Mike Walker is a "one-man media conglomerate," in the words of *New Yorker* magazine, and one of today's most recognized media names in print, radio, TV, and books. Born in Boston, Walker joined the U.S. Air Force and served in Tokyo, remaining in the Far East after discharge to become the youngest-ever foreign correspondent for International News Service—and a staff reporter on Tokyo's *Asahi Shimbun,* the world's biggest daily newspaper.

In the Far East, Walker worked as foreign correspondent for NBC's "Monitor," the award-winning news radio show. Fluent in Japanese, he became a commentator on TV and radio. And he produced an award-winning TV special that finally revealed the fate of twelve missing WW 2 Japanese heroes—after his headline-making discovery of the world's only intact Mitsubishi bomber in the jungles of a remote Pacific island.

After the Far East, Walker worked in Europe and the UK—then returned to the States, joined the *National Enquirer* and launched his two-page gossip column. Read by millions, it quickly became what it still is today—the paper's No. 1 feature.

Known as the "Guru of Gossip," Walker's story-telling ability, coupled with his charm and self-effacing humor, made him a TV and radio favorite. For years, he hosted his own national two-hour "Mike Walker Show" on Westwood One Network (CBS), heard on 165 stations, plus 24 BBC and indie stations in Great Britain. He was seen every Friday as co-anchor on "Geraldo" and made the record number of appearances of any guest ever on that show—264!

He guested on such top TV show as "Nightline," "Larry King Live," "The O'Reilly Factor," "Maury," "Nancy Grace," "A Current Affair," "Entertainment Tonight," "Politically Incorrect," and "Charlie Rose"—then wrote and hosted two one-hour specials for MGM Television.

The first, titled "National Enquirer Presents: 25 Years of Scandals," commanded "phenomenal" ratings, wrote *Daily Variety*—and headlined it "A Syndie Hit!" His second special, "National Enquirer Presents: Love, Marriage & Divorce Hollywood Style," scored the same smash ratings.

Walker then created and hosted the daily series, "National Enquirer TV" that premiered in 94% of US TV markets.

During the O.J. Simpson "Trial of the Century," Walker wrote the headline-making *New York Times* #1 Best Seller, *Nicole Brown Simpson: Private Diary of a Life Interrupted*, with Faye Resnick. Just months later, his book *Private Diary of an OJ Juror*, with Michael Knox, rocketed to #5 on the *NYT* Best Seller list.

That created a world record: He's the *only* reporter known to have written *two* best-selling books on the same major story. He's written several non-fiction books, and the novel, *Malicious Intent*.

Walker delighted millions during a record-breaking 16-year stint as a regular with shock jock Howard Stern, who calls Walker "the Hemingway of Gossip." Stern featured him every Friday on his top-rated show, conducting the famed "Mike Walker Game."

Dubbed "The King of Gossip" by *Publisher's Weekly,* Walker's lectured at such distinguished journalism schools as the University of California at Berkeley and Columbia University. And he scored the prestigious invitation to become a Fellow of Ireland's legendary Trinity College, Dublin.

"I'm an historian," Walker explains, "and I'd love to teach a course in what drives mankind's predilection for gossip. How's 'Professor of Whisperology' sound?"

Facebook: http://www.facebook.com/AuthorMikeWalker
Twitter: @IMwalkergossip

CPSIA information can be obtained at www.ICGtesting.com
Printed in the USA
BVOW02s0852231013

334419BV00004B/12/P